THREE

MMF BISEXUAL MENAGE ROMANCE

CHLOE LYNN ELLIS

D1528287

Three

Three © Chloe Lynn Ellis 2018
Edited by Elizabeth Peters
Cover design by Resplendent Media
ISBN-13: 978-1720361060
ISBN-10: 1720361061

This book contains sexually explicit content which is suitable only for mature readers.

1

JOHNNY

*T*he minute we walk in the door, Matt strips his shirt off. We showered at the firehouse, of course, but I still get a whiff of smoke as he pulls it over his head. Hand to God, that shit gets in your fucking *pores* after a blaze like we had today. One thing I gotta say about our career choice—it's definitely killed some of my appreciation for the Fourth of July.

"What do you want to bet it was fireworks?" I ask, following him inside and tossing my gear bag on the couch.

Matt gives me a look, and I snatch it right back up. He's such a stickler for keeping our place nice, but even though it's fun to bitch and moan about it sometimes, I admit I don't mind that our bachelor pad actually feels like a home, thanks to him.

Of course, wherever Matt is has always felt like home to me.

"No bet," Matt said, sounding tired but still tossing me a smile. "This close to the Fourth? Gotta be. And no way was that apartment complex up to code."

He stretches, the ridges of his hard abs unfurling like an accordion and the smooth curves that define his shoulders and arms mesmerizing me for a second. He goes through what I'm pretty sure is one of the yoga sequences he's been insisting we add to our workouts lately, and I blink, looking away.

I *must* be tired. I've had years of practice making myself not notice him like that.

"Fucking New Hampshire," I say, tossing my gear bag from hand to hand as I bounce on my toes and let adrenaline and exhaustion duke it out inside me. "Not even a half-hour drive over the border and any idiot can pick up as many fireworks as they want. You wanna know what I think? I think it's a fucking *miracle* that no one died today. Every floor we cleared, that's what I'm thinking—*this is a miracle*—you know? A call like that, and not even a single ambulance? Someone's watching over Boston today, that's all I'm saying."

"Yep," Matt says, his lips twitching with humor as he rolls his shoulders a few more times and then scoops his shirt up. "Don't know if you noticed, but I was actually there, too, Johnny. But hey, feel free to recap it for me while I get the laundry started. Just in case I missed anything."

He winks, and I grin, following him back to the laundry room.

"Fuck off," I say, figuring he must've undone the top button of his jeans already, too, the way they're starting to ride low on his hips. Low enough that I can see the two dimples on either side of his spine, just above the curve of his ass.

Not that I'm looking, of course.

Fuck.

"And when you say idiots," Matt asked, looking over his shoulder at me and making me jerk my eyes up fast. "I assume you're including us?"

"That was a long time ago," I say, smirking because I know *exactly* what he's referring to. "Besides, we didn't actually end up *buying* any fireworks, so no."

We both laugh, and I reach down to adjust myself, happy to have a legitimate excuse. Because even without the fireworks, that had been a memorable trip, all right. Plenty of women go crazy over double-dating a couple of firefighters, that's for damn sure, and there have been more than a couple wild nights where things got heated up fast and we'd both find ourselves in the same hotel room with our dates, but back then? We'd just graduated high school, Matty's home life had just imploded, and we'd fucked off to New Hampshire ready to do something stupid.

Instead, we'd both done a girl named Cindy.

Matt starts up the washing machine the minute we step into the laundry room, and I hop up to sit on the dryer.

"We really gotta do laundry now?" I whine, because it sounds horrifically boring even though I know him well enough to guess that the answer will be *yes*. "I'm tired as shit."

Matt laughs, rolling his eyes. "You *should* be tired as shit," he corrects me, holding out a hand and gesturing imperiously.

I know what he wants, and I strip off my shirt and toss it to him. He's got some magic formula he uses in the wash to actually get the smoke smell out of all our stuff, and I'm more than happy to let him boss me around a little if it means I don't have to deal with laundry. Besides, taking care of it makes him happy, the weirdo. I'm not gonna say he's got a little OCD action going on, but then again, I'm not going to say he *doesn't*, either, you know?

"I *am* tired," I insist, because it's true. I can feel every goddamn minute of the last 24-hour shift in my bones. My muscles are like jelly. I mean, you know, jelly that's sort of buzzing and wired and makes me feel like I'm bouncing off the walls, but still, jelly, for sure.

"Pants, too," Matt says, killing me as he strips off his. "And toss whatever's in your gear bag in with this load, too."

I want to whine, but I also want other things I can't have, so I just book it out of the room and grab my bag so I can give him what he wants. I bounce on my toes once I've handed it over, looking over Matty's shoulder as I tense and release my fingers, trying to burn off some of the electricity I can't seem to ever really run out of, even now, when I really *am* exhausted.

3

I've always been this way—some part of me always *on*, some wheel always spinning at a crazy speed inside me. Matt operates at a slower pace most of the time, which sort of balances me out... but I like to think that my hyperactivity is good for him, too. Keeps him on his toes, you know? Otherwise he'd turn into a big homebody.

"Will it do any good to ask you to settle down?" Matt asks, stifling a yawn.

I grin, not bothering to answer since clearly that's a rhetorical question, and then I rest my chin on Matt's shoulder just to irritate him.

He hip bumps me away, snorting. "Back off, buddy. We both know you'll be too damn amped to give me any peace for a while, so let me just take care of business here, yeah?"

I roll my eyes just for show. Matty is such a nester. And yeah, I know, I know, he's also a hundred percent right about me. My mouth goes a mile a minute during the best of times, and even faster when I'm coming down off a rush like today. But what he doesn't know? I've *gotta* keep myself busy right now. Keep my mind on the danger we made it through during the call today, or giving him shit about his homemaking skills, or anything I can latch onto at all... just so I can avoid the danger that simmers right here, under the surface of our friendship, every fucking moment of my life.

Sue me, but yes, I'm gonna keep right on prattling on about the fire and the stupidity of reckless people and anything else I can come up with if it will distract me from staring at my best friend's cut body and thinking about things that would ruin a lifetime of friendship if he were ever to catch on. There'd been a time when I'd figured I'd end up eventually telling him I was bi, but I kept putting it off and putting it off—because high school wasn't the most accepting place for guys who were into guys, you know?— and since I liked girls, too, it had been pretty easy to fly under the radar.

Then his dad had come out, and the backlash from that? I shudder. All I can say is thank God I decided to keep it under wraps, because even if I can't say I agree with how things have gone down between Matt and his father, choosing between a lifetime of repressed feelings or not having Matty in my life at all is a no-brainer.

"Aw, A/C too much for you?" Matt teases, reaching out to pinch my side.

I make a big show of flinching away from the minor sting, rubbing at the spot as I flip him the bird. Secretly, I'm thankful he thinks that's why I shuddered and isn't going to press me on it, though.

Bringing up Matt's estrangement from his dad in any way, shape, or form is something I generally avoid at all costs. Not because Matt would get mad about it, but because he'd shut down and *pretend* he was mad... as if I didn't know him well enough to see that it was just a way to hide how bad his father's betrayal still hurt him, even all these years later.

Not that *I* would call his father leaving the family because the guy had finally decided to be true to himself a *betrayal*, of course, but that opinion was another thing I'd learned to keep to myself.

"A/C is a fucking *god*send," I say, not just to steer clear of sensitive subjects, but because it's the middle of the summer and that statement is nothing more than God's honest truth.

"Amen," Matt says, yawning again.

I pick up a spray bottle and put it back down, then find a stray clothespin and start snapping it open and closed a few thousand times. Matty glares at me, so I grin and do it a few more times before tossing it onto a shelf.

He's loading soap or whatever into the machine, standing there in just the green four-leaf-clover boxer briefs that say "Rub for Luck" that an ex-girlfriend gave him as a gag gift last St. Paddy's Day, and that reminds me that he wanted my pants, too.

I strip them off and pull my phone out of the back pocket before handing them over.

"Wanna play some *Dead Trigger*?" I ask, swiping my phone open since I clearly need a better distraction than anything I've come up with so far. I've known Matty practically since birth—basically grew up at his house until that went to shit when his parents split, and then been roommates in one place or another in the eight years since—and stripping down in front of each other is nothing. Still, for whatever reason, I'm having more trouble than usual repressing certain things today.

Matt yawns again, shaking his head at my offer to kill some zombies together. "What I want to do is tidy up the house—"

My turn to snort, because hello, as if he ever lets it get *un*tidy.

"—and then get some damn rest," he finishes, lips twitching as he ignores my interruption.

"We can rest when we're dead," I quip, even though a little of my adrenaline is starting to wear off and hitting the sack is actually starting to sound appealing. I still need to burn off some excess energy—I'd just toss and turn if I tried to go to bed right now—but there's no doubt that the day's starting to catch up with me now that we're finally home.

Matty drops the lid on the washer as it starts to agitate, and I trail after him, back toward the living room. Normally, he's the one trying to talk me into sitting still long enough to play some video game or other, so I figure if I get the zombie hunting game started I can probably convince him to join in and keep me company until I settle down enough to get the sleep my body needs. But just as I finally get it pulled up, my phone goes and dies.

"Shit," I mutter, tossing it onto the couch and flopping down after it, disrupting the color-coordinated throw pillow display Matt keeps there.

He laughs, grinning down at me as he picks one up off the

floor and throws it onto my lap. "How about you just head to bed?"

"*You* head to bed," I throw back, like I'm twelve or something and he just insulted me. I grab the remote off the coffee table. "Let's watch something."

"Oh my God," Matt says, shaking his head as he leaves me there and goes into the kitchen. "I don't know how I put up with you."

"It's because you love me," I holler after him, clicking on the TV. "You're my brother from another mother."

Which is really what he *should* be, even though I'm feeling far less brotherly about him today than I usually manage.

I don't know what's gotten into me, other than maybe the combination of all the adrenaline from the big fire today and the fact that it's been about a hundred years since I've gotten laid.

Matt yells back a creative insult that I ignore and then says something about us needing to pick up groceries, which I also ignore. Instead, I speed-click through some preset stations, looking for something to help me wind down.

{Click} Nope...

{Click} *Definitely* not...

{Click} Boring...

{Click} Even more boring...

{Click} And, *hel*lo.

My finger freezes on the remote, my free hand drifting down to my lap as the porn channel I've accidentally landed on catches my attention. I mean, how could it not, right?

I lower the volume, throwing a guilty glance in the direction of the kitchen. Not like we both don't watch porn—and this station is in Spanish, even, so obviously it's one of Matty's presets—but after the kind of thoughts that have been plaguing me since we got home, for some reason I feel weirdly self-conscious about him hearing it.

The curvy woman on-screen runs her hands over a gorgeous

pair of breasts, and my cock swells under my hand. If *this* is what I'm gonna do to unwind, I know I need to take it back to my own room, but I mean… doesn't hurt to watch a minute or two here on the big screen, right?

"You want a beer to mellow you out?" Matt calls from the kitchen.

"Sure," I say, already feeling pretty distracted. And the video I've landed on is definitely the right kind of distraction right now, since it seems to be just your straightforward (ha! "straight") guy-girl action, perfect for getting my mind off the place it's been trying to go.

I flex my hand over my stiffening cock, throwing one arm over the back of the couch as I lean back and take it in. It's nothing special, really, just those mouthwatering tits barely contained in a skimpy nightgown, the woman looking horny as all hell as she watches a buff dude in overalls lying under a sink. He's definitely not bad, either—flexing every last bit of muscle that the camera can see as he goes to work—but this isn't the time for my mind to go there.

Doing the plumber.

House call.

Clean my pipes, Big Daddy.

I snicker, entertaining myself by coming up with possible titles as the action starts to heat up.

"Her leg… is potatoes?" I mumble under my breath, pretty sure my limited Spanish is letting me down with that translation.

There'd been a time when I'd actually gotten almost decent with the language. Matt and his dad, Santi, used to speak it at their house all the time, and since I was there as close to 24/7 as they'd put up with me, I picked up a bit over the years. Of course, that shit is use-it-or-lose-it, and, since Matt decided to toss the language out along with his relationship with his father, I've basically lost it.

Not that I really need to keep up with the onscreen dialogue to

8

follow along with what's happening between the plumber and the housewife, of course.

"She's saying she wants him to clean her pipes, bro."

Matt's voice behind me startles the crap out of me, and I nearly jump out of my seat.

"Jesus, buddy, what the hell?" I blurt, my heart pounding a mile a minute. I yank my hand off my dick like I've been burned, but Matt just grins, shaking his head as he hands me the beer he promised.

"Not my fault you're butchering the language," he says, his eyes drifting back to the screen.

"A little warning next time?" I say, even though out of the two of us, I seem to be the only one rattled by him catching me like this. "Besides, I thought you didn't—"

I snap my mouth closed just in time. I may have lost most of my Spanish skills, but he'd spoken it daily for the first eighteen years of his life. Of *course* he remembers it.

Calling him out on the fiction that he'd forgotten—something he's insisted ever since he cut Santi out of his life—isn't where I want to take the conversation, though.

Matt takes a sip of his beer, raising an eyebrow at me. "You thought I didn't what?"

"Uh," I say, scrambling for something to cover my tracks with. "Thought you didn't... didn't like, um, you know..."

I make a vague gesture at the TV screen, mind coming up blank.

Matty laughs, taking a seat in the recliner next to the couch. "You thought I didn't like porn? Hate to break it to you, bro, but I do occasionally indulge."

I gasp, making sure to exaggerate it and get him laughing. "Mateo Alejandro Lopez," I say, widening my eyes and putting a hand over my chest. "I'm *shocked*."

"My full name?" he says dryly, lips twitching. "We're going *there*... Eugene?"

I narrow my eyes, but no denying I brought that one on myself. "It's Johnny to you," I retort, trying to make my voice sound threatening.

Matt just laughs. "Just be thankful your last name wasn't something like Wierzbicki instead of Johnson."

I snort, but he's right. We'd gone to school with a kid named Jason Wierzbicki. Jason's a perfectly fine first name, right? But he was forever "Wierzbicki the Hickey."

I'm fine with being Eugene "Johnny" Johnson, when you put it in perspective like that.

My parents had thought it would be cute to name their kids in alphabetical order, but they'd also figured that they'd stop at four. I'd been their "oops" baby, and I always figured they'd just stuck me with Eugene to punish me for making them deal with diapers nine years after they'd thought they were done with that part of parenting.

Of course, as soon as I'd gotten out of those diapers, they really had been done for all intents and purposes. Not to say they didn't love me, I guess, but they'd been constantly busy with my teenage siblings' busy lives and I'd basically fended for myself until I met Matt. I'd never been sure if my parents had really been okay with me spending all my waking hours at the Lopez house, or if they'd just been too busy to notice that I was never around.

Either way, no complaints from me. I'd been perfectly happy to claim Matty's family as my own.

Matt yawns again, still watching the screen, then sets his beer down and lets his hand drift down to rest over his cock. I jerk my eyes away, which just makes them land on the porn I'd sort of forgotten about for a minute. The woman's nightgown has mysteriously gotten torn while I wasn't paying attention, revealing most of her tits and what looks like a pretty tiny, incredibly sexy G-string. I spread my legs a little wider, needing the room as my body starts to respond.

She says something else I don't catch, then reaches down to

pull the plumber's cock out of his pants. It's uncircumcised, just like I happen to know Matt's is, and I scrub a hand over my face, really wishing my exhaustion would hurry up and kick in right about now and kill all this excess... *energy*.

I cut my eyes over toward Matty. He's got his head cocked to the side as he looks at the screen, hand still in his lap. After a minute, he laughs. "You think that's real?" he asks.

I snort, grinning. "It's *porn*, bro, so I'm gonna go with no." Then, in a high falsetto and *really* bad Spanish accent, I add, "You ask for a pipe wrench, no? Is this the tool you wanted, señor?"

Matt gives me a mock-pitying look, even though I can tell he's trying not to laugh.

"I *know* you know that's not what I meant," he says as the hot moaning and dirty words I can't follow start to escalate in volume. He waves a hand back at the screen. "I'm just saying, look at that guy's cock. There's big, but that's... that's just obscene, amirite? What would you even *do* with a cock that big?"

I blink, my brain sort of shutting down the minute Matt admits he's looking at the guy's cock... or maybe it's shutting down because just the fact that he'd wonder something like that has got all my blood flowing south.

What would you even do *with a cock that big?*

I mean, of course I know he's not *actually* wondering about it, but... what would *I* do with a cock that big? Well, I could think of a few things, actually. My cock starts to leak a little precum, making a wet spot on the front of my boxers, and I jerk my eyes back to the screen, covering my lap with a bright blue throw pillow to preserve a little dignity.

Although okay, Matty's right. Now that I'm really looking? There's big... and then there's run-the-other-way. Some things are definitely best left to fantasy.

"He's a... a freak of nature," I say belatedly, clearing my throat.

Matt laughs, but I hear a hitch in his breath that doesn't help with what the pillow is covering. I mean, I know he's gotta just be getting turned on by the idea of fucking the girl, but hearing his tells while talking about cock doesn't help my problem.

"She doesn't seem to mind," Matt says after a minute, and the telltale tone in his voice has me biting back another groan.

"You sure about that?" I crack, trying to tone things down a little. "I'm not really following the storyline, buddy. She could be asking him to pack it away along with the rest of his tools."

Matty laughs like I hoped he would, eyes still glued to the screen when I glance over. I let my eyes dart down to his lap since he's otherwise occupied, and *yeahhhhhhhhhhhhh*, he's into this, isn't he?

"Has your Spanish really gotten that bad?" he jokes, like he's suddenly too distracted to pretend he doesn't understand it perfectly well himself. His hand is starting to flex and relax as it rests over his cock, so I can't blame him for sounding distracted.

And okay, the expression on the woman's face is obviously pretty damn appreciative as she strokes the plumber's monster cock reverently. It's actually hot as fuck, but I only watch for another few seconds before I sneak another look over at Matty. I grin. Oh, he's definitely distracted. He doesn't have a throw pillow on hand, either. His eyes are stuck on the screen, one hand lazily moving over the words imprinted on top of what is now a truly impressive erection.

I snicker. I can't help it.

"Feeling lucky?" I ask when he looks over, forgetting to worry about getting caught looking.

Matt glances down at his dick encased in the green "Rub for Luck" underwear, then laughs as he gets my joke. "I'm too tired to take this to my room," he says with an easy grin. Then he winks. "It's not like you haven't seen me get off before, but I mean, if *you're* ready to head to bed, I'm pretty sure I can hold down the fort out here on my own."

Oh fucking God, I am one hundred percent thinking with my

dick right now, because I stopped hearing anything after the *ready to head to bed* line.

I *so* want to take it in a way he'll never in a million years mean it.

I rein myself in. It's great that Matty's not self-conscious. Why should he be? Did I mention those hotel rooms we've shared? Not to mention that ridiculously hot threesome with Cindy-from-New-Hampshire. Yeah, I've seen him get off before... and thank God he'll never know how hot I find it. It definitely hadn't been just the girls who were doing it for me.

Although *hell* yeah, they did, too... which is what I need to concentrate on right now. The woman onscreen wraps her lips around that ridiculous foot-long cock, sinking slowly down the shaft, and I push thoughts of Matt aside and focus on that.

"Pretty sure my Spanish is up to *this*," I say, nudging the pillow off my lap and grinding the heel of my hand down against my cock as I watch her deep-throat the guy. It's unreal, and hot as fuck.

I hear Matt starting to breathe a little harder, and after a minute, he says, "That's not Spanish, bro. We call that the universal language."

We both laugh, but it quickly fades away into thick silence as we watch her slide up and down the plumber's shaft, pausing for only brief moments to wrap her fingers around and stroke him.

I shift in my seat, pushing my hips up so I can get a little more friction where I need it. The truth is, the woman onscreen is sexy as hell. Whether or not Matt and I head where I think we are—both taking care of our business right here and now—I can definitely get into this.

She's lost her nightgown and that little lace thong is getting me even hotter. The way she's bending over the guy as she goes down on him gives him easy access to grab a double-handful of her lush breasts, and *man*, they truly are works of art.

I groan, my cock starting to throb to the rhythm of the panting and moaning and wet, slurping sound of suction. The slick head of my dick pushes up out of the top of my boxers, and I can't resist —I go from trying to be discreet and just pressing my hand against it to full-out stroking myself.

The woman onscreen pops off the monster cock and says something that I can't translate even a little bit.

"She says it's a tip for good work," Matt translates, and I can hear more than a hint of huskiness rising in his voice.

I flick my eyes over to peek at him. He has his beer in one hand, but his other hand is just as busy as mine.

He catches me looking.

"You... uh, you want me to get out of here?" I blurt, a sense of self-preservation suddenly kicking in.

When we'd been younger, I'd always assumed Matt would be fine with me being bi since he's generally pretty easygoing about everything, but the way he'd freaked when Santi had come out as gay? No matter how hard my dick is right now, nothing is worth Matt cutting me out of his life like he's done with his dad.

Matt doesn't seem worried about catching me looking, though. He just grins and asks, "You suddenly feeling shy or something, Johnny?" He looks back to the screen and settles into his recliner further. "Because you can go if you want, but I'm thinking this is going to be the only way you're going to unwind enough to let me get any sleep, yeah?"

"Definitely," I manage, my tongue feeling thick in my mouth.

He wants me to stay.

No, he doesn't mind if I stay... those are two totally different things.

There's another long minute or two of heavy, electric silence while we watch the woman finish her blow job and slip her panties off, and when she finally lowers herself onto the guy's cock—moaning like it's the second coming—I hear Matt inhale sharply as that monster cock on the screen slowly disappears deep inside of her.

I groan, squeezing my dick hard as it throbs in my hand. It really *has* been too damn long since I've gotten laid.

"Look," Matt finally says, the husky timbre of his voice making my cock jerk in response. "If you're not... not into this, Johnny, no worries. I can be the one to take it into my room, but—"

"No," I cut him off. "I'm good, bro. Let's just... just get this done."

"Right," he says, his laugh stuttering out and then—

Oh fucking God, I hear the slick sound of him stroking bare flesh. Slow... and then a little faster. His breath picks up and so does mine, mingling with the heavy moaning from the couple onscreen and covering up that distinct sound that can't be mistaken for anything but what it is—hands moving faster and faster over hard cocks.

I rub my thumb over my slit, smearing the precum around the sensitive head, then use it to lubricate the shaft as I thrust into my fist.

Slow.

Then faster.

Matching Matty's rhythm as I start to pant with the rising tide. I'm careful not to look directly over at him as I blank out my mind and just enjoy the sensation. Not gonna lie, the hard fucking onscreen would be enough to get me there—it's hot—but knowing Matt's right here with me?

Everything is heightened.

"Fuck," Matt grunts softly. "That's... that's fucking hot. Damn, but I love it when a girl rides me."

"Yeah," I agree, rubbing my free hand over my chest and sinking further into the moment.

The plumber's hands are roaming all over the woman's curvy body. He cups her breasts... strokes her taut stomach... reaches around to squeeze her ass and rock her forward, taking charge even though she's on top. It's definitely hot enough to get my mind off where I can't let it go. It really has been too long since

I've had any action, and combined with the adrenaline from earlier, I'm already close.

I let my eyelids start to drift down, pushing up into my hand and grazing my nails over my nipples as I get lost in the onscreen action. I'd love to get my mouth on those big tits of hers. Love to feel how tightly her body would squeeze my cock if it were me she was riding. Love to have my hands filled with that lush ass... my cock coated in her slick juices... have all those dirty, exotic-sounding words rain down around me as I drive up into her soft body, again and again and—

"*Fuck*," I gasp, my body jackknifing forward a little as my balls suddenly tighten.

"Yeah," Matt gasps. "Me, too. *Fuck* yeah."

I groan, almost losing it. Shit shit *shit*. I'm *not* looking, but now Matty's back on my mind, and I'm still imagining the woman on-screen riding me... but now I'm imagining Matty walking in on us, too.

I'm imagining *his* hands on her tits.

I'm imagining watching as he positions himself behind her... nibbles at her neck... strokes her clit while I fuck her faster and faster.

He's sharing her with me, the way we did with that little fire-cracker of a redhead back in New Hampshire when we were kids, and even though I can't see his cock, I can feel it—thick and hard and slick—as Matt lines up behind her.

Rubbing.

Thrusting.

Accidentally bumping that gorgeous cock into me, too—

I hiss, heat shooting down my spine like a bolt of lightning, and I cut myself off right there. No way am I going to let myself imagine more.

I don't have to.

Matty groans next to me—long and low and so fucking sexy that the sound alone would have made me lose it, even if I hadn't

16

already been right there—and I throw my head back as the orgasm rips through me. I come hard, shooting onto my chest over and over, until I finally *am* worn out.

"Holy shit," I manage after a few, loosening my grip as a languid warmth starts to fill me and all that restless energy I live with 24/7 dissipates with the afterglow.

"Good one, yeah?" Matt asks with a sleepy laugh.

"Yeah," I murmur, since that's both true and safe enough, I figure.

I see him get up out of my peripheral vision, but I don't look over. The glimpses I caught while we were in the thick of it were one thing, but I've got no excuse now.

"'Night, Johnny," he says, the words all but lost in the sound of another yawn.

He sounds totally normal, and why wouldn't he be? I'm the only one who turned it into something more than just two guys blowing off steam after a long day.

Thank fuck it was only in the privacy of my own mind.

"'Night, bro," I say as he leaves the room.

I groan quietly when I finally hear his bedroom door close a minute later, promising myself *for sure* that I'll get laid at the very next possible opportunity.

And that I'll quit wanting what I'll never have, once and for all.

2

EDEN

*M*y foot lands in some spilled flour as I cross the kitchen, and I almost drop Auntie Maria as I flail about and try to avoid landing on my ass.

"Shit," I say, fumbling the clear drinking glass in my hand as I regain my balance. I manage to catch it, but drop my bucket list instead.

So much for multitasking.

"What happened, honey?" Maria asks, her voice sounding weirdly amplified as it comes out of my phone's tiny speaker and bounces around inside the drinking glass. Since I'd already been halfway through making dinner when she'd called, I'd set the phone inside it so we could video chat while I cook.

Or while I *try* to cook, anyway.

Try to cook... *again.*

I stifle a sigh, shaking my head ruefully as I survey the disaster formerly known as my kitchen. I still have a few months to master this whole cooking thing, so no matter how bad things look at the moment, I remind myself that I'm not ready to give up on it.

"Eden?" Maria says, pulling my attention back to her. "Have you burned the place down yet?"

I raise the glass up so we're eye-to-eye, so to speak, and grin at her. "Don't be silly, Auntie," I say. "Everything's under control."

"Oh, is that what 'shit' means out there in Boston?" she teases, not letting me off the hook.

I laugh. "No, *shit* means that someone spilled flour on my floor, and I swear, that stuff is more slippery than grease! Who knew?"

"Not me," Maria says, holding up her hands like she's warding off cooties. "I still don't know why you didn't just buy pancake mix if you were going to insist on making breakfast for dinner instead of just ordering take-out like a normal person."

"Learning to cook is on The List," I remind her, bending down to retrieve my fallen bucket-list notebook from the floor and then setting both it and Auntie Maria in her glass down on the counter next to the mixing bowl I'd been using.

I turn back to take stock of the situation, biting my lip nervously.

The situation is... a mess.

I sigh, then straighten my shoulders. I can do this. I *can*.

"You know, I'd be excited if I actually thought you *did* have someone there spilling flour on your floor on a Saturday night." Maria's voice sounds from behind me as I grab the broom and dustpan and make quick work of removing the latest safety hazard unleashed by my ongoing efforts to learn to cook. "Especially if that someone happened to be hot as sin, treated you like a queen, and had a huge—"

"Okay, okay," I cut her off, laughing as I sweep up the last of the flour. "Don't make me pine for a guy that doesn't exist."

"I'm sure he *does* exist," Maria said. "And if you ask me, you should be out there finding him right now, preferably wearing a push-up bra and with a couple of condoms in your purse."

"Oh my God," I say, laughing as I blush. "A *couple* of them?"

Good Lord, it's been so long since I've had reason to use even *one* of those that I don't want to think about it. And the idea of going out on the prowl looking... I shake my head. It's just not me. Auntie Maria raised me whenever she wasn't deployed, and while I'm used to her brash teasing and frank talk, I'll just never be as bold as she is.

"All I'm saying, honey, is that you deserve someone. And those Boston boys with their accents..."

I look over at the tiny screen and see her fanning herself, and I blush all over again. I kind of agree about the Boston accent, actually, but I've just never been all that forward with men. Besides, at the moment, I've got other things on my mind.

As Auntie Maria goes on teasing me about my nonexistent love life, I put away the broom and dustpan and approach the ingredients I'd laid out so confidently an hour before. Eggs, heavy cream, bacon, and a lumpy sludge that was *supposed* to be pancake batter... I sigh as I take in the sight, not feeling quite as confident about actually getting this done tonight as when I'd started.

Originally, when I'd decided to tackle #66 on The List, *learn to cook*, I'd been a little overly ambitious—beef Wellington isn't for the faint of heart, and it's *definitely* not for a kitchen novice like me—but I swear tonight's attempt hadn't felt nearly as intimidating back when I still had all dozen eggs in the carton.

How had I broken so *many* of them already?

That first beef Wellington fiasco had been followed by a few attempts at supposedly easier meals, all of which had ended in pure disaster, and while I didn't *give up*, I did decide to postpone. Or, if I don't sugarcoat it: I've been avoiding #66 like the plague... for a few years now, I'm not proud to say.

I'm running out of time, though, and with only three unfinished items on the bucket list I started back when I was sixteen, I figure it's now or never. And I admit that bacon, eggs, and pancakes may not sound like much, but at least it's a legitimate *meal*, right? A breakfast meal, sure, but it really didn't sound that complicated when I'd watched the how-to video online, and I figure if I can just get through it once with an edible end result, I can officially cross that sucker off The List and call it good.

"If you haven't found a man by the time your birthday rolls around, I swear I'm going to fly out there myself and take you to a strip club," Maria says as I adjust the neck on my new apron and smooth it down over my thighs. It had been white to start with, but now it's spattered with all the signs of tonight's failed cooking attempt.

I take a breath. No, I don't get to classify it as a failure yet. I'm still in this thing.

I reach for the spatula, then my brain catches up with the conversation and I whip around to face Maria's image on the tiny screen.

"Don't you dare," I say, wielding the spatula like a weapon.

"What?" she asks with a faux-innocent look I don't buy at all. "You're saying that you *don't* want to spend your twenty-fifth birthday pushing dollar bills under the waistband of some hot, muscled man's skimpy little—"

"Auntie *Maria*," I interrupt, blushing furiously again… even though a tiny part of me actually likes the idea. But even if I *could* bring myself to do it, there's no way I'll let her joke about flying out here.

Not for *this* birthday.

That would be bad.

I swallow back the lump in my throat, not wanting to think about it.

"Oh, honey," she says, her eyes softening into something that's as close to maternal as I've ever known. "All I'm saying is that I want you to be happy, you know that. Live a little. And if you get a chance to do some of that living with a man you can enjoy yourself with, why not go for it? I worry about you all alone out there on the East Coast."

"I'm fine, Auntie," I say, loving her so hard that it hurts. "You know work keeps me busy anyway."

I can see that she wants to argue about that, and I can't blame her for not taking my "career" as a CNA—Certified Nursing Assistant—all that seriously. It really is just a toe-dip into the medical field, and I haven't used it as the entry point I'd told her I would back when I first got certified. Instead, I've treaded water, always bouncing around from city to city and managing to find work, but after growing up a military brat and knowing my family history, can I really be blamed for not putting down roots?

She lets it go, though, but only so she can pull out another old favorite.

"Have you put in that nursing school application yet?" Maria asks, as predictable as clockwork.

I wave off the question—also predictable—and change the subject by asking about her. She's career Navy and currently stationed out in San Diego, and as she launches into some fun and slightly raunchy stories, I get back to work trying to figure out what I'm supposed to do with all the food laid out in front of me.

Maria had told me once that when my father, Maria's older brother, met my mom, he'd fallen in lust at first sight... but then when my mother started cooking for him, it had turned into love. But all signs point to that amazing cooking gene having passed me by completely, and much to my dismay, I can't even remember my mother's face, much less any meals she'd ever made for me.

Both my parents died when I was three, and Auntie Maria had just joined the Navy when she lost her brother to the car accident that took them. It didn't make sense for her to get saddled with the responsibility of a preschooler when she was just eighteen herself and planning from the get-go on going career with her military service. She'd had her whole life ahead of her, and no one could have blamed her if she'd said no to accepting guardianship for me—in fact, I'm pretty sure her recruiter tried to talk her out of getting saddled with the responsibility for a three-year-old— but Maria was my only living relative, and even back then, she'd been fierce and opinionated and determined to make it work...

and in my own way, I'd like to think that I approach life that way, too.

Which means I am *not* going to let #66 get the best of me.

"I've got this," I mutter to myself, taking a deep breath as I turn a few burners on and then boldly grab the bacon. I slap a few slices in a pan.

"Go, girl," Maria says, laughing. "I've got faith in you."

I grin at her—because she always has, hasn't she?—then smooth my apron down and reach back to tuck a stray hair away and prepare to tackle the next step.

"I'm going to *own* these pancakes," I say, the sound of sizzling bacon filling me with confidence.

"Get it," she says, laughing. "I want to see you take the first one off the griddle so I can celebrate with you, but then I've got to get going."

"Hot date?" I ask, picking up the mixing bowl and trying to remember how much batter I'm supposed to use. I really should have printed out a recipe on paper instead of relying on YouTube videos, especially since my phone is now in use and I can't pull up the instructions for a refresher, but oh well, I'm sure I can do it by sight.

I mean, I've *eaten* pancakes, so it can't be that hard, can it?

"Let's just say that your auntie isn't all that much older than you," Maria says, winking. "And it *is* Saturday night."

"Good for you," I say, carefully pouring some batter onto the griddle. It sizzles when it hits, and for a moment, I smile. "This smells like it might actually turn out okay!"

"Oh, that's perfect!" Maria says, clapping her hands in front of her. "Just take your time with it, slow and steady."

I laugh, because I'm sorry, I *do* adore her but how the heck would she know?

"I don't think you've ever advised me to go slow and steady with anything in my life," I tease her, only half focused on the conversation while I watch the batter start to solidify.

I've poured three perfect circles, and I smile, a sense of accomplishment filling me. Then a bunch of little dots start appearing all over the top of each of them, like freckles, and I frown, a much more familiar feeling of apprehension replacing that sense of accomplishment.

Is that supposed to happen?

Some of the freckles are bubbling up and popping, and now my pancakes have *holes* in them. I rub at the spot between my eyebrows, a sense of frustration welling up inside me as I squeeze my eyes closed for a second. I *really* don't want to fail at #66 again.

Maria's voice is a welcome distraction.

"Eden, if you ever take my advice and hook one of those sexy Boston boys, then screw slow and steady—" she laughs wickedly as I blush again, confirming that the innuendo was fully intended, "—but in the kitchen?" I tear my eyes off my now-very-holey pancake just in time to see her shrug. "Slow and steady is probably a sound strategy."

I nod, but my eyes snap open to look at my pancakes again. The batter is smoking now. Is this normal?

"Eden, in all seriousness, I want you to promise me that you'll live a little," Maria says as I start pushing at the sizzling batter with my spatula.

"Uh huh," I answer distractedly. The tops of my pancakes definitely don't look all the way cooked yet, so I can't imagine that they're done... but the smoke suddenly doesn't smell nearly as delicious as it had a few moments earlier, either.

I sense another imminent cooking fail, but I'm not ready to tap out yet. Maybe this is still salvageable.

"I mean it," Maria says, sounding bossy. "You're making breakfast for dinner all alone on a Saturday night. Please find time to put a little adventure in your life. Or at the *least*, a little sex."

I can't even be bothered to blush this time, I'm too busy trying to figure out my chances of pulling off this meal in an edible form as I assess the slowly changing color of the smoke. It isn't black yet, but it's also definitely not white.

I hear the faint sound of a doorbell—not mine—and before I know it, my auntie is wishing me luck with the pancakes and rushing to get off the phone. I smile as the call disconnects, pretty sure she *does* have a hot date and definitely thrilled for her, but then my smile disappears as the smoke turns full-on black and starts puffing up in earnest.

Before I can react, a fire springs to life from the char.

I gasp, jumping back instinctively with my heart in my throat even though it's just a few small flames.

Mistake.

The griddle falls to the floor and lands with a huge clang, and I stand there staring at it for a few seconds in shock.

Really?

I can't even manage to cook the most basic of breakfasts?

My eyes suddenly well up with tears, and I dash them away impatiently. My twenty-fifth birthday is September 21st, the last day of summer, and given that I've still got all of July and August ahead of me, too, I've still got plenty of time to get this. I will *not* give up.

I take a deep breath of smoke-laden air and square my shoulders. I'm *not* giving up, but maybe I've at least earned a pass for the rest of the night. I'll just pick up the griddle and clean up the chunky mess now splattered on my floor and order some take-out, and tackle #66 again tomorrow. Maybe even try doing breakfast for *breakfast*.

Except suddenly, a lick of fire springs up from the mess at my feet.

What?

I'd thought that the whole falling to the floor and splattering thing had put it out, but clearly I'd been wrong. The flame is so small that I'm pretty sure I can just stomp it out... except I'm barefoot, so that doesn't seem like a good option.

Maybe if I throw a towel on it?

Smothering fires is a thing, right?

I grab a dish towel and toss it down, then feel like an idiot a minute later when the towel bursts into even bigger flames. Okay, not just an idiot... now I'm an adrenaline-filled idiot. I turn to the sink, determined to stay calm, and immediately slip on the flour I thought I'd already cleaned up. Apparently I'd missed some, because the next thing I know, I'm flat on the floor with my ears ringing... and the kitchen towel fire is actually starting to scare me a little.

"Shit, shit, shit," I chant, raising my head to survey the situation.

The situation is not good.

It looks like I didn't just fall, I also pulled down the bacon pan on my way down, and now the fire seems to be spreading through the splattered grease, too. I scramble backward to get as far away from it as I can, then come to my senses and lunge for the sink again. It's equipped with one of those nozzles that you can turn into a sprayer and extend on a little hose away from the sink, and I turn it on and yank it out as far as it can go and let the fire have it, full force.

The flames practically explode in front of me, and I gasp, immobile with shock and, for a split second, terror. I swallow, staring at the dancing fire as it spreads across the kitchen floor, blocking me in, and the terror fades away, replaced by a heavy sense of inevitability. I let the useless faucet hose drop out of my hand as resignation washes through me, because hadn't I known this day was coming?

My mother died before she'd turned twenty-five... just like her mother had... and just like her mother's mother before her. It was crazy, and it went back generations, but I'd long ago accepted that I wouldn't live to see my twenty-fifth birthday.

I just hadn't realized that my last day would be *today*.

The fire starts to get loud and I sniffle, not really sure if I'm crying or if it's just the smoke. I swipe at my cheeks, backing up against the edge of the sink until it bites into my back and trying to remember if I'd told Maria I loved her before we hung up.

I bite my lip hard enough to taste blood, because I don't think I did.

And my bucket list... I've been working on it for years and I got *so close*. For a minute, I'm almost mad. It's not *fair*. Even though I never knew how I'd end up going, I guess a part of me had been holding onto that list almost like a talisman, believing that I *couldn't* die before I finished it.

I start to tremble, the heat from the fire making me cringe away from it.

I try to calm myself down. No one gets guarantees in life, and even if I haven't done everything, I've still had a good one. I've done a *lot*. And I honestly thought that I'd already made my peace with this day, so I really shouldn't feel so—

"Oh my God," I gasp, my eyes darting to the ceiling as the fire licks its way up the cabinets.

My little pity party is interrupted by a bolt of pure adrenaline. I've only been in this rental for a few months, but it's this lovely old three-story townhouse with each floor converted into a separate apartment. And above me? A young married couple and their baby just moved in.

I spring into action before I can think. It's one thing to accept my own fate, but no way am I willing to let my destiny hurt that sweet family. I have one of those crazy lifting-a-car-off-a-baby moments and jump over the burning floor like an Olympic athlete, scrabbling at the counter where I left my phone sitting in the drinking glass. The glass is so hot it burns my fingers, but finally I manage to pull the phone out—sending the glass shattering to the floor—and stab at the little screen in desperation.

911. 911. Just dial 911, I think over and over again until my fingers finally comply.

"Nine-one-one," a crisp voice finally answers. "Please state your emergency."

And then I really *am* crying—the big, ugly, scared kind that makes it hard to breathe, much less talk.

I manage it anyway, though, determined to make it work, and ask the operator for help.

And you know what? For all her joking, I know Auntie Maria feels a little guilty sometimes for not teaching me how to cook and a million other "maternal" things, but she taught me *this*—how to make something work when it's important, when you just *have* to—and suddenly failing at #66 doesn't really matter so much anymore.

Screw cooking.

3

MATT

The energy in the truck is pretty high as we race toward the Saturday-night call, all the guys in a buzzing, amped-up state of readiness, but if I'm honest—crammed into the truck like a sardine and weighted down with fifty pounds of gear when it's hot as fuck outside and the siren is wailing—I feel weirdly calm.

"Got any water, bro?" Johnny asks, knee bouncing since he's basically incapable of ever sitting still.

I grin and hand it over without pointing out that he has a water bottle, too, then lean my head back and close my eyes for a second and just... enjoy the moment. Like I said, weird, right? Everyone else gets amped up when we get a call, but each and every time we head out to do what we trained for, it always has the opposite effect on me. Settles me down for some reason, like I know I'm doing what I'm meant to, you know?

It's kind of funny if you think about it, given that back when Johnny first suggested firefighting as a career choice, I wasn't so sure it would be a good fit for me. But the idea of him running into burning buildings all on his own? Oh, hell no. I love Johnny, I do, but the man is reckless as hell and too impulsive for his own

31

good, so once I figured out that he wasn't just talking shit and was actually going through with it, I *had* to come along for the ride... just to make sure he didn't get himself killed saving some damsel in distress or whatever.

"You hydrated enough, Matty?" Johnny asks, pushing the water bottle back into my hands.

"I'm good," I say, taking an extra drink anyway just to make him happy.

"Aw, isn't that cute?" Bill says, giving us shit like he always does. "Your boyfriend gonna wipe your ass for you later, too, 'Matty'?"

He makes stupid kissing sounds and I flip him off, but we all give each other shit all the time, so even the "boyfriend" comment doesn't really bother me like it would under other circumstances. Besides, no matter what anyone says, it's pretty great to know that Johnny always has my back, you know? I mean, of course all the guys in the firehouse do, but Johnny and I have been attached at the hip for as long as I can remember. He's basically the other half of me, even though of course I would never say anything as corny as that out loud.

Someday, I'm sure we'll end up with separate lives, find some girls, get married, whatever, but no point thinking about that now since we've got a pretty sweet setup at the moment. Working and playing side by side with my best friend every day, got the best job in the world, living in the best city in the world... and he even pays half my mortgage? Like I said, life couldn't be sweeter.

Johnny thought I was crazy when I bought the house a few years ago, but I like feeling settled, you know? Not like I'd ever wanna live anywhere but Boston anyway, so it just makes sense to put down some roots. Of course, I *had* roots here—was born and raised all my life in the same house down in Southie—but before I can get all worked up with that line of thinking, the truck starts to slow. I roll my shoulders back, staying loose, and get my head where it needs to be. No room for distractions when we're working, and can't say I mind shutting down where my mind had started to go and refocusing on the here and now.

I look over at Johnny and can't help but grin. He has this look on his face that's just pure adrenaline. He lives for this shit and he's damn good at it—even if he does occasionally take a few too many risks for my taste. And then we're all hopping off the truck and I get in the zone, because it's go-time.

"Class K," someone says as we start grabbing equipment.

It was reported as a kitchen fire, but by the look of things, it's been spreading fast. Doesn't look too out of hand—not like that bitch of an apartment building that burned earlier in the week—but still, you always gotta respect the fire and not assume. Still, I'm sure we can get it under control. It's what we do.

I raise my voice to be heard over the siren and the roar of the flames, getting Johnny's attention as I jerk my chin toward the townhouse. "I'm going to check residents."

"Yep," he replies. "I'll be with the Incident Commander."

I nod and turn to the building, but don't get more than two steps before someone slams right into me. I grab her as she bounces off and then hold her tight when she scrambles frantically to get out of my arms. Looks like she's in a state, and it's a response I've seen before. I've got no idea if this is a resident or a bystander or someone with a loved one inside, but the girl's clearly not thinking right, since she hit me while she was heading *toward* the fire.

"Let me go," she wails, her voice breathy and broken like she's been crying.

I feel for her, I do, but that's not gonna happen.

"Calm down, miss," I say, regulating my voice to try and help her do that as I continue to restrain her. "We've got this under control."

She's breathing hard, generous chest heaving under a thin t-shirt. Her pale skin is flushed, eyes wide as she struggles against me and long blonde hair all disheveled, like she's just been—

Jesus. I clench my jaw when it hits me how fucking unprofessional my thoughts just got and how fast they went there. It's not like me, not when I'm on the job. And yeah, this girl pushes *all* my buttons, if I'm being honest, but I know damn well that this isn't the time or place. She's practically hyperventilating, pupils dilated and jumbled words tumbling out between gasping breaths. She's in a state, all right, but despite my dick's momentary confusion, I know it's a state of panic, not anything else.

"Breathe, miss," I tell her, reining myself in. "I need you to stay away from the building so we can do our jobs," I say, holding her chin steady so she has to look at me as I enunciate the words and try to get through her panic. "Do you know if there are people still inside?"

"N-n-no," she stutters, still struggling like she thinks I'm actually going to let her run back in that direction.

"No, you don't know?"

"No," she says, shaking her head. "I mean, the people upstairs, they... they got out."

"Okay," I say, something inside me relaxing a little. We still gotta check, of course, but I can already see that a couple of the other guys took that on as soon as they saw that I was occupied. "In that case, let's get you over to the—"

She's a little thing, but she jerks away from me with some kind of inhuman strength before I can finish offering to get her out of the way and dashes back toward the building.

"Fuck."

I sprint after her. Almost catch up to her, too, but turns out I don't have to. Johnny steps in front of her before I get there, and she slams into him like he's a brick wall. He grabs her arms, and even though I can't hear what they're saying, I'm pretty sure it's gonna be a repeat of the conversation I just had with her.

He's got it in hand, their two blond heads bent together and his tree-trunk arms holding her steady. There's plenty for me to do, so I should just leave it, but for some reason I don't. Not really sure why, but the degree of her panic is getting to me, and even though I trust Johnny to take care of her, *I* want to make it right.

"I left it, I just *left* it there," she's sobbing to Johnny when I get close enough to hear. "It's all I've done. It's *every*thing, and now it's going to be gone."

An "it" isn't a life, so whatever she left inside, I already know it's not worth her putting herself in the kind of danger she was heading back for.

But I also know that when someone's in the throes of a panic like that, they can't hear reason.

"Right now, all you need to do is calm down," Johnny says to her, his big frame dwarfing her. "Me and the boys are gonna get this fire under control, then *after* that happens—" he stresses the word after, because she's still fighting him, "—we can worry about retrieving any belongings, yeah?"

"But it will *burn*," she wails, not unreasonably. And then in a heartbeat, she goes from sobbing and frantic to hopeless. I've seen that before, too, but for some reason, it stabs me in the heart when the fight suddenly goes out of her and she wilts against Johnny. "Please, please, please," she whispers. "My whole life is in that book. Please don't let it burn."

"A book?" I ask, meeting Johnny's eyes over her head.

I know we're both thinking the same thing. A book isn't worth all this fuss, not even if it were a copy of the Good one hand-written by Jesus himself. We're also thinking that it's a book, so it's paper… so yeah, if it's anywhere near the blaze, it's gonna either burn or get waterlogged as we do our jobs.

Lots of people lose things in fires. Tragic things. And then they figure out how to go on, anyway. I dart my eyes down to her and Johnny gives his head a little shake. As usual, we're on the same page.

Looks like this girl is going to be one of those people.

"Listen," he says to her, tipping her chin up and—damn, I know him so well that I can see it when it happens—he has a split second where he goes down that same unprofessional line of thinking I did when I had her in my arms.

Guess we really are closer than brothers, and since we agree on a lot of things, no surprise, really, that she hits us both like that. Johnny shakes it off fast, though, just like I did.

Not the time, not the place.

"We're going to do our best to contain this fast," Johnny goes on. "Don't lose hope, yeah? But we need you to stay safe out here, can you do that for me, miss...?"

"Eden," she fills in for him. "I'm... I'm Eden Evans."

Eden, huh? A gorgeous name.

Then she starts crying. "I don't... I don't care if I'm safe. It doesn't matter, it's all I've got. Please don't let it burn."

"It *does* matter," I say, kind of pissed about that statement even though I know she's still gotta not be thinking straight to have said such a thing. "Let Johnny get you out of the way so we can—"

"How would *you* feel if you lost your whole life?" she interrupts me, clutching onto my arm like I'm some kind of lifeline. "One minute it's there and the next it's just *gone?*"

She's sandwiched between me and Johnny, and her words hit me like a gut punch. Yeah, I've felt that before. One minute I'm part of a happy family, the next I find out it's all been a lie. I wouldn't compare it to losing a damn book, but then who am I to say what's important to someone else?

I eventually found my way again, but truth? Somewhere inside me, I still feel like something's missing every damn day.

"Your whole life is a book?" Johnny asks, his face crinkling up in confusion.

I can't wrap my head around it, either, but looking at her, at Eden, I'm convinced it's true for *her.*

Her eyes well up again, and she nods, looking back and forth between us beseechingly.

"All the parts that matter. It's... it's on the kitchen counter. Ground floor. A scrapbook with a p-p-pink cover."

I frown. Pretty sure that was the reported ignition point.

Johnny knows it, too, and he shakes his head at me again, then plucks her hand off my arm, still holding her tight like he doesn't trust her not to make another dash for it.

"It's gonna be okay," he says, starting to hustle her out of the way. "Don't worry—Eden, right? We're gonna—"

"We're going to get that book for you," I interrupt without thinking it through, like my mouth doesn't belong to me or something.

Yeah, yeah, I know Johnny was about to reassure her that we had it all under control again, or say some other soothing and meaningless thing. Just trying to keep her calm so we could do our damn jobs. We all know personal effects just aren't worth it, but she turns those big blue eyes on me like I've just sprouted a halo or something, and a whole lifetime of good sense deserts me in an instant.

"What the fuck?" Johnny splutters, staring at me over Eden's head like I've just grown a second one. "Matty, don't be a fucking idiot. Contain and control, bro. No heroics."

I nod, because he's right. Then I turn and sprint toward the building, because some things are more important than being right. No one should ever feel like they've lost everything. Still happens every day, but maybe it doesn't have to be that way this time.

Not for Eden.

Not if I can do something about it.

And I'm really not an idiot—if I can't get in and out safely I'll let it go, but I'm not going to be able to sleep at night if I don't at least try to do something for this girl who hits me in the gut.

Something to fix that look on her face when she lost hope.

Johnny's pissed all to hell behind me, I can hear it, but luckily I'm inside in just a few steps and it becomes a moot point. I know for sure that if I hadn't moved fast and he hadn't had an armful of Eden, he would have put me to the ground before he let me come in here, but I'll take the heat for that later. Right now, my attention has narrowed to one objective, and I pause for a two-count to assess and orient.

I snagged some equipment on my way in, including a silver extinguisher rated for these kinds of fires, and I think I might actually be okay as I work my way past a smoke-damaged front room, deeper into the building. I drop my shield over my face and start moving in, sweeping the extinguisher from side to side as I make my way through the fire in the hallway looking for the first-floor kitchen Eden mentioned. Flames leap out and lick at me, but they're not fast enough for my extinguisher, and before I know it, I find it.

The kitchen is definitely the ignition point, and it's burning worse in here than I initially thought from outside. Still, it's not so bad that I can't justify a quick in-and-out in my gear, just long enough to see if there's any hope for her book. I'm sweating hard as the flames suddenly flare off to my left, and I cough, then clear my throat and move fast, adrenaline surging through me when I spy what I came for.

The book is right where she said, and I shit you not, it shouldn't be. I don't know what stray draft saved it, but it had to have been one sent by a higher power. Three steps to cross the room and I've got it, smacking it hard a few times to put out some of the smaller flames that have just started to get the edges.

It's singed, but doesn't look too worse for the wear at a glance, and a glance is all I can spare. Like Johnny said, no heroics. Time to move. I slip the book into my protective coat and clutch it to me, then spin back toward the kitchen exit, and then I hear a sound I don't like at all.

Something's starting to collapse, and a wall of heat slaps me in the face out of nowhere, flames bursting out of what had been solid wall a second before and something shooting across the room like an overheated javelin. It knocks me on my ass and clears my head. *Shit*. What the hell was I thinking, getting all sentimental on the job?

Nothing for it now, though. I'm in here, and I've got the book so I'm not dropping it, but it's time to get out. I get to my feet just as it all starts to go to hell, dodging furniture and fire as I run toward the front door. It got bad fast, but it's gonna be okay. The door is right there, so close I can practically taste it.

And then it happens. I hear another telltale crackle and the sound of heavy splintering, and years on the job have me jumping out of the way without having to consciously place where it's coming from.

Right over my head.

I almost make it, too, but guess maybe coming in here like this really had been a dumb move, yeah? I go to the ground hard, forced down by the weight of something huge, heavy, and on fire, and my first reaction is pure disbelief.

How many times had I warned Johnny about taking risks on the job, worried about him getting all stupid and heroic, fussed about us always staying up on our training, putting in more hours, dotting all our I's and crossing all our T's to be as prepared as humanly possible to do our jobs and come home after in one piece?

And yet, here I am. And you know what? Every part of me hurts like a bitch.

I suck in some overheated air and get it together, ready to push off whatever the fuck has me pinned and get the fuck out of here. But then I start coughing, and much to my horror, realize my vision is narrowing fast.

Nuh-uh. I can't pass out. I'm getting out of here.

Except when I strain against the weight on top of me, pain shoots through me like a motherfucker, and I start coughing even harder as it all fades to black.

Dammit. Johnny's gonna be so pissed.

4

JOHNNY

I'm still in shock as I burst through the hospital doors and rush the desk to find out where they're keeping Matty. It was hell finishing up at the scene after the ambulance took him away, but training kicked in and we got the situation under control fast. Faster than usual, since we all pulled together to kick that fire's ass for hurting one of our own. But now? Now I'm vibrating with adrenaline as I flash my fire badge to speed along the info I need on where the hell they're keeping Matt in this place.

I need to see him, and I need to see him *now*.

And then I'm gonna kill him.

After a goddamn eternity, the woman at the desk manages to do her job. She looks up from the screen and says, "Mr. Lopez is in the B Wing, it's just dow—"

"Down the hall to the right, I know," I say, already sprinting away from the desk. I've been here a time or three and know the general layout, and it's a good thing, because I have zero patience for waiting on anything that's going to slow me down.

Which makes Saturday night at the busy hospital my own personal hell.

I dodge and weave between people and gurneys and too goddamn many chairs in the waiting room that seem to multiply for the sole purpose of getting in my way. The word is that Matt will be okay, and I trust Chief to have told me if it was different, but I still know *I'm* not going to be all the way okay until I see it for myself.

And then, like I said, he's a dead man for scaring me like this.

What the fuck was he thinking?

How many times has he gotten on me about doing the job by the book?

Not taking unnecessary risks?

Respecting the fire?

Assessing the scene before taking action?

I'm working myself up, and I almost feel sorry for Matty, knowing I'm going to rip into him the minute I find him and chew him a new asshole for putting me through this. Six years we've been on the job, and neither one of us has ever had anything serious happen up until now. And okay, the way I'm vibrating with pent-up energy? I guess I'm not handling it all that well, but can you really blame me? I mean, I always figured *I'd* be the idiot who got taken out by fire, not Matty, and I'm one hundred percent sure that I'd rather be lying in a hospital bed writhing in pain than imagining him doing the same.

My stomach tightens up and I push the image away. He's gonna be fine, dammit.

I finally reach B Wing and start scouring the rooms as I pass them one by one, following the numbers until it finally hits me that I don't have any idea what room he's in.

Well, shit.

I stop right where I am. "Matt!" I shout, because I truly don't give a fuck. "Mateo Lopez!"

It's a madhouse in this wing, nurses and doctors bustling around left and right and all the seating areas crammed full. My loud voice barely gets a second look from anyone, which is frustrating as all hell. I reach out and start tugging on sleeves, things like manners and courtesy going out the window as a fresh wave of adrenaline courses through me. All I want is a minute of someone's attention, *anyone's* attention, but all I get is a whole lot of people being too damn busy to answer a simple fucking question, like which room Matty is in.

I can't believe this. Did God just decide to pick today to have everyone visit the hospital, the one day my best friend goes in? Is Boston really that bad on a Saturday night, that everyone and their brother needs immediate treatment? Why isn't anyone at the desk for this wing? Why isn't anyone stopping to help me? Did Matty fucking *die* and no one has the guts to tell me?

That last one can't be true, it *can't* be, but it almost has me doubling over just to think it. My heartbeat rises fast, and I flash back to the panic that girl felt back at the scene tonight. I get it, I really do. I've got enough training that I know it's not reasonable, but knowing doesn't do a damn bit of good to stop what I'm *feeling*.

I clench my hands into fists, struggling to get a grip, but I'm still about to burst when something breaks through my spiral of freaking the fuck out. A soft touch on my arm, and I look down, totally thrown for a loop.

Not by the touch, but by the *who*.

"What the fuck?" I say, which probably isn't the most gallant of greetings. I scrub a hand over my face, trying again. "Uh, it's Eden, right?"

She nods, and it's like I just conjured her out of thin air with that passing thought I had a second ago. And I mean, Eden appearing out of thin air? That's never gonna be a bad thing, because... damn. But it still kind of shocks me to see her here. Maybe that shock is like the paddles the EMTs use, though, because it kind of helps, actually, sheer surprise knocking me off that crescendo of rising anxiety and overblown fears that had me locked in its grip.

43

"I recognize you from the fire, don't I?" Eden asks tentatively, glancing down at the firehouse logo on my t-shirt and hey, no doubt smelling the smoke and seeing worse on my face, arms, everywhere. But not like I was gonna stop and shower just to pretty up before getting here to see Matty, you know?

"Yeah," I say, suddenly feeling like I'm in this weird limbo where all my emotions are still swirling around me, but I've been knocked out of them for this surreal second, like I've fallen in the eye of the storm or something. "I'm here checking on my—"

My throat closes up, and Eden's eyes fill with sympathy. Her hand tightens on my arm and she bites her lip in a way that under other circumstances would've been hella distracting.

Okay, who am I kidding? Guess I'm a dog, because it *is* hella distracting.

I yank my mind out of her pants though and cover her hand with mine because... okay, I'm working the sympathy angle and not gonna lie, but she doesn't seem to mind, and human touch is good in times of stress, right?

"It's John, right?" she asks, not pulling her hand away.

Win.

"It's Johnny, actually," I tell her. Then I *really* look her over, professionally I mean, as it hits me that she's *here*, in the hospital. "You okay, Eden? Were you hurt on the scene? Have you been treated?"

"I'm fine," she says, smiling up at me like I'm some kind of saint for asking instead of just this side of decent, the way my thoughts keep straying to dirty places. "I wasn't hurt," she goes on, "I just..."

She shakes her head without finishing that sentence, and while I'm genuinely glad to hear she's okay and kind of curious why she *is* here if she's not hurt, my real priorities suddenly kick back in, and that anxiety that had me by the balls earlier takes a hold again.

"Do you know anything about Matt? Mateo Lopez?" I ask her. My voice is rising fast and I can't stop it, words tripping over themselves as they try to get out of me. I clutch at her hands like a drowning man. "I gotta find him, Eden. Chief says he's gonna be okay, but I need to see, you know? I need to find him *now*, and everyone is so fucking busy here. I mean, I know it's Saturday night, but seriously? And Matty... Matt's the one who—"

"The one who saved my book," Eden interrupts, pretty blue eyes welling up with tears that she immediately wipes away. She nods. "He's here in this wing. He's going to be fine."

I squeeze her hands too tight at that. Oh, Christ. Thank God. Thank fucking *God*. But she winces, so I let her go, mumbling a quick *sorry*.

She smiles up at me. "He really *is* okay, Johnny," she says, patting my arm. "I promise."

And I'm not proud of it, but I start to shake. Relief, you know? It's just so good to find someone who *knows*, even though I'm still not sure why her, or *how* she knows, or why she cares, but it's just... it's good.

I look around like I'm going to suddenly see Matt standing there right in front of me, and I try to ask her where he *is*, but I can't get the words out right.

"Eden, can you... is he, uh, where—"

And then, oh my God, kill me now. I'm *crying*. Jesus fuck. Right in front of her. One more reason to kill Matty when I see him, but for a minute, back at the scene, for a minute I'd thought he was just gone. That minute passed fast, and then the whole day sped the fuck up, but that minute hits me again, and it hits me hard, and I can't handle it. If Matt ever dies on me, hand to God, I will chase him into the afterlife and kill him all over again for putting me through this shit.

I scrub at my face, embarrassed as hell, but Eden just wraps herself around me in a hug that I take gratefully.

I need it, not gonna lie.

"It's okay, shh," she says, holding me tight and repeating it a few more times. "He's fine. Matt's really okay, Johnny, I promise. He's hurt, but he's going to recover, okay?"

"Hurt?" I ask, pulling back and giving her a hard stare. I mean, I know he was, and it's a million times better than dead, but I still don't like it. Hearing it helps me get myself under control, though, and I take in a shuddering breath and get it together. I needed reassurance and I got it, but now I need the details. And Eden? She's perfect, because she doesn't mention my breakdown, just gives me something solid to hold onto.

She clears her throat, then lays it out for me. "Matt experienced minor smoke inhalation, only a minimum of soot cleared from inside his nose, and his breathing is stable. Given how long he was in there, it could have been much worse, but he's clear."

I let out a breath slowly, taking it in. That's good news.

"So, are they releasing him?" I ask.

"Not quite," she says, shaking her head. "He also suffered from a closed fracture of the humerus. It's a clean break, but his arm will be casted and in a sling for a bit while he heals up." She pauses a moment, looking sheepish. "I think he might have broken it around my book? They told me he was still holding it when they pulled him out, tight to his chest, and it's thick? So his arm probably fractured around it."

And then *she* bursts into tears.

"Oh God," she gasps, turning away like she wants to hide it. "I'm so sorry. I never should've made such a big deal about that book. I can't believe he got hurt because of me. I'm so *stupid.*"

"Hey, now," I say, not minding at all that I get a chance to turn the tables and comfort her. "It was a high-stress situation there, Eden. Matt was just doing his job. It's not your fault."

That's me being generous about Matt, but as much as I still want to kill *him*, no way do I want Eden to carry this kind of guilt. Maybe Matty can explain to me later why the hell he went off like some Hollywood action hero back there, but that's between him and me—I wasn't lying; this definitely isn't Eden's fault.

"Do you work here?" I ask, trying to pull her out of it. And the question seems logical, the way she recited his stats and all, you know?

She shakes her head, sniffling, and I tug her against my chest. Where... *damn*, she fits so well. Kind of perfectly, actually. But no, down boy. I don't know why this girl keeps knocking me off my priorities—unless it's the whole not-getting-laid thing I've been meaning to do something about—but right now, that's definitely not what Eden needs from me.

"So, you a nurse or something?" I ask, although yeah, maybe I should have said doctor not to be sexist, but she's gotta be a few years younger than me and Matty, so I think I'm safe, because medical school... amirite? Sheesh. What is it, forty years long or something?

Eden shakes her head. "I'm just a CNA," she says, her voice muffled against my smoky t-shirt as she keeps right on letting me hold her. "And... {sniffle} and sometimes I volunteer here. I came because I wanted to get my book back... {sniffle} and apologize to Matt... {sniffle} and I just... {sniffle} just..."

I push her back a little so I can look down at her, curious all over again.

"You just what?"

She shrugs. "It's familiar here?" she says, looking sheepish. "And I guess I couldn't... well, I couldn't really think of anywhere else to go."

I'm confused for a moment, and then it dawns on me and I feel like an idiot, because hello, that townhouse ended up being a total loss. "Oh, right. Your place. Shit, I'm so sorry about that, Eden. I can give you a ride somewhere after I collect Matty? You got family in the area? Have you already called a friend?"

She shakes her head, casting her eyes down just a bit. "No. I haven't been in Boston long, and there's, well, there's no one out here but me."

I frown at that, because that's no way to live. All alone? But before I can figure out how to fix that for her, she takes a step back from me, straightening her shoulders and doing something I can't pinpoint to her body language that suddenly reminds me we're strangers, despite all the hugging and holding that just went on.

Like she's distancing herself.

Protecting herself.

"Anyway, I can get out of your hair," she says little too brightly, as if she didn't just come to my rescue when I was losing my shit. "Your friend's in 14B, and maybe you can... can tell him that I'm sorry when you go in?"

Her lip quivers with the last word, and yeah, we *are* strangers, I guess, but fuck that. We just went through something together, and that busts down a few of the social-nicety walls, in my opinion.

I hold out my hand, even though I kind of just want to yank her back into my arms and tell her we're in this together, whatever it is. Don't wanna spook her, though.

"Come in with me and you can say it yourself, yeah?"

She starts nibbling that lip again, then finally nods, her cheeks blooming pink as she slips her hand into mine.

Another perfect fit.

I lead her across the hall, and maybe I'm still ramped up on adrenaline, my emotions bouncing to the lowest lows and now the highest highs, because no joke, I feel like I just won something.

"You get your book back yet?" I ask, stroking the soft skin on the back of her hand with my thumb because I guess I just can't help myself.

"No," she says, looking up at me as we reach the door to the room. Her eyes start to get suspiciously bright, and I launch in to save the day without stopping to think.

Huh, is that what happened with Matty?

"We'll get it for you," I promise, grinning down at her. "If I know Matty, he kept it safe. We'll track it down before you leave the hospital, yeah?"

Shit. That reminds me that she said she's got nowhere to go, but she just nods and gives me a wobbly smile, then we enter the room and my heart lurches and I forget about her book for a minute, because Matty's all laid out in the hospital bed looking like hell.

"Fucking idiot," I say, shaking my head and crossing the room so fast I'm almost dizzy. I grab onto his hand, the one that's not attached to the arm encased in a cast, and squeeze it into a pancake. "You want to explain yourself, Matty?" I demand, embarrassed all over again that it comes out gravelly and sort of broken when I'd meant to rip into him. "What... what were you *thinking*, buddy?"

I pinch the bridge of my nose hard, because crying once was plenty, okay? But Matt just gives me a sunny smile that's way, *way* too happy, and lifts the hand I've still got wrapped around his up to his cheek, sort of nuzzling against it.

"Eu-gene," he says, kind of sing-song. "You came. Thought you'd be pissed at me, but knew I could count on you to forgive me if... if... if I didn't get dead."

"I don't forgive you," I lie, so damn happy he *didn't* get dead that I'm even going to let the use of my real name slide this time. Besides—I narrow my eyes and look at him more closely, and okay, now I see it—besides looking like toasted roadkill, his eyes are glazed over like they've given him something that's making him loopy. My lips twitch. "You're high on painkillers, bro."

"Yeah," he says, snickering. "Remember sophomore year, when we—"

"Hey now," I interrupt fast, looking back sheepishly at Eden. "We got company, Matty."

He looks over my shoulder, then tries to sit up. "Ow," he says, pouting up at me when that doesn't go so well for him... probably because he forgot to let go of my hand and didn't pay attention to the fact that his other one is in a cast.

I roll my eyes and help him up, and he gives Eden a lazy, appreciative once-over that has her blushing.

"I like this kind of company," Matt says, patting the spot next to him on the narrow hospital bed. "Come on over here and say hello, beautiful."

I shake my head at him, but pretty sure Eden knows as well as I do that he's out of it and will let it slide.

She does, and I like her even more.

"I... I just wanted to apologize for getting you hurt," she says, coming up to stand on Matt's other side and lightly resting a hand on his cast.

"Not your fault," he says with an exaggerated frown. "I'd do it again in a heartbeat."

"No, you wouldn't," I snap. "Not if you want to live."

"I *did* live," he says, moving like he's trying to swim through syrup as he turns away from Eden and grins up at me. He wraps an arm around my neck and pulls me in, forehead-to-forehead. "Look at me, Johnny. I'm alive. Alive. A-*live*."

He starts out solemnly, then breaks down giggling halfway through, and I push him away, not quite trusting my rollercoaster of emotions to be up close and personal like this with a doped-up version of my best friend right now.

"Shut up so I can figure out how to break you out of here, Matty," I tell him, earning another giggle from him that sets Eden off giggling.

I look up at her and she slaps a hand over her mouth, turning red. "Sorry," she says, eyes sparkling. "I just... that giggle. Here he is, this big, bad, tough firefighter—"

I snort back a laugh, shaking my head. "This shrimp?" I return, even though he's not really that much smaller than me.

Matt punches me in the arm. "I'm big, bad, and tough, Johnny, and don't you forget it," he says, mock-glaring at me. Then he turns back to Eden, and flutters his damn eyelashes at her. "Go on, beautiful, you were saying?"

"Don't mind him," I tell her. "Just promise me it'll wear off by morning."

She presses her lips together like she's holding in a laugh, but nods. Then her beautiful face loses that good humor, and she sighs. "It will, and I hope they gave him a good prescription, because he's not going to feel great when it does."

I cringe inside, even though yeah, I should just be thankful Matty's okay—and I *am*, so much I'm almost dizzy with it—but at the same time, Eden's comment reminds me of what I've got to look forward to. Matty is the king of calm, cool, and collected most of the time, but everyone's got their failings, and the minute he gets even the tiniest scratch? Shoot me now. He turns into the biggest, whiniest baby on the planet. Seriously, you'd think whining was an Olympic sport and he's going for the gold, the way he can carry on when he's hurt.

"I think I'm gonna leave you in the hospital," I tell him, backing away from the bed. "Let someone else listen to you bitch and moan for the next few weeks."

He gives me a hurt look, exaggerated as all hell, but then brightens, turning to Eden. "You'll stay with me, won't you, beautiful?" He's practically slurring his words, and it's kind of cute, actually. "Since... since my very best friend in the *world* doesn't... doesn't love me enough not to desert me in... in my time of need?"

Eden's cheeks go pink, and I can't blame her. He really is fucking adorable like this, and hey, I'm not immune to that smile, either.

Then it hits me. God, I'm fucking brilliant sometimes, yeah?

"Eden!" I say, bouncing on my toes. "You ever take on private clients?"

"Clients?" Matt repeats, cocking his head to look at her. "What do you do?"

"I'm hoping she'll take care of *your* ass, bro," I answer before she can. "She's a CNA, and she's got no place to live, remember?"

"Oh," Eden says, looking startled. "No, I... I couldn't."

"No?" I say, more disappointed than I should be even though it was a totally off-the-cuff idea. Then it hits me that she really doesn't know us, and I backpedal fast, hoping I haven't made her too uncomfortable. "I mean, yeah, no, of course not. But I can still help you find a place to stay tonight, if you want. Give you a ride somewhere?"

"Your house burned down," Matt says solemnly. "And we *do* have a spare room."

"I totally get it if you don't want to help out with this big lug, though," I say, trying to make sure she has an out.

"Hey, now," Matt says, a half-hearted protest as his head lolls back. He's looking pretty out of it.

"But seriously, Eden," I say, managing not to wince as I think about what a pain in the butt it's going to be listening to him whine about his arm itching or not being able to alphabetize the soup cans or whatever. "It's late and you do need a place to sleep tonight, so just crash at our place, yeah?"

She bites her lip, and I can see it in her eyes... she's feeling alone, but she's also nervous.

"No strings attached," I rush to add, holding up my hands. I mean, not that I'd mind, but the way I was pawing at her earlier and the way Matty's still looking at her right now, maybe she's worried about what she'd be committing to if she comes home with us, you know?

Eden blushes and looks down but *hel*lo, I caught something in her eye, and it definitely didn't look like a girl who was *scared* she was going to get pounced on... but I rein that shit in for the millionth time and practice my weakest virtue, patience, just so she doesn't feel pressured.

I wait for her to look up.

She nibbles her lip.

I drum my fingers on my thigh, still *waiting* even though I'm seriously biting my tongue not to try to just convince her already.

She finally peeks up and looks back and forth between the two of us. "You guys wouldn't want me in the way..."

"*I'd* want you in the way," Matt says, eyelids starting to drift down as his voice fades. "All the way. Every way. Maybe even a threewa—"

"Okay now," I interrupt before he gets a little too uncensored, slapping a hand over his mouth and using all my willpower for my dick not to react to where he was going there.

And great, Eden's face is bright red now. I figure no way will she feel comfortable coming over after *that*—thanks so much, Matty, Jesus—but still, I really don't like the idea of her all alone tonight after losing her home, so I give it one last try anyway.

"What my boy was *trying* to say," I start, clearing my throat, "is that you wouldn't be in the way, Eden, for real. Matty and I are roommates, so I'll keep him in line, and his place is actually disgustingly clean and well-decorated, despite my best efforts to convert the whole place into a man cave."

Matty mumbles something that's easy to ignore, since it's in Spanish, and Eden giggles.

I grin, sensing a win. "It's a three-bedroom," I tell her. "And the extra room ain't much, but if you don't mind a weight bench in the corner, it's got a bed and a dresser and clean sheets, and we've got every take-out menu in the city at your disposal."

She cracks a real smile at that for some reason. "You... you really wouldn't mind?"

"Not at all." Which I mean with everything in me, one hundred percent.

"Then maybe... just for tonight?" she says hesitantly. "I can figure out somewhere else to go tomorrow."

I'm not going to argue, but there's also no way I'm kicking her out. Of course, it *is* Matt's house, not that he ever lords that over me, but I'm pretty sure that even after the meds wear off, he'll be happy to have Eden there—and not because he wants to get in her pants, although yeah, I can tell he wouldn't mind that any more than I would, but because Matty's a good person like that, and Eden—well, obviously I don't know her, but Christ, I've *cried* in front of her already, and she's good people, too, I can tell.

In fact, as she helps me deal with all the bullshit required to actually get Matty out of the place and track down that book of hers and pick up his prescription for new painkillers, it gets clear pretty damn fast that she's a lot more than just good people... she's a godsend. A sexy-as-fuck blonde bombshell of a godsend that I'm going to have to keep reminding my dick is at the house for a reason—and that that reason does *not* involve us getting naked together.

Unless, you know, she wants to, of course.

5

EDEN

*T*here's something about thinking you're about to die that changes you, and tonight has definitely changed something in me. Of course, ever since I figured out that the women from my mom's family don't make it past twenty-five, the knowledge has both driven me and held me back, and as I sit on the cute twin bed that these sexy saviors of mine have offered me for the night, clutching my bucket list to my chest, I think about that.

I've been driven to do a lot in my short life so far—I'm holding the evidence of it right now—but there are also things I haven't seen the point of putting on The List. Long-term things that I've known just aren't in the cards for me. Things like nursing school, settling down somewhere, letting myself get close to people who I know will just end up hurting when they lose me. So yes, knowing I'm going to die has changed me—or rather, it's *shaped* me—but the immediacy of actually thinking that it was all going to end *tonight* is different.

I bite my lip, heart racing as I look at the closed door. Tonight has made me feel... well, not quite reckless, that's just not me, but a little bit bold, maybe. Johnny was so sweet, all worked up about his friend and still trying to take care of me, too. And Matt, so strong when he needed to be back at the fire, and then so silly once the Tramadol kicked in. And both of them hot enough to make my toes curl... and interested enough, unless I miss my guess, to tempt me into doing something about it.

I put my book down and stand up on shaky knees, knowing that what I *should* feel right now is exhausted. When we got here, I helped Johnny get Matt settled in the master bedroom and accepted a wildly oversized t-shirt from him after giving in to a heavenly shower that I needed more than I'd realized. And now I'm supposed to be getting some rest. Sleeping off this traumatic day. Recouping and figuring out what I'm going to do from here, since I basically only own the clothes on my back, have nowhere to live, and it will probably be a week or two until I can sort anything out with my renter's insurance policy.

So yes, exhausted would make sense... but what I really feel?

I bite my lip, remembering Auntie Maria telling me that if I got a chance to enjoy myself with a man, that I should go for it. And why not? Tonight wasn't my time, and I'm more thankful than I should be, given that I know my days are numbered anyway, but that doesn't change the fact that they *are* numbered. Would it really hurt anything to take her advice?

I open the door before I can second-guess myself, my heart pounding out of my chest as I strain to hear whether or not Johnny's still up. If I'm honest—and I know this probably doesn't sound good—I'd take *either* of these two boys if the option were on the table, but Matt is out for the count, and there's no part of me that's disappointed at the idea of getting to know Johnny a little better.

I blush, twisting my hands together in front of me as I pause in the middle of the hallway. Getting to know him better? Oh, Lord. If I can't even be frank about what I want in my own mind, how am I ever going to start something with him? So okay... I actually *wouldn't* mind getting to know him a little bit better, that's true, but what I really want tonight is something else.

I want to sleep with him.

I want him to take me.

I want to give in to the kind of erotic fantasy I've never indulged outside of the privacy of my own mind, and have him fuck me senseless.

"Eden? You need something?"

"Eep!"

I squeal like a little girl when Johnny pops around the corner, clutching my chest and suddenly all too aware that the t-shirt he loaned me is all I have on. It comes down to my thighs, so I guess you could say I'm decent, but I'm also fresh out of the shower and not looking even remotely like a seductress.

Oh my God. I can't do this.

"Eden?"

"I... I'm hungry," I blurt, which is another thing that should be true, given that I never managed dinner, but now my stomach is so twisted up with nerves that I couldn't eat if you paid me to.

"Oh, yeah, of course," he says, smacking his forehead. "Man, I can't believe I didn't offer you anything. But this whole night, you know?"

"It's okay," I say, feeling bad for making *him* feel bad, but he's already taken ahold of my arm and is leading me into the kitchen, and I go with it, because I *did* just say I was hungry... and maybe, if I'm honest, also because a part of me is hoping I'll find the nerve to follow through with my original plan, too.

Because, wow. Johnny's dressed for bed, too. Soft, low-slung sleep pants and nothing else, and the boy is *built*. I guess fire-fighters have to be—isn't that why they invented calendars?—but seeing his big arms, bigger chest, and eight-pack abs in the flesh has my whole body flushing hot with a flashback to how it felt to be wrapped in those arms back in the hospital.

How good pressing up against him had felt.

How *right*.

"Eden?" Johnny says, jerking my attention back up to his face. His strong jawline is covered by a golden scruff, and it frames lips almost too plush for a man.

"I'm sorry, what?" I say, having no idea what he was asking me.

He laughs, but there's a definite spark of heat in his eyes as he scrubs a hand over his face. "Just asking what you'd like to eat. Truth is, me and Matty do more take-out than actual cooking, but I mean, there's some cold pizza?"

Pizza? It would sit in my stomach like lead.

I shake my head.

"Oh, uh, okay," he says, a little flustered as he turns and opens the fridge. "Um, we've also got—"

"You," I say, my core tightening with excitement as I watch his ass flex under those soft pants.

He whips around to face me, that spark I saw a moment ago igniting into something hotter. "What?"

I shiver. *Anticipation.* And then—

"I want *you*," I say, like I'm someone else completely. Someone who says things like that. And then I lick my lips, because he just looks so unbelievably good, and now I really *am* hungry.

"Yeah," he says, his voice going low and sexy and doing things to me that make me want to crawl all over him. Then he shakes his head and rubs at the back of his neck, looking away. "I mean, uh, it's a natural reaction to stress, right?" he says. "Adrenaline does that to—"

Oh my God.

I'm *mortified*.

He doesn't want me.

I've swum with sharks. I've gone cliff diving. I've hiked into a volcano. But I can't face this, I just can't.

I turn and run.

"Whoa, whoa, whoa, *Eden*," Johnny says, catching up to me just as I reach the guest room. He wraps those big arms around me from behind and pulls me back against his chest, physically stopping me. "Hey, now," he says, his deep voice low and soothing and moving over me like a warm wave. "I didn't mean to scare you off."

"I... I'm not scared," I whisper, because it's the truth.

More embarrassed than I've ever been in my life? Check.

Also more turned on than I've ever been in my life? With his big, hard body plastered against me from behind, my breasts resting on his crossed arms, his hot breath tickling my neck... *big* check.

I want to melt back against him. I want to feel his hands on me. I want those lips... I want them *every*where.

"Eden," he says, shifting slightly without letting me go.

And oh my God, I feel it, growing against my lower back. He does *want* me.

"Johnny?"

He groans, arms tightening deliciously around me. "I wasn't sayin' no," he says, which sends my heart rate rocketing. "I just... I wouldn't want you to feel like there was any expectation, what with you staying here and all."

I wiggle around until I'm facing him, loving how good it feels that he *still* doesn't let go.

"I don't feel like that," I say, breathless. It's true, though. He's been nothing but sweet. "And I'm not usually like this. I don't... I don't *do* this," I add, feeling my face flame with heat. "But right now, maybe it *is* adrenaline—" it's not, but how would I explain anything else? "—but if you wouldn't mind, Johnny, I'd really like—"

"*Mind?*" he says, eyes sparkling as he laughs. And then those huge hands slide right down my back and over my ass and find the hem of the shirt he loaned me, and then they're *on* my ass.

He groans again when he finds me bare, and the hard length of his cock jerks against my stomach, and I gasp, my pussy flooding with slick heat. And then before I can even blink, he's hoisted me up against him, just lifted me clean off the floor, and he's kissing me. I wrap my legs around his waist and hold on for dear life, feeling like things just went from zero to sixty, fast enough to make me dizzy.

And I *love* it.

Oh, Lord, do I ever. Johnny can *kiss*, and those big hands holding me up? That hard body flexing and straining against mine? I don't even realize he's moved until he lays me down on the bed and covers me with his body, plush lips leaving mine and trailing over my jaw and down my neck as he pushes the shirt up higher, exposing me.

"Oh, Christ, Eden, you're killing me," he says, fingers splayed across my hip as he rears back to look at me for a minute. "This shirt is ruined for me now unless you're in it."

I bite my tongue to keep from pointing out that it's threadbare and that I've got no makeup on and that I feel both silly and self-conscious with him staring down at me like this. But then he puts his other hand on me, too, framing my stomach between them and rubbing his thumbs across my skin so slowly it makes me quiver, and he's looking down at me almost *worshipfully*... and suddenly I don't feel silly at all.

I feel wanted.

I feel *sexy*.

I feel wanton and bold and so, *so* turned on I don't think I can stand it.

"Johnny," I whisper, arching up so that I press into his hands and—who *am* I right now?—opening my legs wider in invitation. "Please."

His eyes flare with heat, and he pushes the shirt up until it bares my breasts. "This what you want, princess?" he asks, cupping them in his hands and rolling my nipples between his fingers.

"*Yes*," I gasp, heat shooting straight to my core.

"You sure?" he asks, giving me a wicked smile as he slides one of those big hands down over my stomach to rest on my mound, the heel of his hand pressing right into my center. "Because I wouldn't want to neglect *this*."

I shake my head, *not* saying no. "No," I manage. "Please don't... don't neglect... *ohhhhhh*."

He's not neglecting me. Not at all. His hands are magic, moving over my body firmly... slowly... *relentlessly*. Every touch reassures me that I was wrong. Johnny *does* want me. And he's ramping up a fire inside me that I can tell is going to get out of control if I let it.

And oh, I *want* to let it. I want to just let myself go with him. Let this be a guilt-free pleasure that I can get lost in. Let him have his way with me because even though we just met, there's something about him I trust.

Trust him to take care of me.

Trust him to pleasure me.

Trust him to know what I need, even when I can't bring myself to ask for it... just like he did when he chased me down after I bolted from the kitchen.

"Johnny," I whisper, reaching up to run my hands over the hard ridges of his stomach. Skimming them down toward the thick ridge of his cock where it tents the soft material of his sleep pants.

I stop at his waistband and he shudders, so I rake my nails over his tanned skin, feeling bold.

"Jesus, Eden," he groans, capturing my hand and moving it down over his erection. He pushes into my palm—hot and hard and throbbing, even through the pants—and groans again, throwing his head back and looking like some kind of sex god as he towers over me. "How far... how far do you wanna take this?" he grits, all those big muscles quivering as he holds himself still above me and lets me mold my hand around the shape of him.

His cock is huge. Thick and long and pulsing against my hand. I bite my lip. Is he really going to make me say it?

I squirm, looking up at him, and he grins, reading me like a book. What a perfect, perfect man. He pushes his pants down, cock springing free and slapping against his stomach, and I moan.

I can't help it.

"Is this what you want, princess?" he asks, stroking himself as he looks down at me like I'm candy.

I nod. Oh, Lord, do I ever. He drops his hand, stroking my hips... my thighs... teasing and torturing me as he circles closer and closer to where I need some attention. My pussy is tingling, practically *throbbing*, and suddenly I *want* to say it.

"I want to feel you inside me," I gasp, tightening my thighs around his thick legs because oh my *God*, as good as I feel right now? It doesn't embarrass me at all to say those words, it just makes me feel hotter. *Desperate*, but in a delicious way that feels the best kind of dirty. "Fuck me, Johnny," I pant as his thumbs skim the creases at the top of my thighs. *"Please.* I... I need you."

"I'm yours," he says, dipping his fingers inside me. Rubbing his thumb over my clit. Leaning down to capture my mouth when I gasp with the sudden jolt of pleasure, and then sucking my tongue in an erotic rhythm that has me writhing underneath him, one that matches the naughty things he's doing between my legs.

But he's still not fucking me.

Oh, Lord, I want him to fuck me.

I've never wanted anything as badly in my *life*.

"Johnny, Johnny, Johnny," I moan, rocking against his hand as he moves that hot mouth down to my breasts and starts teasing my nipple. Sucking it lightly. Circling it with his tongue. Biting —*ohhhhhh*. Biting it with just the right hint of pain to make the pleasure spike inside me and make me scream.

"Oh my God," I whisper, freezing. Quivering. "Do you think Matt—"

"Matty's totally out of it," Johnny growls, looking up at me. "You go right ahead and scream for me, princess. I want to hear it over and over tonight."

He rolls my nipple between his fingers before I can respond, kissing his way down my stomach, and I gasp.

Over and over? More than once?

But then he's kissing lower, replacing his thumb on my clit with his incredible tongue while his fingers still work inside me, and suddenly I can't think at all. I arch up against him, my hands scrabbling at the back of his head as my own tips back against the pillows and a whole litany of erotic sounds tumble from my mouth.

I'm begging him.

Making him promises.

Asking for more, more, *more* until suddenly it's too much… too good… and I'm *gone*, pushed right over the edge and flying. Screaming again, just like Johnny wanted me to.

My thighs clamp tight around his head and my whole body shakes with the force of the kind of orgasm I didn't even know existed. The kind that turns me inside out and forgets to put me back together again. The kind that definitely would have been on my bucket list if I'd even known such a thing was possible.

"Oh Christ, Eden," he says, trailing hot kisses up my body until he finds my mouth again. "You are fucking *beautiful* when you come."

I want to blush, but I just feel too darn good to bother. Languid and warm and just… just *perfect*. And then Johnny's kissing me again, the musky scent of my own sex invading my senses as that big, hard body pins me against the mattress… as he rolls his hips into mine, sliding the firm length of his gorgeous cock against my soft folds… as he starts to ignite me all over again, until I'm moaning shamelessly and writhing underneath him, wrapping my legs around his hips and rocking against his hard shaft, letting the sweet, dirty words he whispers push me higher and higher and higher until I can't stand it.

"Please, *please* fuck me," I beg, completely without shame as I pant out the words and clutch him closer. "Oh, God, oh Johnny, I need it... I need it... I need it."

"Anything, princess," he grits out, one hand kneading my ass as I rock against him and the other stretching past my head, toward the nightstand, and coming back with a condom that I'd been too far gone to even think about insisting on.

Oh my God. He *is* perfect.

He opens it with his teeth and covers himself smoothly, and then the thick head of his cock presses into me, opening me up like a flower. I moan, letting my eyes drift shut as the sensation overwhelms me. He's so big that the stretch is just this side of painful, but the first orgasm relaxed me so much that all I feel is bliss.

"You feel so... damn... *good*," Johnny groans, pushing all the way inside me in one long, slow, relentless slide that leaves me gasping.

Overpowers me.

Fills me so completely that nothing else exists.

He kisses me hard, buried to the hilt, and then pulls back and throws one of my legs over his shoulder and tilts my hips up with his other hand and oh Lord oh my God oh yes yes *yes*, he starts fucking me.

Hard and fast and deep.

Just like I asked him to.

Exactly like I *need* him to.

And it's so good I think it might actually kill me, that *this* is how I'll go—and for once, I don't even mind.

But then I can't think at all. He's got me at just the right angle to drive me crazy, every thrust hitting me just right until I'm sobbing with it. Clawing at him. *Begging* him.

I'm right on that edge all over again, so desperate to fly that I can't *breathe*.

"Please please *please*."

"Scream for me again, princess," Johnny growls, driving that thick cock into me one last time as his fingers flick across my clit and—

"*Ohhhhhhhhhhhh!*"

My mouth is open, but I don't even know if any sound comes out, I'm that lost in it. The orgasm spirals through me and explodes, a chain reaction of pleasure as I come apart into a million blissful pieces. And Johnny's right there with me—hips stuttering against me as he thrusts into me a few more times, ramping up my pleasure even further, and then throwing his head back with a shout as he finds his release.

Every muscle in that gorgeous, hard body is rigid for a moment, and if a man can be beautiful, this one *is*. I'm still pulsing around his hard length, but the sharp pleasure that overwhelmed me is giving way to a lazy, lovely afterglow the likes of which I've never known. I run a hand over his back, down his side, skim it over his stomach, and he shudders, finally relaxing against me.

"Oh, fuck," he groans, burying his face against the side of my neck. "Oh, *man*, Eden. So good."

Too good, I almost say, but bite it back just in time.

It's true, though. I'm not that experienced, but I'm no virgin, and this was... well, this was *wow*. So good that it makes me want more, even though Johnny was supposed to be nothing more than a one-time, guilt-free indulgence.

Good thing I'm leaving tomorrow.

"Thank you," I whisper, threading my fingers through his short hair. Enjoying the moment without letting myself wish for more. "It was incredible."

He lifts his head up and grins down at me, and something trembles in my chest.

"Incredible, huh?" he asks, the cocky tone making me giggle.

He *deserves* to be cocky after that... but it can't hide the sweetness in his gaze.

"I'll take incredible," he says, eyes softening as he leans down and kisses me again.

And then again.

Endlessly.

Perfectly.

As if he genuinely wants to do *this* just as much as the other.

Until all that exhaustion finally catches up with me and I start to drift away, too tired and too well-satisfied to protest when he finally gets up to handle cleanup and tucks a blanket around me and places one more sweet, soft kiss on my forehead... and goes. And it's a *good* thing that I'm so tired, because otherwise I might have been tempted to do something dumb, like ask him to stay.

To start hoping we *could* do it again, and that it might start to mean something if we did.

The kind of something that I know better than to add to my bucket list.

The kind of something I've *always* known I won't have enough time for... so I'm not about to let myself start wanting now, so close to the end.

6

MATT

*W*hat I want to know is how it's taken me this long to realize that all six of the decorative pillows I bought for the couch are stuffed with lead. I sit up for the eight hundredth time and shove them all together under where I was lying, piling them up in the dwindling hope that this time, the damn things will actually be comfortable. Of course, I'm doing it all with my left hand, which is frustrating as hell since I keep fumbling, and *then*, when I finally get them somewhat settled and try to relax back on them, the fucking remote is missing.

I literally just had it.

Right.

Here.

I roll a little and try to spot it, and great, there it is. Under the coffee table. Which wouldn't be a problem if I had two working arms, but which *is* a problem, since it means I gotta leave the finally decent pillow setup, twist around to use my only functional arm, stretch to try and get to it while also holding the pillow stack in place with my shoulder, and then—

"Fuck," I hiss, falling off the couch and landing on the damn cast. *"Fuuuuuuuuuuccccckkkkkkkk."*

By the time the pain backs off enough for me to unclench my jaw and open my eyes, Eden's standing over me, looking down like she's not quite sure whether to laugh or sigh. Me, though? I grin, because oh man, the view is *nice*, and suddenly all the pain-in-the-ass bullshit of my one-arm morning quits bugging me.

There are about ten thousand reasons I love Johnny, but these last few days? Top of that list is his stroke of brilliance in getting this girl to come stay with us. I know Eden's been stressing about "overstaying" and other garbage, yapping about getting a hotel room and searching for cheap apartments online every day, but so far, my boy Johnny and I have tag-teamed her with good sense and good looks (me) and ninja take-out ordering skills (him), and we've managed to keep her around.

"What exactly were you trying to do here, Matt?" she asks, hands on her hips even though her lips are twitching.

"I couldn't reach the remote," I say, giving her my best puppy-eyed pleading look in the hopes that she'll get off Johnny's laptop and quit with the apartment hunting already and have some pity on me. In other words, I'm going out of my mind stuck here in the house and incapable of basic two-armed functions while Johnny's back on shift at the firehouse, and Eden is my new favorite distraction.

She laughs, and I let her help me up even though okay, I don't really need it. Cast or not, I still got plenty of core strength and two good legs, but hey, like I'm going to pass on the opportunity for some hands-on from *her*? Like I noted back at the fire, this girl pushes every single one of my buttons, and the only reason I haven't already gotten a whole lot *more* hands-on with her—or at least tried to see if she's open to that—is because I don't want to do anything that might scare her away before I get a chance to sweep her off her feet.

Long-term thinking, baby. That's me. In it to win it.

"Did you hurt yourself?" she asks, those soft hands flitting over me in a kind of slow torture that I can't get enough of.

"Yes," I say, grinning and then wiping it off my face and replacing it with a pitiful look when her head snaps up. I hold out my cast. "Ow."

An adorable little wrinkle appears between her eyebrows, and she starts touching me a whole lot more. I mean, she's pretty damn professional about it—the girl clearly has some training—but I'll take what I can get, right?

"I'm going to get you some Tylenol," she says, massaging my bare shoulder above the cast and giving me all sorts of interesting ideas for more things she could rub. "And I really think you should wear the sling here at home. And *ask* me if you need something, okay?"

"I don't want to bug you," I lie, because personally, I'm totally okay with her taking care of me and my wrecked arm 24/7 if I can talk her into it.

"Oh, stop," she says, laughing. "You and Johnny let me stay here and get in the way all weekend." She blushes, then looks away. "I owe you a little help, don't you think? And I promise, I'll get out of your—"

"Eden," I cut her off, using my good hand to lift her chin and make her look at me. "Look at what happens to me without you —" I hold up my cast and pout, "—and you got no place to go. When are you going to accept that we're a match made in heaven?"

She blushes even more, and I see something spark in her eyes that's got me grinning. Oh, I've got this. I've *totally* got this. I almost lean in and seal the deal, but then she gives a little self-conscious laugh that has me second-guessing the moment and twists away, repeating something about a painkiller for me.

I sigh, sitting back down on the couch and grabbing a pillow. I toss it up in the air and catch it with my left a few times—yeah, skills—and wonder if I'm losing my touch.

I'm pretty sure Eden's as attracted to me as I am to her... but then again, maybe I'm misreading things? Or maybe she's just a little torn. I mean, I'm pretty sure I've also caught her throwing some hot looks Johnny's way... and guess I can't say I blame her. Not to be weird about it, but let's be real, there's a reason he's always so successful with the ladies, and while he's a stand-up guy —the best in the world—seems pretty clear that it has just as much to do with how fucking ripped he is. Johnny's just a good-looking guy, and that's a fact, not me suddenly finding out I've got some stray gay gene that accidentally got passed down or anything.

Eden comes back in and hands me some pills and a glass of water, and I figure if she doesn't want to mess around yet, the next best thing is getting to know her a little better, right? So I figure I'll start with an obvious one, given that she's homeless and staying with two total strangers.

Not that I'm complaining, but just saying, it opens up some questions, yeah?

"So where's your family?" I ask, holding onto her hand after I take the pills from it and tugging her down next to me.

She sits readily enough, folding herself onto the seat with her knees up like she doesn't mind settling in for a chat. She's biting that lip I keep wanting a taste of, though, making me think I might have inadvertently hit a nerve, but before I can shift directions, she answers.

"I've got an aunt out in California," she says. "She's Navy."

"Okay," I say, drawing the word out when it looks like she's just going to leave it at that.

One aunt?

That's all I get?

"You got brothers and sisters? Parents? Come on now, I want to know all about you." I give her a winning smile, but her breath hitches, and I lose it fast. "Hey, sorry," I say, straightening up and feeling like an ass. "I'm just being nosy, it's not my business."

"No, it's fine," she says, not seeming to mind me holding her hand. "But no, no brothers or sisters or... or parents. Mine died when I was young, and I don't remember much about them, to be honest. My Auntie Maria raised me."

"Oh, shit," I say, my ass-status confirmed. I squeeze her hand, no ulterior motive. "I'm sorry, Eden."

She gives me a wobbly smile. "Nothing to be sorry about. You didn't know, and Maria is wonderful. I'm so grateful she took me in."

"Was she always Navy?" I ask, even though I suddenly want to know a bunch of other stuff, too. How did her parents die? How young was she? I don't care how long ago it was—I can see it's still affecting her, and that makes me want to fix it.

Which is stupid, yeah? That's not something you can fix for someone, and sure I think she's hot, but I've only known her for three days... but hey, when did I ever claim to be smart? I want what I want, and right now, I want to be the one who makes it so her smile doesn't wobble like that.

Like I said though, I'm good with playing the long game for things that matter.

Eden's nodding. "I was a military brat, through and through. Between all the places Maria was stationed and the homes I had to stay in while she was deployed, I was always moving."

I shake my head. Can't even imagine it, really.

"That must've been... something," I say, feeling bad for her. Sure, I've hit a few other places for some long weekends. New York. Philly. A pretty fucking memorable one in New Hampshire, back in the day. Johnny and I even did spring break down in Cancun once. But me? I'm a Boston boy, through and through. No place I'd rather be when I got everything I want right here.

She must've heard the pity in my voice, because she laughs, shaking her head. "It wasn't so bad. I got to see a lot, didn't I? And it helped me cross number twenty-four off my bucket list."

Her skin flushes pink at that, just like it has the other few times she's mentioned that list. I know why, too. She feels guilty for me getting hurt retrieving it, but that's crap. I still don't fully get it, but I know it means a lot to her, and hey, I didn't die, so broken arm or not, I'm pretty glad I did it now that it's done.

Still, I'm an opportunist, and I want to know this girl, so I'm not above seizing this one.

"So what does a guy have to do to hear about this list?" I ask, holding up my cast and going for puppy eyes again.

"Oh, Matt," she says, all breathless and sexy as her gorgeous blue eyes fill with guilt again. She leans in, starting to pet my arm... my shoulder... just dripping sympathy.

I bite back a smile.

"I'm so, so sorry."

"Nah, it's all good," I say, since it's true. Still, I manage a pretty slick move on the couch which ends up with my head in her lap and her hands sort of weaving through my hair and making me want to purr. "But I am curious about this list. Heard of 'em, but not sure I get it? Isn't a bucket list all the things you want to do in life before, well, kicking the bucket?"

She nods. "I heard the idea back when I was sixteen," she says. "And I started one right away. I just wanted to make sure I didn't miss out on anything, does that make sense? I wrote down all the amazing things I could think of, and I guess some silly ones, too, and then I just started trying to do them."

"So what was number twenty-four?" I ask, remembering what she'd said a minute ago. "And jeez, twenty-*four*? How many things you got on this list?"

"Twenty-four was visiting every state in the U.S.," Eden tells me, grinning. "And that one has been accomplished. And how many? Well, there are a hundred. You know, 'one hundred things to do before turning twenty-five.'"

"Oh, shit," I say, laughing. "Ambitious much? Everyone else gets a lifetime to do a whole list and you're trying to knock it out before twenty-five? What are you now, twenty-two? Twenty-three?"

"Twenty-four," she says, looking away. "And it seemed smart, given..."

"Given what?" I ask, not sure what I said wrong but not liking the look I put on her face.

She doesn't answer right away and I sit up, tipping her chin to look at me again. "Tell me, Eden."

"Oh, it's just... you know, my mother died before she turned twenty-five, so it just felt like a... like a momentous age to... to do things before."

"Makes sense," I say, pulling her in with my good arm and offering some comfort, since I can tell she's shook up about it, even though it happened so long ago.

And man, she fits against me like she was made to be there.

Guess I'm not overly ambitious. I've never had a bucket list and probably never will, because I'm pretty damn happy with what I've already got, and all I want is to know I get to hold onto it. And here's the thing about me—when something fits? That's it. I know what I like, and when I find it, I *will* do everything I can to keep it. Never gonna need to live anywhere but right here in Boston, right in this house that will hopefully someday have a family in it, and someday after that I'll die in it. I'll retire happy from the firehouse without ever wishing I did something else with my life.

And Eden? She fits, too. I can already tell, so yeah, gotta play the long game here.

"What about you?" she asks, still nestled against me. "Is your family here in Boston?"

I frown, but hey, I can tell she's sort of deflecting all the talk about her late parents, and it's a fair question, so I suck it up and start easy.

"Got Johnny, don't I?"

She looks up at me, surprised. "You're... family? You don't really look alike," she blushes, then rushes on with, "I guess I thought you guys were just friends."

I snort, laughing. There's no "just" for me and Johnny. And I mean, sure, he's not *family*, not by blood—and if I had a bigger word, I'd use it—but he's always been part of me for as long as I can remember, and family's as good a word as any. Especially given the state of my *real* family.

"We are friends," I say, since it's true. "Johnny's family sort of forgot about him, he came along so late and all, but their loss is my win, yeah?"

She looks like she might press me on that, and hey, I'll talk about Johnny all day, no problem, but guess she decides against it, because she goes back to my situation.

"Do you have any actual brothers?" she asks. "Sisters? Parents?"

"Nah," I say, rubbing the bridge of my nose. "I'm an only child. Got a great mom, but as soon as I was out on my own, she took off."

"To where?"

"To everywhere," I tell her, laughing as I shake my head, because I mean, I don't get it, but seems to make Mom happy, so whatever. "She always talked about seeing the world back when I was a kid, but I mean, I thought it was just talk? We had a good life—" My throat closes up for a minute, thinking about how wrong I'd been, back when I'd thought all that comfortable routine I'd thrived on growing up was *real*. Barbecues on the weekends. Bruins games with my dad. Johnny over for dinner practically every night and making *huevos* for breakfast every morning with—

I clear my throat, blinking fast.

"Uh, anyway, she's been traveling for years, now," I go on, hoping Eden doesn't call me on anything. "I get post cards from the craziest places, and once in a while she'll even pop back here to Boston and say hello."

"Oh, wow," Eden says, eyes wide. "That's different."

"No shit," I say, a bit of the old resentment surging up in my chest. Not toward Mom, I mean, whatever floats her boat, right?

But would she really be avoiding Boston like this if Dad hadn't betrayed us?

"What about your father?" Eden asks, resting a hand on my chest. "Is he... is he still in Boston?"

Best thing about this cast? It's the middle of fucking summer and hot as hell, and here I've got the perfect excuse to walk around shirtless around a beautiful woman 24/7. I flex a little, covering her hand with mine—because hey, like I said, opportunist—and sort of rubbing it over my pecs in what I hope comes across as subtle.

And fine, okay, so I'm avoiding the subject, but might as well rip off the Band-Aid, though, since I've got my sights on this girl, yeah?

"Dad's around," I say, keeping her hand pressed against me but letting my head fall back against the couch. I stare up at the ceiling, wondering why the hell they spray ceilings with that stuff that makes it look like they're covered with little bumps. I keep right on wondering and let the words just come out flat, so I can hurry up and tell her about that part of my life without having to think about it, and then hopefully be done with it. "He still lives in the house I grew up in, but with someone else now."

"Oh," Eden says, and I can feel her kind of settle into stillness next to me, like she's hurting for me. "Did he... did he leave your mom for another woman?"

"Nope," I say, popping the "p" sound and wondering if I'd hate him less if he had?

Nah, it would be the same.

Okay, different, but the same.

"You... you don't like his new wife, I take it?" Eden asks tentatively.

I sigh, pinching the bridge of my nose. "No wife. Not remarried, thank Christ, since he's shacked up with another *guy* now."

"Oh," Eden says, her voice a little tight.

"Yeah, no shit," I go on, even though I should drop it. "He went and decided he was gay all of a sudden, like he hadn't had years to figure that shit out if he really had to have some D so bad, yeah? Like he couldn't have saved himself the trouble of starting a family he was just going to bust apart later?" My voice is rising, but there's no helping it now. And *this* is why I don't let myself think about this bullshit on a regular basis. "Or since he *did* go and marry my mom and then lie to her all those years," I spit, the floodgates fully open now. "He couldn't have just… just kept it to himself? Been a fucking *man* and dealt with the responsibilities he had in front of him instead of running off and… and…"

I'm breathing hard all of a sudden, so it takes me a moment to realize that Eden isn't just quiet, she's also stiff. Pulling away from me. And thanks so much, Dad, for one more moment of my life you've ruined.

I take a breath, trying to shake it off.

"Don't worry, beautiful," I say, squeezing her around the shoulders with my good arm and trying to pull her back in. "Gay ain't contagious."

"No," she agrees. "But being a dick might be, and I'm not going to risk it."

She shakes off my arm and stands up, and I don't get it, because this isn't the Eden I've been flirting with and teasing for the last few days. The one who gives me sweet looks and is full of sympathy and caring and… and all those things that make me want to do more than just get in her pants.

But I mean yeah, I want that, too, of course.

"What?" I say, getting to my feet fast when she starts heading down the hall toward the guest room without explaining herself. "Eden—"

She spins around to face me, and—oh, shit. I don't know what I said, but the girl is *pissed.*

"I'm just going to get my purse and my things," she says. "And then I'll be out of here for good. And I'm sorry your parents split up, Matt, I imagine that must be hard, but you know what? Life is too short for me to spend any more of mine around someone who would say such disgusting things."

"I... what?" I repeat, dumbfounded.

For real, what's she talking about? What did I say?

Guess I asked that last one out loud, because she starts stalking back toward me, letting me have it.

"What *didn't* you say?" she snaps. "That you'd rather your father live a lie than try and find happiness? That you think loving someone is only acceptable if it's done in one single way? That you'd rather see both your parents trapped in a marriage where I'm betting *neither* of them was fulfilled, just so you don't have to adjust *your* view of the world?"

She's right in my face now, one finger poking me in the chest with every point, and I'm... I'm frozen. No one's ever said this shit to me, and what the fuck right does *she* have? But just when I start to get a good head of steam worked up to tell her so, she starts crying. It's bad, too, because I don't even think she realizes she's doing it. She's still poking me hard with every other word, but now the tears are just spilling down her cheeks while she talks, and it stops me cold, freezing up all my righteous anger and draining it right out of me. And it's like her tears are washing out my ears or something, too, because suddenly I'm *listening* to what she's saying, instead of just deflecting it.

"You've got two parents who are *alive*," she says, voice cracking. "And you resent them for living those lives on their own terms instead of being thankful every day that you still *have* them? I'm sorry, Matt, but just... no. It may not be my place to say, but I'm going to anyway. You're wasting something precious, and if you think *gay* is the worst thing someone can be—"

"No," I blurt, that last accusation startling the word right out of me before I can stop it.

She stops with her mouth open, and I wipe her cheeks, because it's killing me.

"I'm not... not like, what's the word—"

"An asshole?"

"A bigot," I correct her, even though I can kind of see from her point of view why she thought the other word applied, now that my ears have been washed out.

She crosses her arms in front her chest, calling bullshit with her body language, and I'm dumbfounded. What, she really thinks I... I mean, sure, I don't like that my dad went gay, but... and okay, so, okay. I guess the way I expressed myself could have given her the impression that it was the gay part of my dad's story that I have a problem with.

I scrub my good hand over my face, feeling like the asshole she's just accused me of being. Not the greatest start to getting her to stick around, yeah?

And if I'm *really* honest, I guess I do have a problem with gay... but more like, I can't separate it from the way Dad broke up our family, not what Eden said about me thinking there's only one right way to love someone and all.

I don't really think that, I just... I just... oh, shit.

I'm crying, too. Maybe an aftereffect of the meds they gave me.

"Sorry," I say, ducking away from her and figuring this is it. So much for us fitting together like I thought. This is just... this is a clusterfuck, is what it is.

But then, instead of leaving like she'd just promised, Eden wraps her arms around me from behind, resting her wet face against my back, and sighs.

"I'm sorry, too," she says quietly. "I don't really know the situation with your family, I guess it just touched a nerve. And I... I really don't have patience for bigotry."

I laugh, turning around to face her and happier than I deserve when she lets me wrap my arms around her right back. "Yeah, I got that, you fierce little thing. Do I get points if I apologize?"

"To me, or to your father?" she asks, the question freezing me up all over again.

Because damn, I'd rejected all *his* apologies over the years, but it's never once even crossed my mind that I might owe him one.

I should want Eden gone, the way she keeps blindsiding me with shit I don't want to think about. But what I really want? Yeah, it's not that. Not saying everything she's just hit me with feels good, because it doesn't, but you know what? When I was a kid, maybe eight or nine, Johnny and I were playing baseball and he egged me into sliding for home even though I would have scored the run just fine staying on my feet. And besides winning the game and looking fucking *awesome* in the picture someone snapped for the league calendar, hitting the dirt like that also got me a broken leg... which turned out kind of awesome because of all the sympathy points that cast earned me that summer. But point being, once the cast came off and the physical therapy started, it fucking *hurt*. But it was a good hurt, because as fun as it had been to be pampered and all, I'd missed having two good legs.

Maybe I'm thinking about that now because here I am in a cast all over again, or maybe I'm thinking about it because as pissed off at my dad as I still am, even after all these years, the truth is I miss him just as bad as I ever missed being able to walk that summer.

Maybe worse.

"Just tell me what I've gotta say to get you to stay," I say to Eden, not sure if I'm scared she'll try to force me to tell him I'm sorry... or hoping for it.

She doesn't try to force anything, though. Just looks up at me, startled. "Why on earth would you want me to stay?" she asks, eyes wide.

Oh, man. That's a loaded one, yeah? Too many reasons I shouldn't give; everything from how bad I want her—my dick on high alert even now, when I feel like I've just been through an emotional wringer—to all the stuff that I know damn well it's too soon to even hint at, but that I can already tell I'm hoping will work out.

And then there's this new thing. The way she pushed me and I kind of hope she might keep pushing me.

"Because you make me better," I say, the words slipping out too fast for me to stop them. I lift up my cast, playing it off like that's what I'd meant. "Didn't Johnny say you were a nurse?"

"Just a CNA," she says, shaking her head but kind of smiling, too, so that I think I've still got a chance here.

"You ever take on private clients?"

She laughs out loud at that for some reason, and something inside me feels lighter.

"You and Johnny think a lot alike, don't you?" she asks, grinning like she's in on a joke I missed. "Are you really asking me to stay and take care of you while you've got that thing on? Because you'd be stuck with me for *weeks*."

I grin, because yeah, I've won this one, I can tell. She's going to say yes.

And weeks? I'll take 'em... for a start.

7

JOHNNY

J'm thumbing through a stack of mail as I walk in the door: bills, bills, bills, and then two actual letters, which surprises me, because who mails anything anymore? Well, I know one person who does, and sure enough, I recognize one of the envelopes without needing to look at the return address. Matt's dad, Santiago Lopez, always uses these signature bright orange ones, and it hurts something inside me to know that Matty will just toss it without even opening it. Santi has never given up on Matt, and the thing I've never been sure about is whether Matty knows that his father never gave up on me, either.

I kick the door closed behind me and lean back against it for a second, enjoying the hell out of the A/C. I still keep in touch with Santi, and it's weird as fuck to always do it on the down low, because when have I ever kept anything from Matt, you know? Well, I mean, other than the fact that my sexuality is maybe a little more inclusive than he'll ever realize, of course, but point is, it always feels a little off to know I have secrets from him.

I'm grateful to still have Santi in my life, though. Growing up, he and Brenda, Matt's mom, were way more like parents to me than my own. Brenda sends Matty and me postcards from the craziest places, and she's a riot, but even when we were kids, gotta admit I was maybe a little closer to Santi than to her—mostly because he was the one who was always around, always in our business, but in a good way.

Santi's a nester, just like Matty is. Growing up, Brenda was busy climbing her corporate ladder and dreaming of traveling the world. She was a good mom, but restless, you know? Santi worked from home, still does, and when we were younger, he was always the one cooking for us and getting on me and Matt to keep up with our homework, taking us to Bruins games, helping us pick out our first suits back when we took the Schuster twins to junior prom... he was just *there*, always, and it still kills me that Matty cut him out so completely when he came out.

Nowadays, Santi and I mostly stay in touch by email, even though he lives not twenty minutes away. He keeps it simple, just asking about my life and making sure I know he's there and that he cares. I know the estrangement hurts him, but he's real good about not pressing me about Matt, and even though I'll drop a few comments here and there, I don't say that much. I may not agree with Matty, but I've gotta respect that it's his decision, you know?

Anyway, I think Santi knows that if I ever had to choose sides, there's really only one choice for me, so he doesn't push, and Matty and I just go along with a "don't ask, don't tell" approach when it comes to my relationship with his dad.

I'm just grateful neither one has ever pushed me to actually make that choice, you know? Because I love them both, and for as big as my biological family is, the two of them, plus Brenda, are basically the only family that matters to me.

I hang my keys on the hook by the door, then flip to the other non-bill I noticed and see that it's one of those photo-printed postcards. I huff out a laugh, shaking my head. Speaking of how big the Johnson family is, right? It's from a niece of mine who's a year older than me, and it's a birth announcement for her... what, must be the third baby, I think?

Yeah, we're not exactly close, and it's a nice thought to share her good news with me, I guess, but I know all that's expected of me is to find the online registry and make sure I send something.

I'm about to put the stack of mail in the decorative little tray attached to the wall that Matty's trained me to use when I hear something crash in the kitchen, followed by a muffled *"shit."* I'm not too worried about it—didn't sound like he managed to pull the fridge down on top of himself or anything—but I *am* shaking my head and laughing as I make my way in there. And yep, I find just about what I expected. Matty's broken something and is now being an idiot, trying to deal with things that his arm just ain't up for, not on his own like this.

I fold my arms across my chest, mail still in hand, and lean against the doorjamb as I watch him. Matt is on his side, on the floor, trying to sweep up the remains of what looks like a shattered plate with only one good arm to work with. He's bent in what looks like an extremely uncomfortable position, trying to hold the dustpan with the casted hand and using the broom in slow, awkward movements to get the glass to slide in.

I must've made some sound, because he suddenly looks up and sees me, a guilty look flashing across his face before he quickly replaces it with something far too grumpy to be real. He knows he's a shitty patient. Back when we were kids, he fucked around so much on a broken leg one year that when he finally got the cast off, he had to suffer through a few more months of physical therapy that would've been totally unnecessary if he'd just done what the doctor had told him in the first place.

I raise an eyebrow.

Matty turns red. "You've been letting the dishes pile up," he snaps, as if I'm gonna buy that accusation and let it deflect the shit I plan on giving him for being stupid about his arm.

I grin. Dishes in the sink? Yeah, no. We both know that I wouldn't violate one of his all-time biggest pet peeves like that, not after all these years. I pick my battles, and violating the OCD levels of cleanliness Matty insists on is not a hill I'm willing to die on.

"What, you mean that coffee cup and plate that you haven't managed to break yet?" I retort, shaking my head and trying not to laugh at him. "I'm pretty sure they weren't there when I left this morning, so this isn't on me, buddy."

He makes a sound like a cranky elephant or something, and rolls up to a sitting position, glaring at me for a second. Then he sighs, slumping back against the wall, and I almost feel sorry for him.

"I'm not cut out for sitting on my ass all day," he says, which gotta admit, is God's honest truth. Then he pulls out that cute-but-annoying whiny voice that only and always shows up when he's hurt. "There must be *something* I can do down at the station. Paperwork?"

I snort. "You hate paperwork, and Chief specifically said to remind you that he'll rip you a new one if he sees your face there before that cast comes off."

"That's forever," Matty whines.

"Six weeks," I correct him. "Maybe eight if you keep fucking with it."

The firehouse is kinda like a family, too, and all of us except the new guy know him too damn well. Matty would *say* he'd handle paperwork, and then the minute we took our eyes off him, he'd be out there trying to wash the trucks, or worse.

He looks like he's going to keep arguing for a second, so I distract him.

"Bill and Jimmy have been giving the new guy shit on your behalf, so really nothing you have to rush back for."

"Oh, the new guy started already?" Matt asks, perking up for any news of the station, our home away from home. "He any good?"

"Yep. Knows his shit."

I take the dustpan out of Matt's hands and make quick work of the broken plate, then I wrap one arm around his side and the other around his good arm to help him up, and try to ignore the thrill I get at feeling just how solid he is.

Truth is, I haven't messed around with all that many guys. I mean, I've known I *wanted* to pretty much since puberty hit, but since it became another one of those hide-from-Matt parts of my life that just feel so wrong, I just don't get around to doing it much.

And truth? It feels weird when I do.

I mean, I definitely like it, and I don't mean it feels weird to my *dick*, but I generally end up comparing whoever I'm with to Matt without meaning to, and then I feel... okay, told you this is weird, but I feel like I'm cheating on him.

"Earth to Johnny," Matt says, waving a hand in front of my face and snapping his fingers. "Dude, where are you, bro? I asked you what the new guy's name is."

"What? Oh, yeah," I say, dropping my arm from around him and stepping away. I scrub a hand over my face, thankful he can't read my mind. "Name's Asher."

Matty laughs. "*Asher*? That's the gayest name I've ever heard."

I bristle inside, the comment hitting me harder than usual after where my mind had just gone, but then Matty pinches the bridge of his nose and sighs, shocking the hell out of me.

"Oh, fuck, I *am* an asshole."

"What? No, you're not," I say automatically, even though the little homophobic digs like that, which I'm not even sure Matt realizes he drops all the time, *do* start to wear on me, if I'm being honest. Still, he looks like he just sucked a lemon, genuinely contrite, and I'm a little floored. Has he been spending this down-time on some kind of sensitivity training or something?

"Please tell me this Asher guy isn't *really* gay," Matt goes on, trying to laugh it off. "Because I know I gotta stop saying shit like that, but how ironic would it be if he was, yeah?"

"Uh," I say, because you know what? Hello, irony. Asher actually is. I wasn't the only one who did a double-take when he put up a photo of him and another guy in his locker that looks, well, they don't look just like friends, you know? And when Bill made a snarky comment about it—calling the dude Asher's boyfriend in that tone that says the word's an insult—Asher set him straight without batting an eye.

Said nope, not his boyfriend... his fiancé. Balls of steel, that one.

Bill shut up fast and ended up surprising me, too, by sort of taking Asher under his wing these last few days. Didn't let up on giving him shit, of course, but kept it away from that topic, you know?

Matty obviously figured his own question was rhetorical, since he doesn't push me for an answer on Asher. I'm happy to leave it alone for now. He'll find out whenever he gets back to the station, and that's soon enough for me.

Matt turns back to the sink like he's going to try and finish washing dishes there, and I see him wince.

"Knock it off," I tell him, hip-checking him out of the way. "You take some meds for the pain?"

"Eden gave me some before she left for work," he whines, taking a seat at the kitchen table as I roll my eyes and get to work on the oh-so-offensive dirty dishes.

"Tell me something, Matty," I say conversationally, whipping out the dish soap and scrubber like a boss. "How come you can rush into a burning building and do what you need to, always keep this house looking like something out of *Better Homes & Gardens* even after a long shift at the station, but you get the tiniest boo-boo and suddenly you're reduced to being a toddler? How does that work, exactly? What, you can't find your own pill bottle now?"

"Fuck off," he says from behind me, sounding like he's trying not to laugh. "My arm *hurts*. It's *broken*. A little sympathy, maybe?"

"Awww," I say sarcastically, grinning at the wall as I rinse and dry without bothering to turn around and get the one-fingered salute I'm sure is waiting for me.

"Hey, which one is Tabitha again?" Matt asks after a minute, the question telling me he's flipping through the mail and found that birth announcement. "Is that Abby's daughter or Barb's?"

My two older sisters, and what does it say about my family that I have to stop and think about it?

"Tabitha is Barb's girl," I finally answer, popping the dishes back in the cupboard and then turning to face him. And yep, he's got the mail in his hand... and found Santi's letter, too. I swallow, waiting for the snide remark, but he just pulls it out and stares at it for a second, then starts tapping it against the table.

"Did you know both Eden's parents died when she was a kid?" he asks, seemingly out of nowhere.

"No," I say, my eyes following the bouncing letter. Tap tap tap tap taptaptap.

What's Matty doing with it? He *always* throws them away.

"That book I saved for her, it's a bucket list."

"Huh," I say, curious despite myself. I've heard of them, but never knew someone who actually wrote one out. And the way Eden was carrying on about it? It's obviously important to her, and she's... well, I guess you could say she's important to me.

Silly, right? Just met the girl a week ago and most of the time she's been here, I've been off working, but something about the connection we forged at the hospital got to me.

And then what came after?

Matty laughs. "I know that look. You're thinking about Eden, yeah?"

"'Course I am," I say, rolling my eyes. "We're talking about her, aren't we?"

"You were thinking about *doing* Eden," he clarifies, leaning back in his chair with a shit-eating grin that says he knows he's right.

Which... fine. He is. But for the record, I haven't told him I fucked her that first night and don't plan on spilling those partic-ular beans right now, either.

I probably *would've* said something, not gonna lie, if she'd left the way she kept trying to, but now that Matty's basically invited her to stay with us for a couple of months or however long it takes his arm to heal, sharing those details just seems kind of disrespectful to her, you know?

You might expect that she and I have either been ripping each other's clothes off every night—something I wouldn't mind, but that hasn't happened again after that first time—or else walking on eggshells around each other in the world's most extended morning-after awkwardness ever, but the reality has been differ-ent. I know she's thinking about it sometimes when she looks at me, and damn, do those moments ever get to me, but between the long shifts I've pulled all week, her work schedule, and Matt always being around, there just hasn't really been another private moment, you know?

Matty's still grinning at me, and I just shrug, neither confirming nor denying.

He laughs, still holding the letter from Santi like he forgot about it. "Can't blame you," he says. "I know *I* think about doing her every damn day."

I snort, turning away to rustle around in the fridge as I wonder how I feel about that. Not gonna lie, Matty and I have shared girls before. Not usually at the same time, but I mean, yeah, once that, too. I've never minded it… never felt jealous… if I'm honest, always kind of got off on knowing he was enjoying himself, actually.

But Eden's different.

I mull it over, pulling out a few Chinese cartons left over from last night's dinner.

Nope, I guess I still don't mind.

Not sure Matt would feel the same, though, so I decide to leave it for now and go back to the other interesting subject he brought up.

"She tell you what's on her bucket list?" I ask, dumping the last of the sesame chicken onto a plate and popping it into the microwave. I attack the fried rice cold, because my stomach suddenly reminds me that I need food *now*, not a minute-thirty from now.

"Some of it," Matt says. "You wouldn't believe what she's done already, and she's trying to get through all of it before she turns twenty-five."

"When's that?"

"A couple of months from now... and I think we should give her a hand. You know, help her finish the last few things."

He gets a wicked grin on his face that's sexy as hell, and I ignore what that does to me from long practice and just laugh, seeing right through him.

"I think you mean we should win some points so you can get in her pants," I say, calling him on it.

Matt does a shitty job of looking wounded that I don't buy for a second.

"What, I can't just help out because I want to make her happy?"

"Oh, I've got no doubt you want to make her happy, bro," I say, waggling my eyebrows. "But with one arm out of commish, you're gonna have to get creative on that one."

He flips me off, still grinning.

"So what's left on her list?" I ask as the microwave dings.

Matty waits until I turn back around. "Skydiving."

"Oh, *hell* no," I say, hissing as the plate of chicken burns my hands. Doesn't stop me though... I'm edging past hungry and straight toward *hangry*.

"You gonna share that?" Matt asks.

"Nope," I tell him, taking a seat across from him and shoving the cold rice across as a consolation prize.

He turns his nose up at it and goes back to giving me shit

about my... slight discomfort with high places. "Bet Eden would be *grateful* to have someone jump out of a plane with her," he says, making it sound dirty as fuck. "Extremely... grateful."

My dick sits right up and pays attention, liking that image a lot, but I ignore the randy thing and go to work on the sesame chicken, because there is no way on God's green earth I will ever so much as go up in an airplane if I can help it, much less jump out of one. Sure, I can do ladder work if I have to on the job, but ninety-nine percent of the time the guys make sure I *don't* have to, because adrenaline plus training can only carry you so far, you know? And heights... not gonna lie, they're my kryptonite. Not proud of it, but no point pretending otherwise when lives are at stake.

"We'll just have to make Eden grateful some other way, bro," I say, grabbing the rice back, since he's neglecting it and all. "What else?"

"She wants to learn to cook," he says, eyeing my meal.

I snort, shaking my head. There's a reason we've got all the best take-out on speed-dial.

"I'm guessing you didn't really think through this idea about helping her out," I say around the last mouthful of chicken. "Sounds like she's hand-picking them just to stump us."

"Right, because I'm sure *we* were a consideration when she put that list together," he says, rolling his eyes.

I shrug. "Guess you're out of luck, bro. Do not pass go. Do not get laid. Do not collect two hundred dollars."

He wads up a piece of junk mail and throws it at my head—something I dodge with zero problems, I'd like to point out. Matt is not a lefty.

"There is one other thing she still wants to do," he says, looking up at the ceiling.

"Yeah?"

He's tapping Santi's letter on the table again, and I slap his hand down and hold it flat, because he passed my tapping limit after the first round of that shit. *I* am the antsy one in this relationship, thank you very much. There's only so much I can take when the shoe's on the other foot.

"She wants to learn a foreign language," Matt says after a minute, shrugging. "Says she doesn't care which one, just that she always thought it would be awesome to be able to speak another one."

Well… that's interesting. I stare at him for a second, but he's stuck, I can see it. Still, he's the one who brought it up, and that surprises me as much as the fact that Santi's letter hasn't already found its way into the trash.

Surprises me and kind of makes me hopeful, too.

"Huh," I say, gathering up my plate and the empty rice carton as I get up from the table, more than happy to provide the push he's all but asking me for. "It's too bad you don't remember your Spanish, *hermano*. Guess I'll have to be the one to dredge my memory for some words and find out if Eden's grateful for the help or not."

I wink at him, then turn away to handle cleanup.

The tapping starts up again while I'm washing my plate, and I exercise epic levels of patience as I wait for him to come around to where he obviously wants to go.

"Your accent has always sucked," he finally says from behind me. "How many times I gotta tell you, you don't pronounce the H."

"Don't tell me, tell Eden," I say, grinning since I know he can't see it.

It takes another minute, but then—

"Maybe I will."

This day is just full of surprises, isn't it?

And so far, I'm liking every one.

8

EDEN

*T*here's a part of me that wants to pinch myself to make sure I'm not dreaming, curled up on the couch between two hot firefighters after a long day on my feet like some kind of erotic fantasy that Auntie Maria might tease me about. Of course, it's all perfectly innocent—we're just browsing Instagram food porn and talking about what to have for dinner—but that's even better, isn't it? Because it gives me the perfect excuse for the way my mouth is watering.

"Doesn't the Thai place have some dishes like that?" Matt asks, pointing to the phone Johnny's holding for us. "I think their take-out menu is online."

Johnny shoots down the idea of Thai and the two of them start bickering like an old married couple, and they're so darn cute together that I can't help giggling. The sound cuts them off mid-sentence.

"What?" Johnny asks, looking down at me with a teasing glint in his eye. "Please tell me you don't agree with him on Big Guys Pizza. I'm so done with pizza this week."

"Did you have an opinion you wanted to share, beautiful?" Matt asks from my other side.

I shake my head, worried I'll blurt out something that has nothing to do with food and that would only cause problems if I open my mouth, and they let it slide and go back to arguing, because they're... well, even with their flaws—and after two weeks living under their roof, yes, I've seen those too—I'm having a really hard time not feeling like they're pretty much perfect.

Perfect for *me*.

Which is a problem. I've slept with Johnny and would do it again in a heartbeat, and Matt... oh Lord, Matt. He stars in my fantasies just as often as Johnny does. It's easy to see how close the two of them are, though, and sure, at some point, everyone dates someone's brother, someone's best friend, and so on, but is this really a choice I'm going to have to make?

I bite my lip. The delicious way that the feel of those big, hard bodies sandwiching me between them sets everything inside me to tingling is going to have to be enough, because no, it's not a choice I have to make. It's not one I *get* to make. And even though they both flirt with me relentlessly, neither one pushes me.

I'm grateful, because I wouldn't ever want to come between them.

I mean, maybe in the *literal* sense...

I squeeze my thighs together tightly as that tingle they inspire turns into a wet heat, surging between my legs, and I slap a hand over my mouth to stifle a naughty giggle. Oh my God, I'm just as bad as Auntie Maria.

Of *course* they notice.

Johnny drops a hand to my knee, squeezing it. "If you've got a better idea for dinner than *this* lunkhead, please, for the love of God, spit it out and save me now."

His unbelievable body—that I remember so, *so* vividly—presses against me from thigh to shoulder on my other side. I shake my head, pretty sure if I try and speak, I'll jump him.

"Come on now," Matt teases, letting his left hand—flung across the back of the couch—smooth over the back of my hair. It's deliciously sweet. "You're going to *have* to share whatever that thought was."

I know I have to say something before having both their hands on me at once drives me to distraction, so I make a monumental effort and come up with—

"I was... was just thinking how lucky I am." Not exactly true, but it's definitely not a lie, either. "I still can't believe you're letting me stay here."

"Letting?" Johnny repeats, snorting back a laugh. "Pretty sure we'd both be on our knees begging you to if you tried to skip out on us before Sir Whines-a-lot gets his cast off."

"Shut up, bro," Matt says good-naturedly. He lets his hand slide down my hair to my shoulder, tugging me against his side. "You're just jealous because she gives me sponge baths while you're down at the station."

"What?" I splutter, laughing despite myself as my face flares with heat. "I do not!"

"Do you know how hard it is to shower with this thing?" Matt asks, turning an adorably pleading look on me as he holds up his cast.

Johnny snorts back a laugh, shaking his head at Matt's ridiculousness. "*Hard*, huh, buddy?" And then, winking at me, he adds, "Maybe you *should* help him out, princess. Keep this one happy and we'll all be happier, you know?"

My jaw is on the floor and I can't pick it up. I mean, I know Johnny's just teasing, but that isn't the kind of joke I'd expect from someone I've already slept with.

Is he testing me?

Tempting me?

Torturing me?

The two of them share a look over my head, then Matt uses his one good hand to tip my face toward his. "Did I mention that Johnny's the smart one?" he says, eyes on my mouth. His voice drops low enough to make me shiver. "I mean, you wouldn't want me getting... dirty, now, would you, beautiful?"

My breath hitches.

Yes.

Oh, Lord. *Yes.* I really would... but it would kill me to hurt Johnny, no matter how laid-back he is when we're all flirting like this.

I swallow, jerking my eyes away from the heat I see in Matt's eyes and stabbing blindly at Johnny's phone. "We should... we should have that for dinner," I babble, not caring at all what it is.

It takes them a minute, but then they both turn to look, gracious about letting the sexual tension ease. Or at least... letting it stay under the rug. Nothing inside *me* has eased, that's for sure.

"Tacos?" Johnny asks, tilting his head to the side as he squints at the small screen. "I'm down with that."

"Those aren't just tacos, they're *Pineapple Habenero Pork Carnitas* tacos, bro," Matt says, reading the caption. "And damn, those do look good. Pretty sure we don't have a take-out menu for that, though."

"Let's make them ourselves," I say, suddenly filled with a surge of... motivation.

Yep, sexual frustration is a *great* motivator.

But then I do sort of get excited about the idea of making them. I mean, I still need to knock #66 off The List, don't I? And maybe learning to cook in the company of two actual firefighters will prevent me from, oh, I don't know, burning the house down again?

"Uh," Johnny says, shaking his head back and forth. "I dunno, Eden. Maybe we just all hop in my truck and hit that new Mexican place?"

"Pretty sure we don't have any pineapple here at the house," Matt says, sounding relieved about it. He rubs at the back of his neck. "Or pork. Or cilantro. Or tortillas. Or—"

I laugh, cutting him off. I know I'm in trouble, though, because the fact that they're both so clearly terrified by the idea only makes me all the more attracted.

To.

Both.

Of.

Them.

Lord, what's *wrong* with me?

Nothing I can't ignore. I get to my feet before my libido over-rides my good sense.

"Come on," I say, determined to make it work. "Let's do this. Please?"

"You do know it's Friday the thirteenth, right, Eden?" Johnny says, humoring me anyway and getting to his feet. "You sure you wanna push your luck that way?"

I give him a wounded look... which hopefully covers up how I'm having trouble catching my breath. My heart is racing and those tingles are making me want to do wicked things, because Johnny is *huge*, and now that he's standing, we're far too close.

Not close enough.

So close that it's all I can do not to wrap myself around him and beg him to have his way with me again.

Instead, I get ahold of myself and turn to grab Matt's free hand, tugging on him until he stands, too.

"You really want to do this?" Matt asks, running his thumb over the back of my hand and making me shiver.

"I really do."

I want to do *all* of it, but cooking together will have to be enough.

"Just checking," Matt says, grinning down on me. "Because I know it's on your list and all, but if I remember correctly, the *last* time you cooked something..."

"Oh, you," I say, smacking his shoulder. "I can't believe you went there."

"Hey, did I say burning down your place was a *bad* thing?" he retorts, still grinning. "I've got no complaints about how that turned out, and if you really wanna give it another go tonight... I mean, who knows what we'll get out of it this time, yeah?"

He's still holding my hand, doing distracting things to it, and I'm blushing again, all too aware of Johnny next to me but incapable of pulling away from Matt's touch. Finally, he drops my hand, saying something about finding his wallet, and heads out of the room. I stare at his ass as he leaves, but then catch myself and dart a guilty glance up at Johnny. And... oh.

Oh.

Something trembles inside me. Was Johnny staring at Matt's ass, too?

He catches me looking at him and gives me a sheepish smile, a pink tinge coloring his cheeks as he says, "So, tacos, huh? That sounds... good."

I almost let it slide.

I *should* let it slide.

I can't. Holy shit! Have I totally misread things?

"Johnny, are you..." I bite my lip, suddenly remembering the conversation with Matt about his dad. I lower my voice. "Does Matt know that you're, um, that you—"

"No," he says, and I have to give it to him, he doesn't pretend not to understand.

Or that it isn't true.

He shrugs, glancing down the hall. "Matty's not real open-minded about some things, so, you know, we're just... not ever gonna go there, okay?"

I nod, my heart squeezing tight for him. I *know* how much he cares about Matt. I see it every day.

And then, selfishly, I have another thought, and I go pale. "Does that mean... when we, um, when you and I... were you just... pretending?"

As soon as I ask, I know there's no way. A tiny whimper escapes me before he can answer, and I'm squeezing my thighs together as another surge of desire rocks through me. That was hands down the best sex of my life, and Johnny was one hundred percent into it, too, I know it for sure.

He cups my cheek, eyes hot. "Oh, hell no," he says, the husky tone of his voice confirming it even as he says the words. "Wanting him doesn't take away from how bad I want you, Eden."

How bad he *wants* me.

Still.

Present tense.

He runs his thumb over my lips, and I gasp, the light touch shooting straight to my core. And then he wraps his other huge hand gently around the back of my neck, steadying me, and the rest of what he said hits me.

Wanting him.

Wanting... *him*.

Him. Matt. Johnny wants Matt, too, which is what we've just been talking about, of course, but suddenly I'm actually thinking about what that *means*.

Picturing it.

Panting with it.

This would shock even Auntie Maria, but the vision of the two of them together is so vivid that, for a second, I forget myself completely and moan, eyes locked on Johnny's but mind full of the dirtiest, hottest images I've *ever* fantasized about.

Johnny's big hands on Matt's incredible body.

Matt's teasing smile turning into a greedy moan as Johnny undresses him the way he did with me. But rougher. More urgently. Until Matt turns the tables and pushes Johnny down and straddles him. The two of them grinding together, Johnny's ever-moving mouth silenced under Matt's hot kiss, and then—

"*Jesus*, Eden," Johnny growls, his mouth crashing into mine. One hard kiss and then he backs off, shooting a look toward the hallway as he whispers, "You're killing me, princess."

I touch my mouth, chest heaving. "I... I was picturing the two of you together," I say, too turned on to censor myself. "Matt is so hot."

Oh, Lord. I can*not* believe I just said that to him. But Johnny just laughs, scrubbing a hand over his face, then shakes his head and smiles down at me ruefully.

"You get a chance at helping with those sponge baths, Eden? Let's just say I want you to take it for both of us."

"You... you wouldn't mind?"

Johnny gives me a wicked, wicked smile. "Did *you* mind, princess, when you were thinking of him and me together just now?"

My breath hitches. We both know the answer to that one, and the idea of Johnny getting just as turned on fantasizing about me with Matt... oh my God, can I really have my cake and eat it, too?

Johnny's smile turns even dirtier—and the way his eyes move down my body? I *swear* I can feel it—but before he can say anything else, Matt walks back into the room. Johnny winks at me, and my heart starts to race, because yes, I'm pretty sure he's just given me permission to do *exactly* that. And when he makes a pointed comment about the 24-hour shift he'll be working in a few days?

I know for sure he has.

9

MATT

"*P*lease tell me you're hungry," Eden says, blowing a stray piece of hair out of her face as she looks back at me over her shoulder in a pose that's sexy as hell.

Of course, she probably doesn't mean it to be, but damn, the girl gets to me.

"Absolutely," I say, willing to eat whatever she comes up with... even if it's burned again. The ruffled apron she's wearing while she works on our lunch is giving me dirty ideas, and since I'm pretty sure I actually *am* earning some points after a full weekend of helping her knock *learning to cook* off her bucket list, it's taking a lot for me to stay in my seat and not try and do something about them.

It doesn't help my willpower that it's hot as fuck outside and our air conditioner is on the fritz. She's got nothing but a tiny tank top and short shorts on underneath the apron, and from a certain angle, it's like all these fantasies in my head are already coming to life.

Of course, you could argue that me and my left arm haven't actually been all that helpful here in the kitchen—as evidenced by the fact that I'm sitting here on my ass while I watch hers—but hey, Eden's not complaining. And sure, maybe I haven't been able to do a whole lot with actually cutting vegetables and the like, but I've been pretty good with looking things up online as needed, so I'm claiming credit there.

And as far as the hands-on help? Well, Johnny *does* have two good hands, and he was right here with us all weekend chipping in, but since he's not around today? I figure I'll just seize the opportunity and claim whatever points he earned by proxy.

I grin, liking the math. Seems fair to me, at least.

Eden slides a spatula under the sandwich she's got grilling and carefully transfers it to a plate, then turns and catches me looking. I can't tell if her cheeks are pink from the heat or from something else, but since I like to think of myself as a glass-half-full person most days, I figure I'll go with *something else.*

"What are you smiling about?" she asks, biting that lip I still haven't tasted yet.

"Like I said, I'm hungry," I tell her. My dick perks up since this front-view is the one that makes her look naked under the apron, but I tell it to be patient, and ask, "How did the sandwich turn out?"

"Good?" Eden answers, sounding uncertain as she brings it over to the table. "I mean, it's just grilled cheese…"

"Grilled cheese is my favorite," I say, deciding it's true enough when it wins me a smile. She sets the plate down in front of me, and I add, "This looks great, Eden."

I mean, it's just cheese and bread, so not much to go wrong, amirite? And okay, so the edges are a little… dark. But honestly, it really doesn't look bad at all, and I'm actually pretty proud of suggesting it. Given some of the flubs we had over the weekend, I figured she needed a solid win.

Those flubs, though? Gotta admit, the three of us had about as good of a time as I can imagine, given that all our clothes stayed on. It's kind of amazing, actually, how well Eden fits in here with me and Johnny, and it just makes me more certain than ever that I want to make sure it turns into a more long-term situation.

She's standing close enough that I can count a couple of freckles, high up on her thigh under the edge of those short shorts, and the way she's poking at the sandwich with the spatula and chewing that lip to death make it look like she's trying to figure out what's wrong with it.

I bite back a smile. I wouldn't ever say this out loud, but cooking just isn't that hard. I mean, sure, I don't do much of it *now*, but back when I was a kid, my dad made me help with practically every meal, and the only reason Johnny and I live on take-out is... well, it doesn't matter. Guess I just lost my stomach for working in the kitchen after things went to shit.

But Eden? I don't know; it's like she's got a mental block or something. She really has managed one disaster or another with pretty much everything we've tried, but as far as I'm concerned, that's one part cute and one part opportunity. It's important to her for whatever reason, so if she hasn't gotten it down by the time this damn cast comes off, I've already got plans to start getting a lot more helpful.

This sandwich, though, it's a win.

I take the spatula out of her hand and set it aside. "Stop abusing it, beautiful. It looks good. Smells good. It's gonna be fantastic."

She stares at it for another sixty seconds or so, and then—

"Maybe?" she finally agrees, her lips curving up. "I mean, it actually does look pretty edible, doesn't it?"

"Totally," I agree, although with all this skin showing and right in arm's reach? I'm not thinking about the sandwich at all.

"Are you going to taste it?" she asks, turning big eyes on me.

I rein in my dirty mind. "Not until you do," I say, tugging her down on my lap... because that's really the best place to reach the sandwich from, yeah?

She giggles, but settles on my thighs without protest.

Win.

"So, does this count?" I ask as she takes the first bite. "Can we cross the whole learn-to-cook thing off of your bucket list now?"

She shakes her head. "No. But… oh my God, it's actually good?" She takes another bite, her smile so big it does things to me that have nothing to do with how happy my dick is with our seating arrangement, then she adds, "I think I still want to try something a little more professional before I count this item as done. You can't serve grilled cheese at a dinner party."

"Oh, we're having a dinner party now?" I tease her, grinning. "Who's coming?"

She deflates a little. "Well, I guess it's a stupid idea. Besides you and Johnny, I haven't met all that many people in Boston yet."

"Hey," I say, tipping her chin up. "You want a dinner party, we'll do a dinner party, yeah? Whatever it takes to get number sixty off your list."

An idea flashes through my mind, but Eden's lips twitch and distract me—shiny from the melted cheese and close enough to test my willpower—so I figure I'll come back to it later.

"Cooking is number sixty-six, actually," she says, her eyes sort of glowing at me like I've just earned a few bonus points. "Sixty was riding a mechanical bull."

"*Jesus*, Eden," I say, huffing out a laugh. My cock starts to swell, and the image of *that* doesn't help at all when it comes to my attempt at keeping my hands off her.

Well… hand, singular.

And okay, so my good hand is most definitely *on* her, but I've got to make sure she's balanced, right? I've got it resting low on her back to stabilize her, right where there's a tempting strip of skin showing between her shorts and top, and it's all I can do not to give the apron strings tickling my fingers a tug and undo them.

She's blushing about the mechanical bull comment now, but hello, that's a spark of heat in her eyes, isn't it? I'm pretty sure that underneath that embarrassment, she's picturing something too.

She licks her lips and shifts a little on my lap, and... well, shit. No way she doesn't feel the evidence that's right there and growing by the minute.

"You... you really like grilled cheese, I guess?" she asks, eyes sparkling.

And damn, I'm starting to get so turned on that it takes me a few to realize she's teasing me.

"If I say yes, are you gonna give me some?" I ask, taking a chance and sliding my hand down over her ass. Her breath hitches —so fucking sexy—and I give it a little squeeze as I hold up my cast and turn puppy eyes on her. "I don't have a free hand, now do I?"

She stands up, and for a second, I think I've screwed up—but then she sits right back down, straddling my lap this time so we're face-to-face, and I start thinking maybe I've just hit the jackpot, instead.

She tears off a tiny piece of the sandwich and holds it to my mouth, and you've gotta bet I will take anything she wants me to at this point.

I chew.

I swallow.

I'm hard as fucking stone and more than happy to give that mechanical bull a run for its money if she lets me.

"What do you think?" she asks, voice all breathless and sexy. "Is it... is it any good?"

"Perfect," I say, and suddenly I'm feeling way more coordinated with my left hand than I have for the past couple of weeks. It's back on her ass, and I rock her forward a little to see if this is going where I hope it is, and... yeah.

Fuck yeah.

Her eyelids flutter a little as her hands land on my shoulders for balance, and she makes a cock-hardening sound somewhere between a gasp and a moan, rolling her hips forward even more so that I'm centered right between her legs.

And holy *Christ*, is my dick ever happy right now. The soft heat at her core? Fucking *heaven*.

"Matt," she says, cheeks flushed bright pink and pupils blown wide. "Are you sure we should… should—"

"Yes," I say before she can get the question out. Never been more certain in my life, and not just because I want her so bad I can taste it.

Eden fits everywhere. Here on my lap. Here at the house with me and Johnny. She's in my head and pretty sure she's working her way into my heart already, too. And right now? Oh *hell* yes, I'm one hundred percent sure that we should find out just how well we fit in a few other ways.

Ways that will involve me getting up close and personal with those freckles I saw.

Ways that should have her panting my name if I do it right.

Ways that are going to pretty much guarantee that I start to like cooking again.

I urge her on with my hand, sort of kneading her ass, and she starts putting those bull-riding skills to use, rocking against me until I swear I'm at risk of coming in my pants like a horny teenager. Partly because of how damn good it feels on my cock, and partly because of the expression on her face.

Jesus, she's getting lost in it fast, and watching her is the most erotic thing I've seen in… *ever*.

"You're fucking beautiful, Eden," I grit out, cursing the fact that I'm down an arm. No way am I letting go with my left, but I need to finally get a taste of that mouth she's starting to pant out of, and it kills me that I can't reach up and pull her to me. "Kiss me."

She moans with a kind of pleasure that makes it sound like she's just been waiting for permission, hands coming off my shoulders to grip the back of my head, and when she brings her mouth to mine? Guess I wasn't lying when I told her how hungry I am, because I fucking *devour* her.

Or maybe she's devouring me. Holy hell, guess my first clue

was when she took me to task for my fucked-up thinking about the gay issue the week before, but all that soft sweetness I see on a daily basis? That's definitely not all there is to her. Eden wants this just as bad as I do, and now that we've started, she's just a hair shy of outright aggressive.

It's hot as fuck.

She's still rocking herself on my cock, and it's torture, because there are too many clothes between us, but at the same time, I can't bear to take my hands or my mouth off her long enough to rectify that situation.

My cast is wedged between us, pushed up under her gorgeous breasts and making me curse it all over again since I can't feel a thing there, but when I go to move it out of the way, Eden gasps, jerking back.

"Oh, no, did I hurt you?"

"You're hurting me right now, beautiful," I tell her honestly, trying to rock her forward again with my good hand. "What are you thinking, taking that mouth away from me?"

She goes that pretty shade of pink again, but bites her lip instead of letting me taste it again. "But... your arm?"

I'm about to tell her not to worry about it, but then see an opportunity. "Just means I'm gonna need a little help," I say, running my left hand over her curves. "Can you do that for me?"

That sexy little hitch to her breath again—breasts heaving against me—and she nods. "What... what do you want me to do?"

I skim my fingers under the waistband of her shorts. "These are in my way. Can you take care of that for me, beautiful?"

I love undressing a willing woman, unwrapping her like a present, but when Eden stands up and reaches under that apron to slip those shorts off, and a lacy pair of pale pink panties along with them? It doesn't take me long to discover that I love watching it happen almost just as much.

She reaches behind her, toward those apron strings, and I shake my head.

"Leave it," I tell her, my cock jerking in my pants with the knowledge that she really *is* halfway bare under the cute little thing now. "Can you get your top off without untying the apron?"

"You don't want me to take the apron off?" she asks, pressing her lips together like she's trying not to laugh when I nod.

She does it, tank top and bra landing on the floor next to her other clothes, and then stands there in front of me looking... well, pretty much exactly like she did *with* the apron on, but now I know damn well that there's nothing underneath.

"Fuck, that's hot," I say, not even trying to pretend I'm not turned all kinds of on.

Eden laughs, smoothing the fabric that barely covers her hips. She's blushing with pretty much her whole body now, but I love that she's letting me get away with this.

"Do you know how many times I've imagined this today?" I ask, grinning up at her. "You're doing a good deed here, Eden Evans, helping an injured man live out a fantasy. A real Samaritan."

"Have you seriously been thinking dirty things about me in this apron all weekend?" she asks, biting that lip again as she smiles at me.

"Busted."

She comes closer, standing between my spread legs and then killing me when her voice gets all breathless again and she says, "I'm so glad I'm not the only one."

"Not by a long shot," I say, sliding my good hand up her thigh... skimming over those freckles... exploring underneath the hem of that apron as I start to learn her by touch.

She gasps when I make it to the center and discover just how smooth shaven she is, her hands landing back on my shoulders for balance. "Matt," she whispers, her fingers tightening on me as mine dip into her for the first time. "Oh, *Lord*."

"That's right, beautiful," I say, stroking through her folds. Her face is so gorgeous, so expressive, telegraphing exactly what she needs and telling me just how much she likes it when I give it to her. "Right there, yeah?"

She moans, thighs trembling, and I take that as a yes and do it some more. And damn if discovering just how wet she is doesn't make my dick want to leap right out of my pants—but I ignore it for now, because nothing on God's green earth is better than the sounds she's starting to make as I finger her tight, hot pussy... as I find that little nub that drives her crazy and tease it with my thumb... as I rock the heel of my hand against her until she's practically riding it, head thrown back and fingers digging into my shoulders as pure arousal burns off the last of her self-consciousness.

Fucking... *beautiful.*

I'm so hard it hurts, and I already know I'm not ever gonna be able to see her in this apron again without getting right back in the same state. It's red and covered with little white polka dots—the top shaped like a heart that barely contains her generous breasts and a white, ruffled, lacy bit all along the outer edge that hits the very top of her thighs and hides my hand—and if I wasn't in this damn cast, I'd use my other one to pull her down here. Let the weight of those lush tits fill my palm and get my mouth on her nipples—straining against the material like they're begging for attention—and find out if she likes that, too.

She moves her hands off my shoulders, running them through the back of my hair as she starts to pant with her need. The hot, musky scent of her sex teases me, so close to my face but hidden away, and as much as I'd love to see *all* of her—and you can bet that I'm still counting on that happening sooner rather than later—right now? There's something insanely erotic about discovering her by braille, so to speak.

By learning my way around by touch alone.

By keeping my eyes on hers as she makes all these pretty, pretty sounds that let me know just how good I'm making her feel.

"Matt... Matt... *Matt...*"

The way my name keeps falling out of her mouth makes me think she doesn't even know she's saying it, and suddenly, just touching her isn't enough.

"Turn around for me, beautiful."

She blinks dazed eyes at me like she didn't quite hear, but no problem—I'm already doing it for her, suddenly all kinds of proficient with my left hand as I spin her around to face the table and get my first look at her perfect, heart-shaped ass.

I groan. I've always been a bit of an ass man, and with that sexy little apron tied in a bow right between the two dimples at the base of her spine, ends dangling down to taunt me as they tease her crease? All I can say is that if there's ever a time I wished for two good hands, it's right... fucking... *now.*

"Matt," she says, turning to look down at me over her shoulder. Her breath hitches. *"Please."*

Damn, that *please* gets me. I'm not sure what she's asking for exactly, but I sure as hell know what I'd *like* to give her. I'd like nothing more than to pull my cock out and get some relief, to sink it into her and take us both to heaven, but no way am I interrupting the moment to go find protection.

No condoms... one hand out of play... just means I'll need to get creative.

I grind my good hand against my throbbing cock for all of two seconds—all the time I can bear to not be touching her—and then I'm squeezing that beautiful ass with my one good hand. Moving those little red ribbons aside so I can spread her open a little for an intimate look. Running my palm over all that petal-soft skin... those sweet, bouncy curves... that innocent-looking little red bow.

I'm tracing her spine with a firm hand.

Pressing her down over the table.

Bending her over in front of me until she's exactly where I want her—where I *need* her—to be.

I kiss the tender spot where her ass meets her thigh, and she moans like a porn star, her whole body trembling. Christ. If she's this responsive *here*, I really am gonna be coming in my pants once I get my mouth where I want it.

"You like that, beautiful?" I ask, grinning and doing it on the other side.

"Y-y-yes," she manages, and I swear it feels like that needy, stuttering word strums right over my cock.

Not gonna lie, I'd love to watch her face while I fuck her someday, but there's something about doing a girl from behind that gets me all sorts of fired up. Like I said, I'm an ass man, and when she starts begging me again—

"Please... Matt... *please.*"

—I groan and spread her wider, letting my fingers push into her moist folds exactly the way I already know she likes. And oh yeah, *fuck* yeah, she likes it just as much from behind.

My mouth is watering, but patience brings its own reward, amirite? So instead of allowing myself a taste of what I really want, I start by licking those little freckles I noticed on her thigh earlier. It makes her whimper in the sexiest way, so I nibble on them, working my way toward the inside, chasing the tiny quivers in her soft skin and guided by the rising tone of her panting breaths.

Fuck, she's delicious, and I haven't even gotten a *real* taste yet.

"*Matt,*" she gasps when I find her clit again with my fingers.

"*Fuck,*" I grit out, because I shit you not, I'm in actual pain here. Cock so hard it might cripple me and no way to give myself any attention whatsoever, because Eden? She's so fucking responsive I wouldn't stop now if you paid me. I've got her grinding on my hand like it's a sex toy... rocking back against me and promising me dirty, dirty things as I lick off the sweet juices that coat her thighs... as I circle closer and closer to where I know she really wants my mouth... as she starts begging so prettily for some relief that I can't hardly stand it.

The pain is one hundred percent worth it. So... fucking... *hot*.

"Please," she gasps, practically sobbing as her voice gets more and more desperate. "Oh, Lord, oh God, Matt... please... please... *please*."

I'll never get enough of that sexy hitch in her breath.

"Spread your legs for me, Eden," I growl, wrapping my good hand firmly around one of her thighs and pulling her toward me.

She whimpers, doing what I tell her and then gasping out my name again when I bury my face in her sweet center and finally use my tongue to start doing all the things she loved so much with my fingers.

"Matt."

I flatten it, licking her with long, lazy strokes as I savor my first taste.

"Oh my... oh my *God*," she pants, thighs trembling around my face.

I suck on her delicate folds, parting them with my tongue. Thrusting it inside her. Using my hand to spread her wider and doing it again... and when it makes her cry out... *again*.

"Matt... Matt... oh, Lord, *Matt pleasepleaseplease*."

I find her clit and tease it.

Lick it.

Suck on it until she's begging even louder.

Bite down on it—just enough to make her gasp—and then pull her against my face so I can thrum my tongue against it.

Faster...

Faster...

Faster.

I'm drunk with the taste of her... with the feel of her... with the sound of her sobbing breaths as I push two fingers inside and find that sweet spot that makes her scream, as I fuck those fingers into her over and over, until I feel her pussy start to clench tight around them and then—oh fucking *Christ*, Eden finally comes apart, and I ride it out.

Taste *all* of it.

…and then push her even higher, because I'm a greedy son of a bitch who wants it all. I don't let up until she explodes for me all over again, until she's clawing at the table… gasping out my name… grinding against my face and… and *Jesus*—

"Fuck fuck fucking *Christ*," I gasp.

—and then I'm coming too, totally hands-free. Shaking with it. So damn worked up over how completely Eden let herself go that before I can stop it, I'm groaning against her heated skin, cock pulsing hard, spilling out my release. I'm coming with her taste on my tongue and my pants still zipped and the absolute, rock-solid unquestionable certainty that I was right.

Eden's the girl for me.

She's fucking *perf*ect.

And oh, the things I plan to do to her once I can get *both* my hands on her.

JOHNNY

"*D*idn't I tell you to keep him away from the station?" Chief Masterson pretends to growl, winking at me as he throws an arm over Matty's shoulders. Chief is grinning like the prodigal son has just returned, and has been since the minute he caught sight of us.

It's the station's annual summer barbecue, and every year they do it up like a major holiday. It's a shame Eden had to work, but no way would Matt have considered not coming. And truth? For all the B.S. flying, Chief would've killed me if I'd let Matty miss it.

Classic rock pours out of the speakers, the smell of grilling meat is heavy in the air, and the beer flows freely as firefighters and their spouses mingle with community volunteers, trainees, and so many kids hyped-up on sugar that getting from point A to point B without tripping over one is a serious hazard. Basically, the day is fucking perfect.

Matty shoves the chief off him good-naturedly. "Hey, gotta make sure you guys haven't burned the place down, yeah?"

Chief rolls his eyes at me theatrically, jerking a thumb at Matt. "Next thing you know, this one will be sneaking onto a truck and going for more of those heroics that we try to train out of you assholes," he says, walking with us toward the food.

"Hey, this isn't on me," I try, holding my hands up as a couple of the guys, Bill and Jimmy, catch sight of us and head our way with the kind of grins on their faces that tell me they are absolutely ready, willing, and able to give Matty the three weeks' worth of shit he's missed out on since his accident. "You know I can't keep Matt away when meat is grilling," I add.

"Not on you," Jimmy repeats, obviously overhearing. He shakes his head like he's disappointed in me as he and Bill join us, handing over cold beers to make the day even more perfect. "That's a load of bullshit and you know it. Pretty sure they only gave you a badge so you'd keep Lopez in line, Johnson."

"Hey now," Matty protests, doing his best to look offended. "Pretty sure you got that backward. Last I checked, I'm the one who keeps *Johnny* in line. You guys really want him loose on a scene without my calming influence to keep him from doing something crazy?"

My lips twitch at that. I mean, sure, there may have been an ounce of truth to it, but luckily, one of the guys steps up and points out the obvious.

"*Calming*, he says." Bill snorts, shaking his head as he taps Matty's cast. "Might've believed it before you pulled *this* stunt."

"Needed some vacation time, didn't I?" Matt tosses back, as if he's not going one hundred percent stir-crazy at the house.

Well… maybe not quite one hundred percent anymore, unless I miss my guess. I take a drink from my beer, eyeing him as he banters back and forth with the guys and feeling just about as happy to be right here, right now, as any day I can remember.

Matty looks good. Cast or not, he's definitely keeping himself in shape. Putting in extra time at the gym to make up for all the downtime these last few weeks, and fuck if it doesn't show to a very nice effect. Today—sporting cargo shorts that fit his ass like they were designed to color my balls bright blue and a Red Sox t-shirt that hugs his chest like a second skin—he's a fucking wet dream.

I scrub a hand over my face and look away before I let myself go too far with that line of thinking, but it just brings me to the other reason I'm guessing Matty's started to enjoy his "vacation" time a bit more. I pulled a few 24-hour shifts last week, and the way he and Eden have been exchanging looks? I'm pretty sure that during at least one of my overnights, the girl took my advice and made something happen.

I'm not exactly green about it, but I'm definitely... something. I grin, hiding it behind another sip of beer. Fine, no point pretending I don't know what that *something* is, and it's sure as shit not jealous.

I'm horny as fuck is what I am, not gonna lie, and imagining what might've happened between the two of them has practically worn my right hand out in the shower this past week.

I nearly spit my beer out when the new guy, Asher, sneaks up on me from behind, clapping a hand on my shoulder.

"Hey, Johnny," he says, eyes trained on Matt. "This the infamous Mateo Lopez?"

Well... shit.

"Matty, Asher Campbell. Ash, this is Matt, yeah," I say, managing the introduction.

I'm pretty sure I'm not just imagining the invisible ripple of tension that moves through all the guys. I'm not immune to it, either.

Matty's smiling like he doesn't feel it at all, and I want to groan. Or grab him and leave. Or just... well, I'd never run out on him, of course, but this is definitely one of those moments where I wouldn't mind hiding my eyes from the train wreck I'm pretty sure is barreling toward us.

"Heard about you, buddy," Matt says, holding out his hand.

"Same," Asher says, not cold... but less than warm.

That tension cranks a little higher. The thing is, you gotta trust everyone to have your back in a job like ours, and if these two get off on the wrong foot, we all know it's gonna be rough.

Matty and Ash shake hands, and I can see Matt's eyebrows go up enough to guess that Asher put a little extra something in his grip.

Shit.

Did I mention Asher has balls of steel? Coming over with the obvious intention of dealing with Matty head-on is one hundred percent true to form, but doesn't make it any less nerve-wracking to watch.

I exchange a covert glance with Bill as Matt gives Asher a questioning look. I've already overheard a couple of the guys warning Ash to expect a little standoffishness when Matt gets back to the station—Bill being one of those guys—but Ash wasn't born yesterday. He's obviously correctly interpreted that "stand-offish" for the warning it actually was, because it's no secret around here that Matty's got more than a hint of homophobia in his make-up.

I resort to another swig of my beer, the few seconds those two spend staring at each other feeling like a fucking eternity.

Maybe I *should* have given Matty a heads-up that Asher is gay? Too late to second-guess it now, and while that bigotry is a side of Matt that caught me off guard back when it first came out— because truth is, he generally treats everyone more than decent—I know that a big part of why I didn't mention anything about Asher is that I've never had the guts to call Matt on it directly.

Not that I didn't have my reasons, of course. And sure, maybe it's a cop-out to use how torn up Matty was over his father as a reason to ignore the little digs he throws out whenever the subject comes up, but I guess it's also been a bit of self-preservation. I can't say I like that one piece of him, but it's also not worth losing him over, you know?

Matty and the guys here at the station are the only family that matter to me.

Fuck if the situation here hasn't surprised me when it comes to Asher, though. Not to say that Ash hasn't gotten some shit from some of the guys and won't keep on getting it, because sure, it's Boston—supposedly the eleventh most gay-friendly city in America—but Matty isn't the only one who failed to get the gay-friendly memo. Still, overall? Ash's whole out-and-proud-and-dgaf demeanor has already reduced the bullshit to a mere trickle.

Doesn't hurt that he's a hell of a firefighter. Between that and his refusal to act like *he's* the one with the problem, he's already got a whole slew of allies here at the station... some of them from the likes that I wouldn't have expected in a million years.

Case in point, Bill, who would've been dead last on my list of good ol' boys who'd be okay with men who like men... much less quick to jump to their defense, like it looks like he's primed to do right now as he eyes the standoff between Matty and Asher.

Of course, Matty ain't dumb, either, and he can sense the tension even if he has no clue what it's about yet.

"So, you my welcome wagon?" he asks Asher, the easy grin on his face almost masking his confusion as he tries to figure out why everyone up to the chief is giving him a bit of side-eye.

Asher smiles back, and gotta give it to him, you can tell he's not here to be a dick, he's just not one to wait when he can take action, you know? Seen that about him on the job already, too, and it's a quality I admire... when it's not making my stomach twist into a knot, like right now.

"Just wanted to say hello," Ash tells Matty, pulling another guy forward who I recognize right away from pictures. "This is Quinn, my fiancé."

Matt's eyes widen for a second, but... hello, who *is* this man and where's my best friend? Because sure, I don't expect Matty to be an outright dick, either, but I also most definitely don't expect him to hold out his hand to Quinn the way he does and give both of them what I recognize as a genuine smile.

"Congratulations," Matty says. "You guys got a date set?"

Asher blinks, looking as thrown as I am, and the way I see Quinn sneak a hand onto Ash's lower back in obvious support makes me realize what I probably should've guessed from the beginning: sure, Asher's got those balls I mentioned, but doesn't mean it's easy for him every time he has to swing them around, you know?

Just makes me admire the guy all the more.

I finish off my beer, not sure if the other thing I'm feeling is envy or inspiration... I just know that I'd give a lot to have that kind of confidence in this one area of my life.

Matty, Asher, Quinn and the guys start shooting the shit, the tension dissolving like it had never been there, and I'm joining in, but I'm kinda watching Matt the whole time, too. Looking for signs that he's faking it with this new and sudden gay-comfort level, I guess.

And you know what? I don't see any... and it's got me feeling unsettled in a way I've got no words for.

A good way, maybe.

Matty and I finally give in to the smells from the grill and break away from the little group, heading that direction to grab a couple of burgers.

"We got any plans next weekend, Johnny?" he asks me as we walk that way.

I shrug. "I'm on shift Saturday and Sunday both."

"Friday?" he presses, fumbling a couple of plates off the stack with his one good hand and holding them out so I can take one.

"I'm off Friday," I tell him. "What's up?"

He gets busy building a burger, and I'm so busy trying not to laugh at him doing it one-handed that it takes me a minute to realize he's doing mine. I bite back a smile, knowing damn well that it's little shit like this that Matty doesn't even think about that always has Bill teasing him about us being boyfriends. Bitter-sweet... but mostly sweet, if I'm going to be honest and let my inner romantic out for a second.

Not, of course, that Matty means it as anything like that. He's just always been that way, and I like to think that for all his talk about keeping an eye on me when we're on the job, I do my share to take care of him, too.

We look out for each other, you know?

Although, when it comes to burgers... I shake my head, figuring there will always be things that even the closest of friends agree to disagree on, right? I know Matty appreciates cheese and tomatoes and onions in other contexts, but on a burger? I've never understood it, but I can attest that it's true: he's never been able to stomach the combo of those three on meat, and no amount of me trying to convince him he's missing out has ever gotten him to see the light.

He finishes adding all the condiments I like and hands it over, taking the empty plate from my hands with his one good one and starting on his own. Not that *that* takes long. Cheeseburger, plain and dry.

Heathen.

I almost forgot he was asking me about plans until he tells me what's on his mind.

"Eden was saying something the other day about wanting to try cooking a fancier meal," Matty says. "She wants to be able to do something worthy of a little dinner party, so I've been thinking about how to make that happen."

"Sure," I say, since I'm pretty much down for anything that makes her happy.

"She doesn't know a lot of people here," Matty reminds me. "But I thought maybe we could put something together, yeah? But you know, keep it simple. Just us and... and maybe a couple others."

"Yeah?" I say, muffled around my mouthful of food. Matty knows exactly how I like my meat, and it's fucking delicious. I jump to the obvious conclusion. "Don't tell me you're gonna have Bill and Jimmy over."

Matty snorts, shaking his head. "After the way they got into it over that PlayStation game the last time? I don't think their wives will *let* them come back over."

I laugh, but gotta agree. Then I have a thought, and it's out of my mouth before I can stop it, because hell, I guess I'm still a little shell-shocked from today's version of Matt.

"You're not thinking of inviting Asher and Quinn, are you?"

Matt stops trying to pick up drinks he has no free hand to carry and looks at me like I've grown a second head.

Right. Of *course* he isn't thinking of those two. Doesn't look like I've managed to trigger old-Matt, though, since he just laughs and gives up on the drinks in favor of more food.

"I just met those guys, bro," he says, hip-checking me out of the way so he can scoop up some potato salad. "Didn't I say I've been thinking about this for a bit?"

His efforts with the potato salad aren't going great, given his cast, so I have mercy on him and step in to handle it, grabbing a couple of forks and a bag of chips after I load up both our plates.

We walk over to a picnic table that's set up on the grass before he gets to the point, and it's a good thing we sit down before he does, otherwise I would've fallen right over when I finally hear it.

"I was thinking..." Matty starts, toying with his food. Then he takes a breath and looks up at me, like he's bracing himself. "Got a letter from *Papi*."

I freeze. Matty hasn't called Santi that since we were kids.

"His fiftieth birthday's coming up," he says.

"Yeah," I manage eloquently, because for real, it's all I've got.

Of course I know about the letter. I know Santi's birthday is coming up, too. Already ordered him a bottle of that pricey scotch he likes online, didn't I? What I *don't* know is what's come over my best friend, and how I can keep this version of him around for a bit longer... like forever, maybe.

Matty clears his throat. "Don't know if Dad has any plans—"

"Nick's taking him on a cruise," I blurt, shoving the burger in my mouth right after the words burst out in the hopes that I haven't popped the bubble of never-would've-believed-it-in-a-million years that we seem to be sitting in.

For a second I think I might have. I've never actually come out and point-blank admitted I keep in touch with Santi, and right now, Matt's looking at me like he wants to say something about me breaking our unspoken "don't ask, don't tell" agreement about his dad. Not fair, since he started it—but then he just shakes his head and gets back to making his point.

"Anyway, I thought we might have Dad and his—and *Nick* over," Matty says, proving once again that it truly is my day to have the shit shocked right out of me. "For dinner, you know?" He gives me a smile that turns something over in my chest, adding, "Help Eden knock that cooking thing off her bucket list once and for all."

"So, this is about Eden?" I ask cautiously.

I mean, it's a stupid question, because Matty possibly opening the door to having Santi back in his life? That's about a whole lot of things bigger than just Eden, no matter how amazing she is. But still, seems like the safest way I can think of to respond to this totally unexpected turn of events.

It works, too.

The tension disappears from Matty's shoulders as soon as I say her name, and he gets a shit-eating grin on his face that tells me I'm definitely right about him having gotten into her pants.

Fuck, and now I'm picturing *that...* just a little too vividly, thank you very much.

Vividly enough that I kinda wish I still had a beer in my hand to cool me off. Why didn't we grab a couple more to go with the food? Oh, right. Because Matt's only pulling half his weight in terms of carrying things these days.

I shift on the bench, reaching down to discreetly adjust myself and glad as fuck that he's obviously got other things on his mind right now and doesn't seem to notice.

"Guess you could say it's about Eden," Matty says, popping a chip in his mouth. "She might have pointed out what an ass I was being about... you know. Things." He shoves a whole handful of chips in next, so that it's hard to understand him, but pretty sure his next words are: "Kinda miss having Dad around."

"Pretty sure Santi misses *being* around, buddy," I say.

And instead of giving me shit about being a sentimental sap, or making a joke about it, or doing any of the things I might've expected from him, Matty reaches out and squeezes my arm and looks me in the eye and sends my heart rate fucking *skyrocketing*, even though I couldn't have said why this look feels different than the sixteen million other times he's ever looked at me in the lifetime that we've known each other.

I swallow hard, just... frozen.

"Thanks," Matty says, smiling. "Pretty sure I'm gonna need you to be there if I... if I do this."

"Pretty sure I wouldn't be anywhere else," I tell him, since it's God's honest truth.

He squeezes my arm again, still holding my gaze, then drops his hand and picks up his boring-ass burger and waves Jimmy and his wife over to join us when he sees them wandering around with plates in their hands. Bill joins us a minute later, too... and then Asher and Quinn, who bring an entire six-pack of that cold beer I was just wishing for.

And yeah, I *was* just wishing for one, but I turn it down in favor of a soda, because truth? I feel a little off-kilter right now. Intoxicated, even. But since I've only had the one beer so far, well, maybe it's not really the alcohol.

Can you get drunk on possibility?

Because all the surprises Matty's thrown at me in the last hour are making me think that a lot of things I'd assumed would never happen might be... well, not back on the table, exactly.

But maybe not entirely off it, either.

EDEN

J'm a little in awe as I look at the spread of food we've prepared for tonight's dinner with Matt's father, and I know for sure it never would have happened without these two amazing men in my corner.

Matt's planning and organization skills were in overdrive all week, and his idea of doing a make-ahead menu so we weren't scrambling today was a stroke of genius. And Johnny? The man is a human Energizer Bunny, and the way he jumps in with both feet when something's important to Matt—like tonight is—is a testament to the size of his heart.

Just as big as the rest of his mouthwatering body.

I tear my eyes away, feeling guilty, and then gasp softly when Matt wraps his good arm around me from behind and rests his chin on my shoulder. The way he touches me electrifies me, every time.

"What do you think, beautiful?" he asks, nodding at the food. "Are we good on number sixty-six now?"

I bite my lip as I do my best not to react to his touch too obviously, all too aware of Johnny watching... and of all the things I know about Johnny that Matt doesn't.

That we slept together.

That I want to again.

How mind-blowing it felt to have Johnny fuck me.

How hot it is to know that he wants to be with Matt that way, too.

Matt's hands skim over the silky material of the dress I'm wearing, teasing my hips... my stomach... the base of my ribs. I shiver, biting back a moan. Is he trying to torture me? Tempt me?

It's not the time or place, for so many reasons, and it suddenly occurs to me that maybe Matt is trying to distract himself, too. Seeing his father for the first time in eight years is going to either be hard as heck on him tonight... or amazing.

Maybe both.

Johnny's tossing an apple up in the air and catching it over and over while we all try to pretend we're not watching the clock as we wait for Santiago and Nick to arrive, and when Matt presses a kiss against the side of my neck... well, to say that a part of me still feels conflicted about being openly affectionate with him in front of Johnny is the understatement of the year.

I'm turned on.

I'm guilty.

I'm scared Johnny will see... and pretty sure that I want him to, too.

Oh, Lord. I'm a hot mess, aren't I?

Johnny catches my eye, his gaze sliding down my body like a physical touch, and he grins, eyes going hot when I shiver, and I just *know* he's thinking something that's just as wicked as the thoughts in my own head.

I catch my breath as my whole body reacts to him. I can't pretend I don't want Johnny again... *badly*, because I do. I just can't see a way to have my cake *and* eat it without hurting Matt, who so far seems oblivious to the undercurrents that threaten to sweep me away whenever the three of us are together.

It's like he has a blind spot, one so big that I'd almost think it was intentional if I believed Matt was wired to ever deceive Johnny on purpose. Still, how he's managed not to notice how Johnny feels about him after all their years of friendship is beyond me. Now that *I* know, I can see it in a thousand small moments every day... and God, it's both hot as hell and a little bit heart-breaking.

"You gonna answer the man, princess?" Johnny asks me, that low, sexy timbre his voice drops down to telling me for sure that he knows just how dirty my thoughts were getting.

I blink, pulling myself away from Matt because... well, *not* because I want to. I guess just because no matter how hot my fantasies have gotten lately, I can't really imagine how sleeping with both of them can possibly work out in any way other than someone getting hurt.

I have no idea what Johnny's talking about, though.

"Um... what?" I ask, looking back and forth between these two men who make me want to throw every socially acceptable moral out the window and indulge myself like a greedy, wanton—

Matt laughs, low and dirty, and I feel my face go hot. I swear, I never used to be like this, but lately, I can't be in the same room with either one of them before wanting things I would have been embarrassed even to admit to a few weeks ago.

"Distracted by something, Eden?" Matt asks with the kind of innocent expression I might have fallen for back when I first met him.

"Stop," I say, putting my hands over my cheeks as they heat up. I wrack my brain, trying to remember what the question was. "Um..."

Matt laughs again, crossing over to stand next to Johnny. He snatches the apple out of the air the next time Johnny tosses it up —he's really getting good with his left hand, something I can attest to—and then sets it back in the fruit bowl and throws his good arm around Johnny's shoulders. "Looks like she needs a... *hand* with that one, yeah?"

He manages to make that sound dirty as all heck, and oh, if he could only see the heat that flares in Johnny's eyes. Still, Johnny has mercy on me.

"Matty wants to know if this—" Johnny sweeps a hand out, taking in the meal we've got laid out on the table and which I *still* can't believe turned out so well, "—is good enough that you can check *learn to cook* off your bucket list now."

Oh, right.

I nod, still too distracted by what these two do to me to censor myself when I answer. "I'm officially crossing it off," I say, smoothing a hand down over my dress. "Just in time, too."

Matt and Johnny's eyebrows go up at the same time, both of them looking at me curiously.

"Just in time for what?" Johnny asks.

"In time to get it done before I turn twenty-five," I answer, still distracted. It's my only excuse, because I've never admitted what that birthday means to me to anyone, not even Auntie Maria, and yet I go ahead and add, "Not that I'll make it that far, of course."

Matt and Johnny both have all of their attention focused on me, but the way they're leaning together makes them look... well, *together*. Especially when I notice that Matt's let his hand slide down off Johnny's shoulder and is resting it around his waist now, thumb hooked through Johnny's belt loop and fingers teasing at the hem of Johnny's shirt.

Does he know he's doing that?

Does he know how sexy it looks?

Oh my God... does he have feelings for Johnny, too?

If he does, there's no way Johnny knows. And heck, based on Matt's knee-jerk reaction the first time he told me about his father, maybe he doesn't even know it about himself. Hasn't been able to *admit* it to himself, I mean.

Or maybe I'm just seeing things.

Letting my fantasies color my vision.

Imagining that—

"What are you talking about, Eden?" Matt asks me sharply, straightening up and pinning me with a hard stare that snaps my attention into focus.

"You're not… what? Not gonna make it to your birthday?" Johnny presses, his eyebrows bunching together as he frowns at me. "What the hell does that mean?"

"It's… it's nothing," I say, which is about as opposite of the truth as it's possible to get.

It's *every*thing.

It's shaped my whole life.

"That's not nothing," Matt says, crossing the room in two strides and grabbing me by the arms. "Why would you say something like that?"

"Seriously, Eden," Johnny says, suddenly right next to me, too. His big hand wraps around the back of my neck exactly like it does when he kisses me, fingers tangling in my hair, and he looks down at me like he's not planning on letting me off the hook, either. "That's not funny. What did you mean?"

"I…"

I can't say it. No matter how true it feels in my heart, I *know* it sounds crazy.

"You said your mom died when she was twenty-five, yeah?" Matt suddenly asks, his dark eyes softening as he stares down at me. "Along with your dad?"

I nod. "She was twenty-four," I correct him. "She never made it to twenty-five. And neither… neither did her mother."

"No shit?" Johnny asks, eyebrows going up even though he's looking at me with sympathy, too. "That must've been rough on your mom, to lose her so young and then…"

He doesn't finish it.

"My grandmother died from a fall down the stairs," I tell them, although I'm not sure why. "And *her* mother died in a fire, can you imagine? Both of them when they were twenty-four years old."

Matt's frowning, and Johnny cocks his head to the side like

I've noticed he always does when he's trying to make sense of things.

"I had to do a class project when I was sixteen," I say, the words starting to spill out as if all these years of holding them inside have built up until they *have* to. "It was a genealogy thing. A family tree. And it was really hard to track down the information but... but once I did, I had to keep going back further. Not for school, but for me. I wanted to find someone who lived."

"Your great-grandma?" Johnny asks, his warm tone wrapping around me like a blanket.

I lean against him, held up by Matt's hands still on my arms, and shake my head. "No. My great-grandma drowned, and *her* mother died of influenza. Before that? An accident with a horse. Another fire. Tuberculosis. A drowning at sea. I... I went back generations, until I couldn't anymore."

"All those... those ancestors died young?" Matt asks me, because he still doesn't get it.

"Yes," I say, wiping at my cheeks even though I'm not sure when I started crying. "But not just young. None of them saw their twenty-fifth birthdays, and none of them died younger than I am now. They all died *when* they were twenty-four. Not earlier. Not later. It's... it's my fate. The fate of all the women in my family."

Johnny's shaking his head, that big arm all the way around my waist, and Matt's eyes are boring into me like he's trying to see right through to my soul.

"No," he says firmly. "You mentioned an aunt—"

"She's my father's sister. But all the women on my mother's side?"

"That shit isn't like... I mean, none of that was hereditary genetic type stuff, you know?" Johnny says before I can go on. "Eden, come on now. That really sucks, and I'm not saying it isn't weird as hell that it all happened to them at the same age, but sometimes coincidences just happen, you know? But we're not talking like cancer or anything, though, so there's no reason for you to—"

The doorbell cuts him off, and we all jump.

"Oh my God," I say, shaking. "I'm... I'm so sorry. I need to go fix my face."

I'm a mess, and I can tell they want to stop me from rushing out of the room, but tonight isn't about me. I can't blame the boys for not believing me; I'm also not willing to let my fate take away from what I hope will turn out to be the start of a true reconciliation between Matt and his father.

The doorbell rings again, and I wipe at my wet cheeks and then—I don't know what's gotten into me, it's just too much emotion crammed into too little space, I guess—but I pull Matt to me and kiss him on the mouth, hard.

And then I do the same with Johnny.

They both look dumbfounded, and it's sweet and kind of flattering and I *can't* think about how I'm going to explain that to Matt later, I just can't. But luckily, he's going to have something else on his mind for a while.

"Forget about me right now, okay? Go get the door," I say, cupping both their cheeks as something surges up inside me that I don't want to put a name to.

Not after just knowing them for a month.

Not when I feel it for *both* of them.

And not when I'm running out of time to do anything about it, anyway.

"Eden—"

"I am *not* meeting your father looking like this, Matt," I say firmly, kissing him again because I'm greedy. I turn to Johnny. "And don't think I don't know what tonight means to you, too."

I've picked up on the fact that Santiago has been like a surrogate father to him, and oh, Lord, it's like something broke free inside me and I can't stuff it back where it belongs, because with my hand still on Matt's face, I turn and kiss Johnny again, too.

I don't wait to see their reaction this time, because I'm *sure* my makeup is a mess now and I just... I just need a minute. I do hear Johnny call after me, though.

"We're not done talking about this, Eden."

"About *all* of this," Matt adds, sounding more serious than I'm used to from him... but not *angry*, thank God. And then the doorbell rings a third time, and I'm off the hook for now because they really *do* have to answer it.

I glance back just before ducking into the hall bathroom and see that Johnny's pulled Matt against him in a quick hug.

Thank God they don't look at odds over those kisses. Not at all, in fact. Johnny whispers something in Matt's ear that I can't hear, holding him close for a second, and whatever it is makes Matt relax a little as he glances toward the front door. He nods, and Johnny gives him a little push in that direction.

And me? Oh, Lord, I'm in trouble, because even though I know it's pointless, for the first time since I can remember I want to fight my fate. And not *just* fight it.

These two sexy, big-hearted, overprotective boys of mine?

They make me want to win.

12

MATT

I'm not sure what I expect to feel when I open the door, but the first thing that hits me is that my father has a beard now. When did that happen? It's trim and flattering and peppered with gray, and I should be saying hello, yeah? Or at least *some*thing.

But instead I'm just staring.

It's one thing to know that my father's about to turn fifty, but it's something totally different to realize that he's actually gotten *older*. My throat tightens up, but before I can figure out how I'm gonna manage to get any words out when I'm not sure I'm even breathing, Dad saves me from needing to figure it out by pulling me into a tight hug.

"*Mijo*," he says, sounding like he's just as choked up as I am. "It is so good to see you again. *Ocho años, no lo creo.*"

Oh, shit. Eight years, he says, and even though it's not an accusation, it hits me even harder than the shock of his new beard: eight years, and it's my fault.

My arms tighten around him, and my father feels smaller, but somehow the same, too.

What the fuck had I been *thinking*, letting him get older and smaller like this? Letting so much time pass? And then I remember. Oh, right. I'd been thinking about how my father had always been the most solid thing in my life and I hadn't even realized it until he'd betrayed me.

Except, now I'm also thinking maybe I was wrong.

Maybe Eden was right, and Dad wasn't betraying me at all.

Maybe him coming out had nothing to do with me… and I'm the one who ended up letting *him* down.

"Lo siento, Papá," I whisper. I'm sorry. It's not what I thought the first thing I'd say would be, but I guess it's what it needed to be, because as soon as those words get out, I can suddenly breathe again.

And then Johnny's there, thank God, coming up behind me and clapping a hand on my shoulder. Giving my dad an easy smile and getting a hug of his own as he welcomes him and makes a little chitchat to let me have the minute I need to get a grip.

I know Johnny like the back of my hand, and yeah, its genuine —he's always gotten along with my dad—but I also know he's doing it for me. Jesus, he's a godsend.

"Boys, boys," Dad says, smiling at both of us as he ushers in the man he came with. "This is my Nick. He is looking forward to this dinner as much as I am, no?"

"Good to see you again, Nick," Johnny says, that hand coming back to rest on my shoulder as I wonder for a second if I'm going to feel something ugly, but how can I? The guy doesn't look like a threat. He actually looks like an accountant or something, just an ordinary guy who's maybe wearing a little more pastel than your average CPA, but for real, I don't even really notice that, because he's also looking at my dad like… well, huh. Kind of like the looks Johnny's been sneaking at me.

Like Nick wants to make sure Dad is okay.

And also like he's one hundred percent there for Dad. Like, *really* there. And suddenly it's like a lightbulb goes off in my head, and for the first time in my life it occurs to me that Dad didn't just suddenly decide he liked dick—which I'm sorry, he's still my father, so I can't even—but that maybe he also wanted to go out and find someone who *loves* him.

Maybe—if I'm being honest in the privacy of my own head and all—someone who could love him better than Mom did.

"Nice to meet you, Nick," I say, surprising myself by meaning it. "Hope dinner is okay. None of us are all that good in the kitchen—"

"What?" Dad interrupts me, eyebrows shooting to his hairline. "This I cannot believe. You were always my helper, *mijo*. *¿Que pasó?*"

I know damn well what happened, but admitting that I rejected some of the things that had mattered the most to me just because they were associated with my dad would make me feel like a two-year-old having a tantrum. I'm saved again, though, when Eden comes into the room—jaw-droppingly gorgeous, as always—and Johnny jumps in with introductions.

"Santi, Nick, this is Eden, the inspiration for tonight's dinner."

"Uh-oh, does this mean I'm going to get the blame after we sit down and taste it?" she asks, cheeks going pink as she lets Dad take both her hands in his. "So nice to meet you."

"So nice to meet *you*, Eden," Dad says, beaming at her as he looks back and forth between Eden and me. "You are my Mateo's *novia*...?"

She shrugs, throwing me a questioning look. "I'm sorry, I don't speak Spanish."

"*Yet*," Johnny says confidently, resting a hand on her shoulder as he grins at my dad. "Learning another language is a goal of Eden's. Me and Matty are gonna be helping her with it, ain't that right, bro?"

"We are?" I ask, even though honestly, it sounds like a no-brainer. I don't know why the idea seemed daunting before.

"Of course you are!" Dad says, eyes lighting up. "You cannot let this lovely one go all of her life without the beauty of *Español en su vida, verdad?*" He claps his hands together, rubbing them gleefully. "We can start tonight, *¿sí?*"

Eden starts ushering us all toward the table, and while Dad gushes over the spread and Johnny jokes around with the two of them, I watch Nick.

Nick's watching Dad, and he's got a smile on his face. It's delicate, walking a line somewhere between concern and love. I wonder if my father was just as nervous about tonight as I am. He probably had to work up some serious guts to come out here, let alone knock on the door, and this man helped him do it.

Must have.

"Do you speak any Spanish, Nick?" I ask, suddenly ashamed that I know nothing about this man who's obviously such an important part of my father's life. I'm pretty sure they've been together for six or seven years now, even though I've made a point of not paying attention to the details of my father's new life. Still, I guess I've picked up a few from Johnny here and there, never letting myself really question him about how he was always up on that shit.

"Not as much as I should," Nick answers me with a small smile. "You?"

"Same," I say, suddenly embarrassed about it. Not that I *can't* speak it, of course, but for the last eight years, I haven't. I clear my throat. "Maybe Eden's bucket list will help me correct that though, yeah?"

"Bucket list?" he asks, taking a seat and directing the question toward her with a look of genuine interest. "You've started one of those?"

"Started?" Johnny scoffs, grinning. "She's almost done with it! All she's got left is the language, right?"

Eden starts serving the food, and I laugh, pretty sure Johnny's employing some selective memory on that one. "Yeah, no, bro. She's still gotta go skydiving, too."

He makes a face, and my dad laughs.

"Let me guess, this is not one you will be so quick to help her with, Johnny?" he teases, winking before he turns to explain to Nick. "You wonder where my gray hair came from? It was this one, always too reckless for his own good and getting my Mateo into trouble. Like the time on their bicycles when they decided to race one of the... what are they called?"

"Hey, now," Johnny cuts in, laughing. "The duck boats? How come *I* get the blame for that? Matty's a big boy. He's the one who wanted to—"

"Pfft," Dad interrupts, flapping a hand in the air to dismiss Johnny's attempt at pinning that one on me. "My son only went along to make sure you did not kill yourself, no?"

"Truth," I say, raising a hand in the air like I'm testifying.

Johnny wads up his napkin and throws it at me, grinning, and Eden smacks him on the arm, shaking her head.

"This is supposed to be a *nice* dinner," she admonishes him, lips twitching. "No throwing things."

"What?" Johnny asks with a ridiculous attempt at an innocent look. "I took the napkin ring off first."

Nick laughs, and I see him and my dad exchange a look that... well, that's nice. Not weird. Not over-the-top. Just kind of loving, you know? They kinda remind me of how that new guy down at the station, Asher, was with his fiancé. I mean, not that Dad and Nick *remind* me of those two, but I guess I'm just thinking that here I've seen these two gay couples, two weekends in a row, and they're just... they're just couples. Both guys, sure, but I mean... I guess I'm having trouble remembering why I was so sure that fact bothered me for so long when all I see right now is two people who get along like peas in a pod.

Sort of complementing each other.

Fitting each other.

I'm thinking about that, trying to sort of test out how I feel about it, but my head is still jumbled. Dad is just... it's too close, you know? So I switch for a second and go back to thinking about that guy Asher instead.

At the barbecue, I'd finally caught onto the fact that he'd been waiting on me to be an asshole, and that didn't feel great. But actually seeing him and his man? Truth was, it didn't bother me. I mean, sure, it was odd—you just don't see it every day—but the odd faded fast and then it was just background. Just another couple, yeah?

A couple who seemed to fit each other.

I snicker, grabbing the wine glass Eden's already filled for me to hide it behind. Because I mean, sure, looked like they fit as a couple, but not *all* their parts are gonna… fit, exactly, amirite?

And yeah, my mind went there, but I mean, I'm a guy, so pretty sure I get a pass. Hasn't it been proven that sex is on our minds ninety-nine percent of the time? And yes, that *is* what I'm picturing right now, and two guys together? Kind of funny when you think about how maybe the word *fitting* doesn't exactly fit, because with two dicks involved, there isn't really a place to put—

"You okay, bro?" Johnny asks me when I suddenly start choking.

I nod, and he must see something in my face that tells him I desperately need a save right now even though thank fucking Christ he doesn't know why, because before anyone else can comment about my sudden inability to get my drink to go down the right way, Johnny just rolls the conversation away from me and gives me a minute to get it together.

And holy shit, do I ever need that minute. Because yeah, I'm not ignorant. I know damn well there actually *are* a few places you could put your cock if you happened to have it out and about while getting, uh, you know, getting close to another guy. I mean, obviously there are, because gay sex is a thing, but it wasn't so much the fact that made me choke as it was what those particular images did to my dick.

Dad is going on to Nick about this theory he has that I can't disagree with, all about how God gave Johnny his white-knuckled fear of heights as a last-ditch effort to keep Johnny from getting himself killed, what with how enthusiastic my boy gets about diving headfirst into certain situations and all, and I just let that conversation flow around me while I take a breath and try to calm my suddenly much-too-happy stick while I try to reason out what the fuck just happened to me.

I shift in my seat, and yep, I am legit sporting a semi right now. And I mean… maybe it makes sense that I'd have a bit of a reaction to the line of thinking I'd wandered down, because there are really only a couple of things I can imagine guys doing with each other… and not gonna lie, I do like anal. Not all girls are into it, but damn if it doesn't do it for me when they are. And blow jobs? Sign me up, the more the merrier. So probably it's just the actual sex acts I'm suddenly reacting to, right? Not the… the context.

"You good, bro?" Johnny asks, leaning toward me to ask it quietly while Eden gets busy charming my dad and Nick. He rests a friendly hand on my leg as he leans in, just for balance or whatever, obviously, and oshit.

Clearly, I am *not* good yet. I most definitely don't have this shit under control, so thank God Eden had us put this dangling table-cloth on the table to hide what my best friend's totally innocent touch is doing to me.

He's looking at me all concerned-like, and I nod in the hopes that we can move on. I *know* he doesn't believe me, because he just knows me too damn well. Still, he squeezes my knee and lets it go —thank Christ—and I let out a slow breath, realizing that he probably thinks I'm all tied up in knots because of my dad's visit.

Which… yeah. I'm that, too.

Am I just trying to distract myself from that shit by paying attention to my dick right now? Some sort of coping mechanism, the way they've prattled on about during some of those mental health training days at the station?

Possible, because I've already been doing it, haven't I? I've been kind of trying to distract myself about how I'd feel about seeing *Papi* again all day, and maybe some buried part of my brain just latched onto this particular set of images as yet another avenue of distraction, yeah?

Because fuck if I ever thought about doing *any*thing with my dick in terms of another guy before.

I mean, not all that much, at least.

I scoot a little farther away from Johnny under the pretense of reaching for the salad bowl on the other side of me, suddenly worried that he'll somehow read me a little *too* well and it'll fuck us up. But it's not my fault that I may or may not have occasionally had a stray and totally inappropriate thought when it comes to my best friend, given some of the situations he and I have found ourselves in, yeah?

And it's not like I've ever tried to *act* on those thoughts.

Besides, all guys wonder a little, amirite?

And I mean... some guys are just attractive by like, genetic default or whatever, so it's not gay to just notice that in a purely-factual-fact type of way.

I cut a glance in Johnny's direction, but accidentally catch Nick's eye instead. He's smiling at me with a sort of bemused expression on his face—and for real, does the guy ever *not* smile? —and I'm suddenly irrationally terrified that *he's* going to be the one to read my mind and maybe like... I don't know, lay it out for Johnny about all the things that have crowded into my head just now, maybe as some sort of revenge for the shitty way I'm just now really realizing I've treated my dad over the last few years.

"You like the pork chops, Nick?" I blurt out in an effort to shut him up before he can out me like that.

"They're delicious," he says, the genuine warmth in his eyes instantly making me feel like an ass.

Of course he can't read my mind. And even if he could... guess I don't know the guy yet, but I have to admit, I like him. And now that I'm starting to get my own freak-out under control a bit?

Truth is, I just don't get the impression that Nick's the type who'd try to ruin me and Johnny like that.

Nick turns to my dad. "We should get the recipe for these, Santi, don't you think?"

"*Sí, sí,*" Dad replies, nodding enthusiastically. "We can serve them the next time Brenda is in town, no?" And then to me, with a cautious note in his voice, "Mateo, maybe you will join us?"

I blink, my random moment of misplaced horniness going up in smoke. "You... you wanna have *Mom* over for dinner?" I ask, dumbfounded. "Are you crazy? She—"

I snap my mouth closed while they all just stare at me, but okay, I'm really *not* an asshole, so I'm not gonna just blurt out that Mom hates him. I mean, she must, right? He's the whole reason she's avoided coming home to Boston for so many years.

"She what, *mijo?*" Dad asks after a minute, looking genuinely confused. "You know your mother has always liked pork. Remember how she used to beg us to make *pernil asado* when you were small?"

"Of course I do," I say, feeling totally discombobulated by his laid-back attitude. And oh my God, now my mouth is watering, too. I haven't had *pernil asado*—a Puerto Rican-style roast pork dish—in years. "But..."

"But?" Dad prompts me after a second.

Eden and Nick are both looking a little lost, and when I shoot Johnny a save-me look, I can see that he's confused, too. For once, he's *not* reading me like a book—even though he should know better than anyone why it's surreal to have Dad talking so casually about socializing with Mom. But his constantly moving mouth is glued firmly shut right now as he waits for me to finish my sentence, so I guess I'm on my own.

"But, uh, I guess... guess I didn't realize you two were still in touch," I mumble, shoving a bite of salad in my mouth and hoping that'll be the end of it so we can just move on to a different topic already.

Dad cocks his head to the side, giving me a quizzical look that I'm guessing means moving on is a no-go.

"Why would we not be? She is my best friend, *mijo*. We shared a life together for twenty years. Of course we are in touch." He suddenly grins, stroking his new beard and exchanging a look with Nick that screams *inside joke* before adding, "She is always sending us postcards from her travels. She favors... beaches."

Nick snickers.

"She sends us those, too," Johnny offers, raising an eyebrow. "But why do I get the impression yours are more fun than the ones I get?"

"Eh, you are young," Dad says, waving a dismissive hand as his lips twitch. "Brenda would not want to corrupt you the way she tries to do with my Nick."

Eden suddenly slaps a hand over her mouth, stifling a giggle.

"What am I missing?" I ask, feeling like the answer to that is way bigger than a few postcards.

For real, I can't wrap my head around it. Dad and Mom... I just... *what?*

Eden is looking back and forth between my dad and Nick with a gorgeous pink tint to her cheeks and an ear-splitting grin on her face. "Please tell me she's sending you naughty pictures of naked men on those beaches."

Oh, Christ on the cross... no. My *mother?*

"Brenda, she likes the scenery, no?" my dad says with a twinkle in his eyes that I do *not* want to contemplate.

Eden laughs. "It sounds like she'd get along with my Auntie Maria."

"If your Auntie Maria likes naughty naked men, then I like her already," Nick quips, neither confirming nor denying the thing about my mom that I... just... can't...

I grab for that wine glass again.

Dad's quiet accountant-type boyfriend is joking about naked pictures?

My *mother* is sending dirty postcards to my dad?

Dad wants to make her *dinner*?

Get us all together again?

Have it be like... like... well, definitely not like it was before. How could it be? Because it wouldn't be just the three of us, a family, it would be—

I look around the table trying to figure out what it would be— besides batshit crazy—to try to get us all together. Johnny would have to be there, of course. And Eden—I mean, sure, it hasn't been long, but I already know I want her to be in my life in all the important ways. And it's obvious that Nick and Dad are a package deal—it's evident in every look and touch between them; in the easy way they play off each other—so that would probably be the weirdest part.

Except that Dad makes it sound like they've *already* had dinner with Mom.

That the three of them are... are *friends*.

But if my parents *aren't* at odds, then what the hell have I been doing all these years, carrying around a thousand-pound chip on my shoulder over how he ruined everything? I drain my wine glass and look around for the bottle, even though truth is I'd rather have a beer.

Maybe two beers.

All the beers.

I'm more than a little thrown by having so many of my assumptions shaken up tonight, and I'm still not sure what they'll look like once they settle down again.

"It is good that Brenda can finally travel the way she has always yearned to, no?" my dad is saying, no animosity in his voice at all. "I am happy for her, but—" he clucks his tongue, shaking his head, "—she never eats enough when she is overseas. Eden, you will give us the pork recipe?"

"Of course, Santi," Eden says, smiling like he's just given *her* something. She's glowing, absolutely beautiful, and through all my confusion, I'm suddenly happy for her.

Look at her.

She made a comment the other day that got me thinking about why cooking has been such a beast for her, why it's taken so damn long for her to figure out something so basic, and I've got an idea about that. I know she's close with that aunt that raised her, but there's a longing in her voice, too. A wistfulness. I hear it those few times she mentions her mom—and yeah, she happened to drop that the woman was apparently a killer cook—and Eden also gets that tone when she talks about family.

The kind she didn't ever really have.

The kind *I* had... and thought I'd lost... but now am starting to think I might have actually thrown away, instead.

The kind you cook for.

She looks over and refills my wine glass without me having to ask and Johnny gives my leg another one of those supportive *I'm here for you, buddy* squeezes that had my dick so confused earlier, and as I listen to the four of them banter around the table, it suddenly hits me that tonight *does* feel like family. The kind of family I've missed having all these years of it being just me and Johnny... which is maybe why I can recognize the feeling in Eden.

And that's my theory, which could just be a huge crock of shit, but maybe isn't—that once Eden had a family to cook for, she was able to come through and finally do the thing, yeah?

I kinda hope that's it.

Hope she feels that way about us.

Hope, too, that we *are* that way, or can be. Not just me and her, which I definitely plan on making happen, and not just me and Johnny, which is a given—rock solid as long as I don't mess it up with weird confusions like I was having earlier—but now that I've got him back, it hits me hard: I want *family* to include Dad again, too.

He changed everything when he came out eight years ago...

except right now? Even with different faces around the table, it almost feels like nothing really changed at all. Like it was all just right here waiting for me to see it the whole time; to have the guts to reach for it and claim it and be a part of it again. And sure, it looks different now, and maybe it's just the wine talking—because how many glasses have I had now? I'm starting to lose track—but tonight at least, seems to me like "different" might not be so bad.

Might even grow into something better than it was before.

13

JOHNNY

*J*t's late by the time Santi and Nick leave. I've got to be up early in the morning, but as Matt walks them out to the car I already know I'm not going to be able to get to sleep anytime soon. I'm too wound up. *Buzzing.* Just completely amped from the whole night.

"That went well, didn't it?" Eden says, following me into the kitchen with the salad bowl in her hands as I start loading the dishwasher. She's smiling with her whole body, and I know she's just as happy for Matty as I am.

"It definitely did."

She hands over the empty bowl, then laughs, shaking her head. "Is there a prize for how fast you can stack the dishes in there?"

I grin, knowing damn well that it's going to take more than tidying up to burn off all the excess energy coursing through my veins. I toss a pod of detergent into the machine and hit start, then swing her up in my arms, laughing when it makes her squeal.

"You offering a prize, princess? Because dinner didn't just go well, it went *hella* well. I definitely think we should celebrate."

She giggles, and I'm mostly joking around, but no denying that I'm also genuinely stoked about how the night had gone. It had

147

been about a thousand times better than I could've imagined, and while I'd been a little worried about how Matty would deal— because let's just be real, eight years of resentment is a lot to carry around—he'd actually ended up enjoying himself, as far as I could tell. And sure, all that wine Eden had kept flowing probably helped, but the important thing—the epically awesome thing— was that by the end of the night, there had been an ease between Matt and his dad that I'd once been afraid was lost forever.

It gives me hope that their rift might actually get mended.

Eden wraps her arms around me, still giggling, and I guess I had a fair amount of that wine, too, because I don't even hesitate before setting her on the counter and stepping between her legs to get a taste of what I've been wanting more of for weeks. She kisses me back like she's just as ready for it... but then suddenly gasps and sort of squirms against me in a way that tells me all the theatrics are about something other than how hot I'm making her.

"Johnny," she squeals, pushing at my chest until I back off. "The water!"

I start laughing when I see. Looks like I'd pushed her up against the sink and somehow nudged the faucet on. That sexy little dress she's wearing is half-soaked from the waist down, and of course the first thing that comes to mind is getting her out of it.

She's still sitting on the counter, and she bunches up the material to sort of wring it out into the sink... which basically bares her gorgeous legs all the way up to the tops of her thighs.

I grin. *Perfect.* She's halfway to naked already.

"This the kind of prize you were thinking of, Eden?" I ask, running my hands all the way up those pretty legs until my thumbs slip under the soft material bunched at the top.

She stops what she's doing and sucks in a tiny breath, making my cock sit up and take some real notice, because I can see that she wants to say yes. What she actually does is bite her lip, then whisper my name.

I decide that counts as an invitation.

I wrap one hand around the back of her neck and let her moan into my mouth as my other hand moves higher. I press against her silky little panties, right over the sweet core of her heat—and *hello*, they're wet too... but not from the water.

I don't know whether to blame my blood alcohol level or the relief that feels almost like a high over finally seeing Matty and his dad start to reconcile, but whatever the reason, I'm not thinking about anything but this right here, like I've forgotten all about where we are or the fact that Matt will be back any minute. Eden remembers, though, because after a minute, she jerks her mouth away, panting, and gives me a look that's a jumble of a whole bunch of things all mixed together.

Desire.

Guilt.

Anticipation.

Nerves.

Her eyes dart toward the door, and suddenly I'm thinking of Matt, too. Maybe not like she is, though. I'm thinking of that moment just before Santi rang the bell, when Eden had kissed him. Then me. Then him again...

I've been petting her over the top of that little slip of silky panty, but now I sneak a finger under the edge so I can touch her directly. I'm pretty sure that her kissing Matty confirms that they've done other things, too, and all the blood rushes down to my dick as I imagine it.

"So," I say, smirking at her. "You and Matt?"

Eden blushes.

"Come on now," I whisper, letting my fingers dip into her. "We both know you wanted to... just tell me. Did you?"

Her breath hitches as she rocks against me, and finally she nods, just a tiny one. "Yes," she whispers, spreading her legs wider with a moan as I press my fingers deeper into her.

And *God*, she's so wet. And that one yes? Makes it so fucking easy for me to picture Matty right where I'm at now.

Touching her like this.

Listening to the way her breath starts to quicken.

Feeling his cock swell into a beast with every soft, needy sound she makes.

I keep my eyes locked on hers, imagining the two of them together, and that, plus the way she's rocking against my hand, takes me from aroused all the way to hard as a fucking rock in the blink of an eye.

"Did you like being with him, princess?" I ask in a low voice, wrapping one hand around the back of her neck to pull her close.

She moans, and my cock jerks.

"Tell me how hot it was, Eden."

She makes another needy sound, and I grin, pretty sure I'm gonna have a fantastic way to burn off my excess energy after all. But then—

"How hot what was?"

It's Matty's voice from behind me, and Eden freezes. I can see her pulse fluttering at the base of her throat, as fast as a hummingbird's wings, and a whole bunch of conflicting emotions flit across her face, all variations of the ones I saw earlier. Eden's turned on and worried, both at the same time, but me?

I'm just turned on.

Maybe it's all the wine in me, or maybe it's just how fucking horny I am, but no part of me feels worried about this being a problem for Matt.

I let her go and turn to face him.

"Eden got water on her dress," I tell him. Not a lie, but neutral enough that I'm not going to embarrass her if she wants to try to pretend this wasn't just happening.

Matt's face is a little flushed in a way that reminds me he probably drank twice as much as I did and at only ninety percent of my body weight, and the way his eyes are slightly out-of-focus, I'm not even sure he noticed what we were up to. He crosses the kitchen and leans one hip against the counter right next to Eden and me.

"Water, huh? Shame, that," he says, his voice all relaxed and almost lazy from the wine. "Especially after how well the rest of the night went, yeah? Dinner was... it was good."

"Eden and I were just talking about that," I tell him, also not a lie. I grin, adding, "Went so well, we kinda thought we should celebrate, actually."

I'm still standing between her legs, and she smacks my arm, going pink.

She doesn't deny it, though.

...Interesting.

"Yeah?" Matty says, blinking slowly like he's really feeling that wine. Then he smiles, still slow and relaxed... but maybe with a hint of something dirty there, too. He looks back and forth between the two of us, and intoxicated or not, I can see the wheels turning. I mean, he can't be *that* out of it, right? After all, Eden's dress is practically hiked to her waist and my hand is still resting on her bare leg, right up near the bit where her panties almost peek out.

We both wait on Matty. Swear to God, I can *feel* Eden holding her breath.

"A celebration, huh?" Matt finally says, his eyes zeroing in my hand.

After a minute, he pulls his eyes off it and looks at me again. And... nope, it's not just my imagination. There's *definitely* something dirty in that smile.

"Am I invited to this party?" he asks, slinging his casted arm up to rest on my shoulder as he wraps his good hand around Eden's other thigh, all the way at the top so his fingers nudge the hem of her dress. He looks her in the eye and says point-blank: "You kissed Johnny."

Not sure if he's referring to just now or before dinner, but doesn't really matter, does it?

Eden sucks in a sharp breath, eyes darting to mine for a second before she gives Matty a jerky little nod. A small smile hovers over his mouth at that, and she starts nibbling that lip again, eyes locked on Matt's like she's waiting for the other shoe to drop. He didn't say it like an accusation, though, just a fact. And I know my boy. I know where his mind is probably heading right now, and I—

Well, fuck.

Of *course* I want it. I'm still horny as fuck, aren't I? And it's not like Matty and I haven't shared a girl before. It's been hot when we have, not gonna lie, but God's honest truth?

I'm just not sure if it's really safe for me to go there right now.

Maybe it's because of all those images that were going through my mind a minute ago, thinking about him and Eden together, but whatever the reason—I'm feeling just a little too aware of him at the moment, if you know what I mean. And with as tipsy as *I* am? Sure, not nearly as much as he seems to be, but... yeah. That could be a problem.

Matty smiles at Eden, slow and sexy and dirty as hell, then turns that look on me. And—

Shit.

Dangerous or not, let's just be real: I'm not gonna say no, am I?

"Tell me about kissing Eden, bro," Matty says, the kinky little shit.

He's still got his right arm slung around my shoulders in that cast, and he's stroking her thigh now with his left—fingers brushing against mine as he teases her—and even though I'm doing my damndest not to look, I see the bulge growing in his pants.

The plus side? I can tell that getting turned on is clearing his head a little.

The other side? Fuck if seeing that bulge doesn't ramp me up even higher.

His fingers brush right over Eden's center and she sucks in a sharp breath. She's not pulling away, though, doesn't seem to mind at all that we're all three in this together, and suddenly my dick is pressing *hard* against the too-tight confines of my pants.

"You wanna know about me kissing Eden?" I ask, mesmerized by the sight of Matty's hand on her.

Fuck, wasn't I just fantasizing about him touching her like this?

He makes a horny little sound that gets my cock fully locked and loaded, and I pull my eyes off the action between Eden's legs and stare right into his. "Done more than that, Matty," I admit, because when it comes to ninety-nine percent of my relationship with him, I'm all about full disclosure.

Okay, whatever. This isn't about full disclosure, this is about it being fucking hot.

"Yeah?" he says, grinning at me as that bulge of his gets noticeably bigger. "Tell me about it."

My hand tightens on Eden's other thigh. She's breathing in hot little gasps as Matty plays with her, but she gives me a tiny nod, cheeks going even pinker.

Permission to share.

Makes my cock fucking *throb*.

"The first night we brought Eden back here," I tell Matty, voice raspy because *Jesus*, I'm gonna need some relief soon at this rate, aren't I? "When you were—"

Matt suddenly takes his hand off Eden and slaps it over my mouth, cutting me off… and fuck if that touch doesn't go straight to my cock and almost cause me to embarrass myself.

Matty grins, looking a little sloppy and hella fucking sexy. "I changed my mind," he says. "Let's do show, not tell." He turns his attention to Eden. "You like Johnny, don't you, beautiful?"

Matty's low voice is almost hypnotic, so guess I can't really blame her for not answering right away. Especially when he takes his hand off my mouth and runs a finger over her lips instead.

Back and forth.

Slow and sensual.

Over and over until she finally breaks, pink tongue darting out to taste. She moans, her eyelids fluttering closed, and sucks it into her mouth.

"Fuck, Matty," I mutter, adjusting myself because... well, *fuck*. I have to, don't I?

"You gonna be a good girl and answer me, Eden?" Matty teases her, winking at me as he pulls his finger out of her mouth so slowly it makes my dick want to cry. "I wanna know if you like my boy."

She whimpers, then opens her eyes, looking dazed, and nods. "Yes," she breathes out. "I... I like Johnny."

My cock jerks. Oh, *fuck* yeah. This is really gonna happen, isn't it?

"Don't blame you," Matty says, talking to Eden but keeping his eyes locked on me until I'm fucking crazy with it.

Oh, shit. This *is* gonna happen... and I was right. The way my cock is reacting to *both* of them?

It's going to be dangerous for me.

Matt finally turns back to face Eden just before I do something stupid. He gives her another one of those dirty smiles, using that arm he's got slung around me to pull me closer as he says, "I like Johnny, too, and I want to see you kiss him again. Can you do that for me, beautiful?"

Her eyes go wide, and she licks her lips, chest heaving like she's having just as much trouble catching her breath as I am. Her eyes dart between the two of us, and oh yeah, she wants to.

"I... um, Matt," she starts hesitantly. "You... you really want me to?"

I grin. She just needs permission, and it's a perfect fit, isn't it? Because Matty... let's just say that I have it on good authority that he gets off on taking charge in the bedroom.

"Only if *you* want to," he tells her in a hypnotically soothing voice as he uses his free hand to stroke her jaw... her throat... the long line of her collarbone.

Sure, it *sounds* like he's leaving it up to her, but at the same time, he's pulling at me with that arm, urging me to get in there close to her and do what he wants. His good hand wraps around the back of Eden's neck, pushing her toward me, too, and he leans in to whisper right in her ear.

"But Johnny definitely deserves it, yeah? Just a little kiss? Always there for us, best guy I know, and look at him, huh? You like this? How could you not?"

She's blushing hard now, but doesn't even pretend to resist as he guides her toward me, getting her so close I can almost taste her. "I... I like both of you," she finally whispers in that sexy, breathless tone that makes me wild.

And now I *can* taste it—the sweet warmth of her mouth flavoring the air between us.

"We both like you, too, princess," I tell her, wrapping my hand gently around her throat. I tip Eden's head backward, putting her mouth at the perfect angle to let me give Matty the show he wants.

She moans, pupils blowing wide, but still doesn't close the gap.

"Come on now," Matty urges her softly, kneading the back of her neck, his fingertips brushing against mine.

"It's not... not wrong?" she asks, airing that last fear that must be holding her back from taking what it's pretty damn clear we all want right now.

"Can't be wrong if we all agree, yeah?" Matty says, voice still soft but smile positively wicked. He winks at me, adding, "And Johnny and I agree on just about everything, don't we?"

Hell, yeah we do.

I quit waiting, because fuck, I need her... and knowing Matty's going to be getting off on watching it until he joins in, too? I'm not even going to pretend that that doesn't do it for me.

I take Eden's mouth, and she opens for me with a needy little sob, like she's desperate for it, gasping and sucking my tongue in and wrapping one arm around my neck to hold me against her, so that they've both got me now. And then Matty is kissing her, too. His dark hair tickling my jaw as he drags his mouth down her throat and pushes the dress off her shoulders so he can move lower. I stroke Eden's throat as I kiss her, *inhale* her, and rest my other hand on Matty's hip, because I have to, you know? Where else would I put it?

It's erotic as hell to be kissing her with both their arms around me. To feel Matty moving against her, too. Yeah, we *have* shared girls before… but not like this.

Not at the same time.

Not while I get to touch him, too.

That last thought is like ice water, and I groan, making myself stop and pull away from both of them. I *don't* get to touch him, too. Touching him, too, would pretty much be the death of every-thing good in my life.

Eden looks up at me, eyelids at half-mast and mouth swollen and wet. "Wh-what? Johnny?"

Matty's looking at me oddly, his eyes sliding off mine and right down my body, pausing when they get to where my overeager cock is straining for freedom.

"Fuck," I mutter, scrubbing a hand over my face because a drunk Matty is a horny Matty and him accidentally stopping to stare at my junk is doing all kinds of shit to me.

His eyes jerk up to my face, and I'm not sure what he sees there, but he suddenly smirks, giving me a hot look I can't read, and then tells Eden, "Pretty sure Johnny wants us to have a little more room."

And okay, I'll take that excuse. It's even a good one. Because sure, having her on the kitchen counter between us is hot, but maybe it doesn't provide the best access, you know?

"My room?" Matty asks, not waiting for a response before he tries and fails to scoop her off the counter.

I snort out a laugh, because he's an idiot. "News flash: your arm is still broken, bro."

I push him aside and lift Eden into a modified version of a fireman's carry that has her luscious ass in the air and those soft breasts I'm gonna need to get my hands on soon pressing against my back. She squeals as I head down the hall and Matty gives her a little tap on the ass as he follows, which makes her gasp.

"Quiet, you," he says in the horny, drunk version of what I'm guessing is supposed to be a stern voice. "We're trained professionals here."

Eden giggles, then gasps again when we finally reach his room and I toss her down on the bed. And *dammmmmmmmmmmmmmmmmn* is that a sight. Dress and hair disheveled as fuck, long legs spread like an invitation and a hint of some naughty-looking lingerie peeking out where Matty already pulled her dress down low.

She's panting, looking up at us, and for a minute, it's like all three of us are frozen.

Can't speak for the two of them, but I can tell you for sure why *I'm* not moving. You ever gone to one of those high-class brunch buffets? Everything looks so good, it's like you don't know where to start.

"You never did tell me how you two managed to get her dress all wet like that, Johnny," Matty says, palming himself as he eyes her. "But looks like we should help her get it off, yeah?"

He's grinding the heel of that one good hand against the bulge in his pants, and the sight makes me groan.

I probably shouldn't let on that I'm staring at his cock, but my mouth has a mind of its own. "Looks like you need some help of your own," I say, because I guess *I'm* the idiot.

His eyes jerk up to meet mine, a slow smile spreading over his face, and I rush in with a save before what I meant has a chance to kick in for him.

"You only got one hand to work with, buddy," I remind him, winking. "Use it to get yourself situated. I'll take care of Eden."

Matty grins, but doesn't argue. His hand fumbles at his belt, and for a split second, I have the crazy impulse to say fuck it and *really* offer to help him. I might even get away with it, too, since I mean, it's hard as fuck to do certain things one-handed, you know? But then Eden saves me from myself by making the sexiest fucking sound I've ever heard, and my attention snaps right back to her.

I get to work on following through with Matty's suggestion. Her dress needs to come off.

I push the soft material up to her waist, my cock jerking hard at the sight of the little scrap of black silk that covers her mound. I remember damn well how it felt against my fingers, and it looks just as sexy as it feels.

I run my hand over it again, and she arches up into my touch with a moan. I already know I don't want these coming off. I can fuck her just fine by moving it just a bit to the side... or *damn*, maybe I'd rather watch as Matty does.

I slide my hand higher, pushing the dress up as I go, until it gets locked up around her full breasts and stops my progress. I push them together, making a half-ass effort to get that dress the rest of the way off but I'm pretty fucking distracted, if I'm honest, by the way she starts breathing hard... chest rising and falling under my hands... squirming against my touch as she presses her breasts into my palms.

"Johnny," she says after a minute, flushed and sort of laughing. "It... it has a zipper."

"What does, princess?" I ask, my voice sounding thick and slow as I watch her wiggle under my hands. I'm kinda mesmerized by the dip in her belly as she moves, and I'm just about to give up on getting her all the way naked so I can run my tongue down that soft skin to tease the top of her panties, when she grabs my chin and tilts my face up to look at her.

"My... my dress," she says, gorgeous mouth quivering with laughter. "You were going to help get it off?"

"Anything," I promise her, tilting my head to the side to kiss her palm.

She makes a sexy little sound, then comes up on her elbows and runs a hand over her breasts, pushing them up so they practically spill out of the bunched material trapping them there.

"The zipper's in the back," she says breathlessly, spelling it out for me with sparkling eyes. "Can you...?"

Oh, this girl. She's trying to kill me with that teasing little smile, isn't she?

"Roll over, Eden."

She's quick to do it, sinking down onto the bed with a sigh, and I hear Matt hiss behind me as I finally pull that zipper down and then slide the dress all the way off her, leaving her laid out for us like that buffet I'd been thinking of a minute ago.

"Stay just like that, Eden," Matty growls from behind me.

The mattress dips, and then he's right there next to me. And *fuck*, he managed the undressing thing pretty well with just one arm, didn't he? He's down to wearing just his cast and a tight pair of black boxer briefs, and he's all hard planes and acres of olive skin and mouthwatering muscles that bunch and flex as I try not to look.

Matty runs a hand up the back of Eden's leg, all the way up to her curvy little ass. He molds the shape of it with his palm, groaning, and I almost do embarrass myself then. The two of them together are just as hot as I'd imagined.

"Matt," Eden purrs, pushing back into his touch, and fuck if I don't almost come right then and there.

Those little black panties of hers are a thong, and I know *I* think that's hot, but what else I know? Matty gets off on ass—always has, always will—and right now, his cock is straining like it's trying to bust right out of his boxers as he starts teasing his hands over hers. Slipping a finger under that sexy black strip of silk to trace her crease. Pushing her legs open a little wider and settling himself between them. Dragging his hand over her ass, right down the center, dipping it between her legs and sliding it underneath her to play... making her moan... cursing his lack of two hands under his breath real quiet-like, so I don't even think he realizes he's doing it.

I grab my cock and squeeze it hard for a little relief, realizing I'm the only one still dressed.

"Those aren't coming off," I tell Matty when it looks like that's what he's about to do. "Fuck her just like this."

Eden moans, and yeah, she likes that idea too, doesn't she? But Matty's eyes jerk up to mine like he's just remembering I'm there. He gives me a hot smile, his eyes flicking down to my dick for a second before he takes his hand off Eden's panties to stroke himself through his briefs, holding my gaze while he does it.

Oh, shit. I need to get naked. *Now.* No way am I coming in my pants like a horny teenager.

"This what you want to see, bro?" Matty asks me in that same low, hypnotic voice he'd been using with Eden. He runs his hand up the length of his shaft, pushing it against his body until the head pokes out over the top of his waistband. He lets his thumb swirl over the slick tip, then strokes down again... back up... down...

"You want to see me push this into her—" his voice is getting slower... heavier with lust as he finally breaks eye contact with me and looks back down at Eden's ass, "—right under that sexy little thong? You want to watch me fuck our girl's sweet pussy until she screams?"

"Oh my God," Eden whispers, panting as her hips roll against the bed. "Please, Matt... *please.*"

I hold her down, letting my hand trace her spine from the top of that thong all the way up to the lacy bra she's still wearing. I pop it open, not daring to look at Matt again, but not needing to right now, either.

Fuck, Eden's sexy.

"I like it when Eden screams," I say, pushing the bra off her shoulders and pulling her long hair out of the way so I can kiss the back of her neck. "Do you want to do that for us, princess?"

"Oh, Lord," she says, burying her face in a pillow with a shaky laugh. "I want a whole bunch of things right now that I feel like I shouldn't."

"Sounds good to me," Matty says with a wicked smile.

He grabs onto her hip and rocks her back toward him, pulling her up to her knees, and I take advantage of the moment to slip her bra the rest of the way off and then reach under her to fill my hands with those lush breasts I adore.

Eden whimpers, looking up at me, and I roll her nipples between my fingers until I get her panting.

"There's no *shouldn't* if you want it, Eden," I tell her, needing her to be just as into this as Matty and I are if it's going to be good. "Giving you what you want is hot as hell... and you know you like to scream."

She bites that gorgeous lip of hers, sort of laughing through it, but then it turns into a down and dirty do-me moan, and I look back to see that Matty's got his boxers shoved down around his thighs now.

His cock is out and in hand, and he's rubbing it between her legs, her panties pulled to one side, just like I wanted. He's not inside her yet, just rocking his hips forward and back, letting that thick, uncut cock of his slide over the top of her pussy, getting his shaft nice and wet as he lets her grind down against it. And fuck, is she ever. She's rolling that pretty ass of hers back against him, and when she slips one hand underneath herself, reaching back and under, I know for sure she's giving him some added friction— letting him push his cock through the tight space between her palm and her pussy—by the hot-as-fuck sound of his groan.

"Jesus, Eden," he says, eyes dropping closed as his muscles tense and release, moving with the maddeningly slow rhythm as his breath starts to come a little harder. "Gonna feel so damn good... to be... inside you."

"Oh, fuck." I need to get my own zipper down before my dick explodes. "That's fucking *hot*, Matty."

I shove my pants down to my hips and thrust up through my fist, hard and fast, groaning. Fuck getting all the way naked right now, I need immediate relief.

"Matt," Eden says, moaning. "Oh, God, oh please."

She's rocking back against him, and I can tell she's starting to feel a little urgency, a little desperation, but Matty... he's torturing her.

"You're gonna be so tight when I get inside... so hot... but feels good now, too, doesn't it, beautiful? Just like this? Feels... *nice*," Matt says, drawing out the last word into a slow hiss. He's staring down at his own cock as he rubs it against her, over and over, and his voice is just slurred enough to remind me that he *is* feeling pretty nice right about now.

From the sexy-as-fuck sounds Eden's making, a little intoxication doesn't seem to be hurting his coordination any.

"That feel nice to you, beautiful?" he asks her, taking his hand off his cock to stroke her ass.

He slides his thumb under that sexy black strip of thong and runs it over the crevice between her cheeks, and when she whimpers, his face blooms with a hot smile.

"That a yes, baby?" he teases her, centering in on her pucker. He doesn't wait for an answer, though, just starts pressing his thumb rhythmically against that little back hole while continuing to slide his cock over her pussy.

A little faster now.

Thrusting a little harder.

Practically forcing me to match that rhythm as I grind the heel of my hand against my cock and feel my own hole clench with excitement.

"Fuck fuck fuck," I'm chanting, not even really aware. Breathing hard and fast and fucking *mesmerized*.

Eden's hand is still holding Matty's cock against her as she rocks back against him, and when she starts getting frantic… starts begging him to fuck her… starts promising all sorts of dirty things I didn't know our girl had it in her to say… swear to God, I'm pretty sure *I'm* going to come if he doesn't hurry up and do it.

"You got condoms in here, Matty?" I grit out, squeezing my dick hard to keep it in check. "I think… think our girl wants a little something more, you know?"

He looks up at me with a hot smile, then jerks his head toward the nightstand.

I do him a solid and get one out for him, then ask a question I probably shouldn't as I hand it over.

"You gonna be able to suit up one-handed, bro?"

"Why, you offering to help me out, Johnny?" he asks, pinning me with a look that I'm definitely seeing through my own haze of lust, because fuck if it doesn't make my cock start to leak with excitement as I misread it. Or fuck, maybe I don't? Because then he winks at me and adds, "You know I'm no good as a leftie."

Truth is, he's gotten a hell of a lot better with that left hand over the last month or so, but I'm just lost enough in the moment not to look a gift horse in the mouth. I mean, I guess it would make more sense to have Eden be the one to help him out, you know? But when I look at her, she just gives me a hot look that tells me she's not offering on purpose.

"Hurry up, Johnny," she says, practically panting. "Didn't you say… there's no *shouldn't* if you want it?"

I groan, and she licks her lips, eyes dropping to my cock.

"And I want *both* of you, so come back up here when you're done."

I grin. That, I can definitely do.

Eden laughs, cheeks pinking up again like she's just realized how forward she's been. Which I fucking adore, by the way, but which I'm getting the impression isn't her usual style. Then she gasps when Matty gives her a sharp smack on the ass.

"Naughty, naughty," he says, stroking the pink that blooms on her pale skin where his hand landed. "Quit distracting my help, beautiful. You know what happens to naughty girls, yeah?"

"Oh my God." Her words come out with a breathless little laugh—one part self-conscious, one part turned-the-fuck on—that gets muffled when she buries her face in a pillow and adds, "Please tell me you fuck them."

Matty is still stroking her gorgeous ass, fingers slipping under that little black thong to tease her, but now he's looking at me with an evil grin that I also fucking adore.

"We can start with that," he answers Eden, arching a brow as he holds my gaze. "*If...* my boy ever follows through with that help he promised me."

Oh Jesus, Mary, and Joseph. Does he actually *want* my hands on his cock?

I don't know what Matty's thinking right now and I'm not going to worry about second-guessing it until later, I just move. I use my teeth to open the foil wrapper, reaching for him with my other hand, and then—*holy shit*, I've got his cock in my hand.

The minute I touch it, swear to God, mine swells to double its size and I almost shoot then and there.

Matty hisses through his teeth, staring down at my hand wrapped around him, and his thick length jerks against my palm so I have to bite back a moan that would give me away for sure.

"You boys sound like you're having fun back there," Eden says, twisting around like a cat to stare at us. She licks her lips. "Oh, Lord. That's hot."

"Just... just doing a good deed here," I manage, praying that Matt won't suddenly freak out on me. I shit you not, though, his cock almost feels better in my hand than my own... and damn if I haven't been thinking about touching him like this since we both hit puberty.

The fact that he's not really asking me to help him out the way I'd *like* to doesn't take away one bit from the part of me that's fifty shades of turned-the-fuck on, just to finally have him in my hand,

and when he makes another sound low in his throat, I give him one good stroke without thinking.

Whether I'm trying to distract him from any impending freak-out or drive him to one, I don't know, I just know I can't *not*. But then I realize what the fuck I'm doing and get it together quick, rolling the condom down his shaft with my other hand and... okay, yeah, adding in one more stroke just to make sure it's on there good.

And then one *more*, because after that one, he thrusts up into my hand with a hot groan that makes it impossible not to keep going.

"Oh my God," Eden pants, saving me again before I totally forget myself. "Boys, seriously, keep that up and it will totally do it for me."

She's still up on all fours, still twisted around to watch us, but now she's got one hand between her legs, thighs clenched tight around it as she rocks on her own fingers. Whatever self-consciousness she had before has been completely replaced by something more urgent, and can't say I blame her one bit.

"*Fuck,*" Matty whispers, watching her as she starts to moan, working her fingers faster.

No matter what she says, Eden needs to be fucked, and she needs to be fucked *now*. I make myself let go of Matt's cock, and he immediately spanks her ass.

"*Ohhhhhh,*" she gasps, lurching forward with a hot moan.

He pulls her hand away from herself and pushes her shoulders down to the bed. "We're gonna take care of this for you, beautiful," he says, not leaving any room for argument.

"Please please please," she's whispering, thighs trembling as he starts tracing the back of her thong all the way down to her wet center.

He takes himself in hand, then looks at me.

"Push those aside for me, Johnny."

I'm getting a little desperate to do something about my own

throbbing cock, but not gonna lie—denying myself has never felt so good. If I come just from watching the two of them? Touching the two of them?

No complaints.

None.

"You ready for this, princess?" I ask Eden, my hand brushing Matty's tip as I pull the slip of black silk to one side for him.

"Yes," she says breathlessly. And then, as Matt lines himself up with her entrance and starts easing into her, inch by inch— "Yes yes yes *yes*, oh my *God*, yes."

That thick, beautiful cock of his is forcing the hottest fucking sounds I've ever heard from her mouth, and nope. No more denying myself. I'm on the verge of exploding, my dick throbbing like it's going to go off all on its own if I don't do something about it.

"Jesus *fuck*," I whisper, doing something about it. I lick my lips, stroking myself with a tight grip as I watch him start to fuck her, and even though Eden's telling us without words how much she likes it, I can't stop myself from asking, "That good for you, princess?"

"Y-y-yes," she stutters as Matt bottoms out. And then, when he pulls back and drives himself home again, she moans, making my cock pulse so hard in my hand that for a second, I think I'm done.

Not yet, though.

Not... fucking... *yet*.

"You like... feeling Matty... fill you like this?" I ask her, panting now. Speeding up my own strokes as I unconsciously match the rhythm he's fucking her with. "You like... that big cock inside you, princess?"

"*Fuck*, Johnny," Matty grunts, half-laughing. "You trying to make me go off early?"

"Just making sure the lady's enjoying herself," I say, even though yeah, maybe talking about his cock is more about me stoking my own fire.

Kinda hot to know it works on him, too.

And Eden? Holy hell. She's giving us that same porn-worthy soundtrack I remember from when I fucked her before. The way she lets herself go during sex is such a fucking turn-on. Especially when she pushes herself back up to all fours and pants out my name.

"Johnny," she says, twisting to look back at me. "Come... come... come..."

"Not yet, beautiful," Matty says, spanking her hard on one cheek, then earning another sweet moan when he makes up for it by driving deep into her again. He leans over her, whispering in her ear, "My boy deserves... a little help with coming... yeah?"

She gasps, half-laughing. "I didn't mean... I don't want him to... I want him to come up *here*. So I can... can..."

"Good girl," Matt says, not making her say it. He slows his pace for a minute as he strokes her curves, winking at me. "Take that thing up to Eden," he says, his eyes sliding down my body and landing on my cock.

It tries to leap right out of my hand.

I stare at him staring at me, and don't even realize I'm frozen until he smirks.

"Didn't you hear her say she wants it, Johnny?"

My cock jerks again, and—oh, Jesus. I'm kneeling in front of Eden's face before I even remember moving, my brain shutting down as my dick takes over completely. And Eden... *dammmmm- mmmmmmmmmmn*. The girl doesn't hold back. Has me in her mouth and halfway down her throat before I even know what hits me.

Hot.

Wet.

Fast and sloppy and so good my eyes roll back in my head. I brace one arm on the headboard behind me and guide her head down with my other, up and down, up and down, torn between watching her enraptured face as she swallows me and the sight of Matty, driving into her from behind.

"Fuck," I whisper, heat racing down my spine. Shooting up my thighs. Pooling in my balls until they feel like they're about to burst.

And then they do.

"Fuck fuck *fuck*," I grit out, hips stuttering against Eden's face as my release rips through me. I come, so hard and fast I don't even have a chance to warn her. I'm gasping with it, fucking *wrecked*, and she won't let me go. Swallows as much as she can. Only comes off me when she finally starts to come, too. She falls forward into my arms and she starts to shake with it, sobbing out her release as Matty keeps pounding her from behind.

"Johnny... Matt... Johnny... *Matt.*"

And when Matt finally comes with a hoarse shout, collapsing on top of her and then rolling off to the side, all three of us end up in a sweaty tangle of limbs and perfect fucking satisfaction that even I don't have any excess energy to move away from.

As if I'd want to.

As if I'd *ever* want to.

Because this right here? It's as close to perfect as I'm ever going to get, you know?

At least until Matty wakes us both up in the middle of the night, and we go for perfect all over again.

14

EDEN

*L*ately, Matt with his shirt off is enough to have me thinking dirty thoughts, but when the view is topped by a big old pout? My lips twitch. I guess I shouldn't think it's cute, but I've been thinking all sorts of things about him lately that maybe I shouldn't.

About him and Johnny both.

"Pretty sure Doc Holloway is going to cut me out of this thing today," Matt says, twisting and turning his cast in front of his face, like he thinks he's suddenly developed x-ray vision.

I cover my mouth, stifling a giggle.

"What?" he asks, pinning me with a look. "You don't think so?"

"It hasn't even been five weeks yet, Matt," I say in the soothing voice I sometimes use with patients.

The pout is instantly back, and this time I do laugh. He isn't the world's *worst* patient, as Johnny likes to claim, but if I'm honest, he is a bit of a baby about the whole thing.

Not, of course, that I'd tell him that.

The door to the examination room opens, and Matt's pout disappears in favor of a winning smile that I'm sure he's hoping will get him his way. I shake my head, still smiling. Does he really think charming the doctor is going to magically heal his bones faster?

"Afternoon, you two," the cheerful, white-haired man who enters says, grinning at the two of us.

It's not the first follow-up appointment I've brought Matt to over the last month, and I've yet to see Dr. Holloway with any expression on his face other than a beaming smile.

"Happy one-month cast-iversary, son," he says to Matt. And then, with a wink for me, he adds, "I see you wasted no time stripping down for your girlfriend."

"Just trying to make it easier for you to cut me out of this thing, Doc," Matt replies, not looking thrown at all by the girlfriend comment.

I bite my lip, trying to deny the little thrill I get at the label. Not that I'd mind being Matt's girlfriend, but given what we've done with Johnny? And given that I'd be just as thrilled to be mistaken for *Johnny's* girlfriend? There's a voice in my head that tells me I should be ashamed of myself, but since my twenty-fifth birthday is less than two months away, I've decided to ignore that voice and give myself a pass; permission to enjoy it while it lasts.

And oh Lord, ever since we had Santiago and Nick over for dinner? Let's just say that I've definitely... enjoyed myself.

Repeatedly.

I feel my skin flush with heat at the thought, and of course Matt looks up and catches my eye over the doctor's shoulder right at that moment. He and Dr. Holloway are bantering about his treatment, but that doesn't stop Matt from giving me a look hot enough to make my toes curl.

"Eden here could use an extra hand with a few things," he says to the doctor, holding up his cast. Somehow, he manages to make his voice sound perfectly innocent despite the wicked glint in his eyes. "You're not going to make me disappoint her, now are you, Doc? I like to keep her... happy."

Dr. Holloway chuckles—there's no way he missed the innuendo there—and I try to simultaneously glare daggers at Matt and squeeze my thighs together to contain the rush of heat.

Brat.

Dr. Holloway pats Matt's shoulder. "You'll just have to get creative for a few more weeks, son," he says, turning to wink at me. "Can't rush it if you want to get back in the field in tip-top shape."

I want to sink into the floor with embarrassment, but Matt just laughs.

"Come on now," he says, giving the doctor a winning smile. "Don't I get time off for good behavior?"

"What do you say, sweetheart?" Dr. Holloway asks me, eyes twinkling. "Would you say he's earned that?"

"Not today," I say, smiling at Matt sweetly.

He grumbles adorably, and the doctor laughs.

"Looks like you picked a good one here, Matt. Best hold onto her."

"Could do that better if I had two of these," Matt quips, holding up his good hand.

"Your bones aren't completely set the way they need to be in the healing process," I blurt out, suddenly needing to refocus this appointment on Matt's injury instead of on *us*. I know the doctor is just trying to be nice, but any talk of something longer term, of us lasting... I just can't.

I'm starting to want it too bad.

Dr. Holloway is nodding. "She's right. You could risk deformity that would put you out to pasture for good if you jostle that thing around before it sets properly," he tells Matt. Then, to me, "You ever think of going into a medical field? I can tell you know what you're doing with this one."

"It's because she's a CNA," Matt says before I can answer.

"A CNA?" Holloway replies. "Interesting. I don't normally see many CNAs with the depth of medical knowledge you've displayed during this guy's appointments, young lady. Nursing school might be a good fit, or if you don't mind putting in the time, go for your MD." He winks again. "I know it might seem like a lot of years, but you're young. You still have your whole life ahead of you."

I nibble on my lip, trying to ignore the way the doctor's compliments and friendly suggestion twists my stomach up inside. Before I have to admit how much I'd love to go to nursing school, or why I can't, Matt—bless him—shifts the conversation off me.

He reads me so well, both in and out of the bedroom, and for a second I tear up, thankful that the doctor's back is to me. I've accepted my fate for so long, and it seems absurdly unfair somehow to suddenly want so much right at the end.

Matt throws me a concerned look over Holloway's shoulder, and I get myself together, pulling up a smile for him. I'm being silly. Besides, if I really did still have my whole life ahead of me, I'd be faced with an even worse choice, wouldn't I?

Johnny *or* Matt?

The thought of giving either one of them up makes me want to have a tantrum, and even though I've never thought of myself as either selfish or greedy, I guess coming face to face with my own mortality has brought it out in me.

Matt's appointment wraps up and it isn't until we're in the car again that I realize he hasn't let it go.

He takes my hand as I pull out of the hospital's parking lot, lacing our fingers together. "You ever think of becoming a doctor, like Doc Holloway was saying?"

"No," I answer, because it's true.

"Nurse?"

I huff out a breath, not sure if I love or hate that he does this. He's the same way in the bedroom. Somehow, he can always tell what I really want, and I already know him well enough to realize he won't let up until I admit it.

"I'd like that," I admit, hoping that will satisfy him.

"You'd be good at it," he says, so sincerely that it warms places in me I've always protected from getting too attached to other people. "The way you keep me in line? I'm a fan of your bedside manner."

I laugh, shaking my head as I glance over at him for a second. It's not safe to drive without watching the road, of course, but I can't resist... and sure enough, he's giving me those innocent puppy eyes that are so misleading.

"Stop, you," I say, grinning at him.

He laughs, but doesn't let it go. "Seriously, you should apply to nursing school, yeah? There's some good ones around here, and you really do know your stuff. And that bedside manner?" This time he doesn't make it sound dirty. "You really are good with people, Eden. You ever thought about doing it?"

My throat closes up. "I can't," I manage anyway.

"Sure you can," he says confidently, squeezing my hand. "Even if you gotta do some pre-reqs first, you can... hey now, what is it?"

Oh, Lord. I'm tearing up, and he reaches over to wipe the moisture off my cheeks so gently that I can't stand it. We're at a stoplight, and he grips my chin, turning me to face him.

"Eden, what's going on?" he asks, his liquid chocolate eyes filled with all sorts of things that suddenly make it impossible for me to stop crying. "Pull over, yeah?"

"I... I've got to drop you off and get to work."

"What you need to do is pull the car over and tell me what's going on," he says in a voice I don't even pretend to want to argue with.

He pulls me across the center console and right into his lap once we're stopped, and I'm such a mess that I don't even worry about whether or not he should be doing that with his cast.

He wipes my cheeks again. "What did I say to trigger these? Was it about going to nursing school?"

I nod, because even though I'd rather avoid the subject completely, there's no part of me that wants to lie to him.

"What happened? You applied and got rejected? Because if they need someone to go knock some sense into their heads—"

"No," I say, laughing despite myself. I kiss his cheek, trying to ignore how much he warms my heart. "I... I've never applied."

"Why not?" he asks, brow crinkling in confusion. Then his eyes suddenly widen. "What you said the other night... Eden, you don't *really* believe you're not gonna make it to twenty-five, do you?"

"*No* one in my family has, Matt," I say, my throat so tight this time that it actually hurts to force the words out. "Not for generations."

I half expect him to tell me I'm crazy, because I *know* how it sounds... but I also know it's true. Instead, though, his arms tighten around me and he just looks at me for a long minute, then shakes his head.

"That's not going to happen," he finally says flatly. "Your birthday's in what, a couple of months?"

"Seven weeks."

Fifty-two days.

Less than two months.

He wipes my cheeks again. "Nothing's going to happen to you, Eden," he says quietly. "You think me and Johnny would let it? By the time we get to your birthday, you're—"

"Please don't mention my birthday," I interrupt, panic squeezing my chest so hard I can barely breathe. "I *know* it sounds irrational, Matt. I do. But I just... I can't... you don't understand, I—"

"Okay, okay," he says, giving me a small smile as he starts rubbing my back in slow circles. "Shhhh."

"I just... I don't want to talk about it, is that all right? I don't even want to *think* about it. I just want to enjoy whatever time I have left."

For a moment, he looks like he's going to argue, but then he just smiles, shaking his head, and pulls me in for a kiss. It's not even remotely hot. Instead, the way he's kissing me makes me feel precious.

Cared for.

Safe.

"Okay, beautiful," he finally says. "We'll do it your way for now, but I reserve the right to bring it up again after the big two-five, yeah?" Before I can panic about that, he asks, "How's that bucket list coming? Me and Johnny promised to help you finish it, and if I'm remembering it right, you only had three things left to do before your birthday."

I nod, and he starts ticking them off his fingers.

"We got learning to cook crossed off and *tu español está mejorando.*"

"*Gracias,*" I say, even though I'm not entirely sure whether he just told me that my Spanish is getting better or getting older.

His eyes light up. "So that just leaves—"

"No," I say, pressing a finger against his lips with a laugh. "Matt, honestly, I've had number fourteen on my list for nine years, but even if I do finally manage to get the guts up to do it, *you* are not helping with that one."

"Always wanted to go skydiving," he says, grinning.

"Your arm is broken," I point out, laughing. "*Broken,* Matt. You can't skydive with a broken arm."

"Doc says just another week or so."

"I'm pretty sure he said he would *check* it then, but not to count on getting the cast off for another *three* weeks," I remind him, laughing.

The man is stubborn as hell, isn't he?

"That's still before your birthday, beautiful," he says, pushing a strand of hair out of my face with a soft look that makes me feel... oh, Lord.

No. I'm not going to let myself go there.

"Dr. Holloway isn't going to approve you skydiving right after you get your cast off, either," I say instead, my heart as light as air.

Although how this man has me smiling not two minutes after I felt like I couldn't even breathe, I just don't know.

For a second, I think he's going to keep arguing, but then he gets a truly evil grin on his face and says, "Guess that means Johnny's up, yeah?"

"You're volunteering him to go skydiving with me?" I ask, pretty sure I remember Santiago saying something about Johnny having a fear of heights.

"Absolutely," he says. "It'll be good for him."

I shake my head. "He went a little green when your dad was telling some of those stories."

"We all gotta face our fears sometime, yeah?" Matt says, cupping my face. "He'll do it for you, beautiful. Either one of us would."

The look he's giving me is too much. Too close to what I know I don't have time to have and wouldn't want to have to choose, even if I did. Still, I can't help asking—

"How do you, um, feel about that? About Johnny and me, I mean?"

I hold my breath. The first time the three of us got together, I *know* Matt was a little drunk, but so far, even sober, I haven't seen any sign of jealousy or the kind of problems between him and Johnny I was scared of causing. I wasn't expecting them from Johnny, of course, not after... after what I know, but with Matt— well, he just hasn't said *anything*.

"Johnny likes you," he says now, eyes sparkling. "Can't say I blame him. Pretty sure you know I feel the same."

I bite my lip. Oh, Lord. I like the two of them, too—understatement of the century—and Matt makes it sound so simple. *Easy.* But life doesn't work like that, does it?

"Yes," I say cautiously. "But... that's not... not a problem?"

"I don't think it has to be," Matt says after a minute. "Sure, I know what you're saying, but... I don't know, Eden. It's *Johnny*. Can't really imagine anything important I'd want to do in life without him being a part of it, too. You think it's going to be a problem for you?"

"No," I say, not even having to think. My two firefighters? They're the opposite of a problem. In fact, I'm pretty sure they're the best thing that's ever happened to me.

"Good," Matt says, smiling slow and sexy, and then he kisses me again.

And you know what? Maybe sometimes life *can* be this easy.

At least for this last piece of it.

15

MATT

I'm still thinking about my conversation with Eden after she drops me off at the house. And do I hate having to rely on her to drive me everywhere when *I* should be the one taking care of *her*? Bet your ass I do. And yeah, yeah, that's sexist as hell... but it's still the truth. Sue me, but I can't do anything about how I feel, right? Just like I can't do anything about how *she* feels with this crazy notion that she's gonna die before her birthday.

Which... just no. Like I told her, that's not going to happen.

Still, I get it. Irrational fears can still be very real roadblocks—look at Johnny's fear of heights, yeah?—so I figure I'm not gonna be able to argue her out of it. The only way to prove it to her that she'll be okay is to get to the other side.

And to do that? Might as well focus on that list of hers.

I pause at the door for a second before opening it. Johnny knows me too well—if he sees the evil grin I can feel on my face right now he'll probably run the other way before I can have any fun. Because yep, that's my plan for afternoon entertainment: talking Johnny into skydiving with Eden.

Pretty sure he has a shift today, but his truck is parked out front, so I know he's still home, and once I finally manage to school my face, I head inside to get busy making my case for the whole "facing your fears" thing.

And am I planning on using sexual favors as a carrot when it comes to that? Hell yeah I am.

Eden's sexual favors, of course.

Problem is, when I walk in the front door something goes sideways in my brain, and suddenly I'm feeling all confused about just whose sexual favors need to be on the line here.

It's Johnny's fault.

Oh, he's home all right. Guess he just got out of the shower, because he's walking down the hall straight for me, water still clinging to him. He's got a towel slung low around his hips and nothing else, and his physique is showing the kind of extra definition in the arms, shoulders, and chest that tells me he just finished an upper-body workout.

Which should matter exactly zero to me, amirite?

Except *fuuuuuuuuuuuuuuucccckkkkkkkk*. All of a sudden it feels like it matters a hell of a lot more than that.

I sort of trip over nothing, right there in the doorway, and my brain freezes completely while my body goes into a state that it really shouldn't be in around my best friend. At least, not without Eden there between us.

Thank Christ Johnny doesn't seem to notice.

"Hey, Matty," he greets me, rubbing his short hair with another towel. "You got Gatorade?"

"No," I croak out. Him mentioning Gatorade makes me kinda desperate for some myself all of a sudden, what with how dry my mouth just got.

Don't know what he sees on my face, but I finally kick it into gear before things get weird and turn away to hang my house key on the hook by the door.

I toe my shoes off.

I open the coat closet and line them up on the shoe rack inside.

I'm thankful as fuck for the closet door open between us, blocking my view, because truth? I need a minute to try and get a fucking grip. To settle my randy cock down. To make sure my heart doesn't beat its way out of my chest, the way it's pounding in there.

Seriously, what the fuck just happened to me?

"What the fuck just happened to you?" Johnny asks, plucking those words right out of my skull as he suddenly appears next to me with a shit-eating grin. He latches on to the top of the doorjamb with both hands, leaning forward between his arms so every one of his oversized muscles stands out in sharp relief.

Oshit.

"What—" I clear my throat, trying again. "What do you mean?"

Playing dumb is really the only strategy that comes to mind here.

Johnny widens his eyes to comical proportions. "You?" He gasps dramatically. "Forgetting a basic necessity in life like replenishing the Gatorade? Who are you and where's my Matty?"

Relief floods through me. That's right, he'd asked me to bring some home, hadn't he? I'd gotten distracted by that conversation with Eden and totally forgot.

"For real, bro," he's going on, shaking his head in an exaggerated show of disappointment. "Do you know how hard I just pushed it?" He flexes, grinning, and adds, "Got a new PR on the bench press."

I stare hard as he goes through some jokey bodybuilding poses, then catch myself and mumble an automatic, "Congrats."

Johnny throws his hands up in the air, shaking his head in mock-exasperation. "Congrats, he says. And how's that going to help with no Gatorade? You think I would've pushed so hard if I'd known you were going to flake? You never let me down, Matty, and now this? I've got a shift later, you know. What am I supposed to do if my electrolytes get outta whack?"

"Salt, OJ, honey, and water," I rattle off, not doing so great on getting that grip.

I know he's just hamming it up, giving me shit that I usually toss right back at him, just like he's been doing all my life, but right now? It's like I've never *seen* Johnny before... which has gotta be hands down the dumbest thing I've ever thought, because hello, pretty sure I've seen him just about every day of my life since... what? First grade? Kindergarten? Whenever it was we met.

Johnny makes a face at the electrolyte drink recipe. "Lame," he says, followed immediately by a big-ass grin and... "Make some for me?"

Like I'm his fucking mother or something.

I'm pretty sure the correct response is "fuck off," but since I'm obviously having a surreal moment, that slips my mind and I just nod and brush past him, heading toward the kitchen while I continue my efforts to stop noticing things about him that I'm pretty sure I'm not supposed to when I don't have some kind of, you know, inebriation justification to fall back on.

Is that it?

Did Doc Holloway slip me something?

Johnny follows me to the kitchen, and after I pull the ingredients I need out of the fridge and close it, he's right there, giving me an odd look.

"Hey, for real, buddy, what's up?" he asks, losing the joking tone from earlier. "You okay? Doc give you some bad news? You look a little off."

"No, I'm good," I lie. And since when have I ever lied to Johnny?

But I for damn sure can't let on that I'm suddenly *noticing* him.

I get a pitcher out and measure some orange juice into it, then the salt, then add the honey. Then my brain kicks into gear and I remember my original plan about convincing him to skydive with

Eden. Perfect. He'll get distracted by that and forget whatever *this* was.

"Eden and I were talking about her bucket list in the car," I tell him, grabbing a wooden spoon and mixing the stuff in the pitcher.

"Yeah? She got something new on it?" Johnny asks, lighting up and...

Okay, I'm getting ridiculous now. Sure, he's a good-looking guy, but... *Jesus.* I need to just look away.

I do, but then he leans against the counter right next to me with a look in his eyes that confuses my cock all over again.

"Please tell me it's something kinky," he says, voice dropping low exactly like I've heard it in the bedroom when it's all three of us.

"Uh," I say, freezing up the minute I meet his eyes. And then, like they've got a mind of their own, *my* eyes go on a leisurely journey all the way south. Checking him out exactly like I would a hot chick.

I swallow hard. My best friend is standing next to me talking about kinky sex, and here I am staring at the towel that's about to slip off his hips and hoping it does.

What.

The.

Fuck.

Is.

Wrong.

With.

Me?

"Come on now, don't tease me, bro," he says, taking the pitcher out of my hands and walking it over to the sink to put some water in. "You gonna tell me already?"

My dick takes over my mouth and shoots back, "You gonna make it worth my while if I do?"

There's a way I could have said that that would have been fine.

183

Just giving my buddy a hard time. All good. No harm, no foul. Perfectly innocent.

I did not say it that way.

My dick was talking, and it came through loud and clear in my voice.

Oh fucking Christ, I just *flirted* with Johnny, and for a split second, I hold out the hope that maybe he didn't pick up on it. But no dice. I see the way he sort of tenses up at the sink for a second, then turns off the water too slow before finally turning back to look at me.

And his face? Oh, he caught it all right.

Doesn't call me on it, though.

"You add any lemon to this?" he asks, holding the pitcher up in front of him like a shield as he gives me a wary look. "Might be too sweet without it, you know?"

"No," I say, and then, because something clearly *is* wrong with me, I add, "Ask me nicely though, and I might."

He stares at me like I've grown a second head, and while I *should* be freaking the fuck out about how I'm flushing our friend-ship down the drain right now, what I'm actually doing is just standing there staring right back, noticing how ripped he's gotten lately.

And noticing other things, too.

The hint of golden stubble along his jaw. The way that towel dips down like a tease, right above the swell of his cock. How strong his fingers look, wrapped around the pitcher exactly the way I remember him wrapping them around my—

Jesus. I pivot away from him, jerking open the refrigerator door and pulling out a lemon while I try to pretend I'm not getting hard over the memory of a drunken bit of silliness that meant nothing. Is gay hereditary? Or like, transmittable? Because I'm pretty sure I never looked at Johnny like this before Dad and his boyfriend came to dinner the other night.

I mean, sure, a few times maybe, but only when I was shit-faced and it didn't mean anything.

I can't hide in the refrigerator forever though, and come on now, this is *Johnny*. I've never hidden from him in my life. I gotta trust that I'll be able to dig myself out of this particular hole and save our friendship, right?

He'll give me a pass.

He's got to, yeah?

But when I turn back around, ready to offer to hand-squeeze a fucking lemon just to make it up to him, Johnny's right there, crowded up behind me.

I open my mouth, but nope. I've got nothing. I close it again.

He smiles, just the tiniest bit, and I see something shift in his eyes. It's so fucking subtle that I would have missed it if I didn't know him so damn well... but I *do* know him, and suddenly my heart's racing all over again.

"So, just how nice do I have to ask if I want this?" he asks, eyes locked on mine as he reaches for the lemon. Doesn't take it out of my hand, though. Instead, he just folds his right over it so our fingers sort of tangle together, trapping that lemon like it's in a cage.

He's staring at me hard, and I...

I...

Well, fuck. I chicken out completely. My dick may be on board, but truth is, I'm really not sure if I want this. Hell, I'm not even sure if *he* wants this. I mean, maybe Doc Holloway actually did give me something and I just don't remember, and maybe it was something that's got me all twisted up and imagining things.

Misinterpreting things.

Making me think that I know what Johnny's doing right now with all the staring and hand-holding and lemon-innuendo and all, when in fact it could be—probably *is*—nothing at all like what I'm thinking. And messing us up? Losing him? It's not an option I'm even willing to consider.

That cinches it.

Clears my head fast and finally allows me to get my cock under control.

Johnny raises an eyebrow, and I tap out, because the only thing I *am* sure of—one hundred percent—is how much I'll regret it if I ever fuck up our friendship. I close my hand around the lemon and shove my shoulder into him, grinning as I get him out of my way.

I go grab the citrus juicer out of the cupboard, making quick work of that lemon.

"All you gotta do is be nice to Eden, buddy," I tell him. "Help her out, you know? She hasn't added anything new to that list as far as I know, but she's gotta get it done before turning twenty-five, and that's coming up fast."

Clear head or not, no way do I have it in me to turn and face him yet, and fuck if it doesn't take him too damn long to answer. He finally does, though, and I let out a breath I don't even realize I've been holding.

He sounds normal.

We're fine.

"Before her birthday, huh? Don't tell me she was serious about thinking she wasn't going to make it past that, just because of her mom and the rest?"

I turn and face him, keeping my eyes off that towel and thankful as fuck that we're good again. "Guess she does," I tell him, reaching for the pitcher he's still holding.

I add the lemon juice, give it a stir, then pour him a glass and hand it over.

Huh. I'm actually not so bad with my left anymore, yeah?

"Eden got pretty worked up about the subject," I go on. "So I figure the thing to do is just get her through it, yeah? Distract her by helping her finish off that list."

Johnny takes the glass from me and I don't even notice when our fingers brush together, because for real, didn't I just decide I was done getting confused and all?

He downs half of it in one gulp, then says, "For sure. What's left on the list then?"

I grin.

He freezes with the glass halfway to his mouth, looking at me warily, and... *there* it is. I see exactly the moment he remembers what her last bucket list item is.

"Oh, hell no," he says, shaking his head and laughing. "Your arm is broken, Matty. No way are you skydiving. Pretty sure they wouldn't even let you."

He finishes off the glass and I refill it—because he was right, he really does need to replenish his electrolytes—then put the pitcher away in the fridge.

"When you're right, you're right," I tell him, holding up my cast as Exhibit A and for once not even a little bit annoyed by my temporary disability. I wink. "Guess it's gotta be you, buddy. You know we can't let our girl go alone."

Johnny chokes on his drink. "Nope," he says after a minute. "You know I can't do it, bro. Sorry."

I lean back against the door of the fridge, crossing my arms over my chest and so used to the cast by now that I don't even notice it. Normally, my role is holding Johnny back from doing stupid things, but this? I don't know why I feel so determined to get him to do it, but I do. It's partly Eden, it's partly the joy of seeing him squirm, but it's also something more.

I really think he should do it.

"No," he says again, even though I haven't said a single word to convince him yet. "I *can't*, Matty."

I smile. "Sure you can."

He winces, shaking his head.

"Come on now, what's the worst that can happen, Johnny?"

He laughs, scrubbing a hand over his face. "Uh, death, maybe? What, you trying to get rid of me now?"

I know damn well he's joking, but after coming so close to

maybe fucking things up with us a few minutes ago, that line hits me hard and I end up blurting out something way too intense before I can get my mouth in check.

"*No.* Jesus, Johnny, I'm just trying to hold on to you here."

Johnny's eyes widen a little, and yeah, he heard that undercurrent of desperation in my voice, didn't he? I guess it's really my day to shut him up, and how often does *that* happen? Not that I blame him for being a little dumbfounded, since seems like every time I've opened my mouth since walking through the door something comes out of it that shouldn't.

I force a smile. "Hey now, I just meant—"

"You don't have to hold on to me, Matty," he says, cutting me off before I can dig my way out of this latest one. He's looking at me real steady-like, no hint of joking in his voice anymore. "I'm not going anywhere."

"Yeah, yeah," I say, making myself laugh about it.

Jesus, he must think I'm really losing it.

"No, for real," Johnny says, not laughing along with me. Still staring. Still looking serious as fuck. "Nothing you could do is gonna break us, you know that, right? Not ever. You don't need to worry about that, Matty."

And you know what? I never have before. *Ever.* But it still feels hella good to hear it.

I have to clear my throat twice, and honestly, I'm not even sure what's going to come out of my mouth this time when I finally get the guts to open it again.

Turns out it's this: "Funny you should say that. Eden was just asking me about the three of us, you know?"

Another thing I really wasn't worried about before she brought it up.

One corner of Johnny's lip quirks up, and fuck if it isn't distracting. I am definitely not supposed to be thinking *sexy* in relation to my best friend, yeah?

"It's not a problem for me," he says, and it takes me just that much too long to realize he's answering me about what's going on with the three of us... not reading my mind as I stare at his mouth.

I jerk my eyes off it and back where they belong.

Johnny's still staring at me hard. "*Nothing* we've done with Eden is a problem for me, Matty. Not any of it."

We've done a few things with Eden over the last few days, all hot as fuck, but we haven't ever talked about how he'd helped me with the condom that first time it was the three of us together. But somehow, with him saying that? It's all I can think of right now.

How hot it had been to have his hands on me.

How Eden had egged us on.

How much it had ramped things up to know she was into watching it as Johnny touched me... and oh Christ, how fucking tempted I'd been to let him just finish me off once he started.

I clear my throat. "Nothing, huh?" I'm feeling self-conscious as fuck, but something's shifted here, so I go ahead and add, "Gotta admit, I like the way the three of us are together, too." I clear my throat again. "*All* three of us."

Johnny's eyes heat up fast, and fuck if he doesn't look almost beautiful with it when he smiles, but that's about as much as I've got in me right now, so before he can say anything more direct about the subject I'm pretty sure we're both dancing around here, I hit him with the skydiving thing again out of pure self-preservation.

I just... I need a minute, yeah?

"So, should we book you and Eden in for a jump, bro?"

He laughs, looking away for a second. "You're really pushing me here, buddy."

"Face your fears," I tell him, winking.

Not sure if I'm talking to him or me, though.

Johnny hesitates for a second. "You know this is a big one for me, Matty."

Epic understatement. I do know that, even if I'm not crystal clear on exactly why I'm pushing so hard for it.

"You think you can do it?" I ask. "Eden matters, you know."

"She does," he agrees, looking at me like he's maybe saying something more, too. Something that's got my heart trying to pound its way out of my chest again.

I clear my throat, wondering if the damn thing's going to be raw after this conversation, what with how constricted it keeps getting.

Johnny gives me a small smile, and something inside me relaxes.

"So, you'll do it?" I ask him.

"You think you could, in my shoes?" he asks, raising an eyebrow as he keeps pinning me with this look that says we're having two different conversations at once.

I laugh, looking up at the ceiling just to break that intensity. "What, jump out of a plane?" I joke, figuring he knows me well enough to guess I'd think it would be a rush.

"Is that what I'm asking you, Matty?" He straightens up from where he'd been leaning against the counter and adjusts that towel around his waist as he looks at me, and fuck if that little smile that keeps hovering around his lips doesn't get to me. "Jumping out of a plane really your biggest fear?"

It would be really fucking easy to walk away right now, and knowing us? We'd go right back to normal if I laughed it off.

No harm, no foul.

Instead, I take a breath and answer his real question. "I don't know," I say, as honest as I know how to be right now. "I'm not sure if I could do it, Johnny."

"Might be fun, though," he says, his lip quirking up. Then he throws my own words back at me: "I mean, what's the worst that can happen?"

I laugh, and then thank Christ we're out of time since he has to get to the station, but you know what? He actually agrees to go skydiving with Eden before he goes, and it hits me that maybe *what's the worst that can happen* isn't really the right question. Maybe—if Johnny's willing to do this, to get over something that's held him back his whole life and go for what he really wants—maybe the right question is—

What's the *best* that can happen?

16

JOHNNY

*I*f terror and insanity had a love-child, it would be the icy hot panic that's got me in its grip as the tiny plane takes off over Blackstone River Valley. For real, I think I'm going to hurl.

"You okay?" Eden asks, yelling over the sound of the engine as she leans against me.

Uh, no, I'm most definitely not, but I nod anyway, because I have to, you know? For one thing, we're already in the air, and for another, it's not like I'm going to back out when she's counting on me.

Not to mention what may or may not be riding on me doing this… with Matty, I mean.

I'm still not entirely sure I'm not just imagining how things have changed between us over the last couple of weeks, because nothing's actually *happened*, you know? But somehow it still feels like it has.

Or like it's about to.

Or at least like it *could*.

All of a sudden, my stomach drops out from under me as the plane tries to kill me, dipping and rolling and making me scream

193

like a little girl as I grab on to some metal things jutting out of the wall next to my head. I squeeze my eyes closed and prepare to die... but after a second I'm still alive. The plane seems to even out, and I cut a glance at Eden out of the corner of my eye only to find her trying not to laugh.

"Air pocket, I think," she says, patting my thigh.

"Okay," I say, just to prove I'm still functional. I've heard of those. I mean, I've actually been in planes a few times before, you know? Although as far as I'm concerned, that's already been a few times too many.

Besides, the experience doesn't really compare. For one thing, those other times were in real planes, with normal seats and no engine noise to speak of and a panic button you could push to call the flight attendant at any time. And for another, what got me through those other flights—I mean, besides a shitload of tequila that one time Matty and I did spring break down in Cancun—was the knowledge that I'd be exiting safely through the front door or whatever it's called and getting my feet back on solid ground once the trip was over.

This time, though?

Eden and I were going to jump.

Out of an airplane.

In the sky.

High, *high* up in the sky.

Like, five million miles above the earth or something.

"Oh my God," I mutter as it really hits me. "We're about to die."

Eden laughs, then turns my face to hers and kisses me hard. It's almost hot enough to distract me... but not quite. Because I mean, *death*, you know?

"We're not going to die," she says, which a part of me feels is a bit hypocritical of her, given that ridiculous idea she has about her twenty-fifth birthday and all, but hey, I'm not going to be an ass and point that out.

Plus, not gonna lie, it helps to hear her say it.

"You sure, princess?" I ask, doing my damnedest to cover up the pit of utter terror in my stomach with a shaky laugh.

"I'm sure," she says, twining her fingers through mine and giving my hand a squeeze. "I have a hundred things I want to get done before I... before my birthday, don't I? Not ninety-nine."

She smiles, and I squeeze her hand back, losing a little of my fear by thinking of her instead of myself. She really does believe this shit, but I know Matty's right. All we can do is hold out until after her birthday and prove her wrong.

"So this is number one hundred, huh?" I ask, impressed as all hell, if I'm honest.

She shakes her head, though. "Skydiving is actually number fourteen... I haven't really tried to do them in order, and this one? The truth is it scares me a little bit, too, so I've been putting it off. I mean, what if it's the way I—"

"Hey now," I interrupt, pretty sure I know where she was going with that. "You just said it yourself, we're not going to die today."

I crook my pinky and hold it out to her, and after a second, she laughs.

"Are you asking me to pinky-swear not to die with you?"

"I am," I say somberly, lifting her hand myself and hooking our pinkies together. "You in?"

Her gorgeous blue eyes get soft and sparkly at the same time, and she says, "I'm totally in," shaking on it and giving me a look that kind of makes me fall a little bit in love with her.

As if I'm not halfway there already.

I've never really gotten serious about a girl before, but Eden? She's sexy as hell, but it's more than that. Truth is, she inspires the shit out of me with her bucket list and how she's taken on life wholeheartedly, just jumping in feet-first with all these things she wants to do. I love that she's got all the soft sweetness you'd want in a girl, but that she's down and dirty, too. And the fact that it's all wrapped around something unbreakable inside her? Something that wouldn't bend to Matty's bullshit about his dad? Something that made all three of us better for it?

For real, what's *not* to fall in love with?

"Thank you," she says suddenly, leaning in to kiss me again.

"For what?"

"This. Today. Everything."

I grin, my heart swelling with all these feelings for her until it feels like it's going to burst out of my chest; until it's big enough to blot out the panic I was feeling a few moments ago.

At least, until the pilot turns back to look at us—yeah, that's how small the plane is—and says, "We're coming up on cruising altitude."

Then that panic takes over again with a vengeance, shoving my heart and all that sappiness I was feeling right out of the way as it tries to choke me to death.

"Oh shit," I say, gasping for breath. "Shit shit shit shit shit shit *shit*."

Eden holds up her pinky, waggling it at me as a reminder of what we'd just promised... but I don't know, I mean, sure, pinky-swears are inviolate and all, but suddenly I'm not so certain that even that can hold up against a force as big as, you know, *gravity*.

"All right you two," the jump instructor says, sliding out of the copilot slot and moving into the cabin with us. "Remember everything I told you? Pulling the cord, taking your time, remembering the emergency chute if all else goes wrong?"

Wrong?

Wrong?

Wrong?

Oh *hell* no. Even the jump instructor is admitting that we're about to die.

"We remember," Eden says, smiling at him as she squeezes my hand.

Unfortunately, my hand has become a cold, clammy dead fish,

just lying there without responding, and guess she notices, because she bites her lip and turns to stare hard at me.

"I'm good."

...is what I mean to say. Instead, pretty sure I'm hyperventilating.

"You don't have to do this, Johnny," Eden says. "I can jump on my own."

Not proud of it, but I'm tempted to take her up on it. But then I can't, can I? Because she gets this sweet little smile that's also the tiniest bit sad and drives a nail right through my heart.

"Please don't worry about it," she says, squeezing the dead fish again. "I've done most everything on The List alone. I'm used to it. It's no big deal if I do this one on my own, too."

"Yes, it is," I say, manning up. "I'm jumping, Eden."

Guess maybe I'm already past halfway when it comes to that love thing, you know? Because no way do I ever want to feel like she's on her own when I'm right fucking *here*.

"You don't have to—"

I cover her mouth with my hand, shaking my head. "Eden, you're *not* alone anymore, okay? And you know Matty would be up here, too, if it weren't for that arm of his. We're in this together, all three of us. I don't want to hear any more of this *on your own* nonsense. You've got *us*."

She smiles at me. I can feel her lips curve against my palm and I see it in the way her eyes start to glow, and yeah, I'm still terrified of what we're about to do, but somehow it just stops mattering, you know?

The jump instructor grins at us. "Aw, y'all are gonna be naturals, I ain't even worried a little bit about you two. And remember, I'll be making the jump as well, so if I see any problems, I'll be there to help."

"You promise?" Eden asks him, pulling my hand away from her mouth but keeping a tight hold on it.

"Cross my damn heart," he replies. "You've got another couple of minutes before we start, so if either of you is going to change your mind, just remember, no shame in it. You need to be focused when you step out, got it?"

We both nod, and he moves back over to the cockpit.

I look at Eden. Even in her jump gear, goggles and all, she's beautiful.

"I'm afraid I'll lose everything," I blurt out without thinking, my fear of this moment all tangled up with my fears over driving Matty away if I'm wrong about him.

"I know," Eden says, reaching out and touching my face. "Me, too. But another way to look at it is how blessed we are to *have* something to lose. You know what I was never brave enough to put on my bucket list?"

"What?" I ask, curiosity overriding everything else. I've seen some of the stuff she's done... and there's *more*?

Her cheeks go bright pink, but then she just shakes her head. "Maybe I'll tell you after we make it to the ground."

"Come on now," I say, that blush making me even more curious. "You can't do that to me. What if we don't?"

"Don't what? Make it to the ground?" she says, laughing. "Pretty sure that one way or another, we will."

"One way or another," I repeat, shaking my head. "Now that's just cruel."

"No, that's gravity." She snickers, which is fucking adorable.

I groan.

"Sorry," she says, looking contrite. "I don't mean to joke about it." She pats my hand. "We're going to be fine. You really don't have to—"

"Yeah, I do, Eden," I say, cutting her off. "And if it's a mistake, I mean, at least it'll be the quickest mistake either of us make."

It takes her a minute, then she smacks me, laughing. "Not funny!"

I grin. "A little bit funny."

She sticks her tongue out at me. And damn, that's distracting, because do I ever love what she can do with that tongue.

The jump instructor hops back into the cabin. "Moment of truth," he says, grinning as he looks back and forth between the two of us. "What's your final answer?"

Eden squeezes my hand so tight I figure I've lost the use of it forever, then gives the man a jerky little nod. "I'm in," she says, breathless.

He looks at me, but there's not really a question now, is there? If she's in, I'm in, too.

He must see it on my face, because he just nods and urges us to our feet and runs through a few final reminders with us. And then he opens the door on the side of the plane.

In midair.

Like a fucking crazy person.

And even more crazy? When Eden steps out of that door a minute later, I step out right after her.

Then I scream my head off because I'm falling through the air a million feet over solid ground and hello, physics, that means I'm going to fucking *die*.

But then I keep falling.

And I keep not dying.

And it's loud and cold and wonderful and strangely peaceful, and eventually my throat gets sore so I stop screaming and start looking around, and it's fucking magnificent. I can see out far over the horizon, miles and miles of earth just spread out below me like God's own masterpiece, and we're so high up that the height almost doesn't matter, you know?

It's like time and fear have both been suspended, and I'm just... free.

Eden is below me, looking like she's not moving at all and also like she's spinning with joy, arms and legs spread out like a starfish as she floats like a jumpsuited angel above that amazing landscape, and suddenly it really hits me—

I just jumped out of a damn airplane.

And then I'm laughing uncontrollably in the air as I fall, spreading my limbs out like the instructor taught us and letting the wind slice right through me and cut out all those fears that have held me back from going for things I want. It's not even a decision, it's just a fact: I'm done with that shit. From now on—whether it's only for another couple of minutes if my chute doesn't open, or if I get another hundred years to spend with the people I love—I'm holding onto this feeling right here.

Not not being afraid... but being afraid and still doing it anyway.

17

EDEN

att's good arm is slung around my shoulders and I've got one hand resting on Johnny's hard thigh, and there's truly nowhere I'd rather be than right here, right now, tucked between these two on the bench seat of Johnny's truck as we head back to the city and Johnny gushes on and on and *on* about our jump.

"No, buddy, you so don't understand," he's saying to Matt, the excitement radiating off him in waves. "It was *amazing*. The most intense experience I've ever had, but maybe also the most peaceful one? I don't know, man, it was just wild. Soon as Doc okays it, you've got to go up, too. It was like every last second of that drop was a fucking eternity, like I could see it all stretched out in front of me from start to finish, and I..."

I lean against him as he keeps going, feeling just about happy enough to burst. Skydiving was exhilarating.

Liberating.

Amazing.

Now that I've finally done it, I don't know why on earth I waited so long... except that all of a sudden, I'm suddenly over-come with so much gratitude I feel like I might burst with it.

Thank *God* I waited. If I'd crossed #14 off The List before meeting these two amazing men, it just... it just wouldn't have been the same.

I'm not just happy I've finally done it, I'm happy that I did it with *them*.

Given how scared Johnny was, the fact that he jumped at all was incredible. And the fact that he jumped for *me*? I still don't know what to do with that. It fills something up inside me that's been empty for a long, long time.

And Matt? He insisted on coming with us today even though he had to stay on the ground, and right now, listening as Johnny's exuberance fills the truck with a mile-a-minute recap of our jump, he's glowing, too. He's got this incredible smile on his face as he listens to Johnny, and it's as clear as day to see that he's as happy for the two of us as if he'd done it himself. Who feels that way about other people? I mean, *really* feels that way?

I lean over and kiss his cheek impulsively, and he grins back at me, squeezing my thigh.

Johnny looks over. "Do I get one, princess?" he teases me, one of his big hands dropping down to rest on my other leg.

"Distracted driving is dangerous," I tease him right back, but of course I can't resist giving him what he's asked for.

He turns his head at the last minute so I get his lips, then winks at me and whips his eyes right back to the road, that big hand squeezing my thigh.

He goes right back to telling Matt about skydiving, but me? I'm caught up in a wave of something so sweet it almost makes me tear up. I'm thinking about what he said to me up there. Before I met these two, I *have* always felt alone... and I know darn well that it's my own fault.

I've never been brave enough to put *falling in love* on my bucket list.

The thing is, I know how bad it hurts to have that hole inside you from losing someone, and I've always told myself that I'm not cruel enough to do that to another person. But you know what? Maybe keeping people at a distance all my life hasn't just been because of how much I've moved around or about me trying to protect *them* from the pain of losing me, given how short I know my time here will be. Maybe—like I hinted to Johnny about just before we jumped—maybe it's that I haven't been brave enough to risk having that kind of hole inside me again.

I huff out a breath, earning a comforting squeeze from my boys, and I face the truth I'm dancing around. There's no "maybe" about it. I've been scared to fall in love, and it's kept me alone.

But right now? I've never felt *less* alone.

Right now, I'm practically vibrating with the joy of sharing this moment with Johnny and Matt.

Right now, I'm *fearless*.

A laugh bubbles up inside me, and I want to sing with it. Just take all the adrenaline and exhilaration I feel from having completed this jump, from having found these two boys who make me feel free in so many ways, from having made it through the very last of my bucket list in time—I want to take *all* of it and just... just... *explode*.

But in a good way.

I want to explode in the *best* way.

The trees on either side of the quiet highway are thick and full of leaves, leaning over the road and covering it with a thin canopy that almost makes it feel like the three of us are in our own little world. The sunlight filters down, sprinkling the road ahead with golden patches that look like magic, and all of a sudden I can't stand to be stuck in this truck after falling through the endless sky, not with all the beauty out there and this bubbling excitement inside me, needing to come out.

I need to *do* something.

And I need to do it with Johnny and Matt.

And I need to do it *now*.

"We should celebrate," I say, instantly earning me matching

looks from my boys. Wicked, naughty, *dirty* looks that make my whole body flush with delicious heat.

Yes, I know darn well what that word is making them think of after our "celebration" the night Matt's father came to dinner, and *yes*, that's exactly how I meant it.

"I'm always down to celebrate with you, beautiful," Matt says to me, twining his fingers through mine and lifting my hand up to press a hot kiss against my palm.

A shiver of anticipation shoots through me, and he grins, moving my hand over his lap until I feel something that proves he means it. He's hard and getting harder, and oh Lord, *yes*.

This is what I need.

This is exactly how I want to celebrate and let loose with all the bubbling emotions inside me that I'm so close to feeling brave enough to claim.

To *name*.

I rock my hand against Matt's erection and he spreads his legs wider apart with a happy groan, pushing himself up against my palm, and just like that, I'm wet.

"I want this," I say, closing my hand around the shape of him. "And I... I don't want to wait."

Look at me, so bold. So brave. Wanton and shameless and taking what I want.

I jump out of *airplanes*.

I definitely deserve a reward.

"Christ, you're sexy when you're like this, Eden," Matt whispers, pulling me against him while I continue to stroke him through his shorts. He slips his good hand up under my tank top to squeeze my breast, starting to breathe a little harder, and says, "Maybe we need to take you skydiving every day, yeah?"

"Hey now," Johnny says, grinning as he cuts a glance at us before looking back at the road. "What were we just saying about distracted driving? Because you two are definitely distracting me with all that."

I reach over and find him getting hard, too, and it's a heady feeling to know that I do this to these two.

Even headier to realize that all I need to do is let them know what I need.

Because when I do? They always—*always*—give it to me.

"What if I want to distract you, Johnny?" I ask, my hands still on both of them. And *ohhhhhhhhhhh* what it does to me, the feel of both of them straining against my palms. It's heating me up from the inside out. "Maybe... maybe you should pull over?"

"You're killing me, princess," he says, pressing it against his cock. "There's nothing out here, and still forty minutes to home."

Matt laughs, then leans across me to pluck my hand off Johnny's cock.

"Safety first," he says, a deliciously dirty glint in his eye. "And you know we're not going to make it forty minutes if Eden doesn't want to wait. Pull over like she said, buddy. Our girl wants to celebrate, and she deserves it, yeah?"

I can *feel* how much Johnny's into the idea—the evidence was just in my hand—and he doesn't even pretend to argue.

We're driving past a lake, and the trees that border it thin out up ahead. It's not an actual access road, but as far as I'm concerned, it's perfect.

"Right there," I say, pointing to the spot. "Please, Johnny?"

"Anything," he promises, doing it.

The truck crunches over a few branches and then comes to a stop. Johnny's pulled us deep into the trees, and he's right, there's nothing here at all. Of course, right now? I don't need anything except the men on either side of me.

I need them to share this moment.

I need to show them what they mean to me, even if I'm not sure I can say the words.

I need them inside me. Taking me. Proving to me that they know just how completely I'm theirs.

Johnny's got the A/C blasting and the windows aren't tinted

and the highway isn't all that far behind us, but I don't feel a single inhibition… I just feel *need*. I've never had sex in public. Never done it outside, even in private. And honestly, I never thought I'd want to. But right now? I want *every*thing.

The clinical part of my brain recognizes that I'm having a natural response to an adrenaline high, but I know it's something more than that, too. My bucket list is finally done, and of course I feel good about that… but I don't feel *complete*, the way I've always assumed I would.

Instead, knowing there's nothing left to check off fills me with a new sense of urgency.

It means it's almost over.

I don't know how much time I'll really have left, but my birthday is just over a month away, so it can't be much, and even without any more items left on The List, I'm determined to wring as much as I can out of every last moment that I get.

Starting right now.

Johnny turns the truck off, shifting around in his seat to face me.

"What can we do for you, princess?" he asks, cupping my chin and giving me a dirty smile.

"I… I want that feeling back," I tell him. "The one we had when we jumped. But this time, I want it with *both* of you. I want to fly, Johnny. Can you make me fly?"

"I can do anything, Eden," he says, winking. "I just jumped out of a fucking *plane*." He looks over my shoulder at Matt. "You up to the task, Matty? Wanna make our girl fly?"

"I'm always up around the two of you," Matt jokes, but he holds Johnny's eye for an extra beat, and I swear, something sizzles between the two of them that makes my toes curl.

Then Matt's hand is under my tank top again and Johnny slides his up my thigh and rests it right between my legs, rubbing my pussy over my shorts. I moan, spreading my legs wider and letting my head fall back. They're both kissing me, Johnny pushing my long hair off my neck and driving me crazy as he trails love bites down the side of my neck. Matt takes my mouth with his, and I'm in overload, all that exists is the heat of their mouths... their firm hands... the building excitement inside me and the hot, gasping sounds that come from all three of us, filling the cab of the truck.

Within minutes, I'm panting and filled with a much more immediate urgency.

I'm squirming. Asking them for more. Hands and mouths just aren't enough. We've all got too many clothes on. And oh, Lord. King cab or not, this bench seat was *not* made for three... at least not when two of the three are the size of Johnny and Matt.

And not when they're both determined to give me every single thing I ask for.

Even the things I don't *have* to ask for.

"You still got camping supplies in the back, bro?" Matt finally asks, laughing when his knee slams into the dash for the second time. "I think we're gonna need a little more space to work with here."

Johnny nods, and before I know it, we're out in a clearing by the lakeside. Anyone with a pair of binoculars might see us from their cabin on the other side, or a passerby might get a quick glimpse from the highway, but the way I'm feeling right now? I'm not even sure I'd mind.

I'm not even sure I'd *notice*.

Johnny lays some kind of blanket out on the ground and Matt makes quick work of undressing me. And I've never done anything like this in my life—naked in the middle of the forest?— but suddenly I wonder why the heck not? Why haven't I seized *every* moment? It's almost like I've lived two lives—those moments where I'm pursuing a goal and checking something off The List, and all the rest of my life, where I've kept myself small. Insulated. Lived all *those* parts of my life as if the only purpose was to get to the end.

As if getting one hundred checkmarks in a notebook could somehow be equated with a life well lived.

I wouldn't trade my bucket list experiences for anything, but right now, it's so, *so* obvious to me that it's really the little moments in between that mean the most. Here with these two boys that I can't get enough of, who put me first and have taught me to open my heart as well as my body, I don't just feel alive... I feel *ecstatic* about being alive. They fill me up and complete me, and when I'm with them like this, I truly feel like it doesn't matter how long I've got, as long as I remember not to miss out on *what* I've got.

"So you want Johnny to make you fly, beautiful?" Matt asks, wrapping his arms around me from behind. His casted arm goes around my waist, locking me against him, and he teases my nipples with his good hand while he whispers in my ear. "You want him inside you? Want him to push you higher? Want him to make you scream?"

"Yes," I breathe out, wanting *all* of that and so, so grateful that Matt knows it. That he'll make it happen. That I know they *both* will, and I won't have to ask. That I'm free to just put myself in their hands and trust that they'll get me there, now that they know I want it.

I love how Matt always takes charge when I need him to.

Love how Johnny is so ready to jump into every new experience.

Love their big hearts and sheltering arms and that touch of silliness that lives in both of them.

And oh Lord, do I ever love *this*, too. Hard bodies. Erotic fantasies. The feel of Matt's cock, a hot, hard length pushing against my back.

He groans, rubbing it against me while we both watch Johnny undress. And Johnny getting naked is so, *so* worth watching. The lightest breeze comes off the lake, cooling the hot summer air and spreading a cascade of goosebumps over my naked body, and I drink the moment in, letting go of everything that isn't right here and now.

"Look at what's waiting for you," Matt whispers in my ear, rolling my nipple between his thumb and finger.

I gasp, the feeling shooting straight to my core.

Johnny's got his shirt off and is just kicking his shorts off to the side, and he looks up at the sound, giving us a hot smile that affects me as much as what Matt's doing with those talented fingers of his. His eyes roam my body as Matt plays with me, then Johnny mimics Matt's action, sliding his hand up his own chest and pinching his nipple, too. His eyes half-close as he hisses with pleasure and his cock—long and thick and already pointing to the sky—jerks.

Matt makes a sound too low to hear, but he's holding me so close that I can feel it vibrate right through me.

"Oh my God," I whisper, half-panting. "That's... that's so hot."

Johnny touching himself. Matt reacting to it. Knowing I get to have them both.

"You like that, baby?" Matt says right into my ear. "You like that big cock of his?"

"Yes." It's more a whimper than a word, but I can't help it.

Johnny grins at us and starts stroking himself.

"What do you want to do with it today?" Matt asks, his erection throbbing against my back. "Should we get Johnny down on his back? Get you bent over between his legs so you can have a taste of it? Get him nice and hard with that pretty mouth of yours, then let you climb up and ride him?"

I whimper again, there's really no other word for it, and squeeze my thighs together as the tingling excitement between my legs goes into overdrive. *Yes.* Anything. I just want them, any way, every way.

Both of them.

I love feeling their hands on me at the same time. Love watching their hard bodies move against me. Love it with my eyes closed, too, so I can do nothing but feel. Heat and strength and power, two hot mouths all over me, licking... teasing... biting.

"Is that how we should start, beautiful?" Matt asks me. "You want Johnny's cock in your mouth?"

"Please," I whisper, pressing my fingers between my legs. "Matt, *please*. But you, too. Fuck me. Make him fuck me. *Some*thing."

Now.

"Oh, hell yeah," Matt says, making me moan loud enough to quiet the birds around us when he drops his hand down to cover mine, grinding it against my clit. Then, "You hear that, Johnny? Our girl needs us."

"Wouldn't want to disappoint," Johnny says, giving his cock a long, lazy stroke that makes my mouth water. "Bring her over here."

Matt does, and Johnny's eyes are filled with everything I could ever want as he grins down at me—lust and the joy of our jump and that thing that always makes me feel so cherished when either one of them looks at me.

That thing I've been afraid to name.

Johnny wraps his big hand around my throat the way I love, using it to tip my face up to his. Sandwiching me between the two of them. His hard length grinds against my stomach as Matt whispers dirty things in my ear, and then Matt pushes me down to my knees.

I press my face against Johnny's length, breathing him in, and it's not just my mouth that's watering. I *love* his cock, and as I lick up the shaft and swirl my tongue around the slick head, I slide a hand between my own legs because I *have* to.

I'm so wet.

I need friction there so bad.

But oh Lord, I also need *this*. I take Johnny in my mouth, and his delicious groan makes me shudder with need.

"So good, princess," he whispers, fingers combing through my hair as he looks down at me. "You... you see that, Matty? Fucking... *beautiful.*"

Matt puts his good hand on the back of my head, pushing me forward, urging me to take Johnny deeper, and watching him stare down as I take Johnny's cock in my mouth? Watching the way his pupils dilate... seeing his eyes follow every wet, sloppy motion... noting how he rests his casted arm around Johnny's hips and leans into him and... oh, God.

Oh my *God.*

I whimper, grinding against my own hand as I watch them watching me. The two of them are so hot together. Someday, *someday,* I want to see what happens if Matt ever realizes it. I moan, the blow job starting to get truly sloppy as Matt guides my head faster and faster, and Johnny's eyes roll back in his head.

"*Fuck,* Eden," he groans, thrusting into my mouth once... twice... again... before he suddenly pulls his cock out, breathing hard. "It's... a little... *too* good."

"Oh, she's not done with you yet," Matt says, his tone flipping into that hard, bossy voice he always gets when he's turned on. The one that makes my insides flutter. He's still got a hold of my head, and now he pushes Johnny toward the ground. "Lay down, Johnny."

Johnny groans, one hand wrapped around his own cock, and does it. And once he's on his back? Matt pushes me forward, positioning me right between Johnny's legs, just like he'd told me he would.

"Suck him, Eden," he tells me in that don't-argue voice. "Go on now, you can do it, beautiful. Make him crazy."

I don't *want* to argue. I bend over Johnny's cock, bottom in the air, and do my best to swallow him down. Johnny's hands are back in my hair, his cock swelling inside my mouth until I almost choke on it, and those deep groans, panting breaths, dirty words that slip out of his mouth... they're everything.

I'm lost in it... until suddenly Matt moves behind me and spreads me open from behind and *oh my God*—

I gasp.

Matt's mouth is on me.

I completely lose track of what I'm doing.

"Fucking *hot*," Johnny groans, moving my head to the side to see.

Matt's mouth is always magic, but he's never done *this* to me before. This time, he's not licking his way inside my pussy the way I'm addicted to. Not thrusting that tongue into me until I'm crazy with it. Not sucking on my little button, teasing it unmercifully with tongue and teeth and lips until I break down begging.

This time, he's put that hot mouth of his directly over my little back hole.

And it... feels... *indescribable*.

"Ohhhhhhhhhhhhh," I moan, long and loud and totally shameless. Johnny's cock slips out of my mouth as the most incredible sensations move through me, and suddenly I'm shaking. Panting. Begging, even though I didn't even realize I'd opened my mouth. "Matt... Matt... please... please... *please*..."

Somehow that one spot electrifies my whole body.

Matt licks at me and I quiver, begging him for more. He sucks the delicate skin there and I sob, pushing back against him. His mouth is hot and his tongue is wet and then oh Lord oh my *God* oh *yes*—I shouldn't like it but *I do*—he pushes that tongue deep inside me and I almost come apart.

"Ask him to fuck you," Johnny growls, up on his elbows now, watching. "Jesus fuck, Eden, that's so hot. Ask him to fuck you right there, princess."

Right... *there?*

I feel dazed, but then Matt takes his mouth off me and I whimper, wanting it back.

"Please," I whisper, face flushing with mortification. "I need... I need..."

I can't. I can't ask that.

"You'll get it, beautiful," Matt growls from behind me. "Johnny—"

"I've got you," Johnny says, sitting up and pushing me down onto his cock again.

As soon as it fills my mouth, he leans over me, smoothing a hand down the line of my back… then farther… sliding his hand right between my cheeks, where Matt had just been, and pushing a finger into me.

Into my *bottom*.

I gasp around his cock and he pushes my head back down, thrusting that finger in and out of my little hole as I suck him. The sensation makes my stomach flutter, and for a moment, I'm not sure if I can take it. Not sure if I *like* it.

And then all of a sudden I'm *very* sure I like it.

I'm pushing back against Johnny's hand like I've got no control over my actions whatsoever. My body *needs* it, and I'm trying to fuck myself on his finger, moaning around his cock, only half aware as he tells Matt to get things out of the glove compartment in his truck.

Condoms.

Lube.

A towel.

And before I know it, Matt's back and Johnny takes his finger out of me. Pulls my head up, off his cock. Pulls *me* up, manhandling me right up his body without any effort at all. Giving me a hot kiss that leaves me gasping before quickly suiting up and lying down on his back again.

"You gonna ride this for me now, Princess?" Johnny says, stroking himself as he grins up at me.

"You gonna let me fuck you the way I want to, beautiful?" Matt growls before I can answer, kneeling behind me and wrapping one arm around my waist. He pulls my back flush with his chest and kisses the side of my neck. "Gonna let us make you feel good, both of us together?"

My head is spinning and my body is crying out for relief. Yes is the only possible answer.

"You... you always make me feel good," I say, because it's true. "*Both* of you."

And then, thank God, they don't ask me to answer any more questions. Matt takes over the way I love, urging me forward until I'm straddling Johnny, and Johnny's hands wrap around my hips, guiding me down onto his engorged cock.

"*Nnnnnnnngh,*" I moan, gasping, panting as I ease down onto it. I'm so wet that it goes in easily, but he's so big that it's still slow at first. My body is flooded with sensation. He stretches me, fills me, until I can barely breathe and once I'm fully seated, I need a minute to adjust to his size.

It's almost too much.

It's heaven.

"You like that, princess?" Johnny grits out, eyes hot and every muscle tense as he looks up at me. "You ready to fly?"

His hands are still on my hips, and he lifts me. Thrusts up into me. Guides me against him in a slow roll that presses him deep and grinds my clit against his pubic bone, and does it over and over and *over*, until I'm panting with it.

Until I can't stand it.

Until I'm leaning forward with my hands braced on his hard chest and riding him hard. Getting myself so close, so fast, that I feel like I really *am* going to explode.

My fingers dig into the hard muscles of his chest. "Johnny," I gasp, needing just a little bit more. "Oh, please... please... *please...*"

"*Fuck*, yeah," he says, wrapping one hand around the back of my neck and pulling me down against him.

He captures my mouth, thrusting up into me *hard*, and then Matt's hands are on me again. Stroking my back as he presses me down until I'm totally flush against Johnny's body. Tracing my spine all the way to its base, and then running his strong fingers between my cheeks. Skimming over my sensitive little hole without stopping, going all the way down to play with the spot where Johnny and I are joined. Teasing me there until I'm squirming. Finding my clit until I'm sobbing. Coming back to press against my hole again… stroke it… flick it… tease it until I'm panting into Johnny's mouth. Until I'm pushing back against Matt's hand and begging all over again.

I don't know what I want other than *more*, but I know for sure he'll give me what I need.

"Hold still now, beautiful," Matt says, leaning over me and whispering it in my ear. "I want in on this party, too, yeah?"

Johnny groans beneath me, moving his hands down to cup my ass. He pulls me apart and then holds me there, cock buried inside me while he opens me up for Matt.

"Just like this, princess," he whispers. "Let Matt in too, can you do that?"

I'll do anything for these two.

But oh, Lord. I'm trembling.

There's a little *snick* like something's being opened, and then Matt's finger is pressing into me from behind, just like Johnny's did before. I moan, burying my face against Johnny's neck, and then Matt adds a second finger and I gasp, flinching away.

Which just drives me against Johnny's body, making me gasp and rock my hips to try and get more of him.

Which forces Matt's fingers to go deeper.

Before I know it, I'm shameless. Grinding back and forth between Johnny's cock and Matt's fingers as my orgasm starts to build all over again. It feels like those fingers are pressing on my clit from the inside out, and they ramp up the pleasure from Johnny's cock higher and higher, until I'm sure it's going to wreck me.

Until I *want* it to.

"That's it, that's it, baby," Matt growls in my ear. "You want… want some more?"

"Yes," I gasp, because it feels so good. "Yes, yes, *yes*, Matt."

"Good girl."

That little *snick* again, then he pushes a third finger into me.

I shudder. It's too much. Just this side of pain. But with Johnny's big hands holding me in place as he rocks me on top of him, his hard cock filling me from the front and the burning stretch of Matt's fingers in me from behind, everything's jumbled inside me so that even that hint of pain only serves to make every sensation inside me stronger.

Better.

So good that I can't get enough.

So good that all of a sudden, it *does* wreck me. Shatters me. Explodes me into a million pieces as I come and come and *come*, crying out their names.

I scream, and they don't let up, fucking me through it from both ends.

The waves of my orgasm slam through me, again and again, and every time my body tightens with pleasure, Johnny's hard cock swells even thicker inside me, sending me higher.

Every wave that rocks through me makes my intimate muscles clench tight around Matt's fingers, sending another cascade of pleasure flooding through me.

It goes on and on and *on*, and still my boys don't stop pushing me.

"Fucking beautiful, Eden," Johnny finally grits out, pulling me down and kissing me again like a drowning man.

"So… fucking… *hot*," Matt growls, pulling his fingers out of me and making me whimper at the loss.

Greedy. I'm so greedy.

"You're going to do that for me again," Matt tells me. "But this time, with *both* of us inside you."

I don't know if I can. I can't move. I'm boneless. But of course I'm not going to argue.

Johnny's still thick and hard inside me, and then I feel Matt pressing against my little hole again... but this time, it's not his fingers. The thick head of his cock rubs against my back entrance, back and forth, back and forth—gently, and then more insistently, lighting up all my nerve endings until I'm getting worked up all over again.

I don't know if I can do this, not with Johnny inside me, too, but oh, Lord. I want it.

I'm panting.

Quivering.

Suddenly *desperate* for it.

And then I get it. Matt breaches me from behind, and for a split second, it *is* too much. His cock is a lot bigger than three fingers, and that first slow, shallow thrust makes it feel like I'm being ripped in two. Like there *isn't* room, not when I'm already filled in the front with Johnny's thick length, too.

"Fuck... fuck... *fuck*," Matt chants in a low voice from behind me.

He sounds wrecked, too, and I gasp, tears springing to my eyes as the fullness overwhelms me.

"Bear down, princess, you can take it," Johnny says, eyes locked onto mine. "Let him in."

I *want* to.

And Johnny jumped out of an airplane for me. I can do this for him.

...and for Matt, who's stroking my ass almost reverently as he mutters the sweetest, dirtiest things behind me.

...and oh Lord, for myself, too. I do want this, I do. I never have before, but right now? To have both of them inside me at once? I suddenly can't imagine *any*thing I want more.

A shudder of pure desire goes through me, and I force myself to relax. Matt slips in deeper, letting loose with a low groan that's so deep and sexy that my body can't help but respond.

"Ohhhhhh," I moan, all sorts of pleasure points suddenly bursting to life inside me.

"Oh, fuck," Johnny grits out, eyes locked on mine as he fists one hand in my long hair. "That's it. *Take* it, Eden. Fly, princess. *Fly.*"

Matt pushes in even deeper, a series of shallow thrusts that fill me and fill me and *fill* me, taking me from that first, painful burn to a quivering uncertainty to so amazingly good that my whole body starts to shake with it.

Crave it.

Wonder how I ever survived without it.

"Oh my God," I gasp, flooded with sensation. "Oh... *yes.*"

Both of them inside me? Both of them fucking me at once? It really *is* like flying.

It's overwhelming.

It feels like I'm teetering on the verge of coming apart completely... except that there's nowhere to go. Johnny's got me locked tight in his arms, my breasts flattened against his hard chest, and Matt leaning into me from behind, pinning me between them.

They're both inside me, and their cocks fill me to overflowing.

They're both inside me... and then they start to really *move.*

First Matt, his thrusts deeper... stronger... faster. Then Johnny, staying in perfect sync. Rolling his hips under me. Thrusting up each time Matt pulls back.

Their hard muscles flex against me from all sides, holding me, pushing me, driving me toward something *amazing.*

Something I didn't even know I could have.

Something so big that all I can do is surrender to it.

Surrendering is all I *want* to do, and with the two of them, I know I can. Pinned between them, secure, I feel as weightless and free as I was when I jumped.

And like I'm falling toward something just as fast.

"Christ, that's... that's good," Matt grits out, starting to drive into me a little harder. A little faster. "So... fucking... *good.*"

I start to shake.

"Fuck, Matty, I can *feel* you," Johnny gasps out, fingers digging into my hips. "Feel you... inside her. I'm not... not gonna last like this."

"Eden—"

"Princess—"

"*Yes.*" I'm gasping. Panting out the words. The only words I ever want to say to these two. "Yes yes *yes.*"

I'm going to come again, just like Matt wanted me to. It's building inside me like a tsunami, every inch of me engorged with sensation. Their cocks slide against each other inside my body with each thrust, barely separated by the thin barrier between my two channels, both pressing against my most sensitive places, over and over, and a deep, delicious tension coils tighter and tighter inside of me, consuming me.

It's like nothing I've ever felt before.

It's better.

It's *both* of them.

It's *us.*

"Fuck... *Eden,*" Johnny groans, hips stuttering against me as he slams them home. "*Jesus,* Matty. I'm coming."

Matt shouts out his own release, buried in me to the hilt, and then the tsunami breaks over me, too. Sweeps me away in a beautiful swirling, shuddering, endless wave of bliss.

It's perfect.

It's everything I didn't know I needed.

I really am complete now. I've finally, really *lived*... and despite my fears, even if I never risk telling them, I've finally fallen in love, too. It's the one thing I was never brave enough to put on The List.

It's everything.

18

MATT

*B*ill and Jimmy and all the guys have had fun today, giving me shit about my "extended vacation," but hey, I don't even mind. I'm so damn happy to have full use of my arm again and to be back at the station—my home away from home— that I'll happily put up with all of it and ask for more.

I know I'm trying to do too much when I yank some equipment down for cleaning and wince, joint pain filling me up. I keep forgetting that maybe sudden movements with an arm that's been wedged mostly in the same position for months aren't the best idea. No matter, though, it'll get there.

"What's that look about?" Bill jokes, coming up behind me and clapping me on the shoulder. "First day on the clock and you're already trying to scam yourself back to that couch, eh?"

"You wish you could get rid of me that fast," I say, grinning.

"Hell, no," Jimmy says, walking past with a couple of the other guys. "It's good to have you back, Lopez." He waits a beat, then winks. "You know nobody washes that engine like you do."

"Hey now, that's a probie's job," I say, since he expects it.

He laughs and moves on, but truth is, I'd happily wash engines right now.

Bill heads out, too, and I close my eyes and take a deep breath. All the familiar smells fill me right up like I was never gone. Old soap and hot concrete smell and a thousand other things that my brain latches onto as "home."

I've missed this place. I like being settled. Like knowing I can count on things that matter always being there. Johnny calls it my "nesting instinct," and maybe he's not wrong.

Truth is, I would've hated growing up like Eden did, always moving around. I don't really get my mom and her need to always be on the move, either. I was thinking it was her running away this whole time, but since starting to mend bridges with my dad, now it's starting to seem like maybe I was wrong. Maybe she's running *to*.

To new experiences.

To new horizons.

To things that make her feel just as fulfilled as knowing I've got roots and a place in the world do for me.

Different strokes, amirite?

But even with the guys razzing me here, it just feels good to know that things haven't changed while I've been gone. I finish up the equipment and notice a new *Embrace Diversity* poster on the wall, and it reminds me that actually, some things have.

Or really, just one.

Johnny's had nothing but good things to say about the new guy, and I got a good impression, too, at the barbecue last month, but we're gonna be working together, me and Asher, so I figure a "good impression" isn't enough. He's part of the family here at the station now, and after what I'm ashamed to think he probably heard about me, I need to make sure we're solid.

I know he's on a 24-hour shift right now, same as me and Johnny, so I go looking for him. It's dead today—a blessing since we're still in the middle of an August heat wave—so the guys on shift are scattered in various places around the firehouse, doing housework for the most part, or getting their workouts in like I know Johnny is right now, or just shooting the shit, which is—nine times out of ten—Bill's favorite pastime.

Earlier, I spotted Asher sitting cross-legged on one of the crash beds, scribbling in a notepad, and sure enough, that's where I find him. Figured maybe he could use a small break, so I fixed up a couple cups of coffee. Symbolic of my good intentions, maybe, since it bugs me that he might still think of me as someone who'd give a shit about him being with another guy.

Even though, okay, fine, a couple of months ago? Guess I would have.

"Hey, bro," I say, leaning a hip on the headboard of the empty bed next to where he's sitting.

It takes him a moment to realize I'm talking to him. He looks up from his notepad and blinks, and when he sees it's me he's... well, not unfriendly. Not at all. He smiles, but I can see it's a little guarded.

"Hey, Lopez."

"Take one of these from me," I say, offering one of the coffee mugs. "Hope you take it with cream and sugar."

His smile turns into a relieved grin as he takes one. "You read my mind, I feel like I've been making these notes forever."

I glance down at his pad and have to bite back a smile. Looks like he's dissecting the last call he was out on, breaking down what went right, what went wrong. Things that will eventually be instinct, but it's not a bad sign that he wants to improve his performance.

I use my free hand to pull over one of the wooden chairs, turn it around, and straddle it backward, leaning against the chair back and taking a sip from my mug. Doesn't occur to me until I'm seated that I did it with my left. I hold my right out in front of me, turning it this way and that. It's damn good to have that cast off, but it definitely still needs some work to get back where it needs to be.

Maybe I'll go catch Johnny in the weight room after Asher and I make nice.

"Thinking about how good it is to have it off?" Asher asks, grinning at me.

"Thinking about Johnny," I answer, not sure why that slips out even if it's sort of true. I cough, feeling weird about that, and add a quick, "Yeah, it's great to have the cast off. You ever worn one?"

Asher points to his right leg. "Senior year. Bottom of the ninth. Sliding into home."

I laugh, almost spitting out my coffee. "No shit? Same thing happened to me, a bit younger, though. Guess we've got something in common, yeah?"

He raises his eyebrows, giving me an odd look. "Guess so." He takes a sip from his mug. "This is perfect. Cream and sugar. Guess you and I are gonna be coffeemates."

I roll my eyes and grin at the pun. "Oh, that's hilarious."

"Gotta bring something to the table," he says, raising the mug in mock salute. "I bet you're thinking I could get by on good looks alone, but that doesn't quite cut it with all the guys here."

He's joking, but there's just enough of that edge underneath that I know he's testing me, too. And fine, this is why I wanted to talk to him, yeah? So I go for it.

"Speaking of that, uh, how you settling in?"

"Just fine," he says, raising an eyebrow and not giving me an inch.

Okay, so maybe that version of me *going for it* wasn't really as clear as I'd meant to be. I clear my throat and try again.

"Look, Asher, I just want to make sure that we're good, you and me. I'm looking forward to working with you. I just... just wanted to get that stated up front."

He looks at me for a second, tilting his head to the side like Johnny always does, then offers a smile that's a little less guarded than the last one. "You're not what I was expecting, Lopez."

"Just Matt is fine," I say. It's half-and-half for what the guys here call me, and normally I don't even notice—answer to either one—but somehow, sticking with first names just feels more friendly right now.

"Okay, Matt," Asher says, raising an eyebrow. He lifts the mug. "So this is your olive branch?"

I laugh self-consciously, rubbing at the back of my neck, but yeah, it is. Guess I'm just embarrassed that I need one, now that I'm seeing things a little more clearly. We've never had a gay guy here before, at least, none that I ever knew about, and some of the shit that gets tossed around between us—well, I can guess it might not have felt all that welcoming to Asher.

Worst part? If I'd been on duty when he'd started, I would have been one of the biggest offenders. I know it, and I'm now a hundred percent sure Asher got word, too.

He's just waiting on me, so I nod. "Guess you heard I'd have a problem with the gay action, yeah?"

"No one actually told me how you like your action," he says, so straight-faced it takes me a minute to get that he's joking.

"Oh, you're a riot," I say, grinning. Then I clear my throat again. "But for real, man, the gay... how's that going for you?"

I try to imagine it. Him just dealing with the shit here from the guys, and probably everywhere else, too. Not the first time I've tried to imagine gay, but the other times, I was really just thinking about the sex parts. And okay, so the sex is... it's something that I'm... guess you'd say something I'm not exactly averse to thinking about.

Something my dick is *definitely* not averse to thinking about, not lately.

But these other parts—thinking about how I'd feel in Asher's shoes—it doesn't just make me want to clear the air between the two of us, it also makes me feel pretty low for all those years I treated my dad like that was the part of him I had a problem with. Not to mention any other Ashers that might have come and gone

here at the station, but never had the kind of balls he does to just
be out there like that.

Thank fucking God Eden opened my eyes to what an ass
I'd been.

Asher's kinda laughing at me while trying not to show it, I can
tell, and guess I got a little lost in my own thoughts, because for
the life of me, I'm not sure why.

"What?"

"I guess I just never had anyone ask me how gay is working
out for me before," he says, giving in and letting his laugh out. "I'll
go with ten outta ten. Would recommend."

"Oh, fuck off," I say, laughing. "You know I meant how's it
going here at the *station*. You know, with the guys and all."

He shrugs, losing some of the laughter.

"Fine. Not everyone is comfortable with it, but hey, welcome
to life." He pauses to take a drink of his coffee, eyeing me hard
over the rim of his mug, and then... there it is. "I was told you'd be
one of those people, actually, Lop—Matt."

I nod. Fair enough.

"Yep," I say, pulling the Band-Aid off. "I would've been, but
then someone pulled my head out of my ass, thank Christ."

Asher looks kind of surprised I'm admitting it, but then something behind me catches his attention, and he gets a decidedly evil
grin on his face. "Someone, huh? *He* have anything to do
with that?"

I turn to look and Johnny waves at me and Asher with a
cheerful grin. Looks like he's done with his workout but hasn't
showered yet, and it's obviously been another upper-body day,
given how his shoulders are looking flushed and cut, bursting out
of his sleeveless tee.

"Thought you were going to join me, Matty," he says, leaning
against the doorway and wiping some sweat off his face with a
hand towel. "Don't tell me you're gonna keep babying that broken
wing now."

"Fuck off," I say for the second time in a few minutes, grinning back at him. "Just didn't want to show you up."

He snorts back a laugh, shaking his head. "All talk, bro, all talk."

"You wanna go back down? I'll show you talk."

He laughs, waving me off, and heads to the showers.

I turn back to Asher, still smiling, and find that he's looking at me in the oddest way.

"What?" I ask him, looking down like maybe I spilled some coffee on my shirt.

"So it was him, right?" he asks. "You figured out...?"

His voice just peters out, and what, am I supposed to read his mind now?

"I figured out what? And no, it wasn't Johnny. My... my girlfriend set me straight about how I was a bit messed up in my thinking is all."

Feels a little odd to use that word for Eden, but it fits. She *is* my girlfriend, far as I'm concerned. It's just that she's Johnny's, too. And Johnny's my... well, I mean, he's *Johnny*. I don't really know what to call the three of us, and being home and sort of out of the public eye for the most part while we fell into this, guess I haven't had to think about it too hard up until now.

Asher's eyes go wide for a second when I mention Eden, and suddenly he's backpedaling like crazy and I'm still not sure why. "Oh! I.. Sorry, I thought you, uh, I guess when I saw... I just assumed that—"

"You thought what, bro?" I cut in, feeling weirdly impatient with the way he's suddenly stumbling about. "Spit it out."

His eyes dart to where Johnny was standing a minute ago, then he shakes his head. "Never mind."

I narrow my eyes. Yeah, no. What the fuck is he going on about?

I should just let it go, but it's bugging me for some reason, and I can't.

"*What*, Asher? You thought, you say, you assumed… Jesus, bro, just tell me what you're trying to say already."

For a second, I think he's gonna stonewall me, but then he straightens his shoulders and looks me in the eye. "You and Johnny. I heard you guys were close, and seeing you together… I misinterpreted things. My bad."

Ah. O…kay. So he thinks… he thought me and Johnny… what, now it's *obvious* that I've been thinking about my best friend that way?

Suddenly, I'm wishing I hadn't pushed quite so hard, because yeah… yep. *Yes*, fine, I will admit in the privacy of my own head that there are certain… thoughts there. And I've even thought about maybe sharing those thoughts with Johnny at some point. I've just… well, guess I've just continued to chicken the fuck out, even after he blew my mind by kicking the ass of his own biggest fear with that jump.

But since then, things have just been so good with the three of us that I haven't wanted to rock the boat.

Haven't wanted to risk it.

That whole "what's the best that can happen" scenario I was on fire with a few weeks ago? Somehow that voice got quieter the longer I waited, and now *what's the worst that can happen* is back, loud and proud and telling me daily that the worst that *could* happen would be really, really bad.

The worst is why I backed off the first ten thousand times it could have come up.

The worst is losing Johnny, and I just… I can't.

Asher's still looking at me, all cautious-like, waiting for me to rip his head off for daring to assume I might not be as straight as I've always thought I was.

I clear my throat. "Me and Johnny… we've known each other forever."

"Okay," he says, clearly still on high alert, looking at me like I'm a cornered animal or some bullshit.

"We're best friends."

"Yep, I got that," Asher says.

But he doesn't, because I'm not saying it right. Of *course* Johnny's my best friend, but he's a hell of a lot more than that, too.

"We've lived together since forever. I mean, he was always over anyway, growing up, and then as soon as we moved out after high school, it was me and him. Him and me. The two of us. We're roommates. Always have been."

Asher nods.

"And this job, you know, we went through the Academy together. Been on the job together since day one."

"Okay," Asher repeats, irritating the fuck out of me for some reason.

It's like he keeps agreeing with what I'm saying, but something about the way he's looking at me makes it feel like he's just humoring me, if that makes any sense.

Which no, it does not, which is probably why it's pissing me the fuck off all of a sudden.

"Me and Johnny, we *get* each other is what I'm saying," I tell him. "Whatever you think you see, it's because we *are* close. Like family. He's like—"

Jesus, suddenly I'm sweating. That phrase *he's like a brother to me* sounds so fitting, right?

Except it's not.

I can't make myself say it.

I'm not... not thinking of him like a brother. Not lately.

I clear my throat. "The thing is, you're right about us being close," I tell Asher, suddenly feeling like I'm repeating myself. Did I already say that? But for some reason, I need to make him understand. "It's just that we're... we're—"

Asher holds up his hand, and I snap my mouth closed gratefully.

"Really, it's okay," he says, lowering his voice.

And what the actual fuck? Now he's actually looking at me like maybe he's... what? Pitying me? Sorry for me? Some kind of sympathy, anyway.

"I'll leave it alone, Lopez," he says, and now we're back to that? Wasn't I just Matt a second ago? "I'm not going to ou—not going to say anything, okay? It's not my business. I shouldn't have pushed."

I open my mouth. *There's nothing to say* is what I mean to tell him. Instead, what comes out is—

"Maybe I *need* a push."

Asher's eyebrows shoot straight up to his hairline.

Oshit. Why the hell did I say that? Well, I mean, other than the fact that it's one hundred percent true. Because, what, I'm just supposed to... supposed to have all these feelings and go the rest of my entire fucking life hiding them from Johnny and everyone else? How's that gonna work out?

Not very well, is my guess.

Pretty fucking miserable, might be another way to say it.

Oh, Jesus, I'm fucked, amirite?

"You mentioned, um, a girlfriend," Asher says after a minute, sounding like he's picking and choosing every word carefully. "And I don't know how that will, um, affect things—"

"It won't be a problem."

"O...kay. Well, uh, then I guess, if you're looking for, um, a push...?"

"Asher, Jesus, just spit it out. You're killing me here."

He laughs, running a hand through his hair as some of the tension eases out of him. "Okay, well, look Matt, I don't really know you, but can I just say that gaydar is a real thing?"

"Oh Christ. It *is* genetic."

He gives me an odd look. "I don't know about that, but all I meant is that you and Johnny... I just don't think it's going to be a problem, from what I've seen. Assuming we're talking about the same thing, and it's him that you—"

"It's him."

Oh, sweet baby Jesus, did I actually just say that out loud?

Asher grins, and you know what? The world fails to end. My chest even feels lighter, like the tight band of pressure that was building and building when I was trying to explain me and Johnny to him without just coming out and saying what's real has suddenly disappeared.

"It's him," I say again, grinning like a fucking fool. "Not sure when that happened, or, uh, you know, *why*, but yeah. It's... I want that. Johnny. I want Johnny like... like that."

Eloquent I am not, but it still feels kinda awesome. A little bit terrifying, but mostly awesome.

Asher laughs, face lighting up from the inside out like he's feeling the awesome too—even though I don't know why he'd care about me and mine—and then I'm laughing right along with him. Not funny-laughing so much as just... relief.

Happiness.

Butterflies in my fucking stomach over *Johnny*, which is both the dumbest and truest thing I've ever felt.

Weird that this moment is with Asher, a virtual stranger, but also... nice. It feels good to finally share this thing I've been wrestling with out loud with someone. And on the heels of that thought? Guess it's obvious, yeah? It's probably time to stop being such a pussy—

Uh, chicken. I mean stop being such a *chicken*, because fine, given what I'm admitting about myself and also who I... who I *love*, maybe I shouldn't use that word as a put-down any more than *gay*, amirite?

Anyway, point being, it's time to man up and tell the *right* someone.

And pray like hell that Asher is right.

19

JOHNNY

I love overnight shifts. I fucking *love* them. I don't know why—maybe it's just that need to be *on* for a full twenty-four, it suits me, you know? And yeah, yeah, of course we sleep, but even sleeping is with a sort of underlying awareness that we might have to be up operating at full throttle at any moment.

But right now?

Matty and I are twenty hours into what has got to be hands down the deadest, dullest, most profoundly boring 24-hour shift of my entire life. Nothing is happening, has happened, or looks like it *will* happen.

Nada.

Zip.

Zilch.

It's driving me out of my fucking mind.

"For the love of God, go to *sleep*, Johnson," Jimmy says for the five-hundredth time, rolling over in his crash bed and stuffing a pillow over his head.

"I *am* sleeping, bro," I remind him, folding my hands under my head and staring up into the darkness. "Like I was saying, it's un-fucking-believable that Chara's in his forties. He's gotta be, what, twice as old as half the squad? But get him on the ice—"

A pillow lands on my face, thrown by I don't know who, and someone mutters something blasphemous about not giving two shits about the Bruins.

I remove the pillow from my face. "I'm just saying, there's a reason he's the captain, you know? And after Tampa Bay—"

"Shut *up*, Johnny." I think that one's Bill. "If you can't turn it off, go hit the weights again."

"Dude, it's the middle of the night," I say, sitting up on the crash bed. And for real, normally? No one would be trying to sleep during a twenty-four. There's a reason we've got a big-screen TV in the break room. Tonight, though, between the unrelenting heat outside and the mind-numbing quietude of this shift, the guys are all acting like they're actually trying to, you know, *rest*.

"Come on, bro," Matty says, rolling out of the bed next to me and tugging at my arm. "Let's leave these puss—uh, these guys in peace, yeah?"

"Sure," I say, following him out and thanking God yet again for having blessed me with the good fortune to get Matty for a best friend instead of one of those knuckleheads. And of course thinking of Matty makes me think of Eden, because come on now, you wanna talk about blessed? Not sure how I ended up with these two people to come home to every night, but it makes life pretty close to perfect, you know? Of course, thinking of Eden also makes me horny, and since there's nothing to be done about that for another few hours, that's a little less than perfect, but hey, no complaints.

Well, maybe one complaint.

Matty's walking ahead of me in the darkened hallway, and fuck... *me*. Even in the dark, or maybe especially in the dark, he gets to me.

Don't get me wrong, I love all Eden's softness and lush curves.

Like, *really* love them. But there's something about the hard lines and thick muscles of a man's body—okay, who am I trying to fool here? of *Matty's* body—that gets me going just as hard.

Can't do anything about that complaint though, either.

All signs have been pointing to a total shutdown from Matty, despite the hope I had a few weeks ago that things might go a different direction between us, and am I disappointed? Fuck yeah, I am. And am I still fantasizing about just grabbing him and showing him how good we could be pretty much every other waking moment? Affirmative the Second. But am I that fucking stupid that I'd actually act on that fantasy after making it through my whole damn life up until this point by keeping that shit in check? No, I am not, thank you very much, so looks like once again, I'll just have to channel this particular brand of excess energy in another direction.

I grab Matty's arm, swinging him around to face me and jerking my head in the direction of the weight room. "Come on, bro."

And yeah, yeah, I know I've already hit it twice this shift and muscles need rest and all, but I'm so wired that I figure it will be the lesser of evils, you know?

"Oh, hell no," Matt says, the white of his teeth flashing at me in the dark as he grins. "You trying to kill me, *Eugene?*" He holds up his right arm—sad, skinny little thing that it's become—and even though I can't see him all that well, I'll bet anything I've got that he's giving me that wheedling puppy-dog look of his. "I've already put in my time there today. What happened to *oh, but I just* can't *lift any more heavy weights with my big manly muscles, Bill, because it's the middle of the night and I need my beauty sleep to stay so beautifulll-llllllll?*"

I raise one eyebrow and cross my arms.

Really? Was that supposed to be me, or a Disney Princess on crack?

Matty's muffling his laugh behind his hand and ignoring my

stink-eye, apparently under the impression that he's hilarious, so I finally drop the pose and just roll my eyes, restraining myself from pointing out that his skills do not lie in comedic impressions.

You see how much I love the guy?

"Fine, but I'm not binge watching any more *American Chopper*," I tell him, putting my foot down. "I don't know how Bill got you hooked on that shit—"

"I was stuck at home for two months," he interjects, whining like the big baby he secretly is under that hot-as-fuck exterior.

"You were stuck at home with *Eden*," I remind him, wrapping my hand around the back of his neck and pressing our foreheads together. "And dude, with her there? I'd think you'd want to have put in a little more time on the *chill* side of the Netflix-and-Chill equation, you know?"

"Oh, I put in my time," he says, laughing low and dirty. "I'm the king of… chill."

Of course my cock sits up and takes notice when he sounds like that, so I let go of him quick and scramble for something to say that won't make me think about sex. I come up with—

"Besides, you were only laid up for seven weeks, not two months."

"July and August. Count 'em and weep."

"August ain't over."

"Closer to done than started."

"It's the twentieth."

"You're making my point for me."

"Your point was two months, which *I'm* pointing out is an *exaggeration*."

I wait, but he's got nothing, because I'm right.

"Fuck you," he finally says, proving my point.

See? *Nothing*. I grin. Because please, fuck you? Those two words might as well be a big-ass neon sign that reads *Johnny Just Owned My Ass*.

We've both been keeping our voices down out of respect for Sleeping Beauty and her entourage back there, and suddenly—like him and me are some kind of hive mind or something—we're both laughing, the kind that hurts. The kind that wants to bust out and fill the room, but which you've gotta keep in check out of, like I said, respect for those kindergartners who think four a.m. should be nap time.

All that laughter gets stifled inside, and it's like one of those contained explosions, like the ab workout from hell, like a hockey fight inside your body, complete with sticks.

Matty pokes a finger into my ribs to torture me, and I snort and then choke as I try not to be too loud... which just makes him laugh harder... which hurts my fucking abs even *more*, because he's doing it almost silently and looks hilarious, like anyone who didn't know what was going on would consider giving him the Heimlich, you know?

"Quit it," I gasp out, which makes him go from silent to full-volume before he gets it under control again.

"*You*—" he wheezes, leaning on me, "—quit... it."

I'm *trying*, but oh my God, he's gonna give me a cramp.

Every time he snickers it sets me off again, and I finally get proactive and slap my hand over his mouth.

"Shut *up*, Matty," I manage, which hurts like a bitch to even get out, because my abs are now on *fire*.

"*You* shut up," he says... which I only know because I can feel his lips move and know every single retort he will ever make.

I mean, not that the majority of them are all that original, but I'm just saying, it's not like something's going to suddenly come out of Matty's mouth at this point that shocks me after all these years; not like whatever he's mumbling behind my hand is some kind of huge reveal, where the heavens part and choirs of angels play those long-ass trumpets to announce A New Revelation while a shaft of golden light spears down and spotlights him like some kind of *Ice Capades* solo act or whatever.

And yes, I occasionally watch old *Ice Capades* shows on cable, so sue me.

I'm about to make a comment about that in reference to the Bruins' season, because hello, they both involve skating and yes, I *can* tie them together, but then suddenly I'm still trying not to laugh and Matty's just flat-out *not* laughing, and my eyes are well enough adjusted to the dark now that I can tell he's giving me a really weird look over the top of my hand, too, so I table the *Ice Capades* reference for later, drop my hand, and back off, my pulse suddenly racing with nerves that I will never in a million years admit to.

Guess I *don't* always know what he's about to say, because I missed the bit where we went from having fun to whatever's making him suddenly get all still and quiet-like.

"What?" I whisper, my heart rate still in overdrive for no good reason that I can point to.

He opens his mouth, then closes it again, shaking his head and making this weird little sound that I shit you not, I *feel*. I don't even know what to *call* that sound, but I feel it in my chest, and *fuck* the dark. I mean, I can see him well enough to like, make out general humanoid features, but not enough to *see* him, you know?

Not enough to have a single fucking clue what that weird-ass sound actually meant.

"Oh, *shit*," I say, my heart shriveling up and dying in a single instant as it hits me. "Matty. All that weirdness when you... when you came back from that appointment with Doc Holloway a few weeks ago. Did he give you bad news? Do you... do you have a brain tumor? Did he confirm it when he took your cast off?"

I can't believe Matty wouldn't have fucking just *told* me.

How could he have kept it from me?

From *me*? I fucking *love* him.

"What the fuck?" Matty says, clutching himself around the middle as he busts out laughing again. "Of course I don't have a brain tumor. What the hell, Johnny? How would... like, if I *did*, how would Doc Holloway even have caught it from x-raying my *arm?*"

That one stops me in my tracks, and it's actually a very good point. My poor, dead, shriveled heart re-animates, but not in a disgusting *Walking Dead* way, and I punch Matt in the shoulder, hard.

"Well, quit it then. *Jesus*, Matty, you scared the shit out of me."

He goes for wide-eyed and innocent. "What did I do?"

"You got weird."

"*You* got weird."

"I was—"

Before I can defend myself, because hello, that had totally been him, not me, Jimmy pops his head out into the hall.

"Jesus, Mary, Joseph, and all the Saints who are right now at this very moment turning over in their beds because they can't fucking sleep with you two yapping at each other," Jimmy whisper-yells at us. "Will you two please get the fuck away from this doorway so the rest of us can get some fucking *sleep?*"

Matt and I look at each other.

"Do the saints actually sleep in beds?" he asks me conversationally. "Or do you think they just sort of float around on clouds all the time...?"

"I hate you guys," Jimmy mutters, spinning on his heel and slamming the door behind him.

Matty snickers, and I—

Fuck. I don't just love him, I'm fucking in *love* with him, and it's killing me.

Maybe he sees something on my face, because he gets that weird look on his again and grabs my arm and pulls me down the hall, away from Jimmy's precious cone of silence, but instead of heading to some regular place we can hang out, he goes upstairs. The station's an old-as-fuck brick building and the top floor isn't wired up to code or something so it's basically storage, and no one ever goes there except to send probies on bullshit wild goose chases.

Still, I don't argue, because thank God he doesn't have a brain tumor, but my pulse is right back to trying to win an Olympic gold in racing, just like it had been back before that split second when I'd thought that he did. He's not saying a damn thing or turning on any lights, and I'm about to burst if I don't get the lines of communication open here, so I wrack my brain for a safe topic as I follow him to wherever and whatever he's got in mind.

"We should plan a party for Eden's birthday, right?" I say just as we reach the top floor. "Maybe a surprise one, so she can't get worried about it."

"Good idea," Matt says, opening a few doors like he's looking for something in particular.

For real, I haven't been up here for a couple of years at least, so I've got no clue what the game plan is right now, but the weirdness factor? It's way, *way* too high between us for me to do anything but try to fill the silence in the hope of keeping myself sane until Matty drops whatever bomb he's clearly ready to lob in my direction.

And I mean, Eden *should* have a party, you know? So it's not like I'm just talking for the sake of talking. My feelings for her may not have the kind of years behind them as what's eating me up about Matt, but sometimes when it's right, it doesn't take you all that long to figure it out, you know?

I never felt the way I feel about Eden about any other girl, and knowing Matty feels the same—I mean, I can't untangle how I feel about each of them from how I feel about the other. Not that I'm mixing them up, I don't mean that, but I mean... I don't want her *or* him, I want her *and* him.

And I don't just want them, I *love* them.

Like, I'm pretty damn sure it's the forever kind.

So this business of her thinking she's not going to live to see her

birthday? Oh, *hell* to the *no.* First of all, that's bullshit and I don't care
what's happened in her family. Second, like Matty had said, time is
gonna prove it's bullshit, so we just gotta wait it out a few more
weeks. And third, like I'm saying right now, once that happens, we
need to celebrate and move the fuck forward. Help her see that she's
done some amazing things for twenty-five years, but that she can
make a whole new list of amazing things to do for the next twenty-
five, and the next after that, and maybe even the next after *that.*

And hopefully, if we play our cards right, she'll be doing all
those amazing things with us.

Because yeah, that's the thing, I *will* get over this stuff inside
me for Matt in trade for forever or however many years of it we
get, and I'll be thankful for it.

Before Eden, I always figured we'd eventually find other
people and build separate lives, and I wasn't really in a hurry to,
you know? But how perfect is it that the girl it turns out we both
want to build those lives with is the *same* girl, so we can just... you
know, keep on keeping on?

Keep on, but become better, too?

Because Eden does that for us. Matty and I aren't perfect by a
long shot, but we're good together, and we're better than good
with Eden in the mix, you know? She really does round us out,
balance us and push us and inspire the shit out of us, and now that
we've found her, I don't want to give her up any more than I
do him.

And as long as we can keep making this threesome thing
work? I won't *have* to give him up, maybe ever... even if I also
don't actually get to have him the way I want, maybe ever.

Probably ever.

Okay, fuck. I need to just face facts...

Ever, full stop.

Matt doesn't want me that way and never will.

All of a sudden he snaps his fingers in front of my face, startling me right out of my personal pity party and right back to the here and now.

"Johnny, Jesus, what's up with you?" he asks, his brows crinkled together. "Why'd you get so quiet?"

"What's up with me? What's up with *you*? What are we doing up here? Why were you getting so weird downstairs? Why wouldn't you tell me if you had a fucking brain tumor?"

He rolls his eyes, which I can actually see him do now, because we're in some cramped-ass storage room with old equipment and dusty-ass extra mattresses for the crash beds and a full wall of windows, and the streetlights are almost at eye-level here.

"I don't have a brain tumor, why do you keep saying that?"

"Why are you shaking?" I ask to avoid answering.

Well, and also because he *is*, what the fuck? It's the opposite of cold in here.

"I'm not shaking," Matt flat-out lies, tucking his shaking hands in his pockets.

Then pulling them back out.

Then putting them behind his back.

Then crossing his arms over his chest and tucking them under his armpits.

Then—

"Jesus, Matty," I snap, grabbing them and holding them in mine because he's being ridiculous and they *are* shaking. "You are freaking me the fuck out, and if you need a kidney or something, just fucking say so."

But he doesn't.

He holds my hands right back, but tighter, and then leans right into me and *kisses* me.

Matty's kissing me.

Matt's...

I...

For a second, I'm blinded by that shaft of golden light and all the choir-of-angels bullshit, and I can't move. Then he releases the death grip he's got on my hands and replaces it with a death grip on my hips, shoving me back against one of those equipment lockers and pinning me there—all hot mouth and aggressive tongue and get-my-dick-hard urgency—and I get it together fast.

Matty's fucking *kissing* me, and even if this all just ends up being his way of telling me he needs that kidney after all, I'm not going to waste a single second of it.

I grab him right back, one hand on his ass and the other locked around the back of his skull to hold us together, and I fucking *devour* him.

Drink him in like a starving man.

Revel in the fucking moment. Bask in it. *Savor* it.

I've wanted this for so long it's almost making me dizzy, finally getting to touch him.

Taste him.

Feel his hands on me—strong and demanding and insistent as fuck, as if against all odds, he's desperate for it, too.

That kiss goes on for fucking *ever*, and hand to God, I'm so lost in him that I'm not sure I'd even notice if the bunker lights and bell went off. Matty's grinding against me, taking my mouth like he owns it—his cock just as hard as mine—and fuck if the way he's working me over isn't going to make me shoot right here in my pants.

Especially when he finally rips his mouth off mine and yanks my head back, sucking on my neck as he ruts against me.

I groan, tightening my grip on him.

Jesus, I want this. Want him so bad I'm crazy with it. And Matty? He's gasping, shaking, pressing that hot mouth against me over and over, like he wants to brand me.

I'm so far gone in the moment it takes me a minute to figure out he's also talking.

"You don't hate me?" he mumbles against my fevered skin. "This... this okay, Johnny? You don't hate me?"

What the fuck?

I push him away, which my dick doesn't like one bit, and repeat it out loud. "What the fuck, Matty? Hate you? How could I hate you? I fucking *love* you."

He stares at me, lips swollen and pupils blown and whisker burn already pinking him up, and I want to fucking pinch myself. I want to dive right back into what we were just doing. I want him to fucking *say* something, because of course I know he knows I love him, but not sure if he knew I *loved* him, too, if you know what I mean.

But Jesus, I do. I really do.

He's still staring at me, somber and serious like he wasn't just trying to suck my face off, and finally I see him swallow, and his voice all gritty and tight, he tells me—

"Johnny, I think I'm gay."

I blink.

Then I look down at where his dick is still trying to rip its way out of his shorts to make friends with mine, and I snicker.

He punches me in the shoulder, *hard.* "Johnny, I'm serious."

"You're not gay, bro," I tell him, because hello, Eden. Bi for the win, yo. But before I can get that part out, he grabs my cock and squeezes it, making my entire world shut down as I lurch into him and send us both tumbling down onto one of those dusty-ass old mattresses that should've been thrown out, not stored up here like the health hazard they are.

I instantly start coughing like a maniac because I'm seriously choking to death on the clouds of dust that engulf us, but air? Lungs? Both are secondary, because even while I'm asphyxiating here, Matty keeps hold of my dick and rolls with me so we land together.

And I shit you not, I will gladly choke to death right here and now if it means he keeps touching me like this.

Hands all over me like he can't get enough.

Rolling me under him because he's always been a bossy fuck in the bedroom and guess suddenly wanting some D doesn't change that, despite the fact that I've got three inches and about twenty pounds on him and could pin and hold him easily if I wanted to.

Well, okay, maybe not *easily*, but just sayin'.

I don't want to, though. Matt can fucking *own* me for all I care. He can have any fucking thing he wants right now, because now he's yelling at me, grinding down on me again, turning me so far past on that I'm going to fucking burst as he tries to convince me of something that he should know me well enough to figure out that I am one hundred percent okay with.

One hundred and *ten* percent.

A million percent.

"I *am* gay, Johnny," he says, using that gimpy cast-less arm to trap my wrists over my head like he thinks I'm actually going to try to get away. His left hand fumbles between us, on my dick, on his dick, working them together right through our fucking shorts as he pants out his words in my face. "I fucking *want* you right now. Don't... don't want to ruin us, but Jesus, bro, I can't stop thinking about it. Can't stop imagining this shit. I want... want... *Johnny, fuck.*"

Got my legs around him and flipped him—thank you, four years of high-school wrestling.

I grin down at him. "Dude, I'm all yours," I tell him, doing him a solid and pulling his dick out just to be clear.

And *fuck*, do I ever love his dick. Right now it's practically combusting in my hand, thick and throbbing and with that fat pink head fully exposed, jutting out of his foreskin and pouring out precum like a fucking fire hydrant with its cap off.

I start stroking him off, and he practically comes apart.

"Johnny, *Jesus*, I... fuck... *fuck.*"

He's panting, thrusting into my hand and clawing at the mattress and thrashing about underneath me, and it's like riding a bucking bronco. If I had any patience whatsoever I'd pause and get our clothes off and ride him for real. Or flip him over and top the shit out of him. Or take him in my mouth like I've been wanting to since fucking forev—

"I... I talked to Asher," he grits out, hands digging into my thighs as he drives that gorgeous cock through my fist.

I've got my hand on his cock and he's talking about the new guy?

"Fuck Asher," I tell him sincerely, my hand going still.

Why the fuck is he talking about Asher?

"Fuck Asher?" he repeats, getting an evil glint in his eye that makes me want to sit up and beg. "I don't want to fuck *Asher*."

My mouth goes dry. Matty wants—

He uses my moment of inattention to flip me back over and reverse our positions, the little shit. And how he got my shorts down with that move I do not know, but skin-to-skin frottage?

I... can't... see straight.

"Nnnnnnngh," is all I manage, arching up against him and not minding one single bit that he's got my wrists pinned again like the bossy fuck he is.

"I... don't... want... to... fuck... Asher," he repeats, rocking against me. Mouth on my throat again. All that hard muscle and aggressive power grinding me into the mattress until I can't think and don't want to, I just want *this*.

Forever, this.

Although oh fucking *God*, right now? I also want to come.

Desperately.

"Want to... want to... want to fuck *you*," Matty's going on, like he needs to convince me. "Love *you*. Love you, *too*, Johnny. I need... I need... need—"

"Matty," I gasp, bucking up against him when those words send me right to the edge. "Fuck, *fuck. Matty*."

I jerk one hand out of his grasp—thank you, gimpy right arm of his—and wedge it between us, wrapping it around our dicks as he thrusts against me, and that's it. My whole world explodes.

"*Fuck*," he growls, burying his face against the side of my neck. "Johnny… oh *fuck*."

He shudders on top of me, heat spilling between us as the nuclear fusion lightning strike of my orgasm locks me in its grip.

"*Jesus*," I gasp, every muscle in my body seizing up as I come and come and *come*, shaking underneath him. "*Matt*."

It's endless.

It's hot as fuck.

It's *Matt*, and he's coming, too, still rutting on top of me as he grinds out every drop, pleasure-overloading my sensitized dick as he does his best to crush me into the mattress, still saying all these things that I never fucking believed I'd hear from him.

He wants me.

He *loves* me.

He's just rocked my fucking world, and the only thing keeping me from wanting to die happy right here and now is that promise he sort of made when we were in the middle of it.

Matty wants to fuck me, and the truth is, I've never bottomed before, but for him?

Anything.

Any fucking thing at all.

And the way things are going, looks like that anything might just turn out to be *every*thing, and everything… well, that's one of those words like *forever*, you know? One of those words I've started thinking a lot about ever since meeting Eden.

Those words that only sound right when they include Matt, too.

20

EDEN

"Mrs. Blumenhall's hair looks lovely, Eden," Janet, another CNA says as I pass her on my way out to the nursing home's deserted balcony.

"Thanks," I say, grinning at her. "We decided to try and recreate the hairstyle from her wedding photo."

Janet winks. "You ever get tired of this career, you've got it made as a hairdresser, then."

I laugh, but it's bittersweet, and once the sliding doors close behind me, I lean against the balcony's rail and sigh. I've got a fifteen-minute break from my "career" as a CNA, and while a part of me loves being able to put a smile on someone like Mrs. Blumenhall's face—and I know that caring for her basic needs *does* matter—another part of me is full of a growing dissatisfaction with how little I'm really doing as a CNA.

Nursing school.

My twenty-fifth birthday is barreling down on me, and yet I can't stop thinking about it. Maybe it's the boys. Being with Johnny and Matt has made me feel so many things, and I'd be lying if I said a lot of those things didn't include yearning for a future I always thought I didn't have.

A future I *still* think I don't have.

The truth is, I'm scared. I want it so bad now—want to stay alive and have them both and become a nurse and start a whole new bucket list—but every time I try to look at it objectively, to set my fears aside and see if I can really let myself believe that following in my mother's footsteps *isn't* my fate, despite generations of proof otherwise, I get terrified for a whole new set of reasons.

We agreed I'd live with them until Matt got his cast off. Well, now it's off, and no one's mentioned anything about me leaving... but that still doesn't mean they want me to stay *forever*.

And if they did, because oh, the way they treat me—no one's ever said the words, but I've never felt so loved—how would that work out anyway? In the real world, long-term, three people can't just... just... shack up, right? I've never heard of it, anyway, and I'm pretty sure doing it would mean getting stuck with all sorts of nasty labels.

And even if we managed to do all of that... would it really be fair to them? Johnny's in love with Matt, and hopefully, one day he'll have the guts to tell him. Because Matt? I think it's there, too. I get that he has a whole bunch of stuff in his head that he probably still has to work out, but he's been opening up so beautifully with his dad over the past month, and he and Johnny are so close, I really do think he'll open his eyes to what's right in front of him, eventually.

But if I'm there? Maybe not.

Maybe I *would* mess it up for the two of them, the way I'd been afraid of in the beginning.

A warm breeze ruffles my hair as I stare out at the pretty landscaping around the nursing home, giving me a slight respite from the late-summer humidity, and I don't even realize I have my phone in my hand until I'm already dialing. It's instinct I guess, seeking comfort from the one constant in my life, and even though I haven't even taken a moment to calculate the time-zone difference and figure out if she might be available, my Auntie Maria answers on the first ring.

"Eden, my sugar," she gushes, just as happy to hear from me as always. "You've made my day!"

I laugh, because she's silly and she always says that, but I have to admit it both warms my heart and lifts my spirits... and isn't that really why I called?

"How are you, Auntie?" I ask, already smiling.

"How am *I*? I think the question is how are *you*. Last I heard you were shacked up with two hot firefighters while apartment hunting. Please tell me you managed to heat things up while you were there."

I blush from head to toe, even though I'm alone, because... *yes.* Oh, Lord, a thousand times yes. I clear my throat, not quite ready to admit that, though... or that I'm *still* "shacking up" with them.

Instead, I go for what I know will be an instant distraction—

"I was thinking of applying to nursing school," I blurt out. And it's not a lie, I've thought about it off and on for years, but actually saying the words out loud? Suddenly, it makes me want it in a whole new way. It makes it feel possible, as if just giving voice to it has power, despite the destiny awaiting me.

"Oh, honey!" Maria says excitedly. "Oh, *yes.* How many times have I urged you to do that? Please tell me you're doing more than just thinking about it! Just put in the application, baby girl, take the first step!"

The cascade of encouragement from her sparks a familiar pang in my chest. She really has been encouraging me to do it for a long time, and why wouldn't she? I've never told Maria about my fate. Of *course* I haven't. I've never told *any*one other than the boys, because... well, because it sounds crazy.

This time, though—for the first time—as she bubbles over with excitement with all the shiny possibilities for my future, I feel something new, too. The pang is still there, but there's also something else. Something that has Matt's stubbornness and

Johnny's enthusiasm and a little bit of fierceness that I'm shocked to realize is all me.

I *want* this, and I want *them*, and with less than a month left before my birthday, I want to find a way.

Make a way.

Believe there *can* be a way.

Maybe… maybe *that's* why I called my auntie.

"You know I'm a thousand percent on board with this, sweetheart," she's saying enthusiastically. "And if you need any help with the tuition—"

"No, no," I cut her off, laughing. "I haven't applied yet!"

"Well, get on that, girl! They'll take you. They'd be stupid not to. But tell me, why the sudden change of heart? I've been on you for years about this, honey. What happened?"

"I… I just…"

I turn my back to the railing I've been leaning against, fanning my face as I get all flustered thinking about how to answer that question.

What happened? Johnny and Matt happened.

Janet sees me from inside and gives a friendly wave, then taps her watch. I nod. I've got to go back on shift in a couple of minutes.

"Eden?" Maria pushes me, laughter in her voice. "Stumbling around your answer like that makes me hope that 'what happened' includes a new man."

"You've got a one-track mind, Auntie," I tell her, laughing.

"Mm-hmm," she agrees, not even trying to deny it. "But I still think I'm right."

I cover my face, knowing for sure I'd be busted if this were a video call. "It's just, um, some… some friends. They inspired me to dream bigger, I guess."

"Ooooh, I like these friends," Maria says. She waits a beat, and I can hear it coming in her voice— *"Just* friends? A particular friend, perhaps? A *male* friend?"

I laugh self-consciously, and I don't know how she does it, but somehow she interprets that sound for the admission it is.

"Oh, honey!" she practically squeals. "Tell me about him! *Please* tell me it's one of those hot firefighters."

"Um—"

"Which one? What were their names?"

"Johnny," I say, smiling as I wrap my free arm around my waist in a happy self-hug. "And Matt."

God, those boys get to me, even when they're not around. Just thinking about them does all sorts of things inside me, and I see Janet raising her eyebrows at me through the glass door and miming something about the too-wide smile on my face. I bite my lip and shake my head at her, turning away again so I don't end up having to explain—or really, *dodge*—more than one person on this topic today.

On the other end of the line, Maria is quiet.

Too *quiet*.

Uh-oh. She's not a quiet person... not unless her brain is plotting something. Twisting and turning the pieces of some puzzle again to come up with an answer that usually means trouble for me.

"Maria..." I start, knowing I'm going to need to head her off at the pass even though I'm not sure what on earth I could possibly have said to give myself away.

"Don't you 'Maria' me," she says. "Now tell me what's really going on."

I swallow. Sure, she's always pushing me to live a little and go be adventurous with men, but I'm pretty sure what I've done with the two of them goes past adventurous and all the way to... to... well, to addicting, at least for me.

All the way to *needing*.

All the way to love.

My hand trembles against my phone. That's probably not the word other people would use, though.

"What makes you think anything's going on?" I ask, although why I'm even bothering, I'm not sure. She may not have been born a mother, but Maria definitely has that magical maternal super-power of seeing right through bullshit and calling me on it.

She laughs, and I can picture her shaking her head as she casts her eyes up to the heavens. "Oh, sweetheart. *Something's* going on. Just saying those two boys' names practically made you salivate, and I don't care how good the eye candy is, your mouth doesn't water like *that* unless you've also had a taste. Which one, honey? Spill."

"I... I've got to go back on shift," I say, suddenly sweating.

"Don't you try to dodge me," she says mock-sternly. "Why on earth are you acting like I'll judge you? I think it's fantastic. I mean, unless..." she suddenly pauses, and my heart rate skyrockets.

"Unless what?" I whisper, fearing that she'll tell me that the one thing she *will* judge me for, and judge me harshly, is exactly what I've done.

"Unless one of them is married, Eden? You didn't mention that. Or in a relationship? That's... oh, honey, no matter how tempting they are, that's not going to end well."

I shake my head even though she can't see me and open my mouth to deny it, but then I snap it closed again, because it skirts close to what I was just worrying about, doesn't it? About whether me being in the middle will prevent them from ever figuring out how they feel about each other?

Maria sighs, and the disappointment in that sound stabs me in the heart. "Oh, Eden—"

"*No,*" I blurt, because they *can* still find each other after I'm gone, and I wouldn't do what Maria's accusing me of. Not on purpose, anyway. "No," I repeat. "Neither one of them was seeing anyone else before me."

Silence.

And then—

"*Neither* one of them?"

I... what? Oh, dammit. Dammit! Did I really say that? But she can't assume that means what it means, can she?

"Um, I just meant—"

Maria cuts me off. "Eden Eleanor Evans, are you sleeping with *both* of them?"

"I, well, the thing is—"

"Eden!" And now Maria is laughing so hard I can barely understand the words. "Oh my God, girl, I've been telling you to have some fun for *years*. When you finally listen to me, you go all in, don't you?"

I'm blushing again, and I hear the glass door slide open behind me.

Janet's voice—

"I'm sorry, Eden, but we really do need you back on the floor. It's time for Mr. Sanjay's bath."

I turn and nod, and thankfully she closes the door so I can have one last second of privacy to end my call.

"I've got to go, Auntie, *really*."

"Oh, I bet you do," she says, sounding gleeful. "Tell me, sugar, both of them... at the same *time*?"

"Um—"

"Oh, girl," she says, laughing again. "I approve. I *definitely* approve."

"You do?"

"Of course I do. Get it, honey. You deserve all the love you can get, and fuck anyone who wants to judge you for it. You do you, isn't that what I go to work for every day? Your right to live your life the way that fits you best?"

"I think it might be illegal," I whisper into the phone, blushing so hard I feel like my face might burst into flames. "You know, to... to be with... two men at once?"

Maria makes a rude sound that has me laughing. "That's not illegal, that's every woman's fantasy. And Eden?"

"Yes?"

My heart is pounding. *Pounding.* Somehow, I didn't know how badly I wanted her approval until I got it.

"I know you, honey," Maria says, her voice softening. "So I'm guessing since you actually let yourself go there, it *is* more than just a hot threesome... and when it comes to the rest? The part where the law won't let you make that kind of arrangement official if it ever gets that serious between the three of you?"

I nod, my throat closing up tight.

Thankfully, she doesn't wait for an answer she can actually hear.

"Just remember that love is love, and *that's* something I fight for every day, too. Other people don't need to understand it or even approve of it, because life is just too damn short not to love who you love if you get the chance."

And I *know* she's thinking of my parents, I just know it. They weren't together long, not when you compare it to the lifetime they expected to have together, but from everything I've heard, they were happy. *Really* happy. And you know what? It looks like that's another fate I inherited.

"Promise me you won't give this up if it's working for you, okay?" Maria pushes me. "Just hold on tight. Promise me."

"Okay," I say, wiping at my cheeks. I'm not sure where the tears came from, but despite them, my heart feels lighter, not heavier. "I do promise, Auntie. I'm going to hold on tight for... for as long as I can."

For the rest of my life.

And you know what? Even though a part of me knows that "the rest of my life" won't be long at all, that other part—that stubborn, enthusiastic, fierce part that reared its head earlier—that's in me now, too.

And *that* part?

That part wants to fight, just like my Auntie Maria.

That part is in love, and love *is* worth fighting for, and whether it's just for a few more weeks or for a heck of a lot longer, I'm not going to let myself take that for granted... or let go of it quite so easily.

That part has me pulling up nursing school applications once I'm off shift.

And even though it scares the heck out of me, I even start filling them out.

21

MATT

atching Johnny restlessly fidget around the living room is like trying to keep track of a living, breathing Energizer Bunny. When the man gets tired, he gets *more* wired. But me? After the week we've just had at the firehouse, I'm so damn happy to be home I don't want to even think about moving right now. In fact, with the A/C blasting and a cold beer in my hand, I'd be happy to stay right here on the couch for the rest of the night.

Being tired doesn't stop me from enjoying the view, though.

"And Chief said he's down with us using the firehouse for the party as long as—what's that look for?" Johnny asks suspiciously, interrupting himself when he catches me looking. He glances down at his bare chest, swiping at it. "Did I spill some beer?"

"Nope," I say, my grin getting even wider.

I've been around Johnny all my damn life, but looking at him with new eyes is... nice.

Stimulating, you might even say.

I raise my beer to my mouth, enjoying the hell out of it as I let my free hand drift down to my lap and just sort of... keep things warm.

"You gonna bounce off the walls all night, or you wanna come over here and take a load off?" I ask him, patting the seat next to me. Also means I take my hand off the growing bulge in my shorts, and… yep, Johnny's eyes zero in on it right away.

And the look that comes over his face? I'm suddenly feeling a hell of a lot more than just *warm*.

"I could… I could sit," Johnny says, scrubbing a hand over his face like he actually thinks that's gonna hide the big-ass smile he's got going on there all of a sudden.

I don't even try to hide mine. I fucking *love* putting that look on his face.

Not gonna lie, part of me is still a little mindblown about the shift in status between me and Johnny, but gotta say, I like the new reality. I like it a *lot*. That shit we did at the firehouse earlier in the week, back before every damn building in the city decided to catch on fire and keep us hopping for the last few days? Hands down, that was hotter than any of the blazes we put out, and as tired as I am, if there's one thing that might inspire me to get my ass off this couch, it's the chance for a repeat.

Or maybe I'll get to have my cake and eat it, too—get that chance and *not* have to get my ass off this couch—given that Johnny makes good on his word and flops down right next to me, gaze playing ping-pong as it bounces between my eyes and my dick and back again.

"So, uh, about Eden's party," he says, like he actually thinks he can play it cool.

I grin, throwing an arm around the back of the couch as I spread my legs a little wider and take another sip of my beer. He's not sitting *right* next to me, but he's not far, either, so that arm I've got casually laid out?

Makes it so I can sort of tease him a little.

Fingers in the back of his hair… back of his neck… under his ear.

Figuring out where the spots are that make him squirm.

"Shit, Matty," he says, his cheeks starting to pink up. He doesn't pull away, though. "You trying to kill me here? We gotta... gotta plan this... this party out. We don't do it before Eden gets home, it won't be a surprise."

"We've got time," I remind him. A few weeks still. I quit with the touches, though, leaning back and nudging his thigh with mine. "Chief's onboard, firehouse is booked, we just gotta invite some people and get music and food set up, yeah?"

"Yeah," he says, sounding hella distracted... maybe because he's still staring at my dick.

And Christ, just him looking at me like that has me fully hard now... which isn't to say that it's not also a little weird to be teasing him like this, because it is.

Truth is, there's still an uncomfortable twinge inside me at just how gay I'm being right now, and why that is when I fucking *want* this, I don't know, but I can't pretend it's not there. Doesn't mean the twinge is gonna win, though. If that guy Asher can be out and proud with this kind of shit, then I can definitely step up... even if I'm still not real clear on how to do the whole love thing the right way when it's with another guy.

In my head, loving Johnny is a mash-up of how I'm used to treating him with how I'd want to treat Eden, plus a whole bunch of new stuff that I'm still sorting out.

One thing I don't have to sort out, though, is just how fully onboard my dick is. It has no problem whatsofuckingever with me suddenly going gay, and when Johnny licks his lips and flicks his eyes up to mine for a minute? Looking turned the fuck on, but also with just a hint of uncertainty underneath? I reach my limit. I put my beer down and reach for him, and he makes the sexiest fucking sound in the back of his throat—low and deep and needy as fuck—when I wrap my hand around his arm and pull him toward me.

Not gonna lie, I love getting with girls; love the feel of someone smaller than me, softer, like Eden. I love the way she fits

261

against me—just the right size to manhandle a little, but with this soft delicacy about her that keeps me aware at all times that she's a treasure. That yeah, we're going to do dirty things, but that I need to—*want* to—take care of her, too.

Her softness makes me want to be gentle, even when I'm rough, if that makes any sense.

But with Johnny? Fuck. He brings out a totally different side of me. Not that I'd ever want to hurt him, that's not what I'm saying, but I also kind of love that I don't really have to be careful, you know?

Johnny's the opposite of delicate, and as I tug him toward me, I pull hard and like knowing that I can. His arms are huge. I'm not small, but I can't even pretend to span his bicep. It's all hot, smooth skin over hard, defined muscle, and you know I'd never want to give up Eden, but just saying, being with a guy—being able to bring a little more force to things—is really doing it for me, too.

And you know what else does it for me? Knowing Johnny wants it. And I know that because he's letting me get away with this shit. If he wasn't into it—well, not saying I couldn't take him if I really tried, because what, I'm going to admit that? But he does have about three inches of height and twenty pounds of solid muscle on me, so yeah, it's pretty clear that him letting me manhandle him like this is a huge, non-verbal *hell yes, I want this, too,* amirite?

"We're really doing this?" he asks as I pull him against me. "We're doing this right now, Matty?"

Pretty sure the answer to that is self-explanatory. Johnny braces himself with a hand on my thigh, right below where my shorts are tenting up like a boss, and his hand is literally less than an inch from the huge, non-verbal *hell yes* that my dick is giving him as it tries to bust its way out. Still, I bite back my knee-jerk impulse to answer him with something on the sarcastic side, because you know what? I totally understand why he needs to hear me say it.

Truth is, I was scared as fuck when I finally got the balls to initiate that shit with him at the station the other day. Taking him upstairs like that? I'd meant to just *talk* to him about things... you know, *feelings*-type things. I was all geared up for it after that come-to-Jesus convo with Asher, had my big coming-out speech planned out about a dozen different ways, but once I was finally alone with him? I just couldn't figure out how to get any of the words out past the scared-as-fuck constriction in my throat.

Guess I'm just better with non-verbals sometimes... and not to be cocky about it, but gotta say, that whole coming out to him thing turned out pretty well, yeah?

"Oh, we're doing this," I tell him now. And then, because just saying it gives me a thrill inside that's got everything and nothing to do with my dick, I say it again: "I *want* to do this, Johnny."

He makes another one of those low groans that are like fucking Viagra for me or something, and I move his hand off my thigh and put it where it belongs, rocking up into his palm.

Which feels *amazing*.

Although when he doesn't waste any time and starts jerking me right through my shorts? *Amazing* immediately updates to amazing 2.0. Amazing on steroids. Amazing maxed out to something I don't even have a word for, because holy *shit*, Johnny handles me practically better than I do myself.

My head falls back against the back of the couch and I hiss through my teeth as he works me over. Not sure how I'm going to slow down the insanely hot rush that already has my balls tighter than a fucking drum, but no way am I coming from a hand job without even getting my shorts down.

Not that I couldn't.

Oh, fucking Christ, the way he's going? I *definitely* could.

Feels so damn good that I'm not even sure I've got it in me to stop him, but maybe I can at least slow us down a little. Draw it out. *Savor* it.

I wrap a hand around the back of his neck to try and get some control back and pull him in close.

"What, no... no romance, bro?" I tease him, already panting as I push my hips up to meet his fist. "You think... think you can just grab my junk without... without sweet talking me first?"

"Oh, I'll show you sweet, Matty," he says with a dirty laugh that is hands down the sexiest fucking sound *ever*.

Oh, shit. Maybe I just have to face the fact that I *am* gonna be done in under five.

Especially when he finally pulls me out of my shorts.

Closes that callused hand around my cock, skin-to-skin.

Tugs on me slow enough to have me cursing, then runs his thumb through my slit until I'm practically crying. And then— Jesus *fuck*, then he goes back to stroking me with a firm hand... fast strokes... fucking *perfectly*, like he somehow knows my cock better than I do.

"Fuck," I hiss, clutching onto him hard as I gasp for breath and pray for the strength to make it last even though I'm kinda having trouble thinking anything at all other than *please, baby Jesus, oh please make me come.*

I need to fucking come.

Guess I did more than just think those words, because Johnny doesn't let up at all, but he suddenly gives me this *look* and says, "Shit, Matty. I can do that. I *want* to."

His voice is kinda broken with lust, but also almost *reverent*, and it makes my heart do a weird-ass barrel roll in my chest, leaving me a whole new kind of breathless.

The thing is, I was joking with that business about "romance" and "sweetness" that I was spouting off a minute ago, but maybe I was also being a little bit real, too. And don't get me wrong, of course I don't *need* Johnny to sweet talk me... but maybe I also wouldn't mind?

And maybe I want to sweet talk him a little, too. I mean, I love joking around with him, always have and always will, but now I just feel... I feel *more*, too.

I *want* more.

I want *this*.

And I want to kiss him again, not just get off with him.

Hold onto him.

Fucking *drown* in him.

I've got a lifetime of feelings for Johnny built up inside me, plus now a whole bunch of new ones that I'm just starting to let loose, and even though a fair share of those new feelings are about how good my dick feels around him, they're not *all* about that. Some of them are about... well, about wanting to take care of him a little, just like I do with Eden. Maybe even about wanting some gentle to go along with all the hot-as-fuck rough stuff.

Feelings about... about treasuring him.

Cherishing him.

Loving him.

He smiles at me—slow and sweet and sexy as hell—and the whole time he's still working my cock. Making me twitch and grab onto him and feel almost desperate with what he's building up inside me. The orgasm that's building, yeah, but also all this other sappy stuff that just gets bigger and bigger every time I look at him.

"Johnny," I gasp out, covering his hand with mine to slow the pace for a sec. "I—"

Fuck it. I'm better with non-verbals.

I twist around to face him, flinging a leg over his thighs and knocking his hand loose from me as I straddle his lap.

He laughs—sounding a little breathless, a whole lot turned the fuck on—and steadies me with his hands. He opens his mouth like he's gonna say something, but then I rock my hips forward and grind us together, and he shuts right up, the most beatific look on his face that I've ever seen.

This is what I want.

I want to put that look on his face. *Always.*

I push my fingers through his short hair, forcing his head back a bit so I can take his mouth the way I've been needing to for *days* now, and... *fuck.* Maybe it's all the cheesy chick-flick feelings he's got stirred up in me, but gotta say, kissing Johnny is... well, it's perfect. There's just no other word.

It slows me down and speeds me up, both at the same time.

He's my roots, but he's also wings.

Kissing him is exactly and nothing like kissing a girl. Lips, mouth, tongue—the fundamentals are the same, and they're hot as hell—but there's not even a second of it that I don't know I'm kissing another man.

And not just any other man, but *this* one.

Mine.

Johnny moans into my mouth, his end-of-day stubble scraping my face. Heating up my skin with a rough friction that's the perfect contrast to how soft his lips are. Wouldn't have expected it, as hard as the rest of him is, but they are—soft and fucking delicious as they open up to me, inviting me inside like he knows I belong there.

And Jesus, the taste of him.

I could *live* on it. I want to just breathe him in—*inhale* him— and I know that sounds gay as fuck, but—

"What?" he asks when I start cracking up and roll off him.

"Nothing," I say, still snickering. Just gotta embrace it though, amirite? Get over the bullshit voice inside me and claim my gay. So I tell him: "Just if you could be in my head right now, Johnny. I'm so, *so* fucking gay, like, when the fuck did that happen?"

He's laughing at me, of course he is, but he's also pulled his cock out of his shorts and is stroking it, so... yeah. *That's* distracting.

I lick my lips, staring at it.

Wanting it.

"Gay, huh?" he says, a hitch in his breath as he twists his palm over the slick head of his cock. His hips jerk a little, breath hissing out of him, and I shit you not, my mouth fucking *waters*.

Hell yeah, I'm gay.

"I blame it on that thing," I tell him, fucking mesmerized as I watch. "It's got superpowers, yeah? One touch and it turned me gay. Mega gay. *Super* gay. The gayest."

"Oh, this thing definitely has superpowers," he says, eyelids dropping low and voice rasping, telling me just how good his hand feels to him. And fuck if I don't want it to be *my* hand. "But you're not gay, bro," he adds, which is just ridiculous enough to trip me up, right when I'm about to reach out and take what I want.

I laugh at his crazy, eyes snapping up to meet his.

"Johnny, I want your cock," I tell him baldly, words that a few months ago I legitimately would never have thought would come out of my mouth. "Can I get any gayer?"

He grins, still stroking.

Still mesmerizing me.

"Eden," he says, which just makes my cock all the harder. "You're into her, too, so you're not gay, you're bi."

"Oh, I'm definitely *into* her," I say, making sure it sounds just as dirty as I mean it. "As often as possible... doesn't mean I don't wanna be into you, too."

"Oh, fuck, Matty," Johnny says, huffing out a breathless laugh as his face flushes with heat and his hand goes still on his cock, squeezing it tight like he's trying not to shoot. "You're... you're making my point for me."

Guess he's right with the bi thing, but I can't focus on that right now. I knock his hand aside and finally take over like I want, and that laugh of his turns into another one of those hot groans I can't get enough of.

"*Fuck*, yeah," I growl, my own cock jerking against my stomach at the feel of him... and fuck if he isn't a little thicker than me—which I guess I sort of knew, but didn't really *know*, you know?

A dick is a dick, yeah? So holding him like this doesn't feel strange... except it kind of does, too. Differences in size and shape and the angle I'm holding him at versus when I've got myself in hand, plus his cock is cut, unlike mine.

Johnny's is also long and fat and hard as steel right now, and finally getting it in my hand? No joke, it threatens to set mine off like a rocket... especially when I see what touching him like this does to him.

"Matty," he says, sounding wrecked as he thrusts up through my fist. "Oh, fuck. *Matty.*"

And that tone in his voice? Suddenly, I'm not worried about whether I'm gay or bi, or about romance or sweetness or any other cheesy crap, I'm just thinking one thing: *how fast can we make this happen*? But then the lock turns in the front door, and we're both suddenly staring at each other like a couple of deer caught in the headlights.

Frozen... for a second.

For *less* than a second.

After which we're moving *fast*.

"Oh shit," Johnny breathes out, shoving my hand aside and stuffing his cock back into his shorts so quick I'm almost worried he might have hurt himself.

Of course, I'm not worrying *too* much, since I'm too damn busy doing the same with mine.

Miraculously, we both manage to tuck ourselves away without injury, and we leap to opposite ends of the couch and slap matching throw pillows over our laps like some kind of synchronized Olympic "it wasn't me" team, just as Eden walks in.

We probably look guilty as hell since we're both trying so damn hard for the exact opposite, amirite? And to be honest, I'm not entirely sure *why* we're acting like guilty teenagers. I mean, it's our own home, yeah? And pretty sure neither one of us is plan-

ning on, you know, hiding this new development from Eden or...
or sneaking around.

I guess it's just that we haven't really mentioned it to her yet,
and it still feels so new between us, and—

Hell, I don't know.

Instinct?

Habit?

Stupidity?

Maybe a little bit of all of the above.

Truth is, we've barely even had a spare second to *breathe* all
week, what with how busy it got at the station and the insane
shifts we both pulled. This right here is as close as we've gotten to
even talking about it between ourselves so far, and somehow it
feels like a really big deal... and also like it's really not a big deal
at all.

Because it's me and Johnny, what's more right than that? We
fit. Always have, always will.

Eden comes in, and she looks gorgeous. Flushed from the
heat outside and sporting a sexy little sundress that begs to be
taken off her—and maybe that's the thing, the reason we're
both suddenly being weird about it. Sure, me and Johnny fit,
but it's not *just* me and Johnny, is it? It's about me and Johnny
and *Eden*, and as much as I want to do this new thing with him,
the thought that it might mess things up with her fucking
kills me.

All of that flashes through my mind in about 0.25 seconds, and
from the look in Eden's eyes, that's about how long it takes her to
take in the sight of us and jump to exactly the right conclusion
about what we'd just been up to.

"Oh, Lord," she says, her eyes lighting up as she slaps a hand
over her mouth and looks back and forth between us. "I... I interrupted, didn't I?"

"What? No," Johnny says, lying like a rug.

I look over at him and snicker. Can't help it. Hair mussed up in back and lips still puffed out and wet. Skin flushed red and guess I marked his neck, too. My boy looks a little wrecked.

He looks like temptation.

Definitely fuckable.

Hot.

No way is Eden gonna buy that "no."

My cock twitches again and I push the throw pillow down against it harder, stifling a groan as I drag my eyes off Johnny and look back at her. She's grinning at me like it's Christmas, and suddenly my cock is twice as hard.

Not gonna lie, I fucked her a *lot* while I was stuck at home in that cast and Johnny was away at work, and being with Johnny the other day? That was hot as hell, too. So yeah, I'm never gonna say no if I get a chance to hit it one-on-one with either one of them, but the three of us together? Sweet baby Jesus, all I'm saying is I must have done *some*thing right, because when it's all three of us, it's like I don't even have to wait for the afterlife for the kind of reward that should only be found in heaven.

"I didn't interrupt anything at all, hm?" Eden asks, putting her purse down on the entry table and slipping her shoes off.

She's got this sexy little smile dancing over her lips, and that tone means my favorite kind of trouble.

She glances up at us. "That's... too bad."

I hear Johnny swallow next to me, but I can't take my eyes off her.

"Too bad, huh?" I say, and—fuck it—I move my hand and let the pillow fall off my lap.

This isn't gonna ruin us. We *fit.*

Eden's eyes go wide as she takes in my erection, and I give her a hot smile. "You know I hate disappointing you, beautiful."

"Oh, Matt," she says, her breath starting to come a little faster. "You never disappoint me."

She's still staring, licking her lips now, and I shit you not, my cock is going for full lift-off. There's a wet spot on my shorts already, right over the head, because Johnny just got me going that fast, and when I grind the heel of my hand against it because I *have* to, Eden's eyes dart up to mine.

She smiles, definitely turned on, but then she flicks her gaze over to Johnny and a look of uncertainty crosses her face. "Do you... do you want me to, um, give you guys some privacy? I can—"

"*No,*" Johnny cuts her off. They do some kind of weird eye contact thing, and then he gets a wicked smile on his face and says, "Now that you're home—"

"I get to watch?" she interrupts him, all breathless and yearning and instantly making it the number one thing on my to-do list.

Put on a gay porn show for our girlfriend? *Fuck* yeah.

"What do you want to see, beautiful?" I ask her, my mind suddenly filled with all sorts of ideas as I stand up and shuck off my shorts and briefs.

Johnny and I had already stripped down to just those when we'd gotten home, because even with the A/C, it's fucking ridiculous out, yeah? End of summer in Boston is God's test for the righteous. But hey, closer to naked is just that much closer to happy, amirite? So guess there's always some glass-half-full if you just take a minute and look for it.

Both Eden and Johnny are staring at me with hungry eyes, and can't say it doesn't feel good. I run my hand down my chest real slow, enjoying putting on a little show, and sure enough, I've got them both breathing hard by the time I make it down past my abs and wrap that hand around my happy stick.

"You wanna see something happen here, Eden?" I ask her, giving it a slow stroke. "You want me to do something with this, baby? Something to Johnny?"

He mutters a quiet "oh fuck" from the couch that's got me throbbing, and Eden licks her lips, nodding as she looks back and forth between us with hungry, horny eyes.

I know my girl's tells. Her nipples are trying to poke two holes in her dress, and that gorgeous chest of hers is rising and falling so fast she's gonna make herself dizzy. She squeezes those pretty thighs of hers together, and I know she wants to touch herself.

I *know* it.

"You're wet now, aren't you?" I say, still stroking.

It's not really a question, but she nods like a good girl anyway, and the way she's so quick to give me what I want in the bedroom is such a fucking turn-on it makes me crazy.

"Johnny, take that dress off her, yeah?" I say, keeping my eyes on her just so I can enjoy the way those words make her start to pant. "If we're going to give her a show, seems fair that we get to enjoy the view, too."

He's already on his feet. Got her in front of him, those big hands of his sliding up her bare thighs and pushing the little skirt up to show off today's scrap of lace. She's so fucking sexy I can't stand it, and by the time Johnny gets her all the way naked, I'm thrusting into my fist hard.

"This working for you, princess?" he asks, towering over her from behind. Hands overflowing with her breasts as he pushes them together and leans down to nip at the long line of her throat. "You gonna watch me and Matty?"

"Yes," she says, all breathless and sexy. "Oh, Lord, yes... *please.*"

"You gonna touch yourself while you watch?" he asks, taking one of her hands in his and pushing it between her legs.

She whimpers, doing just that, and it's all I can do not to cross the space between us and slide into that sweet pussy of hers, right there while she's in his arms.

Eden cranes her head around to look up at him, panting as she fingers herself, and it's like they're having some kind of silent communication on a whole different level. After a minute, she bites that delectable lip of hers and cuts her eyes in my direction. "Johnny, are you two really—"

"Yeah," he says, tilting her head back so he can take her mouth.

Fuck, they're hot together. My dick jerks against my stomach, and I'm almost tempted to tell them to keep going. Just take care of myself while I watch Johnny push her to her knees. I want to see him get that thick cock of his out again. I want to watch as that sweet mouth of hers gets him even harder. I want to see him bend her over the coffee table between us and fuck her the way I can tell she needs.

I'm about to say it, but then Johnny pulls away from her pretty mouth and gives me a look that has mine going dry.

"Go," Eden says, giving him a sexy smile and a little push. "You've wanted this forever."

Johnny's halfway to me when her words register, and my hand goes still on my cock out of sheer surprise.

"What's this now?" I ask, looking between the two of them. "Eden knew that you and I... I mean, are you saying that even before we—"

"Yeah," Johnny says, cutting me off as I stumble over the idea. He's stopped just out of arm's reach, and he gives me a wary look. "She's, uh, she's known for a while now."

Oh, shit. I'm killing the mood, yeah? But I can't stop my mouth, still trying to wrap my head around it.

"A while?" I repeat, feeling... well, not sure what I'm feeling, actually.

I guess the thing is that I thought me and Johnny was sort of *my* idea. I was relieved as all hell that he got on board so fast, but is he actually saying he wanted it before I did?

Or at least, before I let myself *admit* that I did?

He's nodding, and Eden's biting that lip of hers, and both of them are looking at me like they're not sure what to expect from me... which makes three of us.

"How long?" I ask him, although why it matters I'm not sure.

He goes a little pale, and I suddenly realize I'm being a dick. Because it *doesn't* matter, why would it? It just... well, guess it just caught me off guard is all.

I don't like being the one to make him look like that, though, and I'm moving before I even realize it. One arm around his waist and the other pulling his head down to mine, forehead to forehead, so I can look right in his eyes.

"Hey," I say, feeling all sorts of things for him that almost seem too big for words. "That's hot, yeah? You really wanted this? Thought about this? Even before we hooked up at the station?"

"At the station?" Eden whispers, following the words with a sexy little sound that's got my cock reminding me just how ready for action it is right now.

Gonna get some, too... but not yet. Not with my boy still all tense and worried and it being my fault.

Johnny's sort of frozen, but my arms are locked around him and I look into his eyes and wait, because we both know that I'm not going to let it go until he answers me.

"Yeah," he finally says quietly. "I've... I've wanted you for... for a while, Matty."

And now it's my turn to go still. Not gonna say that hearing that from him doesn't turn me on, because it does, but it also does some other things, too.

It warms something inside me... but it hurts a little, too.

This is *Johnny*, and the idea of him having something so big inside him and not feeling like he could share it with me... I don't like that. I don't like that at *all*. And worse? Looking back at what a dick I've been about things, I know it wasn't just about him keeping a secret. It was about me hurting him... and that kills me.

You know what else it kills, though? That twinge about the gay —*bi*, whatever—thing. Fuck that. That's not gonna happen anymore. Not even a little bit.

I squeeze my eyes closed, and—well, not gonna lie, my dick is still hard as fuck, but for a second I'm not thinking about it. Then Eden's running a soft hand over me. Soothing me. Turning me on. I open my eyes and she's doing the same to Johnny, and suddenly—well, I'm a guy, yeah?—other considerations are sort of pushed aside and I'm right back to thinking with my dick.

She comes up on her tiptoes and kisses me, sweet and hot and dirty, her mouth curving into a smile against mine. Then she turns and does the same to Johnny.

"You two... hooked up... at the... the station."

Eden's sort of breathing out the words under her breath, breathing a little harder now as she touches us, and fuck if I can't read her mind. Still got my eyes locked on Johnny, but I can see it out of the corner of my eye—she licks her lips and looks between the two of us, and I can't help grinning.

Yeah, I can read her mind all right... but kinda wish I could *see* into it right now, too, because I have no doubt that I'd get off on whatever she's picturing me and Johnny doing together.

"Dirty girl," I whisper to her, loosening my grip on Johnny and winking at her as I slide the hand I had around his waist onto hers, then down to squeeze her sweet little ass.

She laughs, breathless and low, but doesn't deny it, and I finally feel Johnny relax.

"How long have you wanted Matt, Johnny?" Eden asks him, sounding breathless and horny and like she's on the verge of coming just thinking about it. "Since... since before you met me?"

He nods, and *fuuuuuuuuuuck*. Really? *That's* hot to think about, yeah?

"Since... since you both became firefighters?" she asks, obviously agreeing with me on the hot factor, given how she's practically moaning now.

Johnny nods again, then groans when she shoves his shorts out of the way and gets his cock in her hand. She does the same to me, stroking us both, and I'm groaning right along with him. Pushing into her grip. Feeling a little staggered on the inside, too, though. Johnny's wanted me for six *years*?

No shit?

"Did you want Matt back when you were in high school, Johnny?" Eden asks, panting as she gets us there. "Did you... did you watch him in the locker room? Want to touch him back then? Did you want—"

"Yeah," he grits out, cutting her off. He's got his eyes locked on hers this whole time, and Eden's biting that lip of hers again, clearly turned the fuck on but also doing some more of that serious, silent, eyeball-to-eyeball communication with him.

"I wanted all of it," Johnny says, staring right at her. "Still do."

Then they both smile, and those are some dirty, dirty smiles that make me want to do even dirtier things to both of them. Guess they make Eden feel the same, because suddenly she's sinking to her knees.

Taking him in her mouth while she keeps jerking me with her hand.

Moaning around that fat cock of his and making me just about lose it when she switches and swallows me down, too.

I've still got a hold of Johnny, my hand wrapped around the back of his neck, and I tighten my grip until he looks at me, and fuck if it isn't hot to be this close to him while she takes care of both of us like this.

Something I need to know, though, and I want to *see* his answer, not just hear it. I pin him with my eyes. "How... how long, bro? How long you wanted this?"

Johnny's eyes are glazing over from Eden's attention, but he holds my gaze. "Since forever, Matty."

I swallow. I've been a fucking idiot, then. Why the hell did I waste so much time?

"You ever... ever jerk off thinking of me?" I ask, and now I've got one hand tangled in Eden's hair and the other on his cock while she's back to sucking mine.

I stroke him.

Once.

Twice.

Just giving a demo of what I'm asking about, yeah?

That telltale pink stain spreads across Johnny's cheeks again and he laughs—the low, shaky one that gets me going hard—and tries to look away... but nope. This is *my* show right now. I keep a tight grip on the back of his neck, still stroking, and keep him looking right at me.

Eden rocks back on her heels, letting my dick slide out of her mouth with a wet plop, and looks up at us.

"Oh, please," she says, practically moaning as she looks up at us. "*Please* say yes."

Johnny gets even pinker, giving me my answer, and fuck if that isn't hot to think about.

"Come on now," I say, real quiet-like since we're all three already up close and personal and my mouth is suddenly dry as fuck with *wanting*. "Tell me... tell me about it, bro."

And look at me, suddenly the breathless one.

"Shit, Matty," he whispers, which isn't an answer... but kind of is, too, what with the way his voice came out as pure, unadulterated sex and all. "I—"

"You used to imagine us together?" I push him. "Me right in the other room and you rubbing one out on the other side of the wall? Thinking about... what? The two of us... fucking? Touching each other, like we were today?"

Johnny's breathing hard, Eden panting at our feet, and we're so close I can taste his breath.

So close that my cock is rubbing against his.

So close it's making me crazy. Greedy. I want it *all*.

"You ever... ever think of being down on your knees like Eden is, Johnny? You ever wanted to suck my—"

He moans so loud it shuts me up, squeezing his eyes closed and giving me a tiny nod, and fuck if I don't just about come right there.

"Do it," Eden says breathlessly. "Oh, Lord, Johnny. Come do it."

She's touching herself. I've still got my eyes locked on my boy, but I hear her hand moving, fast and wet between her legs, I hear those gasping breaths of hers that give her away, and fuck if knowing she's watching doesn't ramp me up even higher.

"You wanna suck my cock, Johnny?" I ask him, and I've gotta wrap my hand around it *tight,* just to keep from shooting off as I say it. "Do you want—"

"*Fuck,* yeah," he says, not even letting me finish before he's on his knees.

And then—

Oh fuck oh Christ oh my fucking *God,* Johnny's got my cock in his mouth.

My eyes roll back in my head.

My legs almost give out.

Johnny swallows me down like he *needs* it, and the sight is so fucking hot I almost can't stand it.

"*Shit,* Johnny," I croak, grabbing on for dear life. It's so fucking good that for a moment, the rest of my body ceases to exist. There's just my cock, halfway down his throat, and that hot, wet, *perfect* mouth of his, stretched around it.

Jesus, it looks amazing to see him on my dick like this. Lips spread wide, cheeks hollowed out, eyes glued to mine. I can't fucking *breathe.* Johnny knows exactly what he's doing to me... and fully intends on wrecking me, doesn't he?

And Christ, *yes, wreck me, please.*

I want him to.

I'll thank him after.

I'll promise him my firstborn just for just the possibility of a chance that he might want to do it again.

"Johnny," I grit out, the end rushing at me fast and furious as he goes to work. "Johnny, bro, I'm gonna... you're... oh, *Christ.*"

So good.

So... fucking... *good.*

"You're going to come," Eden whispers, sounding just as wrecked as I feel. "Matt, you're going to come in his mouth, aren't you?"

Oh, fuck, I want to. More than life.

Eden's gasping now as she watches, and I can tell she's getting herself close, too.

"You're... you're going to come right down his throat?" she asks, panting.

Johnny moans around my cock, and I almost do. Is Eden trying to *make* me?

"Please say you're not going to pull out. Say he can... can taste it."

Oh fuck. *Fuck.* I'm panting right along with her. Knees shaking. Fingers digging into Johnny's skull as my balls pull up, heavy and tight.

Eden's killing me. *Johnny's* killing me. And oh my fucking *God*, this is exactly the death I want.

Every day.

Over and over.

I'm in fucking *heaven*.

And then Johnny's hand is on my balls, his touch shooting sweet fire through them.

Priming them.

Getting them ready to blow.

And then he swallows me all the way down—*all* the way—face pressed against me and throat tight around my cock, gagging himself.

"Oh *fuck*," I gasp, seeing stars.

"Let him swallow it," Eden pants, leaning against my thigh and sounding just as wrecked as I feel. "Let him swallow *all* of it."

Johnny pulls off, gasping for breath, then does it again, and I moan like a fucking porn star. He's got one arm locked around my hip, holding me in place, and he keeps taking me deep... sucking me hard... doing some shit with his tongue that's straight-up magic and looking so damn into it that I don't think I'm gonna have a choice.

I can't hold out like this.

I *can't.*

He's sexy as hell, and he's not letting up, not even with Eden egging me on.

Not even when my balls finally clench tight and that sweet fire inside them starts to spread.

Not even when I start to shake, knowing for sure that it's already too late as I try to gasp out a warning anyway.

"So... so fucking *good*, baby. I can't—" *Jesus, did I just call him baby?* "—I can't last... like this... Johnny, fuck fuck fuck *Johnny. I'm gonna... I'm coming. I'm coming, baby, shit shit shit SHIT YESSSSSSSSSSSSSSSSSSSSSSS.*"

Oh, Jesus. Oh my fucking *God.* I come so hard I'm shaking with it. He's got me pinned with relentless eye contact the whole time, making me crazy, and fuck *yes*, he does swallow it. It's sloppy as hell, but he takes as much as he can and just keeps looking up at me like he wants even more. He chokes on some of it and some spills down his chin, but that hot mouth of his just keeps milking me through it like a rockstar, sucking out every drop until it's finally too much for me to take, and my knees really *do* give out.

"Fucking hell, Johnny," I whisper, sinking down to the couch and looking at him with a whole new set of eyes. "That was—"

"So hot," Eden breathes out, finishing for me. "Oh, Lord, Johnny, that was *amazing.*"

Fuck yeah, it was.

He's amazing, and so is she.

"Love your cock, Matty," Johnny says, voice raw. Rasping. *Wrecked.*

Then he gives Eden the tiniest push and she tumbles right onto my lap, her lush ass landing on my spent cock. Pretty sure she already made herself come once, but she spreads her legs for him with a moan, greedy little thing.

"Love this, too," Johnny says, dipping his head to press a hot, sloppy kiss against her wet center.

Our girl starts to tremble, burying her hands in Johnny's thick hair, and I pull her back against me—her back flush with my chest. I fill my hands with her lush breasts and watch Johnny eat her out, and when she starts to moan, I can feel her whole body vibrate in my arms.

"*Johnny*," she gasps, arching up against him, grinding that ass down on me. "Oh, *yes*. Oh, *please*."

God, she's incredible. Uninhibited and beautiful and *ours*.

Johnny has her coming hard in moments with that magic mouth of his, and then he's up on his knees and spreading her thighs even wider, right there on my lap.

"Jesus, Eden," he groans. "Need you."

Made sure a week ago that we're all in the clear for bareback, so he doesn't wait. Just drives that fat cock of his deep into her with one thrust, and the look on his face when he buries himself to the hilt in that sweet, tight pussy of hers has my spent dick doing its damnedest to come back to life.

Can't quite manage it yet, but with the two of them as motivation?

Soon.

Hella soon.

Eden moans, wrapping her legs around Johnny's waist, and I hold her hips steady as Johnny starts to pound into her.

"Please please *please*," she sobs, that pretty, pretty begging of hers that always means she's close.

He's about to make her come *again*.

"Jesus, that's fucking hot, Johnny," I whisper.

He gives me a scorching smile over her head. "Not as hot... as it will be... when I make her... *scream*."

Oh, fuck.

I groan, my recovery time improving by the second. I'm already half-hard again.

Johnny wraps one of those big hands around Eden's thigh,

shifting her leg higher and then holding it up at an angle. He gets one of his feet under him for leverage, and then—

Holy *Christ*, the man can fuck.

"Ohhhhhh," Eden moans, writhing on my lap. She's begging him again in no time. Desperate for it. Panting and clutching Johnny tight, shaking in my arms as he pushes her hard.

Pushes her right up to the edge.

And *Jesus*, does it ever get me going to have him fucking her right between my legs. My hands are full of Eden's lush curves, and fucking hell, the way he's got her going? It's like holding onto a live wire—hot as hell and energizing the fuck out of my cock.

Eden's sweet, soft ass grinds against me over and over as Johnny pistons into her, and her needy cries overlap his ragged, gasping breaths, filling the air around the three of us until it's like *swimming* in sex.

"Johnny… *Johnny…* John—*ohhhhhhhhhhhh.*"

When Eden finally screams for him, I'm hard all over again, and I only get harder as Johnny slams into her again and again, fucking her right through it as she comes.

And then he's coming, too. It's fucking *beautiful*. Hard body taut with ecstasy. Groaning. Grinding against her. Giving her everything he's got and gasping with the aftermath as he finally starts to come down from it.

And me? I'm groaning right along with him, locked and loaded and ready for another round. And you want to know what heaven really is? It's these two. Johnny taking her mouth in a wet, sloppy kiss right in front of me after he comes… Eden's happy sigh as she turns her head and gives me one, too… me pulling Johnny in close so I can kiss him, too… tasting *both* of us on his tongue.

"You done, princess?" Johnny whispers in Eden's ear when he finally pulls out. "'Cause seems like Matty's ready to take you there all over again."

She's boneless. Completely fucked out. But she's ours, and she's fucking *perfect*, so she looks over her shoulder at me—lip caught between her teeth—and asks in that breathy, sexy voice of hers: "Oh, Matt. Could you?"

Johnny knew our girl would be a yes. He's already lifting her off me... turning her around to face me, and oh... *fuck.*

It's so good.

Eden sinks right down onto my cock—tight, hot, and so wet I'm dizzy with it—and with Johnny's hands on her ass, rocking her against me, and her mouth back on mine, tasting like heaven, I know for sure that I'm gonna die happy.

Could I, she asks? For these two? That would be a *hell* to the *yes.*

Anytime.

Anywhere.

Always.

They really *are* my heaven, and all I ask out of life is that I get to hold onto them both, for—

Well, guess *for forever* is the only thing that sounds right there, yeah?

22

JOHNNY

A day off from work, home all day with the two people I'm crazy about? If we weren't all three stuck here waiting for the repair guy to show, and if the A/C wasn't out while the in-house temperature tries to melt my face off, I'd have no complaints. But as it is—

"Ninety-six degrees," I say, tapping the thermostat in disbelief. "Are you fucking kidding me?"

And this is *with* the windows open.

Matty laughs, the fucker, but I notice he doesn't even pretend to try to move. He looks like he's melted right onto the kitchen stool, parked next to one of those open windows with a fan that's as good as useless blowing toward him and Eden.

Well, useless except the way it keeps fucking with the Monopoly money we got laid out, because for real, isn't the heat enough? I gotta be tortured with my least favorite board game of all time, too?

I'd happily take double this heatwave to get out of playing... except of course I can't say that, since Eden's having fun with it and Matty's having even *more* fun, since apparently he likes seeing me suffer.

And okay, maybe I'm not actually down with double the heat, since I'm pretty sure twice the temperature we've got going here would turn the place into a *literal* oven, instead of just this feels-so-close-that-who-gives-a-fuck-about-the-difference business.

Although gotta say, if there's one upside to living in an oven today, it's the view.

Matty's stripped down to just a loose pair of gym shorts that hang low on his hips, right below the cut, and Eden? No bra, loose tank tied up and barely holding her tits in, and shorts so short I'm pretty sure they're illegal. They're both looking flushed and lazy and sexy as hell, so maybe all things considered, I've actually got no complaints after all, you know?

Especially since I'm currently doing pretty good at dodging the next round of Monopoly. Dodging it... and getting inspired about some way funner things we could be doing right now, what with the two of them looking like that and all.

Matty snorts back a laugh, pouring his six millionth glass of lemonade as he shakes his head at me.

"What?" I ask.

He grins. "Stop it."

He hands the glass to Eden, then pours another one and presses it against his face.

We're all so over-hydrated at this point that I'm pretty sure he'd float away if he tried to actually drink it, but can't blame him for trying to get a little relief from the insane heat.

Still—

"*What?*" I say again, bouncing on my toes to see if that'll help turn the breeze from the fan any cooler.

Annnnnnd... that would be a negative.

Matty's laughing at me, so I give up on finding any patch of air that's not combustible and cross my arms in front of my chest, glaring at him.

"Stop *what?*" I ask for the third time. I mean, come on now, if

I'm gonna get called out on something, I've got a right to know the offense, you know?

"You were looking at Eden like she's candy, bro," he finally says, leaning back against the wall like the poster child for temptation.

Jesus, Mary, and Joseph, he is hands down the sexiest man alive... not that I need to stroke his ego with that particular factoid right now.

Instead, I grin, because he's right about the eye candy.

"Look at her," I point out, even though I'd technically been looking at *both* of them that way. "You gonna try and tell me you don't want to peel those shorts off our girl and—"

"Oh, you," Eden cuts in, laughing as she fans herself and turns even pinker. "You know I'd normally agree, but..."

Matty eyes her appreciatively, but then turns back to me with a lazy smile and an entirely too accurate: "It's too damn hot for that shit today, Johnny."

I refuse to admit the truth of that statement.

"When is the repair guy gonna get here again?" I ask instead, sticking the kitchen towel I'm holding under the faucet for the five millionth time and then slinging it around the back of my neck.

Blessed, blessed coolness... all 0.5 seconds of it before the damn thing is right back to room temperature.

Matty rolls his eyes, and Eden giggles.

"Does he ask 'are we there yet' when you guys road trip, too?" Eden asks Matt, the sexy little Judas.

"Endlessly," Matty says dryly, fishing a slice of lemon out of his glass and chucking it at me.

I dodge like a pro, then smack it in midair in the direction of the sink, sinking it in one.

Skills, yo.

I grin, triumphant, and Matty snorts back a laugh at my victory dance. A laugh that I ignore, because I'm gracious like that.

Then of course I fish the lemon wedge out of the sink and put it in the trash can, because I know how particular Matty gets about those things. And *then* I get my neck-towel wet again, because turns out that my dazzling display of athletic skill was actually a bit too much exertion for a nine-thousand-degree day like this.

"Come over here and sit down, Johnny," Matty says, sounding half-asleep from the heat. "And don't think I don't know that you're trying to pretend you didn't just land on my railroad."

I ignore the accusation because he's right, and then wet the towel yet a-fucking-gain, which causes inspiration to strike me.

"Hey, I know," I say. "Let's all go fuck in the shower."

Cool water? Check.

Naked bodies? Check and check.

Passing the time doing something other than dying from heat-stroke or suffering through the never-ending board game from hell? Checkity check check.

Yep, pretty sure I get the award for best idea of the day.

I grin, raising my eyebrows at the two of them.

"And who's going to listen for the doorbell?" Matt asks like the party pooper he's apparently set on being today. "We definitely don't want the repair guy to have to come back tomorrow."

Huh. Good point.

I'm about to suggest doorbell equals the short straw when Eden points to my nemesis, the Monopoly board laid out on the counter between them.

"Is this just your way of trying to avoid declaring bankruptcy?" she asks, giving me a smile far too sweet for someone who apparently lives a secret double life as a closeted board game real estate tycoon.

I grimace, pulling the towel off my neck and covering my face with it. Satan is known by many names—Lucifer, the Devil, some weird, unpronounceable things I vaguely remember from Sunday school... and *that* guy, the inventor of Monopoly.

Seems obvious to me, at least.

I hear Matty laugh. "Johnny's *always* hated this game, Eden. You should have heard some of the crazy shit he'd come up with, trying to wheedle his way out of debt back when we were kids."

"Your mom charged some crazy prices for a night in a hotel, bro," I point out, my voice muffled by the towel. "Just sayin', there should be room for negotiation, you know?"

"But you're the one who suggested we play, Johnny," Eden says, laughing.

I let the towel drop off my face and put it under the faucet again. "Not true," I say, defending myself. "I believe *I* said let's play strip poker."

"Couldn't find the deck of cards," Matty says, which is beside the point.

"And you know, it really wouldn't have lasted long anyway," Eden adds, those gorgeous blue eyes of hers sparkling as she looks between the three of us. "I don't think we have more than a half-dozen pieces of clothing on between us."

She's right, but I still think it would have ended up being a hell of a lot more fun than the torture which is *this* endless slog of a game.

The next time Matty has us go on a spring cleaning kick? I'm totally going to accidentally on purpose put it in the "donate" box. For real, why do we even own it? Because I'm pretty sure I've already used that strategy at least twice in the past. It's like one of those... what are they called? That mythical beast where every time you cut off its head, another two appear?

"I think he's forfeiting," Matty says to Eden, downing his lemonade and then pushing the empty pitcher toward me with a serious dose of puppy eyes.

What, he thinks those are gonna work on me?

...it's like he knows me or something.

"*You're* forfeiting," I say, not worried in the slightest that the comeback makes no sense.

I snatch the pitcher off the counter and open the fridge,

pulling out some more lemons because of course I'm gonna help him out. I'm a sucker for him and he knows it. Besides, neither one of them looks capable of unpeeling themselves from the stools they've melted onto, so *some*one's gotta take care of business, you know?

I'm tempted to spike it, but since it's been too hot to eat all day and is *still* too hot to fuck, the alcohol would probably be less fun than I imagine... or else too much fun, given our empty stomachs.

We are still waiting on the repair guy, after all.

I table the idea and decide to revisit it after he finally shows up and does his thing, assuming that ever happens.

"You can close the fridge door any time now, bro," Matty says from behind me, obviously jealous that I'm actually enjoying a moment's grace.

"I'm looking for the sugar," I lie, leaning in to the tiny patch of frigid air and wishing like hell I could just fold myself up and fit inside the fridge completely.

Eden laughs. "We keep it in the fridge now? Last I checked, the sugar was in the cupboard."

I give up and close the fridge, turning to face her with a grin. "You would know," I say, winking. "Aren't you the chef in the family now? What was *learning to cook*, number sixty or something on your bucket list?"

"Nah," Matty says, giving her a hot look. "Pretty sure sixty was something else."

Eden pinks up at that, so I'm guessing #60 was something fun.

"Cooking was number sixty-six," she says. "And I still can't believe I've actually done it. I've checked every single thing off my bucket list." Her eyes are glowing, and she's smiling with her whole body as she goes on. "It's been in front of me for so many years, and some of those things I really wasn't sure I'd manage. Even though, um, I'm not really... I mean, *mi español todavía está... está...*"

"It's good," I say when she flounders, jumping in before Matty does even though all I really got was the bit where she said something about speaking Spanish. "Doesn't have to be perfect yet, you know? I still say checking off the language one counts, since you've been practicing so much."

"Agreed," Matty says, pulling her in for a quick kiss that makes me rethink the whole "too hot to fuck" thing.

But... no. It really is, dammit.

I finish mixing up the lemonade and pour them each another glass, then go back to the sink for another pointless round of wet-the-towel.

"You know where I want to be right now?" I ask. "Alaska. Give me a glacier, please."

Eden grins. "I've been to Alaska. It's actually really nice in the summer. Not too cold, and the glaciers really are beautiful."

"You've been to Alaska?" Matty asks, downing half his lemonade in one gulp. He must have the bladder of a camel. "*Please* tell us all about the cold parts. In great detail. Along with every other cold place you've ever been to. Iceland, maybe? Antarctica?"

She laughs, shaking her head. "I've never been out of the country, actually, other than a few day trips across the border to Canada, but visiting all fifty states was number twenty-two on my bucket list."

"What else you have on there that we don't know about?" I ask, giving the Monopoly board a side-eye. I'd *much* rather talk about Eden and her list than give the two of them a chance to talk me into another round of that bullshit. "You ever ridden in a hot-air balloon?"

She laughs, nodding. "Yep. Number fifty-two."

"Sang karaoke?" Matt asks, raising his eyebrows.

Eden smiles. "Number seventy."

"How about ride an elephant?" I ask.

"Well, I know she's ridden a mechanical bull," Matty says before she can answer, and of *course* he makes it sound dirty.

Which okay, fine, can't blame him. The image is hot.

Eden presses her glass of lemonade against her forehead, blushing like she knows it, but all she says is: "I've, um, ridden a few things. Number thirty-three for the elephant, number sixty for the bull. I even toured the Grand Canyon in a helicopter, which meant I got to check off both number forty-two and number eleven."

"I should do a bucket list," I say, because hello, who wouldn't want to ride on an elephant? Also because I've got to get my mind off her on that mechanical bull... at least until the repair guys shows up like he said he would five hours ago and cools the house down enough for me to properly fantasize about reenacting her on top of it.

"You *should*," Eden exclaims, her eyes lighting up as she looks at me. "What would you put on it?"

"Season tickets to the Bruins," Matty says, which sounds good to me.

"Riding an elephant," I add, grinning. I eye Matty's glass. Empty again. "And maybe a camel?"

He snorts, shaking his head. "I think they spit."

"And bite," Eden says, wincing.

Matty shudders. "And *smell*."

"Camels don't smell," I say, offended on their behalf. Even though, okay, truth is I have no clue, but come on now, why are they suddenly hating on camels?

Although if I do put it on the list, clearly I should specify a two-hump camel, because my balls would not be happy if I had to perch on top of a bony one-hump for the duration.

Are their humps made of bone?

Are their humps actually their *bladders*?

Would I be riding on a pee-hump?

That... might be gross, actually. Not gonna back down now, though.

"Sign me up," I say in camel-solidarity, determined to love on them regardless of their actual hump status.

"You should *totally* start a bucket list, Johnny," Eden says excitedly. And she obviously really likes the idea, because she actually unfolds herself from her melted puddle and plucks the magnetized notepad and pen that Matty uses for a grocery list off the fridge door, then plops back down at the counter and starts scribbling on it. "What's number one? The camel?"

"*Hell* no," Matty says, grabbing her hand before she can write it. "Something that doesn't involve zoo animals, please."

"It's *my* list, bro," I remind him. "You can start your own."

"You're going to drag us along to all this shit, I already know it, so I think that entitles me to have a say."

"Sorry, Matt, but you're wrong," Eden says, because she's a goddess of truth, wisdom, and beauty. "This is Johnny's list, and he can do whatever he wants to." She swats away Matty's hand and writes *#1 — Ride A Camel* on the page, then grins up at me. "Next?"

Easy. "I want to see the world's largest ball of twine."

Matty rolls his eyes, but you know he wants to, too.

"*And* go to the top of the Statue of Liberty," I tell Eden, pouring myself a glass of lemonade even though I'm pretty sure it's gonna make my tonsils float.

Matty's lips twitch. "You've already been to the top of the Statue of Liberty."

"That doesn't count."

"So what you're saying is, this time you're gonna keep your eyes open?"

I raise an eyebrow, looking carefully between him and Eden, and then down at myself. "Bro, two out of three people in this room have jumped out of a plane, just sayin'."

He snorts, but I ignore it.

"Do you want me to add the season tickets to the Blue Ones?" Eden asks, making me blink.

"To the what?"

Eden bites her lip, looking back and forth between Matty and me. "Um, the... whatever Matt said. The... Brewers? Is that a sportsball team?"

Matty's eyebrows shoot up, and a deep pang of sympathy enshrouds my heart as the yawning abyss of Eden's ignorance becomes clear.

"Dude," I say, shaking my head sadly as my eyes meet Matt's. "This is a problem."

"I mean, if she was *too* perfect, that would be scary, too, yeah?"

Eden smacks Matt's arm, but I dodge like a pro when she tries to do the same to me and snatch up the pen and notepad while I dance out of the way. She laughs, refilling her lemonade glass, and I scribble a few quick items before tossing it back down on the counter.

#4 - Bruins season tickets
#5 - Take Eden to a Bruins game
#6 - Teach Eden the difference between a puck and a ball
#7 - Ride an elephant
#8 - Make Matty ride an elephant... and a camel
#9 - Duck boat!!!

Matty picks up my list, eyes scanning it quickly before he looks up at me. "I'm not riding a damn camel, Johnny," he says, shaking his head like he honestly believes that to be true.

I grin. He's so cute when he's wrong.

He frowns. "I'm *not*."

"Hey, *you're* the one who said Bucket List Rules include you guys doing all this shit *with* me," I remind him.

"I didn't say that," he lies.

"Yes, you did," I say, because he did.

"No, I didn't," he says, because apparently he likes to be wrong.

"*Yes*, you did."

"No, I *didn't*."

"Yes... you *did*, Matty," I say, grinning because first of all, I'm right, and second, we're not playing Monopoly right now, and third, oh, I *am* getting him on that damn camel, and by this point, we both know it.

"No, I—*Jesus*, Johnny," Matty finally says, throwing up his hands and laughing. "There aren't even any camels *in* Boston."

Even if that's true, I already know I've won... and better yet, he knows it, too.

"You guys," Eden says, laughing as she plucks the list out of Matt's hand and looks it over. "What's a duck boat?"

Matt and I share another look, both shaking our heads sadly. This girl really isn't from Boston.

I'm about to explain it to her when the doorbell *finally* rings, and Eden pops right up off her stool with a look of utter relief on her face, untucking her tank top and smoothing it down, as if she thinks that makes her look any less delicious.

Can only help with the repair guy's motivation though, you know? As long as he's into girls, at least.

"I'll get it," she says, already halfway out of the kitchen and sounding just as breathless and excited as she does when we fuck her.

Matty laughs, watching her go. "Want to bet we get good service?"

"Hey, whatever it takes. This heat is fucking *ridiculous*."

"*You're* ridiculous. The duck boat? Seriously?"

I shrug. "We see them all the time. You ever been?"

Matty rolls his eyes. "Of course not, it's a tourist thing."

I shake my head, tapping my finger on the list in an effort to point out just how ignorant our girl is about our hometown. "Eden needs a little Boston in her, you know?"

He looks at me, and then we both snicker, because of course we're both thinking of the same dirty joke.

"How about you?" I ask, looking mine over and already

thinking of some other cool shit to add. "You gonna start a list, Matty?"

He's quiet enough that I look up, and he's got this expression on his face that does weird things to my heart. *Good*-weird things.

Matty shakes his head.

"Why not?" I ask, holding my breath for some reason.

One side of his mouth quirks up in a sexy little half-smile, and he shrugs. "Don't need to, I guess. Already got everything I want, yeah?"

The snarky part of me wants to point out that hello, neither one of us has ever had Bruins season tickets before and there's a *ton* of other cool shit we could all do together, too, but my heart tells that part of me to shut the hell up, because I see what Matty's saying here.

Jeez, he's a cheeseball.

My cheeseball.

"Love you," I mumble, pulling him in to rest my forehead against his, even though it's still too fucking hot for that shit.

"See what I mean?" he says, grinning at me.

And I do. I really do.

Doesn't mean he's gonna get out of riding that camel, though.

23

EDEN

 $\mathcal{M}$ y twenty-fifth birthday is less than three weeks away, but for the first time in my life, I'm barely thinking about it. Not that I don't know it's coming, because of course I do, but I'm just having such a good time with these two that it feels like the weight of my fate has been lifted off me.

"You ready for this, princess?" Johnny asks me excitedly, pulling me against his side with a cheek-splitting grin on his face.

"It's a duck boat, not the second coming," Matt says, rolling his eyes at Johnny as the tour bus pulls up in front of us.

I laugh, feeling almost giddy, because it's so, so obvious that he's having a good time, too, despite the way he's teasing Johnny.

Matt's got a possessive hand resting casually on Johnny's lower back while they bicker, and seeing that gives me all sorts of thrills. They're going to be just fine without me, aren't they?

I push that thought aside when my throat tries to close up, because I am *not* ruining this day, or any part of whatever time I still get with them.

I step away from Johnny for a second, pulling out my phone with a smile and snapping a picture of the two of them together like this, then quickly set it as my lockscreen. *This* makes me happy.

"Oh, come on now," Matt says, reaching out to grab me. "That's not gonna do. It's gotta be all three of us."

"*And* we need the duck boat in the background," Johnny says, maneuvering us all around until we're facing the other way, the duck boat parked behind us like Johnny wanted and me sandwiched between the two of them, as usual.

I've seen the duck boats everywhere since moving here, big hulking machines that are part tour bus, part boat. There's nothing that looks quite like them, but I'm still not sure what to call them.

"*Is* it a boat?" I ask, laughing as Johnny grabs my phone out of my hand and starts snapping selfies. "Or is it actually a bus?"

"Yes!" they both answer at the same time, looking down at me with matching grins.

Oh, Lord. I *love* these boys. It hits me all over again, and without thinking I go up on my toes so I can kiss the smile off Johnny's face, then turn and do the same to Matt.

"Guess doing the duck tour was a pretty good idea, huh, Matty?" Johnny says, winking at Matt over my head as I squeeze both their hands in mine.

"It hasn't even started yet, bro," Matt says, getting that look on his face that I know means he's trying not to give in and laugh.

"So just think how much better it's going to get from here on out," Johnny shoots back, reaching around me to goose Matt's side.

They've got me laughing again, as usual, and I take my phone back from Johnny and turn to an older couple standing next to us, holding it out.

"Would you mind getting a picture of the three of us?" I ask them, because Matt's right, it *would* be nice to have one… and I've seen Johnny's selfies before. They're fun, but generally tend to include someone's chin getting cut off, or extreme close-ups of facial features that are much easier to appreciate when we don't get to see quite so *much* of them, so to speak.

I'm fully expecting the couple in front of us to smile and say yes—they're the same ones who just asked Matt to take a picture for them a few minutes ago, aren't they?—but instead, I just get a couple of hard, disapproving looks followed by a quick, negative jerk of the woman's head.

"I don't think so," she says tightly, turning her back on me as her husband does the same.

My mouth drops open in surprise, and I'm left standing there with my phone out for a second while I recover.

What on earth did I do to offend those two? The boys are still joking with each other and I don't even think they noticed the exchange. I'm certainly not going to let some sour stranger spoil my day, though, so I give up on getting the picture and just decide to forget about it. As long as we don't sit near that couple, we're still guaranteed to have a good time.

"All aboard!" comes the call from the duck boat parked in front of us. "Watch your step, and make sure to fill every seat you can, we've got a busy, busy day ahead of us, folks!"

Before I can dwell on it any longer, we fall in line, climbing up into the boat. The three of us sit together—me right in the middle the way Johnny and Matt seem to like having me—and before I know it I really have forgotten about that brief moment of unpleasantness, swept up in the silliness and excitement radiating off my boys.

"Can't wait to see what all of this looks like while we're floating on the Charles," Johnny says, doing his best to unfold his large frame in the tight seat. He flings an arm around me and uses his other one to make an expansive gesture that I'm guessing is meant to encompass the entire city.

Matty laughs, reaching across me to punch Johnny's shoulder. "Here's my guess: same as it looks every day."

"Nothing is the same when you're in a duck," Johnny insists. "Bet the Pru looks taller."

I giggle and shake my head, leaning back and settling in with a happy exhale. It didn't take much for them to make me feel better, and as the tour gets underway, even Matt can't hide that he's enjoying himself. They both really love this city, and cheesy or not, seeing it this way with the running commentary from the two of them is making me fall in love with it, too.

"See, it *does* look taller," Johnny says as we circle the Prudential Center, pointing up at the sheer, breathtaking height. "One day we'll hit that restaurant at the top, okay? Remind me to add it to my bucket list when we get home."

Johnny's jumped into the idea of having a bucket list with both feet, because of course he has. I'm not sure he knows how to live life any other way. Unlike mine, though, his is full of light-hearted fun without any urgency, and it's kept the three of us hopping for the last week.

"Look at you," I say, leaning into him and stealing another kiss. "You're going to have my one hundred beat in no time."

"Guess you'll have to catch up," he says, winking at me. "Add a few more to yours, you know?"

I press my lips together, holding in a smile. For once, I'm not thinking of how I don't have any time for that. I'm thinking that #101 should be *fall in love…* the thing I was never brave enough to put on there, but that I seem to have managed anyway.

I want to say it to them, but I keep holding back. If I really don't make it past my twenty-fifth, then it still seems like an unnecessary cruelty, and if I *do*—

I clamp down hard on the surge of hope and wanting that blossoms within me. The only way I'm going to manage is just staying present in the present. One day at a time. Enjoy what I've got while I've got it, and *not* get my hopes up for more. Not let myself start daydreaming about a real future with these two, even though that's where my mind drifts more and more often lately.

"So, you've really never eaten at the restaurant up there?" I ask, pointing back at the Pru. "Is it because of the height?"

"Nah," Johnny says, cheeks going a little pink. "I mean, maybe a little. But mostly—"

"Oh, he's been angling to eat at that restaurant for *years*," Matt cuts in, laughing. "Then he sees the prices and we end up going to Outback instead."

"Well, let's definitely put it on your list then," I say. "Life is too short."

The two of them exchange a look over my head, and Matt presses a kiss against my temple without saying anything. For a second, I think I've put a pall over the day, but pretty soon they're laughing and joking again, pointing out all the major landmarks, complete with color commentary as they both snuggle a little closer to me.

My heart leaps, and I rest my head on Matt's shoulder, holding Johnny's hand as the tour circles the Boston Common. Johnny's going on about some trouble he and Matt got into there back when they were in high school, and just when he's got us both laughing, I hear the distinctive sound of a loud scoff.

Neither of the boys seem to have noticed, but I stiffen at the sound, my eyes finding the perpetrator immediately. It's the woman I asked to take our photo. She's sitting a few seats forward, across the aisle, and she gives me a dirty look of disapproval before turning back around to face front.

I shrink backward instinctively, pressing into Matt's side and squeezing Johnny's hand too tightly, and even though I didn't really catch on before, I get it now. It's *us*, that's what I did to offend her. I've gotten so used to being with these two that I forgot how it would look to others.

I guess most people fundamentally understand one level of relationship—the type between one person and another—but seeing me all over Matt and Johnny, and the way they haven't been hiding that *they're* together, too... well, at least Boston is

progressive enough that most people won't act openly homophobic in public anymore, but the same can't be said for whatever
it is that the three of us are doing together.

"Hey, you okay, princess?" Johnny asks, big arm squeezing me
around the shoulders.

"No, she's not," Matt says, tipping my face up to look at him.
"What just happened, beautiful?"

"It's nothing," I say, because in a perfect world, that would
be true.

"Quit lying," Matt says, giving me a small smile. "Is it about
your birthday?"

Oh, Lord, his eyes are so full of real concern that my own start
to sting. I didn't even know whether he or Johnny remembered
what I'd told them about my birthday—about my fate—but for
once, it's not that.

I shake my head. "It's silly," I say, keeping my voice low. as I
dart another glance at the stiff back of the nasty woman up ahead.
I swipe at my cheeks, hating every word as I say it. "I just... maybe
we shouldn't be so open with each other when we're, um, not at
the house? I mean, what we're doing... people aren't exactly going
to think it's... normal."

And if I *do* get more time with them, if I somehow make it past
twenty-five, is that what I'll be consigning myself to? A lifetime of
speaking in hushed whispers when we're out in public? Choosing
which of their hands I get to hold? Pretending my heart doesn't
belong to *both* of them?

"That really what you want?" Matt asks me, looking serious.
"You want 'normal'? You want us to back off and make it seem
like, what, like the three of us are just friends?"

"Fuck that," Johnny says, squeezing me even tighter. "You
know what it's like to keep it buried inside? It's like... like fucking
cancer."

Matt looks up at him sharply and I have to catch my breath at
the fierceness I see there. Over Matt's shoulder, That Woman is

looking back at us again, but this time, I just glare right back at her. She doesn't get to win, and Johnny's right... hiding what we are to each other *does* feel like that.

She huffs out a breath and turns away again.

"I'm sorry," Matt says, looking straight at Johnny. "Shit, Johnny, I did that, didn't I? Made it have to be a secret?"

"Nah," Johnny says, almost squirming in his seat. "It's just—"

"No, it was me," Matt cuts him off. "Jesus, guess my dad really had some balls, didn't he? Living the way he needed to even though I was such an ass." He looks back at me. "Eden, I don't want that either, not ever again. Like Johnny said, fuck normal. This is *our* normal. We're not hurting anybody."

"I figure we're actually *helping* people," Johnny says, grinning again. "You know, like a public service. Who wouldn't want to see a little more love in the world, huh? Especially when it's dressed in one of these sexy sundress things our girl likes to rock."

I can feel myself blushing, but you know what? I can also feel something else. That tight constriction in my chest is easing up, and I know they're right. I *know* it. And whether I only end up getting another few weeks, or a whole lot longer, I'm not going to let someone else's small-minded opinion stop me from being happy every single remaining moment of my life that I've got these two.

That I *love* these two.

"I'm adding something to my bucket list," I say without stopping to think, sitting up a little straighter.

I've already gone and done it, haven't I? But I'm going to stop being scared about it, and about what it might mean, or how long it can last. And if I'm really brave? One of these days I'm even going to write it on The List and make it official.

#101.

I've fallen in love... and I'm going to tell them, too.

They both look at me with expectant smiles, but then the tour takes us into the river, and I miss my chance because we're all laughing as the bus becomes a boat and the cold water splashes up around us, soaking Johnny most of all but getting me and Matt, too.

"This is a good look on you, Eden," Matt says, staring down at my sundress lasciviously. He glances over at Johnny, then reaches out and wipes some of the water off Johnny's face, grinning. "I take back all the shit I gave you about doing the duck boat, bro. Good call. We need to take Eden on one of these every weekend, yeah?"

Johnny shakes his head with mock sorrow. "Sorry, Matty. Got too much else on my list. Topsfield Fair's coming up, and guess what they've got there?"

"No," Matt says, laughing and holding his hands up like he's trying to ward Johnny off.

"What?" I ask, laughing too, because I don't even care what it turns out to be, I already know it will be fun.

"Don't encourage him, beautiful," Matt says, pulling me right up onto his lap as the tour conductor's voice drones on in the background.

Johnny beams at the two of us. "Camels."

And the resigned look on Matt's face at that makes me laugh even harder. Hard enough that I don't even have to stop and think when The Woman looks back again. I just pull Matt's face toward mine and lay one on him. And when I come up for air and he reaches around my shoulder to pull Johnny closer? I kiss Johnny, too, and then—right in front of me—*Matt* kisses Johnny.

Johnny is startled as heck, that's easy to tell, but when they break the kiss, he's also beaming even more brightly than he did about the camels. He and Matt stare at each other for a minute, and then Matt winks.

"Public service, amirite?"

Johnny laughs, and I do, too… but I also can't help it, I take a quick survey of the boat patrons as the boys start arguing about what a camel's hump is made of.

The Woman is still staring at us, still disgusted, and it's not a perfect world, so I catch another couple of judgmental looks, too, although way lower key. But you know what? I also spot a few wide smiles... and a few secretive ones. And everyone else? They're minding their own business, caught up in the tour and their own lives and busy with whatever variation of normal *they're* living in, and that's just fine.

"I love you," I say, interrupting the argument.

They both turn to look at me, and my face has to be bright red, but I say it again anyway, because they make me feel brave.

"I love you. Both of you. I really do."

Johnny's arm is around my shoulders again, and he gives me a squeeze. "Love you, too, princess."

"Ditto," Matt says easily, grinning at us like it's the easiest, most normal thing in the world. "Love you both."

And maybe it really can be that easy.

Maybe it *is*.

24

MATT

I can hear music coming from the other side of the door, and I wipe my palms on the sides of my shorts for the third time, telling myself to hurry up and knock already. I'm being ridiculous, and I know it. First, because I should have just called, and second because here I am, standing on the doorstep of the house I lived in for the first eighteen years of my life, and I'm staring at the front door like it might bite me.

The door is *turquoise*, for Christ's sake. Pretty sure nothing turquoise is allowed to be dangerous, amirite? It's like, a law of the universe.

Mom would have made such a fuss if Dad had painted the door this color back when I was a kid, but gotta admit, I can see how he'd love it. Looks good, too, not really my thing maybe, but it suits him. Suits the house. Makes the whole decor around the porch sort of pop.

And okay, I'm stalling again. I man up and make myself knock, then straighten my shoulders and remind myself that Dad and I are good now.

The music inside gets muted, and a moment later, the door swings open. It's Nick, my dad's… partner? Boyfriend? And to his credit, the shock on his face only lasts for a split second before it turns into a welcoming smile.

"Mateo!" he says, the smile turning sheepish as he quickly adds, "I guess you go by Matt, actually? Sorry, your father always calls you Mateo."

It catches me off guard, and instead of something normal like *hello*, first thing out of my mouth ends up being: "Dad talk about me a lot?"

Nick's eyes soften, and he nods. "All the time, ever since I met him. Come in, come in! He'll be so happy you stopped by."

He steps out of the doorway and motions me inside, and I have a brief twinge of resentment at this man acting like he gets to welcome me into my own home, and then I step over the threshold and realize what a jerk I am. It *was* my home, but I stormed out eight years ago. Nick's making it more than clear that I'm still welcome back, but it's *his* home now. His and Dad's.

"Thanks," I say, shoving my hands in my pockets once I make it inside.

I immediately want to kick myself for not thinking to bring something. A bottle of wine? That scotch Dad always liked? A peace offering? Olive branch? Anything at all to keep my hands occupied?

"Are you—" Nick starts talking at the same time I do.

"Sorry I didn't call first—"

"Oh, nonsense," Nick interrupts, waving his hand. "Let me just go get Santi. He's in the kitchen, making—"

"*Pasteles*," I finish before he can. I can smell them, and even though the house looks hella different inside, that smell is *home*.

Shit. I'm gonna do something embarrassing here, like get all choked up, aren't I?

I cough into my hand, trying to stave it off, and Nick reaches out and squeezes my shoulder with another warm smile. He drops the touch just as quick as he offered it, then he tells me to make myself at home and has mercy, disappearing off to the kitchen and giving me a moment to collect myself.

Maybe I should be planning something to say, but instead, I'm just staring at the floors. Dad redid them. Used to be old carpeting that I'm embarrassed to say I don't even remember the color of— beige or gray, something bland—but now it's gorgeous hardwood floors as far as I can see, broken up with a few brightly colored rugs. Stylish couches, classy wood and metal for the coffee tables and end tables, a gorgeous entertainment center... every single thing looks modern and redone.

I roll back my shoulders a few times, trying to loosen up, and as I stop looking at all the differences I realize how much still feels familiar. The decor may have been updated, but the colors haven't changed. Everything's still washed over in the bright, tropical colors my dad loves—oranges, limes, more turquoise—they all just live on new surfaces. And now that I'm really looking, I still see a few familiar things around the living room, too. Some of the framed photos on the wall are new—Dad and Nick and a few people I don't know—but I recognize most of the others. Me and Johnny, of course, but Dad's still got a bunch of him and Mom up, too. Huh. Still boggles my mind, but I've talked to Mom a few times since we first had Dad and Nick over for dinner, and I guess they *are* still friends.

I was wrong about a lot of things, which doesn't feel great to admit... but also kind of *does*, yeah?

"Mateo!"

My father emerges from the kitchen entryway wearing comfortable-looking light pants, a loose poet shirt, and a smile that stretches from ear to ear. It's... very much a style I would never have pictured my father in, what with the jeans and button-down shirts he was always sporting when I grew up, but wow, he certainly looks great.

He looks happy.

Comfortable in his own skin comes to mind.

He's holding his arms out wide, and I finally get my feet to unglue themselves from those slick new hardwood floors and meet him halfway, right in the middle of the living room. He pulls me in tight, and now that I've seen him a few times—we met for lunch twice after that first dinner and talked on the phone a few other times—I'm almost used to him feeling just that much smaller than I remember.

"You conning Nick into helping you make the *pasteles, papá?*" I ask, pulling back and suddenly feeling at ease.

The turquoise door didn't bite me and there's nothing here that will, either.

It feels good to be back here. Different, but good.

"Pfft," Dad says, waving a hand through the air. "He is too slow, *mijo!* Your mother, she packs *pasteles* so fast, probably better than anyone else I have ever met before. But *this* one," he continues, pointing at Nick with an affectionate smile. "I do not know that he will ever get the hang of it. Maybe you will come into the kitchen and help me, no?"

"Oh hush, Santi," Nick says, walking over to my father and slipping an arm around his waist. He lays a chaste peck on Dad's cheek, then brushes off a bit of *masa* from my father's beard. "You're not putting your son to work the first time he comes over. The food will wait."

"Yes, yes, fine then," Dad says. "We will cook another time."

The smile they share is full of years of history that I missed out on, but then Dad looks my way again and steps away from Nick, a flash of hesitance coming over his face.

Well, shit. That's for me, isn't it?

Here in his own home, and Dad's concerned about how I'm going to react to seeing the two of them together?

I deserve it, I do, but all I can think of is how rattled Eden was the week before when the three of us got a few dirty looks on the duck tour. That sucked, not gonna lie, and the idea that that's me —or that it *was*, at least—sucks even harder. No way do I want to fuck up this brand-new reconciliation with my dad by letting him think I'm still that asshole, especially now that I've pulled my head out of my ass and realized how much I don't care who he's with, as long as he's happy.

Wish everyone felt that way. I can't pretend I'm totally unaffected by some of the reactions we get when Eden, Johnny, and I go out together—it made me crazy to see Eden so shook up on the duck boat—but I sure as hell don't care enough to give up either Eden or Johnny. Still, it gives me some empathy toward Dad's moment of hesitation, yeah?

I wish I could say something to him now, something to make it clear that I really *am* okay with him and Nick being together. More importantly, something to let him know that I finally got it through my thick head that whether I'm okay with it or not, them being together doesn't really have anything to do with me. But I'm not sure what the right words are, so I just hook my thumbs into my belt loops and rock back on my heels and smile at the two of them, trying to put all the happiness I'm feeling lately into the look to maybe get my point across non-verbally.

Guess it works a little, because Nick gives me a smile right back, and after a moment, I see some tension let loose in Dad's shoulders.

"You are good, *mijo?*" he asks, smiling at me. "You look well. You are happy, no?"

"I'm very good," I say, meaning it one hundred percent. "Couldn't be better."

"Ah, this is good. Very good," he says, and then we all three stand there sort of smiling and nodding at each other like a gift shop bobblehead display for a minute. It's like we're all walking on eggshells around each other with this friendly but stilted conversation, and just when I remember that I actually stopped by for a reason, Dad and I talk over each other.

"Hey, Dad, I came over to—"

"So, why are you here, Mateo?"

311

"Don't be rude, Santi," Nick says, laughing as he bumps his hip into Dad's. "Maybe we can offer Mateo—um, Matt, something to drink before we grill him on his intentions?"

Dad rushes over to me and has both my hands in his before Nick even finishes talking. "No, I did not mean it like that, *mijo*," he says, shaking his head. "Of course I am glad to see you here. Very glad. Why ever you are here, you are welcome. I just meant—"

"I know, *papi*," I cut him off, laughing. "It's all good. I was just, uh, in the neighborhood."

Dad's eyebrows go up and his lips twitch like he's gonna laugh, but he lets the white lie slide.

"Oh, well, yes, I am glad you made it out this way then, *mijo*," he says, not calling me on the fact that we live only twenty minutes away and yet I've never managed to be "in the neighborhood" even once over the past eight years. "You know you are welcome here any time. Everything is okay for you, then?"

"Yeah, everything's totally fine," I say, and I can't help but smile big as I think about just how good things actually *are*. "Better than fine, actually. Things are going really good, and that's sort of related to why I'm here. I wanted to drop by and invite you both to a surprise party me and Johnny are throwing in a couple of weeks."

"Oh, a surprise party!" Nick exclaims, beaming at the two of us. "That sounds fun."

"Surprise party?" my father asks, tilting his head to the side. "Who is it a surprise for?"

I grin, kind of loving how it's coming together to pull this thing off. Eden has no clue, far as I can tell.

"You remember Eden, right?" I ask Dad, getting a nod back. "Well, her birthday's coming up."

I give them the details, and Dad's just glowing. Makes me happy to see and also makes me feel a little shitty for all the years I messed this up between us, but I've apologized, right? And now we're here, so time to move forward.

"September twenty-first, that is a Friday night, no?" Dad asks.

"I think so, yeah," I say. "But if you guys already have plans—"

"I'll check our calendar," Nick cuts in, sounding excited as he starts bustling out of the room.

"No, no," my father says, putting a hand on Nick's arm to stop him. He turns to me, still beaming. "The date will be okay for us. We will work it out, no matter what. We will be there, and you will have to tell your pretty *novia* to save me a dance, no?"

"I'll definitely tell her," I tell him, smiling.

Dad's grin gets even bigger. "Ah, you are not correcting me. The two of you, you are a couple then?"

"Yeah, I mean... well, yes."

We're not a *couple*, because a couple is only two, but I get what he's asking.

For some reason Nick looks surprised at my answer, though. "Oh!" he exclaims, looking from me to my father with a hint of confusion on his face.

"What, *querido*?" Dad asks Nick. "What is the matter? You remember this Eden, of course. She is lovely."

"Of course she is," Nick agrees quickly.

Something's still off with him, though, and I can tell Dad thinks so, too.

"What?" I ask after two beats of silence, looking between the two of them.

Dad shrugs, but guess Nick can tell I'm not gonna let it go, so after a slight hesitation he says, "I just... I guess I just misread things. When we were over, I thought you were together with... with Johnny. As a couple."

I start to grin, but Dad looks horrified.

"No! No no *no*," my father says, waving his hands at Nick urgently as he shoots me an apologetic look. "No, Nick, Johnny is family. He has always been around. Mateo is not... he and Johnny are not... *son comos hermanos, no?*"

Like brothers. I snort back a laugh, but yeah, of course Dad would think that, and obviously he also thinks I'm gonna flip out at being labeled gay, doesn't he? And again, can't blame the guy. It's almost sweet to see him so concerned about Nick scaring me off. Just goes to prove that *I'm* the one who screwed up the relationship between me and my dad. It's clear as day now that my blinders are off that he wants me around, and it feels good.

Great, actually.

Nick's all wide-eyed and stumbling through an apology, so I cut in before things get awkward.

"Actually, things have kinda changed with me and Johnny, Dad. We *are* together now. Not like brothers, but um, you know. Also... together. Same as with Eden. Johnny, *él es mi novio.*"

I grin. Never said it like that. Johnny's my boyfriend.

Definitely weird... and I definitely like it.

Nick's grinning, too, so guess his Spanish is decent, but Dad—

I swallow, my smile starting to slip as Dad stares at me.

"*¿Qué?*" he finally says. "*¿Qué quieres decir?*"

What does he mean, what do I mean? Not sure how I could've said it any clearer, and Christ, Dad's *gay*... I shouldn't have to spell it out for him, yeah? Guess I'm gonna try, though.

"I mean, you know, I'm saying that me and Johnny, we're—"

"*¿Estás bromeando?*" he asks, cutting me off. "This is not a funny joke, Mateo."

My mouth drops open, and truth? I'm a little offended. But okay, okay. He's just had eight years of me mad at him for being gay, guess I can cut him a little slack for not congratulating me right out of the gate. I rub the back of my neck, taking a breath, then try again to explain, pretty proud that I'm keeping an even tone.

"It's *not* a joke," I say. "Why would I joke about something like that, huh? I'm... I'm in love with him. In love with Johnny."

My face flushes with heat as I put it out there like that, but I'm not hiding this, not from my dad of all people... and *Jesus*, not when I can still hear Johnny's voice telling Eden that hiding it felt like cancer.

Like motherfucking *cancer*?

It still kills me.

I won't ever be the one to make either one of them feel like that, even if it takes some getting used to, just flat-out saying shit this way. I wanna take care of them, though. *Both* of them. And part of that is being able to do this whole out and proud thing, amirite? To make sure I'm never the one who makes them feel like there's something to hide here.

Right now, though? The way Dad's staring at me is really putting that to the test. And guess I'm slow on the uptake, because for the life of me, I don't actually get why. I'm still thinking he's being a hypocrite about me and Johnny, at least, until he finally speaks and I realize his flavor of bullshit is the same one we ran into on the duck tour.

"*No*," Dad says, shaking his head as his hand slashes through the air. "No, Mateo. You say you are with Eden, and now you say you are with Johnny. Which is it, *mijo*? It cannot be both. I raised you better than to be doing this."

"Doing what?" I ask, rearing back as if he'd slapped me. "I am with them. *Both* of them. And I'm happy, Dad, we all are. Johnny and Eden are into each other, too. We *love* each other, why are you being like this? Are you just trying to get back at me for how I treated you, back when *you* came out?"

"Of course I am not! But you all three cannot be... this... this way with each other," my father sputters, looking flustered. "*Tres es un problema*. Three is a problem, it is not a relationship. It cannot last."

"Santi," Nick says, putting a hand on my father's arm and shaking his head. "Maybe this isn't our place to—"

Dad ignores him, on a roll. "*No puedes amar a dos personas. No es*

315

posible. No estás en una relación real. Solo dos personas pueden amarse el uno al otro románticamente. Tres personas no pueden. Eso está mal."

Those words feel like a gut-punch, coming from him.

It's impossible to be in love with three people.

It's not a real relationship.

Only two people, not three, can have romantic love for one another.

It's wrong.

It's one thing to blow off some stranger's dirty looks, but gotta be honest, I wasn't even worried about this, not from my father of all people. It blindsides me. He's still going, getting red in the face, but it's getting hard to hear him over the rushing in my ears. I'm hurt, but I'm getting mad, too. Who the hell is *he* to judge who I'm in love with?

"Santi, knock it off," Nick finally interjects sharply. *"Stop."*

Dad's mouth snaps closed at that, and he and I stand there glaring at each other. I'm gonna say something ugly if I open my mouth right now, I know it, and I'm really, really trying not to.

I've said too many ugly things to him already.

A lot of the same ugly things he's just said to me, with a slightly different twist.

He's being bullheaded about something he doesn't understand, and when I come here hoping for some kind of open-armed welcome—a little support, maybe—he hits me with *this* bullshit. It's so unfair that I want to shout, maybe hit something, but the shittiest part?

I can't say a word.

I want to—*badly*—but as mad as I am right now, I'm also just too fucking aware that his ignorance and this whole fight is like looking in the mirror at my own damn self, eight years ago.

Telling him he couldn't love a man, not like that.

That it wouldn't be real.

That it was *wrong*.

I pinch the bridge of my nose, taking a slow breath, but it doesn't help how fucking tight my chest is right now.

"Dad," I start. "Let me just explain—"

He cuts me off with a dismissive noise, throwing his hand up. "There is no explanation. It is simply something that will not work. You cannot—"

"But I *do*," I snap, interrupting him. "I love them. It *does* work."

Fuck. I'm trying to keep my cool, but I'm getting close to a meltdown here.

"Alright," Nick says, still holding onto my dad. "Maybe we can all calm down? If the two of you talk this through, maybe you can—"

"*No,*" my father says, cutting Nick off, too, since apparently he's gotten too pigheaded to let anyone else get a fucking word in edgewise. "This thing you are doing, it is bad, *mijo*. It is a bad idea and bad for… for your hearts. You three are going to hurt one another. You will lose Johnny's friendship. You will hurt this girl. Jealousy will grow between you. You will—"

"Shut *UP.*"

To my shock, he does. I want to keep shouting. Want to tell him that I put the time in to deal with my fucked-up feelings about his relationship. I worked through it. I realized that I was wrong. I apologized. I reached out and brought him back into my life and he has *no right*, after all of that, to say any of this shit to me.

I want him to be there for me, for all three of us, the way I wasn't for him.

But I don't say any of that, because it will come out ugly and twisted, I know it will. Instead, I just leave. And this time, when I slam the door behind me, there's no question that this isn't my home anymore. It hasn't been for a long time, and despite my best efforts, it looks like it never will be again.

This time, I've lost my father for good.

25

JOHNNY

"Sorry, but we are severely short in the grocery department, princess," I inform Eden, plopping down on the couch with the minuscule hoard of alcohol I managed to scrounge up. Not even really sure it counts, since the sum total is half a bottle of cooking sherry that she made us buy for one of her recipes last month and a single, solitary, warm beer that was in the back of the soup cupboard for some reason.

"Does this mean we don't have to watch the show?" she asks, looking entirely too hopeful.

"Oh, hell no," I say, putting an arm around her and tugging her close. "For real, Eden, how did you manage to make it this far in life without any *Walking Dead*?"

She shudders, and I grin. This is gonna be fun, even if the drinking game I'd originally proposed looks like it may end up falling a bit short of my original intentions.

"So remember," I tell her. "You gotta drink anytime someone takes a headshot at a walker—"

"How will I know which ones are walkers?"

I ignore that question and continue, since hello, she'll know.

"And anytime Rick yells out '*Carl!*' you gotta—"

"Which one is Rick again?"

I sigh and grab the remote, clicking it to restart the episode and then zooming ahead a bit until I can pause and show her.

"That guy."

Eden squeals and hides her head against my chest.

"Oh my God, that's disgusting," she says, all muffled-like. "How about we do another season of *Orange Is the New Black* instead? Or one of the superhero ones?"

I groan, letting my head flop back against the couch. Although okay, not gonna lie, I did like *The Flash* when she made me watch it. She pops her head back up and looks at me like she's been practicing Matty's puppy eyes or something, and fuck if I can't already tell that I'm going to cave... not without a fight, though.

Or at least, you know, a negotiation.

"Okay," I say. "How about this. You pick the show, I pick the game."

She laughs. "Johnny, you know you're predictable, right?"

I'm about to defend myself, but then she's gotta go and prove it.

"No matter what show I pick, you're going to find a way to turn watching it into the equivalent of strip poker, aren't you?"

"No," I lie, picking her up and moving her across the couch so that there's a good foot of empty space between us. I point to it as Exhibit A. "A little space, please? I'd like to point out that you're the one all over *me*. Why you always gotta make everything about sex, Eden? Maybe I just want to enjoy a quiet evening of entertainment together, you know?"

Her eyes are sparkling as she tries hard not to laugh, and she goes, "Mmhmm. Okay, *Eugene*."

I gasp. "Oh, no, you did *not* just call me that, Eden Evans."

She grins, looking proud of herself, so I reach over and grab her leg—bare and long and sexy as hell under another one of the short, flowery dresses she has about a billion of—and yank her toward me.

"You wanna rethink that, princess?" I ask, getting her flat on her back and underneath me before she can stop laughing. "I can think of some other things you can call me."

She's still giggling, and I was just teasing, but now that I'm laid out on top of her, I kinda don't want to get off again.

"I know," I say, because I'm fucking brilliant at coming up with ways to pass the time, if I do say so myself. "How about we play how many times can I make you come before Matty gets home?"

She laughs again, but I know her well enough to see it. Pupils already widening, that pretty flush to her cheeks... oh yeah, she's definitely down with the idea.

"I... I knew you'd make this about getting naked," she says, starting to go all breathless like she does when she's horny.

I grin, because she's right, but then I grin even bigger, because there are ways to get what I want and still not have to *admit* that she's right.

"Who said anything about naked, princess? Maybe I'm gonna see how many times I can make you come with your clothes *on*."

She laughs like she thinks I'm kidding, but what's life without a little challenge? Besides, just because I said she could keep them on, doesn't mean I can't still play around underneath them.

Loopholes for the win, yo.

I've got my hand between her legs and pretty sure I'm more than halfway to getting my first win on the board when we hear the lock turn, and if you wanna know why I fucking love Eden— well, maybe not "why," because not like it's the one and only reason, but for sure it's one of THE reasons, you know?—anyway, like I was saying, one of the reasons I adore this girl is what a little freak she is under all that genuine sweetness and her overall air of being such a good person, you know?

Case in point on the freakiness? The minute she hears Matty coming in, does she—

A) Give a sexy little squeaky gasp, like she's suddenly gone shy?

B) Blush and try to sort of hide underneath me?

C) Bite that luscious lip of hers and get one of those "oh, I've been a bad, bad girl" looks on her face?

Hell yeah, she does. In other words, the correct answer is D) All of the above—even though we've all three been going at it like porn stars for what, a couple of months now?—but since she *is* a sexy little freak, my and Matty's sexy little freak, to be precise, the awesome part is that she also gets fifty shades of turned-on-even-*more* by him walking in on us, and without further ado, she comes hard, grinding up against my hand and sounding like that chick in the old eighties movie—you know, the one who faked it in the diner?

So here we are, her all warm and soft and relaxed the way she always gets after round one and me hard and horny as fuck and getting even more turned on than I started with—since now, of course, I'm thinking that round two will include all three of us—but instead of Matty shucking off his clothes like he should and coming over to join us, he just mumbles something that might've been hello and then heads back to his room, barely even looking at us.

"What the fuck?" I say, sitting up and staring after him.

"Is he… is he okay, do you think?" Eden asks, pushing her hair out of her face as she scrambles up to her knees and leans over the back of the couch to look down the hall, too. "Just tired, maybe?"

"No, he's not tired," I say, because why the fuck would he be tired?

He had the whole day off and mentioned doing a few errands —not that I see any grocery bags having come inside with him, thank you very much—but definitely nothing that would tire him out. Besides, if he *was* tired, he'd be compelled to clean something before heading to his room, I know this for a fact.

I frown, considering leaving him alone for a sum total of half a second, then hop to my feet, because let's just be real, that's not gonna happen. Something's wrong or else Matty wouldn't be acting weird, and I'm still a little scarred by that scare he gave me back before he jumped me in the firehouse that first time. You know, the whole withholding-important-brain-tumor-information-from-me thing? I mean, sure, turned out that he didn't have one after all *that* time, thank fuck, but just sayin'... I'm not taking any chances.

"I'm going to get him a cup of hot tea," Eden says, because for one thing, she's almost as much of a nester in her own way as Matty is and seems convinced that all things you might call *cozy* are cure-alls, and for another, even though she's not gonna say it out loud, I know she wants to send me in as like, advance reconnaissance or whatnot. Use my vast knowledge of all things Matty to feel out the terrain before she comes in as reinforcements, you know?

I'm down with that. Actually, I think we make a pretty good team, if you want to know the truth.

So Eden heads off to the kitchen to do her tea thing and I tuck my overly hard dick up into my waistband—wouldn't want it pointing out at Matty like some kind of divining rod when I go check on him and giving him the wrong idea of my intentions, you know?—and then I head back and knock on his bedroom door.

His closed bedroom door.

Closed and *locked*, which I find out when he doesn't answer me immediately and so naturally I try to let myself in.

"Matty, what the fuck?" I say, leaning against the door as visions of kidney transplants dance in my head. "Open up, bro. What's going on? You okay? And shut up before you lie about that because I know you're not, so just get it over with and let me see you already. Seriously, Matty, open the damn door. You know I'm not leaving until you—"

"I *know*," he says, finally opening the damn thing. He gives me a ghost of a smile, but I can see he's trying not to laugh, at least a little. "Of course you're not leaving. Jesus, Johnny, you ever think a locked door might mean something like, I don't know, *privacy, please*, maybe?"

"Uh, no," I say, because hello. No. "Pretty sure it means *I'm freaking out the two people who love me the most in the whole world but thank God I know Johnny won't let me get away with that crap.*"

And Matty actually does laugh at that, which makes me hope that I might get to keep both my kidneys after all... but then not even a full second later, his face sort of crumples like I've only ever seen happen one time before *ever*, and I've got my arms around him before I even know what's happening.

"Matty," I say, holding onto him so tight it's like we're one person. "Jesus, what happened?"

"Nothing," he says, which is so blatantly dumb that I ignore it.

Matty is not a big crier, which is pretty much the understatement of the century, so while the last time he scared me the end result was pretty fucking epic, I can already tell that this time it's gonna be something different.

All thoughts of my dick disappear—well, okay maybe ninety-nine percent of dick-related thoughts, because I'm pretty sure the constant one percent is like, just baseline, you know?—and I manage to get us over to his bed and repositioned without letting go—me leaning up against his headboard and him in my arms. He's sort of on my lap, too, but basically the two of us are in a big old tangle that almost scares me even more, given the way he's legit clinging to me now.

Hand to God, I'm starting to feel like *I* need to cry now. I don't need to know the specifics of what's wrong in order to know that when something *is* this wrong for him, it's wrong for me, too, you know? On the plus side, I can tell that all his limbs are intact, and I know Eden's not hurt—because hello, she's here—so barring that brain-tumor diagnosis, I figure anything else is fixable. But still, knowing it *will* be okay isn't the same as knowing how the hell to make him stop hurting right here and now.

He's lying half across me, head on my chest and hands digging into me hard enough that I'm pretty sure there will be bruises later, but I just try to wrap him up even tighter, pulling him against me, and let him be there.

Kiss the top of his head.

Smooth a hand down his back.

Wish I had a relevant superpower—like maybe mind-reading, or one of those ones where you can go one hour into the future but not actually affect anything, but just kind of look around to help figure out what's up and reassure yourself that it'll turn out okay. Or wait, maybe it would be better to go one hour into the past? I mean, Matty wasn't gone all that long, and there's no way all this is about grocery shopping. The only other time I've seen him like this was when his dad came out.

And... oh shit, now I'm wondering if Santi *died* or something.

Before I start to freak out myself, though, I just shut that right down and hold onto him tighter. Clearly I'm gonna get nothing until he calms down, so I kiss the top of his head again and do my best to wrap myself around him so he knows he's not alone, even though he's not all that small, despite me teasing him about it sometimes.

"Matty," I say, which is all I got.

Okay, maybe it's not all, actually, because then I end up saying a whole bunch of other stuff that doesn't really make sense, just sort of petting and holding him and telling him it'll be all right in like a million ways, even though I have no idea whatsoever whether I'm lying or not, given that he's not yet disclosed what's got his heart breaking like this.

At some point Eden comes in with the tea and sets it down on the nightstand and wraps herself around him, too, until the three of us get so tangled together that I'm not sure whose parts belong to whom, but that's okay.

Feels right.

Feels *necessary*.

And eventually, Matty gets all cried out and none of us want to move, because lying still and doing nothing but this is fucking exhausting, you know? So even though a part of me wants to press him for details and figure out how to go about fixing whatever the hell just happened, before I know it, we're all asleep. But you know what? Even though me and Eden ended up doing basically nothing at all and Matty still hasn't told us what was wrong in the first place, it kind of *does* feel like something got fixed, just us being together like this.

Pretty sure as long as we hold onto that, nothing else can really be wrong, you know?

26

EDEN

*I*t's the third time I've woken up this morning, and just like the previous two, I sit up with a start, heart racing and filled with disbelief. Early morning sun fills my room, the kind that means the sun has barely made it over the horizon, and when I look at the clock on the bedside table, there's just no way I can deny it.

I'm awake.

I'm *alive.*

And it's my birthday.

"My" room is Matt's guest room, the boys' weight bench still in one corner and the few belongings I've accumulated since the fire neatly tucked away and not intruding on the space much. What was the point in spending much of the insurance money or really making myself at home here when I knew it wouldn't be for long? Besides, most nights I sleep in one or the other of their bedrooms, with one or both of them.

Not last night, though, despite how they pushed me a little. I just couldn't bear the thought of them waking up next to me if I wasn't going to wake up at all.

But I *did.*

I'm still here.

I push the covers aside and stand up cautiously, a part of me still expecting something to happen. Some unforeseeable crazy accident to just *end* me, despite the fact that the room is peaceful and quiet and that I've never felt safer or more at home than here in this house. But as soon as I'm on my feet, all the hope that I've been doing my best to deny for the last few weeks wells up at once, filling me with something that feels like champagne bubbles.

Like possibility.

Like *joy*.

I've always known that there wasn't really a *reason* for me to die before twenty-five, not in the terminal-illness sense, but I've *never*—not once since I was sixteen—truly been able to believe I'd make it to this age. And now? I've done it. I've actually made it! Even if I walk out of this room and it all ends, I'm already older than generations of women in my family. It *wasn't* my fate to die before my twenty-fifth birthday, and for the first time, it really, truly feels like I've got my whole life ahead of me.

I wrap my arms around myself, trying to hold in this feeling that fills me, but I can't. It permeates every part of me, it over-flows, it makes me feel like I'm *sparkling*. A smile spreads across my face that's so wide I'm almost sure my cheeks aren't big enough to contain it, and then I'm laughing, flinging my arms out and spinning around like a crazy person.

I'm *alive*.

And oh, Lord. There's so much I want to do.

I grab The List off the top of my dresser and flip it open. So many blank pages still to be filled.

#101 - Fall in love!
#102 - Apply to nursing school
#103 -

I put my pen down abruptly. I've already done #101, but I

still wanted to write it down and be brave enough to claim it. The same with #102. I haven't done it yet, but now I've got a *future*. Now I'm brave enough to try. And beyond that? Well, I can easily think of fifty *more* things to add to The List, but the truth is, I don't want to spend my birthday planning for the future.

I want to go out and *live* it.

The boys are probably still asleep, but we've all three got the day off and I know they won't mind me waking them up. My heart still breaks for the way Matt's father treated him when he found out about us, but the sad truth is that we'll probably always run into people who just don't understand how what the three of us have can be real. If there's any bright side to that rejection, though, it's that the past couple of weeks have only made us closer.

Knit us together more tightly.

Proven just how real this relationship really *is*—and that it's so much more than just sex.

A familiar heat rushes through me—because I mean, yes, it's more than just sex, but it definitely *is* sex, too. Amazing, mind-blowing sex that I don't know if I'll ever get enough of. But making it all the sweeter is that it's also the kind of true, lasting love that I never let myself dream of having before.

It's supporting each other.

It's being there for each other.

It's taking care of one another and believing in *us*, no matter what anyone else thinks.

Some might say it's still too new to be sure, but I already know. Our triad? It's unbreakable. And the idea that I get to have more of it... more of *them*... that it *doesn't* have to end... well, I almost don't know what to do with that.

It almost feels unfair that one person could be so blessed, be given so much.

Fair or not, though, I'll take it. I'm going to be selfish when it comes to this. I'm going to keep them. Hold on as tight as I can and hope like heck that my boys don't ever let me let go.

I've already got my hand on the doorknob, this impossible-to-stop smile still on my face, when I suddenly pivot, switching directions. I can't wait to go give myself the birthday present of sharing today with Matt and Johnny, but first, I'm going to do something else. Something that I've never allowed myself to do because it would mean I'd need a future to do it in. Something that means I know it's real. Something just for *me*.

I'm going to check #102 off my list right now.

I fire up my laptop with a giddy sense of euphoria. All that hope that I've been trying to deny? Despite my best efforts, it's been brewing inside me for a while now, fed and watered by the love of my boys, even when I tried to keep it from getting out of hand. And even though I kept trying to tell myself that I *wasn't* getting my hopes up, the truth is it's been spilling out of me in little ways. I've been doing my research into nursing programs in fits and starts and started the process of filling out a nursing school application even though I didn't really trust that there would be any point to it. I just kept plugging away at it anyway, though—dotted all the I's and crossed all the T's—and somehow now I've ended up with the whole thing ready to go.

I just couldn't bring myself to actually submit it, not when I didn't really believe I'd be around to see it through.

I do now, though.

I hope… I believe… I'm *alive*.

A silly, staccato rhythm sounds on my bedroom door and startles me just as I hit the button to send the nursing school application in, and I look up as Johnny and Matt walk in, knowing I must look just as elated as I feel.

I've done it. I've really done it!

And oh, Lord. *Look* at them. Both wearing the same smile I am; arms overflowing with flowers; awake far, far too early—which means they've planned this.

They're up for *me*.

They believed, even when I didn't, and that's… that's everything.

They burst into a horribly off-key and distinctly naughty version of "Happy Birthday," swooping me up in their silliness and tossing me onto the bed with all those flowers. Of course they join me, because they always know what I need, don't they? And before I know it they've got me laughing and breathless, showering me with silly little gifts that warm my heart as they crowd in next to me on the tiny mattress.

"I don't think this bed was made for three," I say, laughing as they sandwich me between them and hand me another awkwardly wrapped little box with a cockeyed ribbon.

"'Course it wasn't," Matt says, a wicked smile on his face. "Here's how it breaks down. Johnny's bed's gonna be for sleeping, because he's the only one with a king. My bed's for fucking—" Matt has a queen-sized bed, "—because there's just enough space for all of us to have a good time, yeah? And this one—"

"Let's get rid of it and turn this into a full weight room," Johnny interrupts, plucking at the ribbon on my last gift. "No more of this sleeping apart bullshit, okay?"

"Agreed on that, but we're not getting rid of this bed," Matt says. "This one is where we get… *creative*."

The way he says it makes everything inside me hum to life with anticipation, but just when I want to suggest setting aside the gifts for later and moving on to some of that *creativity*, Matt knocks Johnny's hands away from the gift box with a wink.

"Quit it, bro, this is hers." Matt rolls his eyes. "You're always so grabby with gifts."

"I'm just *helping*," Johnny says, going for an innocent look that's so overdone that it has me laughing. "Just want to hurry up with this part and get on to, you know, other ways of celebrating."

I have to agree, especially when Johnny says it in *that* tone, but Matt holds firm.

"Not until after she opens her presents," he says in that bossy sex-voice that always has me wanting to beg him for things I still get shy asking for.

"I've got a present right here," Johnny says, plucking my hand off the tiny box and putting it on top of his erection. He gives me a dirty smile that I adore. "You want to open this one, princess?"

"Yes, please," I tell him honestly, starting to feel a little breathless as I shape my hand around his hard length. It practically singes my skin even through the soft material of the sleep pants he's wearing, and when he tangles his fingers through the back of my hair and pulls me in for a hot kiss, thrusting up against my palm, I let the little box in my hand tumble to the mattress.

Matt laughs, pulling my hand off Johnny's cock and keeping it trapped in his grip. He was squished in on the wall-side of the bed, but now he gets to his knees and rolls me over onto my stomach to swat my bottom.

"Ohhhhhh," I gasp, the deliciously hot sting of it spreading through me with the promise of very, *very* good things to come.

I squeeze my thighs together as my center starts to throb, and Matt laughs.

"Naughty girl," he says. "You're going to make me start your birthday spankings early if you keep that up." He sits back on his heels and pulls me up in front of him, whispering into my ear from behind. "First, your present."

"Thought that's what I was giving her," Johnny says with an unrepentant grin, folding his hands behind his head as he smirks up at us.

Johnny's leaning against the little twin bed's headboard looking absolutely decadent, and the way Matt's cock is suddenly pushing against me from behind, I'm pretty sure he thinks so, too.

"We'll definitely be giving her that one, too," Matt says, the pure lust in his voice making me shiver. He picks up the little box and hands it to me. "Just want to make sure we're all on the same page first, yeah?"

I'm not sure what that means, but I can hear it in Matt's tone—see it in Johnny's face—whatever it is inside the box, it's got their usual cocky assurance colored by a hint of uncertainty.

Do they really think I won't like anything they give me?

"Matty's right. Open it, princess," Johnny says, sitting up straight as he reaches for the box again. "We know you already have one, but—"

"*Spoiler,*" Matt interrupts, swatting Johnny's hand away again when Johnny tries to pull the ribbon off. "Let her... let her just see if she wants... you know."

"If I want what?" I ask, scooting off Matt's lap so I can look between the two of them. "I want everything. I want *you*, both of you. Anything you... you can think of, I'm in."

"Even camels?" Johnny asks, grinning.

I laugh, but Matt takes my chin in his hand and tilts my head to face him, pinning me with a serious look. "We want everything, too, Eden," he says. "We know what you thought about today. About your birthday, and all. And you know, none of us have ever really talked about much past this point. About what we're really doing here, yeah?"

I nod, swallowing past the sudden lump in my throat. He's right. It's all felt so easy in some ways, being with the two of them, but a part of that was the freedom I gave myself when I didn't believe I *had* a future.

Of *course* I haven't wanted to think ahead. Couldn't bring myself to, and every time I tried... well, I just couldn't see how it could work, as if my vision was no better than Matt's father's. But it *does* work. *We* work, and I'm not giving that up. Not if Matt's serious, and he and Johnny really do feel the same.

I'm not sure how it's supposed to look, a relationship with all three of us—or if "supposed to" even applies—but I know I want it. I know I'll fight for it, even when it's uncomfortable. And I know that with these two beside me, I'll be brave enough to hold onto it, no matter what anyone else thinks.

"We want you to stay, Eden," Johnny says, plucking the box out of my hand and unwrapping it quickly, before Matt can stop him this time. He pops the top open and holds it out to me. "Hoping you want that, too?"

It's a house key.

I do already have one. Matt gave me one so I could come and go, back when I first came to stay with them three months ago.

"I know you've moved around a lot," Matt says, pulling it out and putting it in my hand. "You said you never really had a place you felt like you were from, yeah? A place where you had roots? A place you could see yourself staying and putting some down?"

It's true, and I'm just as touched to know that they both paid attention, that they really *care*, as I am by what this key seems to mean. I swipe at my eyes when they start to get blurry, turning it over in my hand.

There's engraving on the key, a heart with the infinity symbol looping through it.

It's beautiful.

"Boston's nice," Johnny says, winking at me. "You've seen all the options, right? Been to all fifty states? Got your whole life ahead of you to keep exploring, but Matty and me, we were kinda hoping you'd stay here. You know, on a permanent basis."

"I want to," I say, closing my hand around the key. "I want that. I want *you*. Both of you. You're... you're my home. The only one I want."

Johnny grins, and Matt laughs, pulling me against him and kissing me hard.

"Sounds like we've got something to celebrate then, right, beautiful? The three of us making this a long-term thing?"

"How long-term are we talking about?" I tease him, tracing the infinity symbol on my new key. "Because a girl could get ideas with this bit here..."

"Get them," Matt says, and the way he smiles at me has my heart singing. "We want this to be forever."

"Forever works for me," I say, meaning it with all my heart.

"You got that one a little wrong, princess," Johnny says, taking the key out of my hand. He sets it aside, kissing me, touching me, and somehow managing to get me naked, too, while he melts my heart with his next words. "Forever doesn't work *for* you. The right way to say it is that forever only works *with* you. With you and Matty both. Ain't no other kind of forever *I'm* interested in, at least."

And then they're both giving me even more reasons to celebrate. Laying me down among all the soft petals scattered around us and using hands and mouths and lips and tongues all over me.

It's bliss.

It's heaven.

They take me there twice before I can even catch my breath... but it's still not enough. And of course, because these two men are perfect for me, they know it.

Know I need *more*.

"You want us to fuck you, beautiful?" Matt asks, looking up at me with a wicked smile from where he's positioned between my legs.

I'm still trembling from the things he did to me with his mouth, and between that and the way Johnny's huge hands are stroking me... teasing me... keeping me poised on the edge of even more, I'm not sure I can answer.

"She doesn't just want us to, Matty," Johnny says, winking at me. "Pretty sure she *needs* us to. Can't disappoint our girl, now can we?"

"Never will," Matt says, palming himself as he looks down at me with hungry eyes. "Like we did before, bro? Both in her at the same time?"

I moan, my whole body flushing with heat at the memory.

Having them take me that way is *amazing*. We've done it that way a few times, and every time, I'm not sure I can take it... and every time, it's the most incredible, perfect feeling to find out that I can.

But this time—

"No," I say, coming up on my elbows as I try to catch my breath.

The word freezes both of them, catching them in the act of shucking off their clothes, and I lick my lips as they stop and look at me.

"How do you want it then, princess?" Johnny asks as he unfreezes and finishes stripping down. "It's your day. Happy to give you whatever you want."

"Always," Matt says forcefully, the heat in his eyes doing things to me.

He's off the bed now, because it really *is* too small, and watching him get naked only fires up my determination to get what I want.

Or at least to ask for it.

Matt must see that determination in my eyes, because he gives me a dirty, dirty look and starts stroking himself.

"But you *sure* you don't want us together, baby? Don't want Johnny's big cock making you scream? Don't want to let me in the back door, pushing you higher as he does?"

Oh, Lord. I *do*. A selfish, selfish part of me really does, and Matt can always tell, can't he? He always knows what I really want... except that this time, I want something else, too.

Something that's like that infinity loop, connecting all three of us together.

"Johnny, let her ride you," Matt says, words that make me moan.

Johnny reaches for me, ready to flip us both around the way Matt wants, but I put a hand on his chest to stop him.

Yes, that would feel incredible, but—

"Um, if you two are into it... I'd kind of like to do something else?" I tell them. "If you're willing, I mean. For... for my birthday?"

"Told you, princess. I'm always into making you happy," Johnny says, covering my hand with his and rubbing it against the hard contours of his chest. "Anything that does that, I'm game."

"Absolutely," Matt agrees, his eyes heating up as he watches the two of us.

I get it, too, because watching is *amazing*. It was so unbelievably hot, the first time I realized Johnny wanted Matt this way. And actually seeing the two of them together?

Watching them suck...

Touch...

Kiss...

These two big, hard men with such sweet, soft hearts getting each other off?

Loving each other?

Making each other moan?

It's by far the most erotic thing *ever*... especially when I get to do both—watch *and* be a part of it. Which is exactly what I want right now.

"I want all three of us to... to be connected," I say, having trouble catching my breath. I scrape my nails across Johnny's chest, making him hiss out his breath as I clench my thighs together, and I tell them again when they don't both immediately jump on the idea. "All three of us to fuck at the same time."

"How, baby?"

I pull Johnny down on top of me, arching up to rub myself against his deliciously hard body. "Fuck me like this, Johnny, will you?" I ask, wrapping my legs around his hips.

The heavy length of his cock is trapped between us, making me crazy, and he groans, dipping his head down to bite at the side of my neck as he instantly starts moving on top of me. Rubbing himself against me. Almost making me forget the rest as he rocks that big body against mine.

I gasp. *This.* Yes. *Always.*

"I'll fuck you, princess," he says, the vibration of his voice against my skin making me whimper as he trails his hot mouth down my throat. "Anytime. Any way. Don't gotta ask me twice."

"And… and I want… want Matt to fuck you," I manage to get out just as Johnny rolls his hips, lining up the head of his cock with my entrance.

Johnny goes still.

"You want me… inside Johnny?" Matt asks, his voice sounding strained.

Strained and *hungry*.

I slide my hands down the impossibly wide length of Johnny's back and grip his hard ass, pulling as I rock my hips up to bring him inside me.

"*Jesus*, Eden," he groans, and I'm so wet that he slides all the way in, right up to the hilt.

Oh, Lord. Oh, *yes*. Johnny's so thick that it's always a stretch with him, even when I'm relaxed, but I love the way he fills me up. Love the way there's no room for anything but this when either one of them take me. Love it from behind, too, even though I'd never considered doing it that way before Matt showed me how much I'd like it.

But the way Matt likes to fuck me sometimes? Taking charge of my back entrance; filling me up there, too; showing me just how good it is when I give up control and let him push me that way?

It's incredible.

Liberating.

So, *so* erotic… like nothing I've ever experienced before.

Almost as erotic as wondering whether Johnny will like it, too.

Have the two of them ever done it that way?

Not when I'm with them, at least, but suddenly I'm almost desperate to have it happen.

To *see* it.

To know that the two men I love are connecting that way, too.

And oh God, oh *please*, I'm also desperate to find out what it feels like to have Johnny inside me while Matt pounds into him from behind. To have the three of us joined in our bodies the way we are in our hearts. To watch Johnny's face and hear Matt's delicious excitement and feel *all* of it, get all of it, have everything I want because—with these two, with my whole life ahead of me —I *can*.

"You... you really want that, princess?" Johnny asks, holding himself still inside me. "You want that to happen here?"

His voice is strained, too, but I can see it in his eyes. I can *hear* it. He's just as desperate for it as I am.

"Please," I pant, running my hands over him. Wrapping my legs around him. Feeling all sorts of hot and bothered, even though they've already made me come twice. "Would you... would *you* want that, Johnny? Want Matt inside you? Want him to fuck you while you're in me?"

I know he does, but I *am* a naughty girl, aren't I? Because I want to say it.

I want to see what it does to Johnny when I do.

I want to egg Matt on, get him all worked up about the idea, see what happens when he flips into that bossy mode I'm pretty sure Johnny loves just as much as I do in the bedroom.

Johnny groans, his thick cock throbbing inside me, and I rock against him, clutching his ass to pull him against me even harder. To get him inside me even deeper. To feel all that strength and power and size that I'm suddenly greedy for.

And then Matt's hands are there, too. Running over the hard curve of Johnny's ass. Pulling him open. Touching him intimately. I can feel it all, and even though I can't *see* what Matt's doing, oh... Lord, I *can* see Johnny's face.

"This mine, Johnny?" Matt asks, his voice low and husky and sounding like pure sex.

I whimper, and Johnny's eyes almost roll back in his head.

"Yessssssssssss," he answers, drawing out the word in a long, erotic hiss even though it's a rhetorical question, and we all know it.

Johnny buries his face against my neck, the heat of his hard, panting breaths skittering across my skin and shooting straight down to my core.

"You want this just as bad as Eden does, don't you, Johnny?" Matt asks, and I can hear in his voice how bad *he* does. "You want us to do it this way? You want me inside you? Want to feel me fuck you?"

Johnny nods, mouth open and hot against my collarbone.

"Love... love your cock, Matty," he pants, arms tightening around me as he shifts position. Spreads his knees. Drives himself deeper inside me as he opens up for Matt to take him. *"Want* it."

I hear the snick of the lube bottle—my boys came prepared— and then Johnny's kissing me. Cock sliding in and out just enough to tease me with short, stuttering little thrusts as he whimpers into my mouth.

Matt's stretching him open.

Touching him.

Egging Johnny on as he tells him how good he feels... as he pushes a finger inside him, just like he did with me... whispering the dirtiest, most delicious things... and after a minute, adding another finger.

Johnny stiffens, then groans.

"Jesus Jesus *Jesus,"* he chants, eyes squeezed closed as his huge body jerks against me, flushed and hot and vibrating with both power and need. "Want this. *Want* it."

"Can't wait until it's my cock," Matt growls over the slick sound of his thrusting fingers. "You're so fucking tight, Johnny, *Christ."*

Johnny's panting hard, and Matt leans over Johnny's back so that I'm pinned under the weight of both of them, forcing John-ny's head up so he can kiss him while Johnny grinds back against those fingers, fucking himself on them while he fucks me, too.

I moan, arching up underneath them, and Johnny gasps, shuddering.

"Oh, *fuck*," he says, bucking against me even harder. "*More*, Matty. Jesus *fuck. Please.*"

I guess it's true that guys have something like a G-spot inside them, and oh, Lord, there's no doubt at all that Matt just found it.

"You like that, baby?" Matt asks, doing something that has Johnny practically sobbing. "You want it harder? Want more? Ready for my cock now?"

"Please," I beg, shaking now. "Oh, God, *please* Matt. Please fuck him. Fuck him right now. Fuck him right into me. Matt, *please—*"

Johnny cuts me off by taking my mouth again, and a moment later, I *feel* it.

Matt enters him.

Johnny's entire frame tightens up as Matt groans with pleasure, the sound drawn out into a timeless, endless moment that has my whole body quivering in response. And then the tension in Johnny gives way to a deep, full-body shiver, wracking his body from head to toe.

"Oh God," he gasps, shuddering on top of me. "Fuck, Matty, *fuck.*"

"That... that good for you, Johnny?" Matt grits out, sounding wrecked. "You good? You good, baby?"

Johnny makes the sexiest sound I've ever heard—half whimper, half groan, pure *yes*—and then Matt starts to *move.*

Slowly at first, then faster.

Thrusting harder.

Driving himself deeper.

Leaning over Johnny... kissing the back of his neck as Johnny's hot mouth takes mine... hands moving from Johnny's hips to mine and back again... stroking us.

Fucking us.

Forcing Johnny to turn his head so Matt can kiss him, too.

They rock above me in perfect sync, Johnny letting Matt set the pace at first. Taking Matt's cock with shuddering gasps and low, needy groans. Letting Matt fuck the both of us, his thrusts sending Johnny's cock deeper into me, driving me into the mattress, grinding against all the spots inside me that light me up.

That have me begging.

That send me closer and closer to the edge I know they're going to make me fly from... the same edge both my boys are rushing toward themselves.

We're going to *soar.*

And suddenly Johnny's not just taking it, he's chasing it. Thrusting himself back onto Matt's cock with hot, dirty curses, driving himself forward to bury his hard length inside me, doing it over and over until I'm clawing at him, my whole body shaking with the soul-deep need that the two of them are building inside me. The delicious tension that has me close to snapping... shattering... breaking into a million pieces that only fit *here*, with these two perfect, perfect men.

I've *never* been fucked like this.

"Oh God," I gasp, starting to come apart. "Oh *please*, please please *please*please*please*."

"So... *good*," Matt growls, going up on his knees behind Johnny. He slams forward again and again, pounding into Johnny faster and faster, and just when I don't think I can take it, he grits out an order to the both of us. "*Come*. Fucking *Christ*. Come for me. *Both* of you."

I already am.

I'm *lost.*

It rushes through me and swirls me into pure bliss, and then Johnny's cock is swelling inside me, taking me even higher. His arms tighten into two steel bands around me and he's groaning. Hot breath shuddering against my neck as he fucks me through it and then that huge body locking in pleasure, pinning me down as the wave takes him, too.

Matt cries out, cursing up a blue streak and slamming us both into the mattress, the last to come... and this is it.

This is perfection.

The three of us, joined just like this, hearts connected by the infinite loop of our love. And the most perfect thing of all?

Today isn't the end, the way I've thought for so long.

It's just the beginning.

27

MATT

*B*lindfolding Eden and getting her here to the firehouse has got to have been some of the funniest shit me and Johnny have ever pulled. Funny… and yeah, it also gave me a few ideas for some things we've gotta try at home one of these days.

You'd think my dick would be sated after what the three of us got up to at the crack of dawn this morning, but damn. I've wanted Johnny like that for a while now, just wasn't sure he'd be into it. And truth is, around those two? Guess I don't just want him one way or her another, I want them both *all* the ways, all the time.

I don't know that I'll ever get enough.

Johnny leans over all casual-like as the two of us watch Eden.

She takes my breath away.

She's beautiful.

She's *glowing*.

"Was that a tear I saw there, bro?" Johnny whispers, smirking.

"Fuck off," I say, because I have to, right? Truth is though, taking that blindfold off Eden and watching her face when the whole crew yelled out "happy birthday"? Not gonna lie, I did get a little choked up. And yes, fine, I may have even gotten a little more than just choked up—may have actually teared up the tiniest bit, not that I'm formally admitting anything here—when Eden caught sight of her Aunt Maria a minute ago.

Our girl lost it. Ugly crying for a minute, but also looking fucking radiant at the same time. And yeah, I *do* think that's beautiful, even with her face a little blotchy and her makeup smudged.

Can't help it. Guess that's love, yeah?

But for real, making her happy, taking care of her like that, pretty sure that's what I'm built for. I don't need a crazy bucket list to feel like I'm living life to the fullest, not as long as I've got her and Johnny. They're mine, and I'm theirs, and there's honestly nothing else I need in life, far as I'm concerned.

Eden finally pulls her aunt over to meet us, and I'm all set to be on my best behavior when Maria pulls me into a hug, kissing my cheek, then does the same to Johnny.

"So you're the two hot firefighters who are keeping my Eden's sheets warm, hm?" she asks after the handsy greeting, grinning up at the two of us.

My jaw is on the floor, and Johnny looks fucking adorable, all flustered and tongue-tied. Eden's blushing, too, but she just laughs and covers her eyes for a second, lowering her voice as she hisses out a scandalized-sounding: "Auntie *Maria.*"

"What?" Maria responds, not lowering *her* voice at all. Her eyes are sparkling, and there's nothing but goodwill rolling off her as she pulls Eden in for a quick, one-armed hug. "Don't be shy about it, baby girl. Look at them! I can't blame you, and I'm not going to say I'm *jealous*, but I will say you should hold on tight and think about not letting go. The way they set this all up for you?"

She sweeps a hand out, encompassing the station and all the guys. The music. The food. It's not super fancy, but it's not bad if I do say so myself.

Maria's still clearly talking to Eden, but she pins me and Johnny with her gaze. "Looks like love to me, hm?"

"Yes, ma'am," Johnny answers promptly, all but saluting.

I bite back a laugh at that, not that I can blame him for how he's reacting to her, of course. Maybe it's all those years in the Navy? Eden's aunt is small, but *I* wouldn't want to cross her.

"We're hoping to hold on to Eden, too," I tell Maria, part of me a little amazed at the direction this first conversation is starting out in. "Permanently, I hope, long as Johnny and I don't fuck it up."

Maria's smile gets even wider, and she nods in approval, then beckons me closer.

"Just be advised," she says, still smiling but with a hard glint in her eye that has my spine straightening out of respect. "If either of you so much as puts a hairline fracture in her heart, I promise to unleash the full fury of hell upon both of you, is that clear?"

She cuts her eyes at Johnny to include him, too, and I see him go pale and nod.

She turns back to me.

"Trust me," I say, meaning it with all my heart. "I'd die first. No one's hurting either Eden *or* Johnny, not on my watch."

"Aw," Maria says, eyes instantly softening as she pulls me in for a hug again. "I knew I liked you boys. It's official. I approve, not that you should give a shit about that, but you're family now, okay?"

And then I really do get choked up for a second. I guess I didn't realize that Eden had told her aunt about us quite so openly, but you know what? After what went down with my dad, it feels good to have some familial support, even if it's not from my own.

Chief comes over to wish our girl a happy birthday, and *hello—* he's got more than a spark of interest in his eyes when Eden introduces him to Maria. My guess is that's part of his motivation as he drags the two Evans women off to meet some more of the guys, and based on the looks he's getting back from Eden's aunt? Just saying, maybe Maria will be visiting Boston more often than not, if things heat up there the way I can see the potential for between those two.

"How'd Eden turn out so sweet when her aunt's got my balls shriveling up with just one look?" Johnny asks, shoving his hands in his pockets and rocking back on his heels as we watch them make the rounds. He's smiling, though, and I can tell he doesn't mean it.

Well, I mean, he *does*, but I can also tell he likes knowing Eden's got that in her corner just as much as I do.

Truth is, Johnny's family ain't bad, but they're definitely a total letdown when it comes to taking care of him the way he deserves. They always have been, like he was some kind of afterthought that they kept forgetting about. All the better for me, I guess, since me and mine took him in, but now? We aren't close with the Johnsons and never will be. Mom is great, but at this point I doubt she'll ever be around for more than a hot second, what with how much she likes exploring new places. And my dad is... well, you know.

I'm just not gonna think about it.

So basically, we've got no family but the three of us, you know?

And now Maria, even though she's not around on a regular basis.

And, of course, the boys at the station.

I look around, watching Bill and Jimmy and their wives out on the makeshift dance floor, cutting a rug. Asher and his fiancé joking around with some of the other guys by the buffet table. Chief already with his arm around Maria and saying something that makes Eden blush so pretty my heart squeezes at the sight.

Hits me all of a sudden that yeah, this *is* our family... and here I am standing next to the man I'm in love with, watching the girl we're both in love with, and something's wrong. Asher's got me beat, holding his man's hand like that and making no bones about the fact that they're together. But me and Johnny? Here I am, all determined to be *us*, to live out and proud and fuck what anyone thinks, including my dad, and I can't share this with the only other family I've got? The one here at the station?

Are him and me always gonna be hidden, right here in this one place that I know we've both felt at home since day one?

That... sucks.

And what sucks even more? For a second, I'm not sure I've got the balls to risk rocking this particular boat.

"You okay, bro?" Johnny asks me quietly, leaning close, but not touching me, of course. Catching on right away that something's not right for me, because there's no doubt that he loves me right back just as hard, but obeying this unspoken agreement that despite everything else we've done—despite me being *inside* him, just a few hours ago—we're still just buds or something here at the station.

Fuck *that*.

Maybe it's prophetic or something, but Asher looks over and catches my eye at that very moment, throwing me a wink. It either bolsters my courage or sends my good sense right out the window, but either way, I don't let myself stop to think, just reach over and pull Johnny's hand out of his pocket, twining our fingers together and holding tight, palm to palm.

He looks at me, startled—looking a bit like a hot-as-fuck deer in the headlights, if you want to know the truth—and I lean in and plant a quick, hard kiss right on his mouth, in front of God and everyone.

Not gonna lie, doing it kinda scares the shit out of me, but it also eases something tight in my chest that I didn't even realize was restricting me like that until this very moment. I don't look around yet to see what kind of reactions we're getting, but holding Johnny's gaze for a second, I already know that no part of me is gonna regret this, regardless.

He's still all deer-in-the-headlights, but he's also mine, and seeing it so clearly in his eyes, that's everything.

I grin at him, squeezing his hand.

"I'm okay now," I say, answering his question now that I can. "Better, at least."

He blinks, a dusky pink stain spreading across his cheeks as his hand tightens in mine, but he doesn't pull it away.

"Okay," he says, swallowing hard but definitely smiling, too. "Okay, then, Matty. We're doing this, huh? Right here?"

"We're doing this everywhere," I tell him, pulling him a bit closer as Eden, her aunt, and the chief circle back around to us. "This is who we are, Johnny, yeah? And anyone who has an opinion can either get on board or get the fuck out of the way."

And now he's glowing just like Eden was earlier, and when she reaches us? Guess the three of us are a happiness hat-trick.

"Best birthday present *ever*," Eden says, her eyes flicking down to my and Johnny's hands before she comes up on her tiptoes and gives us a pair of hot kisses that no one could mistake for anything other than what they are.

Our girl, staking her claim, too, to *both* of us.

Chief clears his throat, raising an eyebrow, and I raise mine right back.

I respect the man, I do, but like I just said to Johnny, on-board or gtfo. As far as I'm concerned, those are the only two options on the table.

"Come on now, guys. Gotta keep the party family-friendly, don't we?" Chief says in a low voice, glancing around and double-taking when he sees the hard look Maria's giving him. He clears his throat again, backpedaling at full speed under the weight of it. "Not that we aren't inclusive and all here, of course. We've got Campbell and his fiancé as part of the station family now, you know."

"Nothing more family-friendly than people who love each other, last I checked," Maria says, crossing her arms over her chest and giving Chief a look that makes *me* want to salute.

"Right. Completely. Agreed on that one, Maria," Chief says. His eyes flick down to me holding Johnny's hand again, and he claps me on the shoulder, winking. "Guess what I should've said is, we *are* a family here, you know that, Lopez, Johnson. Anyone gets out of line, I'm not gonna put up with it any more than I did when Campbell came on board. You just let me know, okay?"

"I knew I liked you, Kenneth," Maria says, hooking her arm through his. "Do you like to dance?"

Takes me a second to realize "Kenneth" means the chief, but by then, Maria's got him heading to the dance floor and Eden's snuggled right up to me and Johnny with a gorgeous smile on her beautiful face.

"I love you guys," she says, leaning against us. "Thank you so much for doing this. I can't believe you set it all up without me knowing."

"We work here, don't we?" Johnny says, grinning down on her and looking... looking just *transcendent*. No other word.

Just like she does.

I could get used to this, making these two happy. Seems pretty clear that it's what I want to spend the next fifty or sixty years doing, and even if that means riding a damn camel or drinking endless cups of that tasteless tea that Eden pushes on me, I'm down. It's all I want, really.

They're joking around about the chief and Eden's aunt, Johnny getting downright dirty and Eden blushing as red as one of the engines that the boys shined up and parked out front to make the place look more festive, when all of a sudden the hairs on the back of my neck stand up. You ever get that? A sense of being watched when there's just no earthly reason for you to know it's happening?

Eden's doing her damnedest to drag Johnny out to the dance floor, and he's digging in his heels—because he knows damn well that he'll look like a spastic moose on crack if he sets foot out there and probably drive Eden away forever, thereby ruining things for the both of us—when suddenly she catches sight of something over my shoulder that's got her eyes widening.

Exactly the direction I had that *feeling* from.

"Oh!" she exclaims, dropping Johnny's arm as her eyes dart to mine and then back over my shoulder again. She sucks that lower lip into her mouth and starts chewing on it, and me and Johnny turn at the same time.

"*Santi,*" Johnny says, the first to recover. "Hey there. Hey, Nick. Uh…"

He looks between me and Dad—Dad all stiff and uncomfortable-looking and me looking like I don't know what, but probably not anything good as my stomach does its best to regurgitate itself —and I can read Johnny as easy as I always can. He's torn. He's pissed at Dad, I can tell and I love him for it, but Dad is also basically like *his* dad, and Johnny wants things to be right. Wants our *family* to be right again, so bad he's practically vibrating with it.

"It is good to see you, Johnny," Dad says, sounding strained. "And… and you, Eden. *Feliz cumpleaños.*" Happy birthday. Then a stiff nod to me. *"Mijo."*

"You came," I say, stating the obvious and managing to do it without puking, even though I feel a whole bunch of shit inside that's the opposite of how happy I was just a moment ago.

Why *did* he come?

Is he gonna make a scene?

Disown me, the way I guess I did to him all those years ago?

I haven't talked to him since storming out of his house a couple of weeks ago, and truth is, I can't even think about him since then without wanting to shut down. For some reason, this last two weeks of estrangement hurts more than the previous eight years.

Hurts more… but has also been more bearable, because of who I've got with me.

Johnny and Eden sort of close ranks around me, both touching me in some way or another. A hand on my waist. An arm around me. Both making it clear where things stand by body language alone. And then we all just sort of stand there staring at one another for who knows how long.

A minute?

Ten?

Fucking *eternity*, the way it feels?

Finally, Nick clears his throat like he's going to try to move us all along toward whatever purpose the two of them had in coming here today, and Eden springs into action, reminding me of her aunt for a minute even though nothing about her could ever be intimidating.

"Johnny was just going to dance with me," she says, holding a hand out to Nick and latching on to Johnny's arm again with what looks like a grip of steel. "Join us, Nick?"

It's not an invitation, no matter how sweetly she's smiling, and Nick gets it right away. I almost *do* expect to see him salute her, and I'm not sure if I'm relieved, grateful, or scared shitless when Eden hustles them away and leaves me and Dad alone a second later.

I don't get much time to think about it.

Scratch that, I get *none*.

"I am an ass, my Mateo," my father begins, adjusting his sport coat and looking distinctly uncomfortable. He certainly fancied himself up for this. Broke out the hair gel and everything. "Nick tells me this, but he does not need to, no? I know it, and I am sorry it has taken me so many days to say it."

Oshit. Now I really *am* choking up.

"I am an ass," he repeats, reaching out to grip my upper arms. "But I am not an ass who is willing to give up eight more years with you because of it. Please forgive me. I do not want to lose you again, *mijo*. Not you or *el hijo de mi corazón*. Johnny, the son of my heart, no?"

I want to forgive him. I want him back, too. But not wanting to lose me isn't the same as accepting me, yeah?

"We're a package deal, Dad," I say tightly, and we both know I don't just mean me and Johnny. "This is *real* for me. They're my forever. Both of them."

He sighs, letting go of me to pinch the bridge of his nose.

For a minute, he doesn't just look older... he looks *old*.

"I know this, Mateo," he finally says, looking up at me. "Nick and I, we come here. We do not know what to say or how to say it. I watch you with Johnny and with your Eden. I do not understand, but I see that what you say is true for you. You love them, and with love... well, it does not matter what I think, no?"

"It matters to me," I say, because no matter how much I might wish it weren't true, it *does*.

To my surprise, that makes Dad smile. The tension eases out of his shoulders and he claps me on the shoulders again. "I *do* understand this. It matters to me what you think, too. I will not give Nick up or live a lie for myself—"

"I don't want you to!" I cut in, because hello, I'm over that. I thought he was clear on that.

Dad's smile gets even wider. "*Sí, sí*, I see that this is true now, Mateo, and it means so much. So I will try to understand, too. To believe that it will work out and not hurt you, this love with so many people, no?"

I snort back a laugh at that. I know the laughter is just my nerves, but for real, Dad makes it sound like I've got a harem or something. So many people? Last I checked, it was just Eden and Johnny.

"It *will* work out," I tell him, because that's just God's honest truth.

Nothing else is gonna work for me, so whatever it takes, it's going to happen.

Dad shrugs one shoulder, but he's still smiling. "I hope so, I do. And I am only telling you the truth right now, *mijo*. I *don't* understand, but I will try. And more importantly, I know that I do not need an understanding. I just need to love my son, and that is something I have never stopped doing. It is why I don't want things to be hard on you, not when it comes to who you love."

My turn to shrug. "Got no choice, do I?"

Can't have been any easier for him. Different, sure, but not *easy*.

He laughs, and his eyes seek Nick out, out on the dance floor making even Johnny's spastic moves look smooth.

"Oh, shit," I say, laughing as I catch sight. "Did you know about this?"

"You see that I know about how things can be hard?" Dad jokes. "Taking him dancing causes injury." Then he gets more serious, gripping my shoulders again. "I was scared of how it would be for you when you told me of your love, but I was wrong. You will get looks. You will get judgment. I know how this feels, but I *was* wrong. You have to do what makes you happy. You have to be with *who* makes you happy. Living any other way eats at you from the inside out."

I swallow. Dad's saying that he felt it too, the thing Johnny said —that hiding it felt like cancer, growing inside him every day.

Doing this today, letting the chief see where things stand with Eden and Johnny and me—letting *everyone* see—hands down, it was the right choice, no matter what comes at us in the future from some of the less open-minded guys around here.

"Thanks, Dad," I say, meaning it. Pulling him to me and hugging him tight. "Thank you."

"You forgive me, then?" he says after a minute, sounding choked up, too.

"There's nothing to forgive," I say, realizing it's true. "I love you, *Papa*. I should have been the one to come to you. I'm the one who wasted eight years. I should have tried harder to keep you in my life this time."

"Pfft," he says, waving me off as he blinks away the shine in his eyes. "With age comes wisdom, no?" He winks, then sighs, adding, "All love can be hard, Mateo, but it is even harder when we love different than others. That is all I wanted to protect you from, *mijo*. I still do, even though I know I cannot."

"But it's worth it," I say, looking back at the dance floor.

Spastic moose or not, these people we both love look *happy* out there, and that's what matters. I turn back to my father. "Right, *Papa*? It's worth it?"

He's looking out at the dance floor, too, and guess I don't really need an answer, not when it's written so clearly on his face.

"*Sí*," he says simply, giving me that answer anyway. "It is worth every second of it. Every single one, Mateo. Don't give up even one of them."

And I won't.

Not even one.

Not ever.

EPILOGUE

JOHNNY—ONE YEAR LATER

*E*den gives my hand an excited squeeze as Matty stands up to give his toast as best man. He looks sharp, kinda making me think we need to get him in a nice suit more often. Of course, the problem with that idea is that if *he* wears a suit, then it probably means I'll have to, too—and just the thought of it makes me wince.

"Stop tugging at your collar," Eden whispers, taking a second to press a kiss against the side of my neck since she's right there whispering and all.

Best.

Girlfriend.

Ever.

And no, I'm not just saying that because of the emergency blow job she gave me before the ceremony to help settle my nerves. There's a ton of reasons, and hand to God, over the last year? Feels like I fall a little bit more in love with her and Matty both, every single day.

Although, fine, if I'm being totally honest, the emergency BJ definitely makes it onto the leaderboard.

I tug at my collar again without realizing it, and Eden laughs softly, taking my hand in both of hers this time. I already popped the top two buttons and loosened the stranglehold of a tie I had to wear as soon as the ceremony was done, so it's not really that I'm actually feeling short on air, it's just more nerves I guess. And not even *my* nerves… I'm just feeling it for Matty, since I know he was stressed about coming up with a good toast for his dad, you know?

And… great. Now I've been fussing with this damn monkey suit so much that I missed the first bit of his speech. Not that I haven't heard him practice it about ten million times over the last few weeks, but still, I do sort of feel like a shitty boyfriend for zoning out when I should be at a hundred percent, for like, supportive purposes and all.

Matty looks like he's got this, though.

He looks solid.

He looks hot as fuck, actually, but I mean, on the emotional front, he looks like he's gonna make it through.

"I wasn't around the first time Nick asked my father to marry him," Matty's saying, and yeah, his voice goes a little husky, but he's not bawling like a baby or anything, so I'm pretty sure he's good. He clears his throat and goes on: "And that… that was my fault. The way I hear it, though, he put Nick off with a weak excuse that Nick chalked up to cold feet. Nick didn't give up, though—"

"Never," Nick interjects, raising Santi's hand to his lips and kissing the tips of his new husband's fingers.

The room titters with happy laughter, and Santi smiles at Nick like the two of them are the only people on the planet.

And shit, seeing that? I've been teasing Matty all week about the possibility of him losing it mid-speech, but now it looks like *I'm* gonna?

Unfair.

Pretty sure he must've planned it this way.

"Nick didn't give up," Matty repeats, smiling at the newlyweds

—so big that it seriously starts to fuck with my ability to hold it together, what with him looking so happy and all. "And he asked Dad to marry him all over again a year later."

Matty pauses for dramatic effect, and Eden—a.k.a. Best Girl-friend Ever—pushes a tissue into my hand.

"Dad said no," Matty says, shaking his head in obvious disbe-lief at the poor decision. "Nick didn't give up, though."

"Never," a few people call out, laughingly repeating Nick's earlier interruption.

Matty laughs too. "That's right. Nick may look unassuming, but that mild-mannered exterior covers a stubborn heart of gold. He asked my father to marry him again the next year, and again the year after that, and then the year after *that,* too. And every single time, Santiago Lopez said—"

"No," I mouth, right along with half the wedding guests.

Santi's laughing, cheeks a little red, but Nick's looking at him like he hung the moon, and the two lean together and whisper something to each other that of course I can't hear, but I kinda don't need to, you know? Because it's not the words that matter, it's what I see on their faces. And since it's exactly what I feel every single day for Eden and Matty? Catching a glimpse of that private moment's got me dabbing at my eyes with that tissue Eden gave me, dammit.

I mean, it's dusty in here, just sayin'.

"You're such a sap," Eden says, leaning against my arm with a happy smile.

"You're a sap," I say back automatically, to which she smiles and laughs and gives me a happy sigh and whispers "I know" under her breath, like I just complimented her or something.

Which, fine, not saying it's a *bad* thing.

I turn my head and press a kiss to her temple, since that's all I can reach while sneaking it in on the sly in front of everyone like this, and besides, this isn't the time or place for anything more. But it's enough, you know? Enough to tell her I'm thinking of her,

I hope. That I love and appreciate her. That she's *my* sap... which, I mean, if you're gonna go and get all technical about it, I suppose actually just proves her point about me being one in the first place.

She looks up at me and smiles, and... yep. Fine. I'm a sap.

"When Nick first told me how many times he'd asked my father to marry him, he was sitting at zero-for-six," Matty's going on. "I asked him if he was going to let it go. Because not great odds, yeah?"

The guests chuckle as Matty goes on.

"I asked Nick if he couldn't just be happy with the life they'd already built together. If it was really so important to him to make it legal, to get a piece of paper with their names on it, to be able to use the word *husband*."

Matty's been looking at Santi and Nick this whole time, but now his eyes find me and Eden and his voice gets quieter. Softer. Kinda makes it sound like he's talking just to us, even though he's got the whole room leaning forward to hear.

"I asked Nick whether 'husband' would mean they loved each other any more. Whether getting married would change things. And do you know what he said?"

"*I* do not know what he said," Santi calls out, eyes sparkling. "I know that I was a fool for saying no so many times when my heart belongs to this man, to my love, but tell me, Mateo, *¿Qué dijo mi marido?*"

"*What did my husband say,*" Eden leans in and translates for me, since her Spanish is about two billionty times better than mine, even though she's only been practicing for less than a year and I practically grew up on it.

Well, you know, *around* it, anyway.

"Nick told me that getting married wouldn't change the things that matter," Matt says, talking straight to his dad. "He said that being your husband wouldn't make him love you any more. He said that that was impossible, because he already loved you with every breath. With every beat of his heart. That he had from the beginning and would until the end, and that whether or not you had a ring on your finger when that final day came, Nick planned on being by your side on that day—and every single one leading up to it, God willing."

"Damnnnnnnn," I whisper under my breath, kinda feeling like I should be taking notes.

Matty and Eden like to tease me about never shutting up, but truth is, when it comes to telling them what they mean to me? Which would be *everything*, thank you very much. Anyway, when it comes to that shit, truth is I'm not always the most poetic. I pretty much rely on the L-word to do the heavy lifting, and then go for things like trying to make them come a lot to get my point across a little further.

I'm gonna have to remember that "every breath" and "every heartbeat" stuff, though, because you know what? That's it exactly. Nick nailed it in one. Pretty much wouldn't need either breath *or* heartbeat without these two, because what would be the point, you know?

Eden squeezes my hand. "I love this part," she whispers, dabbing at her eyes. "Santi's so lucky. Nick's such a romantic."

And okay, so two things here. One, guess I zoned out a little during the five gagillion times Matty practiced this shit because I don't really remember this part of the speech, if I'm being honest, and since Eden does, guess that's on me. And two, mental note: Eden wants more romance. I'm gonna have to give Matty a heads-up so we can do some planning, you know? Up our sap quotient and make our girl happy.

Well, happ*ier*. Just sayin', seems like the three of us do pretty damn good on the happy front, most days.

Eden gives a happy little sigh again—happy, see?—and wipes at the corner of her eye, and I can see Santi doing the same. Oh, God. We're a whole family of saps, aren't we? How'd *that* happen?

"Nick told me two more things," Matty's saying, still staring right at his dad. "He told me that he'd never stop asking you, even if it meant getting *sixty* no's, because he never wanted you to doubt that this is forever for him."

"And for me, *mijo*, and for me," Santi says, sounding all kinds of choked up.

"You... uh, you got any more tissues, princess?" I whisper to Eden. Just, you know, out of curiosity and all.

She squeezes my arm and slips another one into my hand, like she's got some kind of tissue-producing superpower or something, since I'm pretty sure she's got no pockets on her whatsoever, and right then and there I decide never to go to a wedding without her...or watch a Disney flick without her, if we're talking situations which occasionally require tissue.

I mean, just sayin', she got me hooked on them a few months ago, and have you *seen* the end of *Frozen*?

And actually, since I'm on a roll, maybe I should just make that a blanket statement covering any movie that doesn't involve zombies or like, shit blowing up. Seriously, Eden conned me and Matty into renting one about a reincarnating dog last month, and I shit you not, my eyes were swollen for days.

Coulda just been pollen in the air, though.

I mean, maybe.

"Don't leave us hanging, Matt. What else did Nick tell you?" someone calls out from the back of the room.

Matt clears his throat, then grins. "Nick told me that he wanted my blessing before he asked Dad to marry him again."

"And *you* told me I didn't need it," Nick says, a smile hovering over his lips.

"That's right, because love *is* the blessing," Matty says, raising his glass to Nick. "And it doesn't require a ring, or anyone else's approval, or anything at all outside the miracle of discovering that person who God made just for you. And I believe that. I believe there are people in the world who just *fit* together, and when you find them, it's like coming home and discovering a brand-new adventure, both in the exact same place."

Feels like Matty's talking to me and Eden. Feels like he's talking about *us*.

"This is the kind of love my father found with Nick," he says, looking out at all of us. "The kind that they both deserve to be blessed with until death do they part. The kind that my father had the courage to reach for, and that Nick had the persistence to pursue. The kind that today—as we all come together to celebrate the union of their love—blesses each of us, too, because having a love like this out in the world lifts *all* of us up.

"Dad, Nick, if you ever needed my blessing, you would have it ten times over, but you *are* the blessing. I'm honored to have the chance to acknowledge that, touched to be included in your circle of love, and inspired by the depth of what you've found with each other. May the blessing only grow, every day of your lives. Friends, please join me in raising a glass to my father and his husband, to Santi and Nick!"

And then we all raise our glasses and repeat it, toasting the shit out of Santi and Nick, and Eden slips me *another* tissue, because, you know, that damn pollen.

It's *every*where.

I'M trading camel-riding stories with Brenda, Matty's mom—and to be honest, feeling a tiny bit jealous that she got to actually ride one in Egypt while me, Matty, and Eden had to make do with some local action—when Matty and Eden come off the dance floor looking so flushed and gorgeous and *happy* that I kinda lose my train of thought for a second.

Dammmmmmnnnnnnnnnnnn.

Just sayin', all that poetic shit Matty was spouting earlier about love being blessed and all? With the two of them in my life, it applies to me in spades.

"What are you two up to?" Eden asks me and Brenda, her eyes just glazed enough to remind me that she's had a *lot* of champagne... and also to get me kinda excited for all the celebrating I'm guessing we'll be doing later.

"Johnny was just telling me about some of the adventures the three of you have gotten up to," Brenda says, pulling Eden in for a quick hug. "It sounds like you've been a good influence on my boys, Eden."

Gotta admit, I zone out on the chitchat for a second. Not my fault, though. For one thing, I've had plenty of champagne myself, and for another... well, let's just say that Eden and Matty are looking hot as fuck right now.

It's distracting.

Suddenly, I realize they're all looking at me like I missed a conversational cue or something. Problem is, I really did miss it. I'm not even sure what the topic is, to be honest, but since they've all got these expectant looks on their faces, it's not like I can just stay silent, you know?

"I'm putting a trip to Egypt on my bucket list," I blurt out, since it's the first thing that pops to mind.

At least, the first thing that I can actually say out loud in front of *Brenda*.

I mean, come on now—sure we're all adults here, but she's still sort of like a mom-figure to me, you know? And no matter how much I've had to drink tonight, I'm not going to say the shit I was *really* thinking—like how skipping out on the rest of the reception to go fuck like bunnies is sounding pretty good right now, what with the two of them looking like they do and me full of all this champagne and the mushy love-vibes from the wedding atmosphere and all.

"Egypt, hm?" Eden says, wrapping an arm around my waist as she smiles up at me. "That sounds fun."

"Oh, Christ," Matty says, shaking his head with a laugh. "I am *not* going to Egypt."

I grin, and he holds his hands up like he thinks he's gonna be able to ward me off or something.

"*No*, Johnny."

You know what never gets old? Proving Matty wrong. Not sure why he keeps thinking he's actually going to get out of doing all the cool stuff me and Eden come up with, but watching him squirm until he finally accepts the truth is always hella cute.

"Sorry, bro," I say, shrugging. "You're going. Bucket List Rules."

He opens his mouth to argue, but snaps it closed again without saying anything—because he knows I'm right—then he turns on Brenda. "*Egypt?*" he says, like it's her fault. "Mom, will you please stop putting ideas in his head?"

Brenda laughs and pats his cheek. "Oh, honey, lighten up. I think these bucket lists Johnny was telling me about sound wonderful! I think I'll start one myself. What's on yours?"

Eden shakes her head before Matty can answer. "Matt doesn't have—" she starts.

"Just one thing," Matty says, talking over Eden and shocking the shit out of both of us.

Eden recovers first. "You're starting a bucket list?" she squeals, throwing her arms around his neck and planting a kiss on him that brings back to mind the whole fucking like bunnies game plan.

"I am," Matty says, getting a little handsy with her, despite his mom standing right there.

And okay, so maybe we've *all* indulged a bit tonight.

"Isn't that *fantastic*, Johnny?" Eden asks me, slinging one of her arms around my neck without letting go of Matty. She pulls me in to her other side and I get the same enthusiastic kiss treatment that she gave our boy, proving that Eden has definitely had the most champagne-per-body-weight of the three of us.

I reach down and discreetly adjust myself, cutting a glance

over at Brenda. And it's not that I'm not happy to see her—
because I am, for real—but it's just that at *this* moment, if she were
to say, wander over to the open bar or decide she needed to catch
up with people who weren't us, I wouldn't mind, because
suddenly I'm *really* wanting to suggest the whole skipping-out-
on-the-reception-early thing to Matty and Eden.

Or hey, I'm not picky—maybe we could find an unused coat
closet or whatever, you know?

Not sure if Brenda's got superpowers of perception or if I
really *am* blessed, but for whatever reason, I get my wish. Santi
comes up and asks her to dance, and she says something about
wanting to hear all about Matty's bucket list later and then heads
off with him, leaving the three of us alone.

"You know what we should do?" I say, about to spring my brilliance on them.

"Yes," Matty says, giving me a smile that stops me in my tracks.

I mean, my question wasn't really meant as a question, you
know? It was more like a… a segue. But that's not what shuts me
up. It's that *look* Matty's giving me.

The look he's giving *us*.

He's looking at me and Eden the way Nick looked at Santi
during Matty's toast. The way all those pretty words I'll probably
never manage to come up with on my own made my heart feel,
you know? And yeah, I still want us to go fuck, but suddenly I
can't breathe quite right, because it feels like all the room in my
chest that's normally supposed to be for air is taken up by this
other thing. By loving him and Eden so hard it doesn't leave room
for anything else… and by knowing I'm loved that way right back.

"I do know what you should do, Johnny," Matt says, still
smiling at me like that. "I'm starting a bucket list, and Bucket List
Rules. You and Eden should say yes to me."

"Okay," I say, because for real, I've got no clue what he's talking
about but first of all, Bucket List Rules, right? And second… *Jesus.*
How could I *ever* not say yes to him?

"What are we saying yes to, Matt?" Eden asks, her voice all sweet and breathless and making me think she's feeling all the same can't-breathe-no-room-love-too-big shit that I am.

And *then*... well, guess I don't need to give Matty a heads-up on the getting more romantic and sappy thing, after all, because clearly he's already got it down. Because then, before I can even blink, Matty's down on one knee. I can't make sense of it, because that's a classic pose, you know? But he can't... we can't... is he really doing this?

"There's just one thing on my bucket list," he says, looking up at us like it's just the three of us there even though all of a sudden a whole lot of other people are paying attention and gathering round. "Eden, Johnny, will you both marry me?"

Eden gasps, and my heart straight-up stops.

Matty winks. "You should say yes. Bucket List Rules."

"Yes," Eden says... right at the same time that I blurt out *"Matty, we can't,"* because I'm an idiot.

An idiot who feels like he's about to start bawling, just like at the end of *Frozen*.

Matty just smiles. "Neither could Dad and Nick, once upon a time," he says.

Well, that's not true. I mean, technically it *is* true in the sense of marriage equality in *general*, but even though it took the rest of the country a while to catch up, here in Massachusetts gay marriage has been legal since 2004, and Nick and Santi didn't even know each other yet back then. I'm not a total idiot, though, because I don't blurt that out. Instead, I get what Matty's really saying, and—

Oh, shit. Now I really *am* crying. It's worse than at that dog movie.

Eden uses her superpower to pull a tissue out of thin air for me, but she's crying, too, and Matty's still down on one knee, so I'm pretty sure I'm not gonna be able to stop any time soon. Especially with Matty still looking up at us like he means it.

He wants to get *married*.

This is *Matty*, so I know two things. One, he'll stay down on that knee forever if he has to, waiting on the *yeses* he's holding out for. And two, when it comes to actually doing the thing? The three of us getting married, all to each other?

If Matty says he wants it, he'll hold out forever to get *that*, too.

"Johnny, Eden, you two *are* my breath," he says, stealing mine all over again. "You're not just the beat of my heart, you're the other pieces of it, fitting with mine and making me whole. And you both know I never saw the point in starting a bucket list of my own, but only because I thought I already had everything I wanted. Except here? Now? Today? It hit me that I *do* want something more. I want to marry you, both of you, not because it will change us or make me love you both better, but because you *are* my forever."

"Oh, Matt," Eden says, eyes glowing like everything inside her is too bright to keep inside.

"*Jesus*, Matty," I say, knowing exactly how she feels but lacking all the right words to do the glow justice.

Matty smiles at us. "I know it's not legal yet, but I'm playing the long game here, yeah? And as long as you both say yes, I know I'm gonna win." He winks. "Already have, even if it ends up taking the world a while to catch up with us. I love you two with everything I've got. Come on now, say you'll marry me?"

And sometimes the right words don't have to be all that poetic after all. Sometimes they can actually be pretty simple, you know?

"Yes," Eden says, melting against the two of us happily.

"Dude, *yes*," I say, because Bucket List Rules. Well, that and the whole loving these two more than life itself thing.

"Yes," Matty says, even though he's the one who asked.

He stands up, pulling us in and looking at both of us like he's full of glow, too. And this? Whether we ever get to put rings on each other's fingers or not, this right here is enough.

This is *everything*.

ALSO BY CHLOE LYNN ELLIS

His

Mine

ABOUT THE AUTHOR

Once upon a time, there were two authors who loved writing steamy love stories. Between them, they had published a fair number of books *(more than eighty, less than a hundred... but really, who's counting?)* in a variety of genres *(M/M contemporary romance, M/F paranormal romance, mpreg, and lots of hot and dirty erotica with all the "M" and "F" combinations a reader could wish for)* but, sadly, neither author felt that their writing accomplishments were complete.

Then, one day, fate smiled on these two.

They found each other, became fast friends, and eventually decided that trying their hand at MMF romance was an adventure best done balls out, feet first, and most of all... together.

And thus, the writing team that is Chloe Lynn Ellis was born.

Made in the
USA
Columbia, SC